STEFANIE LOZINSKI

Majesty

(Storm & Spire Book 2)

This novel is entirely a work of fiction. The names,
characters and incidents portrayed in it are the work of the
author's imagination. Any resemblance to actual persons,
living or dead, events or localities is entirely coincidental.

Cover by Etheric Designs.

Map created in Wonderdraft, using assets by Evitcani &
Nexoness.

Ave Christus Rex. ✝

First edition

This book was professionally typeset on Reedsy.
Find out more at reedsy.com

To Jordan

Thank you for steadfastly believing
in my ability to write books,
even when (especially when)
I'm convinced that I'll never finish another one.

I love you.

"We men and women are all in the same boat, upon a stormy sea. We owe to each other a terrible and tragic loyalty."

G.K. CHESTERTON

The glorious realm of
KAVERYTH
and the Four Kingdoms

GALEHARBOR

Windshear

Graveholm

Kaurmere Lake

High Keep

BONESHIRE

Redvale

Rill

ARIDMOOR

Vaevar

Edgcairn

Dread Ruins

SILVERFELL

Waymere River

Rivachfall

Strongshollow

Old Hill

Briarcliffe

Claywind

UMRYM

Whitespire

Helmin

The Black Bend

Auranthe

The West Strait

NOX

ii

Prologue

Gramnok Beastbane raised the pickaxe over his shoulder and brought it down against the wall, relishing the satisfying crack as the rock gave way. He wiped his brow with the back of his dirt-caked hand, wondering to himself if he would hit the vein of valuable iron ore before dinner. After taking a few moments to catch his breath, he raised the heavy tool once more, setting his feet as firmly as he could in order to make a solid strike. Before he could swing, however, he felt a telltale prickle of hair rising on the back of his neck.

He wasn't alone.

He forced himself to take a deep breath before turning to face the intruder, grabbing his lamp and allowing the flickering circle of yellow light to illuminate the narrow mine passage.

He did not drop the pickaxe.

"Hello, Gramnok," the stranger said, a smile playing across his lips. It was a fellow dwarf, as one would expect so deep in the mines. He didn't recognize this individual, but that didn't surprise him. It was almost always someone different when they came for him, always another poor sap willing to take on one of the easier tasks. "I'm told it's time for you to come in for another chat."

He said nothing. For a moment, all he heard was a gentle plinking sound as unseen water dripped from the damp ceiling and onto the rocky floor.

"You won't be needing that, I assure you," he added with a short chuckle.

Gramnok glanced at the pickaxe in his hand, his knuckles grasping the wooden shaft so hard that they had gone white. His palms were as slick as the cave walls. He felt his heart begin to thunder within his chest as his head began to swim. He tried to breathe, but the air felt thick, too thick to fill his lungs, a miasma of smoke and fear.

It was dark.

* * *

It had been dark the first time, too.

They had come for him several months before, after his best friend Celesyria had fled Umrym, leaving chaos behind her.

He had dropped his weapon immediately then, having no reason to distrust his superior. He'd followed like an obedient pet, watching the back of the dwarf who summoned him as he led him along winding paths and into a plain room he did not recognize. He'd imagined there had been some kind of problem in the mine that he had to fix, or perhaps he'd been promoted. He hadn't thought of Celesyria's journey out of Umrym, or the High One, or of any of the other recent happenings that had intruded upon his comfortable life.

But then three elves had walked through the door, two women and a man, all so strange and so beautiful that he'd been able to do nothing but gape at them.

A part of his mind, the logical part of it, knew that something must be very, very wrong. The elves did not dare to leave

Nox. That they would venture into the caverns of Whitespire, home of the very dragons who defended Kaveryth from them, was unthinkable. And yet, the rational part of his mind had been silenced, replaced by an insatiable curiosity, a thirst for beauty that crowded out all other desires.

One of the women was especially enchanting. Her hair was as dark and shimmering as polished black onyx, and her silvery skin seemed almost to glow in the dimness of the room. She looked much younger than the others, and though elves lived well into the hundreds, Gramnok would have guessed that she was about sixteen in human years.

The other woman elf finally spoke. "Alright, Aelrie. Why don't you tell him why he's here?"

Gramnok noticed that though she was nearly as beautiful as the first, with a shock of red hair and bright green eyes, there was a hardness to her that repelled him. He blinked a few times, trying to clear the fog and reclaim his bearings. His mind was screaming at him, but his body was more calm than he could ever remember being. Every nerve seemed to flow with cool water, the usual anxieties of life fading away.

He looked toward the lovely elf they called Aelrie, and for a moment, their eyes met. He thought he saw a sadness behind the pools of blue, but before he could attempt to decipher it further, she shied away from his gaze and stared down at her boots.

"We know about your friend Celesyria," she said quickly, looking over at her companions for a moment before continuing. The male elf said nothing, instead moving to stand by the door with a bored expression on his handsome face. "We know everything. There's no point lying. We need you to tell us where she is."

Gramnok listened, thinking to himself that the woman's voice was far too sweet to be delivering such a threatening message.

He looked at his feet, forcing himself to breathe, to think. As he looked away from the beautiful creatures, he felt his mind returning, and the thoughts that bubbled to the surface would ordinarily have set his heart to pounding.

There were elves in Umrym, and they were coming for his best friend. They were going to hurt her. He could not let that happen, even if the foolish dragon had brought these troubles upon herself.

"I don't know anything," he said, raising his head just long enough to meet the redhead's eyes without allowing himself to really look at her.

"You're lying," she said, glaring at Aelrie until she nodded, taking a few steps toward the dwarf.

"You need to tell us the truth, or it is going to be very bad for you." Her voice wavered as she spoke.

"I am telling the truth. I don't know anything. I mean, I know Celesyria, but I don't know what you're talking about, and I don't know where she is."

Gramnok found that as long as he didn't let his mind consider the beauty of the elves, he was able to keep his wits. The senses of his body were a different story, but he could get past that.

My brain is in charge here, surely.

He tried to ignore the oppressive calm that the elves' presence engendered, but the effect was disorienting nonetheless. There wasn't even any sweat beading up beneath his heavy mining helmet. He felt instead that he was just waking up from a wonderful dream and not quite ready to leave sleep behind. It was like moving through a thick cloud, unable to see what lay just a few feet ahead.

"She has put the stability of all of Kaveryth at risk," Aelrie continued, pausing for a moment to glance over at the male elf guard near the door. "I'm—I'm not going to keep asking. Tell me where she is. Now."

He clenched his fists intentionally, trying to force a defiance that he couldn't feel into his voice.

"You're an elf. I figure you would love to see Kaveryth destabilized. What's the problem?"

For a half of a second, Aelrie stared at him, a smile stirring at the edge of her lips, but her companion acted before he could say anything else.

The red-haired elf was kneeling in front of him now, her green eyes mere inches from his own. He tried to turn his head, to look away, but she took hold of his beard with both hands, forcing him to gaze straight into her face. Gramnok felt the sting of her long fingernails against his neck and cheek, but somehow the sensation was pleasant. She smelled like nectar, flowers, grass, and sunshine. It was like spring had been bottled up and carried into the depths of the dank, humid mine.

And then there was pain.

His nostrils were filled with the scent of ash, choking him as he tried to keep breathing, to focus on what was happening, but it was no use.

He was falling, and soon there was only oblivion.

* * *

He heard a crash as the pickaxe fell from his hands, slick with sweat, jolting him from his memories.

"Sorry," he muttered to the other dwarf, reaching down to grasp it before deciding against it. "Let's get this over with."

This time, it would be just a chat, as promised. There would be no beguiling elves, no strange room in the pits of Whitespire, and best of all, no pain. No torture. They had no need for it, not anymore.

He always listened.

He'd already betrayed his best friend to the sworn enemies of Kaveryth to save his own skin. He had no secrets left to give them.

But that didn't mean he had no plans for his revenge. He needed only to wait for the time to be right.

Chapter 1

Wes Cervos held on as another giant gust of wind whipped across his body, threatening to send him flying toward the ground below. He felt his stomach lurch as Celesyria tilted her body, adjusting her wings this way and that so as not to be thrown off course by the huge gusts of air.

"Woo!" Alder crowed from behind him, no doubt with only one hand clutching lazily at the leather bands strapped to the orange dragon beneath. Not that Wes dared to look back at him, not even for even a single second.

"I wish we could travel in the daylight. I want to soak in this view."

Wes didn't comment, instead clamping his jaw shut against the nausea as Celesyria contorted herself into another position and rode a current of air leading upward. After a few more uncomfortable motions, her body stabilized again, and he enjoyed a rare moment of calm.

The dragon flew evenly, allowing the gentle current of wind to carry her along without making any sudden movements. Wes kept his fingers tight on the leather straps, but at least he could breathe without feeling like he was going to be sick.

Far away in the distance, barely visible in the lingering shadow of night, he could just make out the North Sea. He watched the dawn sunlight filling the horizon with pink and the palest green, and he had to admit Alder was right. It was a shame to have to make camp and spend such a beautiful day sleeping.

"I miss riding my deer," he said finally, allowing his hands to relax their grip slightly. "Even a horse would be great. Travel by dragon-flight is, without a doubt, the worst method of transportation in the world."

"Don't worry," Alder said, clapping him on the shoulder. Wes could almost hear the teasing smile in his voice. "The next time we hit a rough patch, I'll hold onto you so you can't jostle about as much."

"First of all, no," Wes said, failing to keep his cheerful mood from showing in his voice. "I'm not a hugger, and even if I was, you wouldn't be my first choice. Second of all, I've lost weight, but not that much. We'd probably both end up falling off."

"You worry too much. You're telling me that the legendary Celesyria, Keeper of the Codex, would let us fall?"

Celesyria gave a snort, her keen hearing allowing her to hear the conversation whenever the wind slowed. "That name would work better if I actually had the Codex in my possession."

Wes was about to make a snarky comment of his own when

he was interrupted by yet another gust of wind, followed by even more stomach-twisting movement from Celesyria. He tightened his grip and leaned forward, closer to her neck, narrowly avoiding being hit full force with the secondary gust that followed.

"You good?" Alder shouted over the noise. Wes managed to nod in response as he pressed his face down against the cool orange scales. Alder always insisted that looking out at his surroundings was the only way to overcome his motion sickness, but so far, it had been terrible advice.

He pressed his eyes closed, trying to relax and to pretend that he wasn't so high up in the air. He stayed that way for quite a long time, enjoying the silence, until he began to feel an annoying prickle of pain on his right cheek. Even with his eyes closed, he could feel the gentle warmth of the summer sunlight against his eyelids. Even after three weeks of healing time, that soft light was enough to make his fresh scar itch and burn.

He'd never much liked his moonscar, the telltale mark of the Envoy and the seal of his fate, but he couldn't decide if this wound was worse. He'd been born with the moonscar. Nothing he had done or didn't do had anything to do with it. It simply was.

This mark was different. Had he simply stayed on the path laid out for him since birth, he never would have been involved in the prison escape and subsequent battle that had led to this new scar. He never would have burned down half of an ancient forest, leaving a similarly ugly wound upon his Kingdom's territory, a wound that would take decades to heal.

He never would have known that Elder Dorold Eli was so willing to betray a boy that he claimed to love as a son.

3

But there was no time for such thoughts. Not anymore.

Every person in the world could second-guess the roads they had trod, driving themselves mad with possible sorrow avoided and joys gained, and it would never make a bit of difference.

His parents and brother were dead, his Kingdom was in peril, and as of this moment, his family consisted of a pretty-boy warrior from Aridmoor, a misfit dragon, and a beautiful princess he absolutely did not want to marry.

The thought made his stomach lurch just in time for the dragon to take another sharp turn across a current of air.

"Hey, Celesyria," he called toward her. Usually, he and the dragon spoke to each other within their minds, but since Alder had not yet mastered the skill, they tried their best to speak out loud while in his presence. "Can you refrain from showing off any more until we land? Please?"

"I'm telling you, you'll get used to it. You just have to face it head on," Alder chimed in as Celesyria straightened out her back as best she could, gliding gently along the breeze.

"Your way has led to nothing but vomit," Wes snapped before he could stop himself. He felt a blush of guilt redden his cheeks when his jab was not met with one of Alder's usual jokes. Not that he thought he could have possibly hurt the man's feelings too badly. He wasn't exactly the sensitive type.

"He's just trying to help," Celesyria said within his head, her voice softer and more girlish when she wasn't trying to shout over the wind. *"We can't afford to bicker with our allies. We're very lucky to have any at all."*

She was right. Alder, a soldier of King Kylan Ursa's personal Protectorate army, had chosen to change sides at the eleventh hour and rescue Celesyria from prison. He was a good man, and without his help, Wes doubted that either of them would be free now. *Yet another person who has sacrificed everything for me. Yet another debt that I will never be able to repay.*

Wes forced his body to sit up straight again, keeping his eyes on the brightening sky ahead rather than the ground thousands of feet below. They were high enough up that the few trees he saw looked no bigger than shrubs. He turned to face Alder, keeping a tight grip on the straps of the saddle.

"I'm sorry."

"For what?" Alder said, flashing him a half smile. Wes allowed his gaze to linger for a few moments, taking in the soldier's muscled arms, fully exposed beneath the grubby brown farmer's tunic he was wearing. *He'd probably annoy me less if he didn't insist on looking so perfect all the time.*

He turned to face forward again, trying not to think about what Kessara's reaction to meeting him would be. Wes was no replacement for his older brother who she had loved so deeply, and he couldn't bear the thought of a living suitor for her to compare him to along with the dead one.

Despite growing up in a palace and being given everything she'd ever asked for, Kessara had a strong practical streak and was one of the smartest people Wes knew. Still, she was not blind.

Celesyria's voice boomed ahead. "I see a good place. Directly to the east."

"Probably the best we'll get this close to Windshear," Alder said. "Let's get there and set up, I'm starving."

Wes dared a glance toward the ground ahead, noticing a small cluster of trees with a creek passing nearby before vertigo forced him to look away. Alder was right, of course—like Aridmoor, much of the Kingdom of Galeharbor, especially the northern half, was comprised of plains with few trees—but he couldn't help but wish his opinion had been asked for.

"I'm still not used to having to hide like this," Alder said.

"Me neither," Wes swallowed his annoyance, glad for the change of subject. His friend didn't deserve his ire. "I've spent my entire life being welcomed everywhere I went. Banquets, gifts, the best of everything. It's strange to go from that to…" He waved a hand to encompass the sky.

Like Kessara, he'd grown up in the palace, though he was raised in Stronghollow rather than Windshear. Despite the economic difficulties that had swept through their respective Kingdoms, they both led very privileged lives as greater House nobles.

Ever since meeting Celesyria and learning about the High One, his life had become much more difficult. He wondered if he'd ever become entirely used to it.

"At least Auranth was nice," Celesyria said. "Well, nice for everyone but me."

Alder chuckled at that, and Wes couldn't resist joining in himself. After he and Celesyria had escaped, the three of them had fled to the small city of Auranth in the far north of Silverfell. Wes had a family friend there, a childhood friend of his father called Bargren, and he'd taken the two men in, offering them every bit of Auranthian hospitality he could muster.

They'd laid as low as they could, and it had worked out well enough. The city was too remote to have heard any news of Wes's imprisonment or pending trial, so in the eyes of Bargren and his servants, nothing was amiss.

Of course, they hadn't been able to bring Celesyria with them.

While they'd dined on bear steak, drank ale, and slept until noon, the dragon had been forced to camp alone in the mountains, far enough from Auranth that she hadn't even been able to communicate with Wes until the men returned.

"Don't worry, Celesyria," Alder said. "One day, the Keeper of the Codex will have a palace of her own. I'll serve you grapes on a platter."

"Do you have any idea how many grapes she would need to eat?" Wes said, laughing.

"I just want to find the Codex in the first place. As long as the High One reigns in Kaveryth again, I don't care if I have to hide away forever."

Alder laughed. "You're far too noble for the likes of us, you know that?"

"It's true," Wes said, squinting at the sky ahead of them. The sun had fully risen now, but there was something strange about the way the air looked, almost like it was visibly moving in front of them. "Wait. Do you see that?"

"See what?"

"That, right there! How it looks like it's—"

Before he could so much as close his mouth, the tiny pieces of undulating sky crashed into him, wriggling and skittering across his face.

* * *

Celesyria blinked her huge eyes as quickly as she could, trying to free herself from the tiny insects that had landed on her. She wanted so badly to use her wings to create a gust of air and push them away, but if she did, she risked letting Alder and Wes fall.

7

"Just hold on," she said to Wes, feeling him press his body against her neck as several of the insects flew into her mouth and settled on her teeth. Alder was doing the same behind him, and their flailing motions as they tried to swat away the creatures was almost enough to upset her balance. Flying with the weight of one human along with the manacles on her ankles made her slower and less agile. With two, it became downright dangerous. *"I'm heading down."*

After a few more blinks, she dove downward and let her wings spread out as far as they could go, allowing them to glide toward the grass below. She felt a shiver run across her spine as pinpricks of pain bloomed on her wing membranes. She could see that the insects were tiny, but with so many of them, she feared they could actually cause real damage if they all chose to bite at once.

As soon as her front claws touched down, her companions scrambled off of her back, and she gave a great shake, wanting to be sure every one of the miserable beasts were evacuated. To her relief, the creatures flew off to join their companions higher in the sky.

She could see that Wes was doing the same, running his hands through his thick brown curls, swatting phantom insects along the back of his neck, and shaking the hem of his shirt. Alder had gone the more direct route, stripping his tunic off and whipping it through the air until the last insect had fallen off. She looked away, blushing at the sight of his chiseled torso. Even though she was over a hundred years his senior and, of course, a dragon, she couldn't deny that he was unreasonably handsome for a human.

"What in the Wrathlands were those?" Alder asked as he pulled his clothes back on.

8

"Elder Dorold told me a while back that swarms of insects were destroying Galeharbor's crops in the summertime. I guess these must be the culprits," Wes said.

"They don't seem to be doing any harm," Alder said, raising a hand to his forehead and looking off into the distance. "Well, aside from grossing us out."

"And biting me," Celesyria chimed in. "I guess they like the taste of piping hot dragon blood."

They began to walk toward the cluster of trees they had spotted from above, making their way through tall grass and the occasional patch of flowers. Up above, she could still see the strange, glimmering clouds of locusts, but they did not seem to have any interest in destroying the infinite carpet of plant life that lay below them.

To the east, past the trees, Celesyria could see the distant towers of Windshear's palace. She had seen pictures of the capital of Galeharbor in books, and for now, at least, that was the best view she was going to get. She understood why she could not join her friends—she wasn't exactly built for stealth—but still, it frustrated her. She was by far the most physically powerful ally that the Envoy of Silverfell had, and yet here she was, letting Wes put himself in danger while she stayed safely behind.

"So, brother," Alder said, bumping Wes with his shoulder as they walked ahead. "What are you going to say to Kessara? Have you decided to marry her yet?"

"I don't know. On both counts."

"It's going to be fine. You'll see," Celesyria added, blowing a warm puff of air from her nostrils that made Wes' hair flutter. "She'll just be glad to see you."

"If she's even here," Wes muttered under his breath.

She would be there, safe in her palace with her parents. Celesyria couldn't bear to entertain any other possibility. It had been a dangerous decision to come back here, to fly right over some of the most populous areas in Kaveryth, but they'd had little choice. Kessara Manta had risked everything to free Wes from prison, and they'd already abandoned her for far too long.

Alder coughed. "Well, if she's not here, she's still in Stronghollow Penitentiary. At least we know she's safe."

"If half of what Wes told me about Kessara is true, she'll be here. She had a plan before she ever stepped foot in that prison. I know she did," Celesyria said, surprised at the edge she heard in her voice.

A companionable silence fell as they continued moving toward the stand of trees. Now that they were closer, Celesyria could see that this variety was very different from most of the ones she had seen before, all broad waxy leaves and scrawny trunks that barely seemed thick enough to hold the weight of the boughs. She had never been so far east, and since they had been traveling at night to avoid detection, most of what she had seen of Galeharbor had been illuminated only by moonlight.

"I see the creek," Wes called out, pointing to a spot somewhere off to the left. The day was going to be hot. Already, even by the early morning light, Celesyria could see ripples of heat adorning the horizon. She had not been thirsty until that very moment, but now she began to notice the dryness of her tongue.

Within a few strides she had caught up to her friends, joining them as they knelt at the edge of the sliver of water, drinking deeply, too exhausted to be bothered to dig around

10

in their packs in search of a proper drinking vessel. She had just put her head down to drink, narrowly avoiding letting her tongue scrape at the pebbles on the bottom, when she heard a woman's voice sounding behind her.

Celesyria whipped her head around, her entire body tense, her instinct to fly kicking in without any conscious need to summon it. She had to force herself to remain on the ground, waiting.

"Show yourself!" Alder shouted into the emptiness. For a few seconds, they heard nothing else. The creek lay in one of the few shallow valleys they'd seen dotting the landscape, and even at her full height, Celesyria could not see anyone standing in the waving grasses above.

"I'm old, not deaf," came a voice in their midst. Celesyria let out a growl of surprise as a fat older woman clambered out from between her front legs. "Sorry to startle you, young man, but I didn't exactly have time to explain."

"Explain what?" Wes asked, taking a few steps closer to the woman. She had a wrinkly, tanned face and wore her curly gray hair beneath a bright blue scarf. Celesyria said nothing, momentarily stunned into silence. The woman had not even seemed to notice the dragon's presence.

"There's still no time, but thank the Dracodei that I found you, at any rate. It seems, how do the city doctors say it, 'dose dependent'. Quite right." The woman strode up to Alder and took his jaw between her hands, turning his head back and forth as though examining a statue she was planning to display on the mantle. Wes coughed as she reached for a leather bag she held at her side and began rooting around for something in it. "But in any case, not even the scientists at Vaevar know for sure how much will kill you, let alone how to reverse the

11

effects. But how could they know? Ancient maladies require ancient remedies. They think only of what is new, of the things that they have mixed and measured. No wisdom in that."

"What are you talking about?" Alder asked rather bluntly, staring at the woman as she plopped her bottom onto the grass and began mixing various powders and bits of dried plants into a bottle of what Celesyria immediately identified as some kind of strong-smelling spirit.

After adding a few more pinches of indistinguishable black powders she stuck a cork in the bottle and began to shake it hard enough to bring sweat to her brow.

"The water, boy," the woman said, casting a brief glance at Alder before returning to her task. "Or has that particular angel of death passed Aridmoor by?"

Celesyria noticed a smirk playing across Wes' face. Though Alder was dressed like a local farmer, a keen eye wouldn't have had much trouble noticing the bits of red hair sticking out from under his hat or the freckles that dotted his arms. They would have to be much more careful with their disguises when they entered Windshear.

"There have been dozens of reports of formerly safe water sources going bad," Wes spoke finally. "I knew it was happening in Boneshire, and even in the more rural areas of Silverfell, but here? Nearly at the gates of Windshear?"

"Well, it wasn't, not before," the woman said as she stood, holding out the murky bottle toward anyone who would take it. "It started up here, maybe a month ago, or even less than that. Hmm. I hadn't thought of it 'til now... well, isn't that a strange thing. Right around the time when our good Envoy was imprisoned."

No one moved for the bottle, but she did not lower it. Celesyria wondered if her arm was beginning to hurt.

"She doesn't recognize me," Wes' voice sounded in her head. She focused straight ahead at the little grove of trees, not wanting to let anyone else see her eyes meeting his.

"Or she's lying, or most likely, she's batty," she replied.

Alder took a step forward and took the bottle.

Satisfied, the woman spoke again, giving a quick nod to each of them in turn as though they had passed some final test. "Anyway, that's enough chatter. I have to get back. My duskturnips will be awake by now."

Celesyria had a thousand questions that she wanted to ask, but before she could say anything, Alder cut in.

"Alright then," he said quickly.

"Safe travels, ma'am," Wes added.

With a final nod, the woman marched over to Celesyria and addressed her directly. "One spoonful in any wild water you're going to drink. You look like the brains of this outfit, dragon. Don't forget."

"Thank you. We appreciate your aid," Wes said after a moment. Celesyria found herself unable to find any words at all.

"There's a change in the world," the woman continued as though no one had spoken, her eyes looking off at something Celesyria could not see. "Something has shifted. Yes. I can feel it beneath my toes. Perhaps the Dracodei have abandoned us. Or maybe we've driven them out."

With a final lingering glance at Wes, she walked off toward higher ground and disappeared into the wavering grass.

Chapter 2

Kessara Manta sat up with a start, her heart pounding in her ears. Someone was knocking on the door of her chambers, and though it was far too early in the morning, she was relieved to have been interrupted. The dream that had haunted her for weeks had returned, leaving her shaken.

"Coming!" she called out, slipping out of her nest of silk blankets and pulling on a robe. She moved to the window, yanking the curtains out of the way and allowing the gentle morning light to fill the bedroom. No matter how many times she awoke to the same view, it still managed to amaze her. The palace of Windshear was set on a huge hill, enabling her to see for miles and miles. Off in the distance, she could see the sun glinting off of the North Sea.

Striding across the room, she opened the door, surprised to see a young boy wearing a stablehand's uniform. "Sorry to wake you, my Princess," he said, stepping from foot to foot. "I've been given a message. Two farmers are here to see you. They traveled all the way from the south, near the border of Boneshire, they told me."

"They asked for me? Are you sure they aren't seeking an audience with my parents?"

The boy knit his fingers together and glanced down at his toes. "No, my Princess. They asked specifically for you. They even made me promise that I wouldn't say a word to the King and Queen."

"Alright," she said, frowning.

"They paid me a little," the boy said, his words tumbling out on top of each other. "My mother has been ill, and father has been away in Kova, trying to sell our spring crops. Even with the sale prices going up, everything else has gone up right at the same time. We can't afford our dry goods. I figured I could help, you know? Surprise my mother with a little extra."

Kessara knelt down, smiling at the child as guilt flashed within her belly. How easy it was to fall back into this life. To forget the world that her family's servants went home to when they exited the palace gates. "I understand. You did nothing wrong."

She wanted to give the boy some coins of her own, but she didn't have any currency laying around at the moment. She made a mental note to look for the child later on.

"They're waiting at the gate near the kitchen gardens," he added, returning her smile. "Anyway, my Princess, I need to get back to the stables. If Mister Corran knew I left before the horses were turned out for the day…"

She rested a hand on his arm. "I will make sure you are paid a little extra this week, alright? I hope your mother feels better soon."

In a moment she was alone again, and as she began to dress for the day, she couldn't shake the worry that had settled in the pit of her stomach. It was a strange request. Though she had returned more or less to her duties as Princess, her mother and father were not exactly advertising the fact.

Though they supported her in her questioning of the Dracodei and even in the illegal aid she'd provided to Wes Cervos, she knew that it was putting the whole royal family at risk. Relations with the Septemvirate and with King Kylan Ursa had already deteriorated, and she was not sure what her father's next move would be.

She pulled a blue dress over her head and gave herself her customary spray of perfume, relishing the smell of daisies and leather on her tanned skin. As she headed out into the hall, she was struck by a memory. She had worn a dress almost exactly like this one, in black, on the day she'd helped her friend and maybe-future-husband Wes escape prison. Less than a month had passed, but it felt like a lifetime ago. As she headed for the back gate, she couldn't seem to summon the same courage she'd had then. Whoever was waiting for her would meet a spoiled princess, nothing more. Maybe there was nothing more. Maybe that was all she was— a privileged girl who did one brave thing.

"Excuse us, my Princess," one of the servant women said loudly as Kessara stepped into the kitchen. The rest of them stopped working, staring up at her for a moment before setting their bowls and cloths and half-cut vegetables down and curtsying in their work aprons. "We didn't expect you. The kitchen is not fit to be seen."

"Please, it's quite alright," Kessara said with a pinched smile.

"I'm just passing by. I wanted to… see the carrots coming up in the garden, if that's alright."

A couple of the women passed a look between them. "Oh, yes, the gardens are lovely now. Enjoy, my Princess."

As she stepped outside, she could hear the swell of gossip already beginning. She caught a few words, enough to know that her brief engagement with the Envoy was still very much a topic of interest. *Perhaps they think he's coming to meet me in secret, to whisk me away for a romantic ride across the—*

Her thoughts were cut short as she saw who stood beyond the gate. She threw open the bolt and rushed through, stepping on the hem of her dress as she went. Without thinking about how it must look, she threw her arms around the dirty young man in farm clothes and pressed her head against his shoulder. "Oh, Wes," she whispered. "Thank the High One you're alright."

"Hello, my Princess," he said a little too loud, pulling back from her embrace. One of the gardeners looked up, narrowing his eyes at them for a minute before he returned to picking weeds. "Thank you for meeting with us personally."

"I'd love to show you our new hybrid crops while we talk," she said smoothly, pointing toward one of the smaller gardens that lay behind a stone wall. She eyed the other man with Wes out of the corner of her eye as they walked, curiosity piqued. "The gardeners tell me that they've been adapted for warm climates. I'm sure that this innovation will be even more important for those living farther south."

As soon as they were out of sight and earshot, she leaned in for another quick hug. "I've been so worried. I heard that you'd escaped King Kylan's men in the fire, but after that, no one knew where you went."

"Good," Wes said, giving her a brief smile. For a split second, she forgot that she wasn't looking at his older brother Roven, the man she'd loved. He smiled at her that very same way, with the same quirk of an eyebrow. Even after these five long years, she still missed him. She doubted that that wound would ever heal, not completely. She knew that Wes experienced that pain even more than she did. He'd lost not only a brother, but both of his parents as well. "We were hiding in Auranth for a while. My father grew up there, and one of his childhood friends took us in. And then we had to travel here, of course."

"Well, I'll say one thing, you look a lot better in farm clothes than in a dress," she laughed. "How's Celesyria?"

The other man coughed, giving her a quick smile.

"She's hiding out nearby, and not particularly thrilled about it," he said, closing the distance between them in two long strides and holding out his hand. She took it, noticing straight away that his hand was large enough to nearly enclose her own. Up close, she could see the telltale freckles of an Aridmoorian dotting his handsome face. "It's nice to meet you. I'm Alder Cadogen."

* * *

Alder took the Princess's hand in his own, giving it a gentle shake. He tried not to stare at her. Wes had told him that she was lovely, but clearly he had underestimated just how true that description was. She was wearing her pale blonde hair loose, and it flowed over the shoulders of a bright blue dress that matched her eyes. They met his own as she glanced up at him from her much shorter height.

"Forgive me," she said, smiling, the muscles in her face

relaxing into the placid mask of a born diplomat. *She doesn't trust me.*

"It's good to meet you."

"He is a former member of King Ursa's Protectorate," Wes said, taking a couple of steps toward them as he let Kessara's hand go. "He was assigned to guard Celesyria in the dungeon, until the High One found him in a dream."

He winced, thinking that such a description made him sound insane, but he didn't wish to argue at the moment.

"I've heard a lot about you," he said easily. "Wes speaks of you often. Though he can't seem to tell me for certain if you two are getting married or not."

Wes gave him a death stare. He smirked back. *What can I say. I'm a man who likes to get the important stuff out in the open.*

Ordinarily, he would have complimented her beauty, or asked whether or not Wes had told her of his own good looks, but in this case, it seemed unwise.

Before Wes could say anything else, a man rolling a wheelbarrow came whistling along the little path toward them. Kessara gave the man a quick wave as he passed. "Well, Mr. Wheat, I assure you that your local council will be happy to help with—er—any property line disputes," she said loudly to no one in particular, looking at the man's retreating back.

"Mr. *Wheat?*" Alder shook his head, suppressing a grin. "It really is incredible that you managed to break Wes here out of jail."

"In my defense, I had a little more time to plan that one out," she said politely, her lips pursing as though she'd tasted something sour. "How did you free Celesyria?"

A little sensitive, aren't we. Well, I suppose it's to be expected from someone who has always gotten everything that she wants.

"She was a little big for a disguise, so I just did it the old-fashioned way," he replied.

"He unlocked her cell door," Wes said, rolling his eyes. "Anyway, I want to know how you escaped yourself."

The Princess smiled then, all hints of moodiness vanishing from her expression. Alder watched her face as she spoke, trying to figure out what lay beneath the surface. Men were so much easier to understand. He and Wes butted heads, but at least with him, he could always figure out where he stood. He had a feeling that Kessara would be different. He only hoped that he could trust her.

"It wasn't very impressive," she started, giving Alder the briefest of glances. "I told the guard—who happens to be an old friend—that if he tells the truth about how Wes broke free he'd be blamed for letting me into a prisoner's cell in the first place."

"So, I assume you had a cover story planned out for him ahead of time. Was it brilliant? Did it involve the code name 'Mr. Soldier'?" Alder asked, giving the princess a wink. She rolled her eyes. It was hard not to tease when her exasperated look was so adorable. He chided himself. *She's going to marry Wes, and I need to let it be.*

"He told the other guards that Wes held me hostage, using my own knife that I'd accidentally brought into the prison."

"How do you accidentally bring a knife to Stronghollow Penitentiary?" Alder asked. For all of his ribbing, he had to admit he was impressed with how well Kessara and Wes had pulled the whole thing off.

"Yeah, I'm not sure that fingernail file you brought into my cell counts as a knife," Wes added. She grinned and punched him on the shoulder as another servant passed by, pretending to be very interested in the basket of potatoes he was carrying. Alder tried not to wish that she would look at him the same way, offer him the same playfulness. She was a distraction. He had to get his thoughts straight.

"Anyway, Moorn told them he'd felt compelled to go along with the swap in order to protect me from harm," Kessara continued. "I hope his story holds up. Actually, I hope he left the Red Army and found another job."

"It's not as easy as you think. Sometimes you can't just walk away," Alder said.

"You did," Wes pointed out. "Not only from Aridmoor's army, but from your King's own Protectorate. You gave up being a Junior Captain."

"And it was the most difficult thing I've ever done in my life," he snapped before he could stop himself. His voice was always deep, but when he was angry, it came out as a rumble. Wes lifted up both hands in mock surrender as Kessara looked down at the dirty hem of her dress. No one spoke for several seconds.

"I'm—I'm sorry. It's nothing. Can we just pretend I didn't just growl at you all like a wild dog?" Alder said finally, forcing himself to look straight at his companions rather than at his boots. He attempted a smile, but he was certain that it came off as more of a grimace.

The emotionless politician's expression had returned to Kessara's face, making it impossible to read her emotions. He would have considered it impressive were it not so maddening.

A few minutes later, as they walked into the palace and toward the throne room, Alder found himself lost in memory.

Despite everything that had happened, despite all of the pain he had both seen and caused, there was a part of him that missed his life as a soldier. It was like a wound that would almost heal, only to be torn open again by the most unlikely, stupid cause.

He glanced beside him at Wes, pretending not to stare at the ugly pink burn that covered most of his cheek. The worst of his own scars were hidden beneath the surface, but that didn't make them any less real.

The Princess strode ahead of them, her long blonde hair falling between her shoulder blades as she walked with the perfect posture of the noble-born.

Perhaps he and Kessara were not so different after all. Both of them were used to giving orders, to making demands, to being listened to by those around them. He suspected that Kessara's authority had made her softer and more willing to notice the needs of those around her. He was different. His years in the army had taught him to be stingy with his trust and to hide his brokenness beneath the veneer of a joke.

He could only hope that with the help of the High One, he'd be able to become more like the boy that he once was. He was so very tired of pushing people away.

* * *

"Let's speak alone," King Errol Manta said, placing a leathery hand on his shoulder. Wes felt the stubs of his missing left fingers pressing against him. "We can visit in my study."

They had been able to enter the palace without much difficulty. Only Wes' face was known to the general population, and he'd been able to hide beneath the shadow of his farmer's cap. In any case, anyone who knew what he looked like would have been expecting to see the silvery-smooth flesh of his moonscar, not the burn mark that now marred it.

Kessara's mother, Queen Jinna Manta, had recognized him right away, giving him a warm hug and immediately asking him if he'd eaten. King Manta had stood off to the side, arms crossed over his chest, eyeing Alder warily until the soldier strode up to bow and kiss his rings.

Introductions made, the others sat at the Queen's table and were offered tea and breakfast. Wes wished desperately that he could join them. Aside from the terror of having to face the grizzly King alone, he was hungry for some decent food.

"Well, the Envoy lives," King Manta said as he sat down in a dark blue armchair and beckoned Wes to sit across from him. "And, to my astonishment, he's free."

Several seconds passed as the man examined Wes from beneath his eyebrows. Wes couldn't help but to notice how much the King had aged since he'd last seen him. His once-handsome face was weatherbeaten, with crows' feet resting at the corners of his sharp blue eyes, and his once blonde hair had largely gone gray.

"Yes," Wes said finally, unsure what else to add.

"My wife is beginning to believe in this High One business," the King said as he pulled a cigar from a box sitting nearby, letting it rest between his lips. "I don't."

"What has Kessara told her?"

"Everything, I suspect. There is much that passes between those two that I've never been able to understand. It's always been that way."

The King paused to light his cigar. Within a few breaths, the room was hazy with fragrant smoke. The only windows

23

were set high in the back wall, and the shafts of sunlight only served to illuminate the upper shelves of the King's bookcases. Smoke aside, Wes couldn't decide if the study was cozy or suffocating.

"Would you like one? Just got them delivered from Port Keyes. Apparently they're importing them from this little town in Boneshire called Rill. Good tobacco grows in strange places."

Wes felt a flicker of sadness in his chest. He knew of the place. It was the home of two children, Holga and Gohr, who he had freed from dwarf bandits in the desert. He hoped that they were well.

"I'm fine, thank you," Wes said, trying to stop himself from coughing. He wondered if the King noticed how much he had aged, as well. He was no longer the fat little brother of the man his daughter loved. He was a man himself, now, at seventeen—though he wasn't sure he felt like one.

"Suit yourself. Anyway, like I said, I don't have time for gods. Men keep me busy enough. But I do trust my daughter. She's one of the smartest people I've ever met."

"She is. And more importantly when it comes to matters such as this, she's sincere."

"Exactly. I want this to be clear, son," he said, leaning a few inches toward Wes, his cigar dangling in his hand and dripping bits of ash on the gleaming wood floor beneath.

"The only reason I have even considered allowing this meeting to pass in secret from the Septemvirate and from the new Steward of Silverfell is because of my regard for Kessara. I would not ordinarily allow men wanted on crimes of blasphemy and treason to wander into my palace."

He cringed at the mention of the Steward, otherwise known

as King Kylan Ursa of Aridmoor. Before Wes had been imprisoned, the man had taken over control of his Kingdom, claiming that his usurpation was only temporary. He wanted to believe that the citizens of Silverfell would resist, but he knew that the bulk of the people would have already accepted this new state of affairs without protest. It was for their own good, if Kylan Ursa was to be believed, and that was enough for most.

"I understand, my King."

"Good. Well, boy, how did you enjoy the locusts on the way in?"

Wes paused for a moment, trying to stop himself from stammering his answer. He knew the King to be a good man, but that didn't make him any less intimidating. He'd spent much of his younger years at sea, fighting off pirates, and he'd lost several fingers doing so. Wes didn't want to imagine what other hidden wounds he'd likely suffered.

"They were disgusting," he offered.

"Those were the babies, Wes," the King said, a fierceness gleaming in his eyes. "They will return at the end of their season, all grown up, and most of our crop fields will resemble the forest that you and the dragon burned down."

"I didn't realize—"

"You need to realize one thing," he said, leaning forward in his chair. "This little secret alliance that we have forged cannot last. Even if my daughter and now my wife wish for it to be so. We rely on Aridmoor's crop to feed our people. I cannot ask them to starve in order to protect you."

"I know."

"Do you?" the King raised his voice. Every fiber of Wes' being urged him to stare at his feet, but he refused. He looked the old sailor straight in the eye.

"Many have sacrificed for me, my King. They've sacrificed even their lives. I live with the weight of that every day that I yet breathe."

Faces rushed through his mind, far too many. Familiar faces. Happy faces of people who had more life to live. People he loved, whose broken bodies were now in the ground.

"King Ursa holds all of the power here. We are at his mercy. At least as things stand now."

Their eyes met for several seconds until Wes finally shriveled away beneath his gaze.

"There is one option, Wes. And you know very well what it is."

* * *

Celesyria tried to sleep, but rest would not come. The sun was high in the sky, and the strange trees provided too little shade to shield her massive form. She found herself tossing and turning, returning to the creek every hour in an attempt to drink enough water to cool off. She kept an eye out for the woman they'd met, but so far, the whole area had remained deserted. As usual, she was alone, hidden away, her very existence enough to put her friends in peril. She lay on her back, trying to let the sun's rays land on her pale belly rather than continuing to fry her wings and neck.

To pass the time, she thought about ways she could teach Alder to speak within his mind. Though she had a special connection with Wes, she wanted to be able to communicate with Alder without always needing to include him in the conversation, especially when the two men were bickering.

26

She found the Aridmoorian hilarious, but she understood why Wes sometimes reacted poorly to his levity. He'd been through more at twelve than most people suffered in a lifetime, and his troubles had hardly ended there. It didn't surprise her that he was still insecure about certain things. In her eyes, he was a hero like few she'd read about. But it was another thing to help him see that, especially when most of the world still saw him as nothing more than a blasphemer and a traitor.

I suppose I'll have to teach Kessara, too. She wanted so badly to meet her. Being the sole dragon everywhere she went was lonely enough. It would be nice to not have to be the only female as well.

She thought of her mother. She had no idea if she was alright, no idea if she and her father had been imperiled by her actions. She wanted desperately to go to them, but how could she? They would lock her up, and a dragon prison would not be so easy to escape. Worse, her parents would probably have disowned her already anyway.

She tried once again to reach out to Wes, hoping for some update on how things were going in Windshear or at least a distraction from her worries, but he was still too far away. She hoped that if she could learn to speak to the others, perhaps there was a way to strengthen her and Wes' skill at speaking from a distance. She sighed in frustration, rolling back over onto her feet and deciding it was about time for another drink from the creek.

As she moved to leave the relative safety of the trees, she noticed something that made her cold blood catch in her chest.

A group of red-clad soldiers were passing near the top of the valley, headed straight for the city.

27

Chapter 3

"If you marry Kessara, she will become the legitimate monarch of Silverfell, and Kylan Ursa will be forced to step down as Steward," the King said, stubbing out his cigar and tossing it into an ashtray on the side table. "We'd still have Elder Dorold and the rest of the Septemvirate to contend with, but at least we'd have a Queen in your Kingdom that both of our people would trust."

"Right," Wes said faintly. He wondered if he should ask for a cigar, after all. He abhorred the smell of tobacco, but he'd heard that it calmed the nerves.

"It would permit a real alliance between Galeharbor and Silverfell rather than a shadowed one. King Ursa would lose much of his strategic advantage. Better yet, your homeland still has at least some functional farmland that we could all benefit from."

"Not enough."

"No," the King said, rubbing at his temples. Wes caught himself staring at his disfigured hand again before looking away. "But it's better than what we have now, and significantly so."

"I had figured that your original plan was no longer an option, considering I spent months in prison. Not to mention the fact that everyone thinks I threatened your daughter at knifepoint in order to escape."

The King waved a hand. "Everyone knows a young couple in love that has gone through worse and come out on the other side. You're overthinking things. Nothing has changed."

"Kessara told the Septemvirate that the engagement was off. It's the only reason that they allowed her to remain free. Even a Princess is not immune from charges of blasphemy. If they wanted to punish her, they could do it."

"Wes," the King said, closing his eyes and pressing his fingers into his skull as though explaining something very simple to someone very stupid. "I'm not sure if you realize this, but your actions and the actions of my daughter have made a diplomatic resolution to this problem an impossibility."

"Fair enough."

We were defending the truth, my King, whether or not you choose to believe in it. Our people have needs that run deeper than food or drink or even peace.

"We may as well take any advantage that we can get. Our options are few. You marrying Kessara won't solve all of our problems, but it will go a long way to help. Elder Dorold will be furious," the King paused, and Wes noticed a sparkle in his eyes as a smile tugged at his lips. "I've always considered him to be a bit of a pompous windbag, if we're speaking the truth. I may enjoy seeing him squirm when he realizes just how much borrowed power that he wields."

"I understand," Wes said, biding time. How could he refuse the King's request? Without the consideration of the High One, the man's logic was sound.

Mere weeks ago, he had proposed to the Princess himself, in front of half of Stronghollow. Did he still have the guts to go through with it, or had fear tempted him into making a promise he never intended to keep? It was impossible to know.

He hoped that he had meant it at the time, at least.

Kessara deserved that much.

"I know she's quite a few years older than you. That has to be emasculating, but—"

Wes couldn't help but to chuckle for a moment before King Manta's stunned gaze fell upon him. He was not a man accustomed to being interrupted.

"My King," he started. "Forgive me, I shouldn't have laughed. But it's nothing like that. Kessara is one of the most beautiful women in Kaveryth, and I do not say that merely because she is your daughter. Even if she is older than I am."

King Manta rapped his remaining fingers along the leather armrest, probably following the beat of some sea shanty, the lyrics lost to memory.

"She loved Roven," Wes said, surprised at the catch in his voice. "I know he loved her, too. He loved her right into his grave. And I know that you probably think the Eternal Lands are nothing but some story we tell ourselves to make everything alright, but you're wrong."

Wes paused, half expecting a scolding, or at least a glare of disapproval, but there was none. His eyes were filled with nothing but shadow, hurt and loss reflected in two turquoise pools.

"I hope and I pray that Roven is there. And in the end, when Kessara dies an old lady who lived a long, happy life, I want her to be able to go back to him. Even if love doesn't look the same as it does for us down here, I know they'll find each other. I'm not naive. I know there will be a husband for her in this life, maybe even a few blue eyed children running around your palace, but I don't want it to be me."

Wes tried to stop himself from crying, but as usual, he couldn't help himself. He brushed away the tears that had spilled down his face, cheeks burning with shame. After taking a few deep breaths into his lungs, he looked up, expecting to see the same vulnerability that had flashed in the King's eyes a mere moment before.

It was gone.

"Do you think that you were Kessara's first choice, Wes?" King Manta said, his voice dangerously calm.

"Of course not. I can't compare to Roven. He's ten times the man I was, and probably will ever be," Wes said, trying not to let his annoyance show on his face. Ever since that terrible day when he'd lost his family, he'd spent most of his time hating himself. It was only more recently that he'd been able to begin to believe his life was even worth living. "Forgive me, my King, but nothing you can say about me could ever be worse than what I'd say about myself. I know that I'm not good enough for her, I know she doesn't—"

"You're missing the point," King Manta snapped, standing up from his chair so fast that it screeched against the floor-boards. "Even if you weren't good enough for my daughter, it doesn't matter."

Wes said nothing, unsure whether he should stand up himself as the King began to pace around the room. He watched as thousands of tiny dust particles glimmered in the light pouring in from the windows near the ceiling, wishing that he could run away from all of his problems and never look back.

"Kessara isn't perfect. I love her more than anything, but that doesn't mean she's without flaws. But there's one thing she does have, and that's the courage to do what's right for the sake of her homeland and her people."

"I know. I'm—"

"You need to learn to listen," the King said, walking over and placing his hand upon Wes' shoulder once more. His voice was softer now. "Wes, I care about you. And I cared about Roven very much. That's why I need to tell you the truth when no one else will."

The King looked at him, unblinking, a deep sadness in his eyes that made Wes want to turn away.

"Men have to make the hard choices, Wes."

"Don't you think I know that? I have made hard choices. I have. More than most fully grown men will ever have to make."

"You still don't understand," the King shook his head, his voice gentle. "Kessara is willing to marry you because it's the right thing to do, because she puts what's right over what she wants. I am proud of her for that. But if she refused to marry you…"

His voice trailed off. He moved for the door, placing his hand on the knob and looking back at Wes.

"If she refused to marry you, I would tell her that she was going to do it anyway. And if she still would not, I would tell her that she would no longer be permitted to live in our home. Because I am a man, and a man must be willing to do what is necessary. Even if it breaks his heart."

Before he could say more, there was a knock at the study door. King Manta looked up, shaking his head as though trying to remove the unpleasant thoughts within. "Come in."

"My King," a young man in servant garb said, bowing low against the wooden floor. "Captain Drohma is here."

* * *

Kessara sat at a small table in the throne room with Alder and her mother, watching absently as a glob of jam fell from her biscuit and onto the pristine blue tablecloth. They had just been informed that King Ursa's army was here in Windshear, and that one of their leaders was waiting outside to speak to the King and Queen. She hoped that Celesyria was somewhere safe, far from whichever road the soldiers would have taken into the city.

Finally, her mother spoke. She cleared her throat and stood up from the table, brushing invisible crumbs off of the front of her beaded blue day dress. "Alright. You two will go up to the balcony for the time being. I will handle this."

From the shadows at the far end of the room, she saw her father exit his study and head toward them, his footfalls echoing against the stone walls of the vast space. "Do you have any idea what this is about?"

"No, darling. I think you should let me take care of it."

For a moment, Kessara and Alder watched as two monarchs faced off, the Queen putting her hands on her trim waist and meeting her husband's gaze.

To Kessara's surprise, there were none of the usual arguments.

"You're right, my love. I'll be in my study."

"Smart man," Alder whispered to Kessara as the King returned to the far end of the throne room. "Beauty is the honey required for such situations."

"Or maybe my father knows that my mother is a skilled diplomat," Kessara said, glowering at him. Before they could say more, however, they heard a cheery trumpet call from just outside the entrance doors.

"Go."

Kessara pointed to a swirling set of stairs between two of the huge glass windows that lined the walls. Alder headed toward them, moving up to the second level with steps so quiet that the ancient wood hardly made a sound. She followed with less success, her skirt catching on an old nail before she was able to shake it loose.

The queen glanced up at her daughter with a finger to her lips. With a final raise of her eyebrows at Alder, she turned, fixed her hair, and moved for the door. "Please, my dear soldier," she said, her voice syrupy-sweet. "I'm just powdering my nose. One moment, if you would."

Kessara scrambled onto the balcony floor after Alder, pressing her body tight against the solid wood rail. "Perfect," Alder whispered as he moved in beside her, pressing one of his eyes against the small, seashell-shaped holes that perforated the top edge of the railing.

"My mother has done her own spying from up here, I'm sure," she whispered back, finding a place to look a couple of paces away.

"On your father?"

"Probably. He has his own way of doing things sometimes. I wonder what he's saying to Wes."

Alder shrugged. "Probably telling him to stop being a loser and agree to marry you," he said. She rolled her eyes.

It's not as easy as everyone thinks it is to choose a person to spend the rest of your life with. She wished that she knew how to say as much. Not that she really thought Alder would understand Wes's objections. *Then again, it's not like I understand them, either.*

"He's not a loser," she said instead.

"I was joking. I'm sure your father had his reasons for wanting to talk to him alone. Some things need to be man to man."

"Easy for you to say when you are one."

"That's true. I don't think I'd want to be a woman."

"Probably not. It's harder than you think it is."

"Maybe."

She smirked as she watched Alder adjusting his position. He was far too tall to sit comfortably and remain hidden from view. Here, his long limbs made him look more like a stumbling new fawn than a warrior of the plains Kingdom.

"What's so funny?" he hissed, pulling back from the peeping hole. She shook her head, pointing back toward the ground level just as the doors swung open.

"My Queen," the man said as he and the several soldiers with him dropped to their knees, heads bent low. "Your hospitality is most appreciated, though it would have been ideal if your husband was here as well. I know that we didn't give you much notice of our arrival."

"You mean no notice—" Kessara started to whisper, but the look on Alder's face as he stepped back from the railing stopped her short. "It's Captain Drohma," he said, setting his jaw. "My superior in the Protectorate. I thought they sent Lieutenant Daas, or even Major Lowell, from the regular army…" His voice trailed off as he moved back to the peephole.

"My Captain, you know that you are always welcome to visit my Kingdom," the Queen said, waving a hand across the throne room as though showing off just how much she was willing to offer an ally. "I regret that my husband is indisposed, I'm sure he would have been very keen on having a cigar with you. But I must confess I am confused as to why you are here."

"King Ursa asked me to convey his regrets. I know that he very much wished to speak to you himself."

"He's a busy man."

"He is indeed, and that is precisely why he wished for me to speak to you about a proposal that he's had in mind for quite some months."

Kessara watched as her mother beckoned her visitors toward a seating area on the opposite side of the room, far from the remnants of their breakfast that could lead to questions, while still facing Alder and Kessara's hiding place above.

"Now," she said, sitting primly in what Kessara knew to be the King's favorite chair. "I would love to hear what our good King of Aridmoor and Steward of Silverfell has been considering."

"To be frank, my Queen, the situation in my own country and increasingly in Silverfell has become quite dire. There are more criminal raids than I have ever seen in my lifetime. The slavers have struck near my childhood home, just east of High Keep. I fear for my family members that do not live within the safety of the city walls."

He's good. Both her mother and her father had a heart for those who fell victim to violence and pillage. She could read no insincerity in his face, and she suspected that he was telling the truth.

"I am sorry to hear that. We have had many troubles of our own. I've had more than one of my subjects tell me that they've seen elves and dwarves, traveling way out in the wilderlands. Right here in Galeharbor. Can you believe it?" the Queen leaned forward in her chair, her eyes wide. Kessara smiled. *That's it, mom. Make sure that he underestimates you. Always ends up being a mistake in the end.*

"I believe him, but that doesn't make King Ursa one of the good guys," she heard Alder hiss from beside her.

"I agree. But she knows what she's doing," she whispered back. "Just trust me on this."

"We have seen the non-human races within our territory as well. How much our world has changed, in so short a time."

"But our dear King Ursa has a solution, I take it?" Queen Manta crooned.

"He does. And if I may say so, my Queen," Drohma leaned toward her, a wolfish smile on his face. "It's the only solution, and I urge you to command your men to take part in it. I can't imagine a beautiful woman such as yourself would have any difficulty convincing your husband of the necessity."

The Queen gave the Captain a smile, brushing a stray hair back behind her ear.

"Ah. The King desires to expand his army," she said, the lighthearted smile still dancing on her lips. "Now that he's Steward of Silverfell, he has more men to command, but he would like to expand that number."

"Precisely. He wishes to create an allied force, strong enough to push back against the dangers that molest us from every side as of late. The King is referring to it as the Red Army."

"You're not strong enough now, I take it?"

Captain Drohma chuckled, but even from the balcony, Kessara could see that his smile never touched his eyes. She felt a shiver run down her back.

"If I'm being honest, no, my Queen, we are not. Our army is large, but before the Silverfell soldiers joined our ranks, we struggled with training and discipline."

"And of course King Ursa is well aware of our soldiers' skill with munitions, not to mention our naval power," she finished for him.

Galeharbor was known across Kaveryth for crafting the best liquid fire and the most destructive bombs, but until recently, such weapons had not been in high demand. The method of their manufacture more closely resembled the work of an artist and his apprentice rather than a well-oiled machine of well-priced death. Kessara doubted that they would be able to produce their arms at the sort of scale that the King would prefer, at least not on short notice.

No. He doesn't care about our weapons. King Ursa wants our navy. Kessara watched as her mother smoothed her skirt and flashed the Captain another regal smile.

The elves in Nox had always been dangerous, and they always would be. They could prepare themselves. But when Kessara looked out at the North Sea, she knew that it was a very different beast. Pirates and slavers were bad enough, but no one really knew what else was out there.

No map was perfect, and no map told tales of what might

lurk below the surface. They needed a navy that was ready for anything.

"A thousand ships, surrounding all of Kaveryth," she heard Alder mutter from beside her. "Red sails on every one."

No monarch in Galeharbor's history had ever dared to neglect their navy, and now it served as a promise that King Ursa would never let them be, never let them remain neutral. He needed Galeharbor, and sometimes being an ally was more dangerous than being an enemy.

* * *

"My Queen, perhaps you should have served in the navy alongside King Manta," Captain Drohma said, giving her a half smile. "You know the strength of your men so very well. As a soldier myself, I can say with certainty that they appreciate being held in such esteem by their ruling monarch."

Alder gritted his teeth, glad that Kessara wouldn't be able to see the blood rushing to his face with his eye pressed against the peephole. Listening to Drohma's attempts at flattering the Queen filled him with rage. He knew better than most how the man really felt about women, especially women whose beauty met his taste. He doubted that the Captain's respect for her stature would spare her from being the subject of his wicked fantasies. It made his skin crawl.

"I understand why King Ursa wishes to broker such an alliance," the Queen said. "These dangers are real, and they threaten the security of all of the people of the Four Kingdoms. For too long, we have allowed Boneshire to suffer under the corruption of their leaders, unwilling or unable to protect their citizens from violence. I admit that the idea of being able to do such good appeals to me. It will appeal to the King, as well."

Alder pulled back and looked over at Kessara. She shook her head. "Trust me," she hissed under her breath before continuing to look out over the balcony. Alder hoped that whatever brilliant plan Kessara was convinced that her mother had would come to fruition soon. His legs were falling asleep and his neck ached from crouching.

"Oh, wonderful, my Queen," Drohma oozed. "I couldn't agree more. Even the poor deserve to be able to conduct their lives without fear of crime and violence."

"Of course. But I assume that our good King must understand that this request puts us in a rather delicate position."

Captain Drohma said nothing, and Alder noticed a brief flash of annoyance crossing his face before he composed himself again.

"My daughter Kessara is a supporter of the Envoy's cause. I'm not sure how much she believes in this High One business herself, but in any case, she's made it clear where her loyalties lie."

"A parent must—" Captain Drohma began, closing his mouth as quickly as he had opened it when Queen Manta held up a hand in front of him.

"I'm sure that your advice on raising a princess is most enlightening, but whatever our opinion is on the allegations against Wes Cervos and the dragon Celesyria, the King and I have no intention of turning our backs on our daughter."

"My Queen, you misunderstand," Drohma started, shaking his head as though the whole matter was quite silly. "King Ursa would not dream of putting such conditions on our proposal. The crimes committed by Wes Cervos and the dragon are a separate matter. The King wished for me to make it very clear to you that he is committed to leaving the Princess out of it."

Kessara made a face. Alder wanted to ask what she meant, but the conversation below continued without pause.

"These threats we have discussed were what led King Ursa to seek Stewardship of Silverfell in the first place," Captain Drohma continued. "I'm sure you can see that things are worse now than ever before. The scent of war has not been so strong since the fall of Boneshire."

The Queen let out a slow breath. "The King foresees a war with Nox?"

Drohma nodded. "It is not certain, but we have seen enough of the signs to believe that is what they are planning. Things are changing, and the race of men must be willing to place our bets upon the future if we wish to survive."

"Yet we must be prudent in our gambling," the Queen said easily. "It is no small thing for me to ask my men to put their lives on the line."

"My Queen," the Captain began, leaning forward in his chair and giving her a sad smile. "For the first time in memory, we have an Envoy on the run who is refusing to offer sacrifices to the Dracodei. Without the sacrifices, we have no reason to expect that the Guardians will continue to protect us. We are on our own, and that changes the stakes."

"I understand."

"My people are beginning to panic. I suspect your subjects are as well, and if not, they will be soon. The summer Feast of Offering draws near. When that day comes, if Wes Cervos has not been found, fear will light our world on fire. We need to be ready."

41

Chapter 4

Kessara watched as her mother asked for a moment to think and headed toward the study at the back of the room. The soldiers remained where they were, though they all relaxed their postures at a wave of the Captain's hand as soon as the heavy door to her father's study closed behind her.

The whole exchange was troubling. She had assured Alder that her mother had a plan, but hearing what Captain Drohma said, she was no longer sure. She had to admit that King Ursa's desire for an allied army made sense, but she did not trust his loyalty to the Four Kingdoms. Furthermore, they refused to understand the true nature of what was going on in regard to the High One and the sacrifices. But was it possible that they could succeed in defending Kaveryth against the forces of Nox, even if they continued to insist upon worshiping false gods?

"We need to talk," Alder whispered, gesturing toward the back of the balcony, behind the rows of seats. It was dark, and the thick tapestries that hung on the walls would muffle their voices as long as they stayed quiet.

"Don't you want to hear what they say?"

"No. And you don't either. Come on," he said firmly.

"Don't tell me what to do," she hissed at him, pressing her eye back up against the peephole. "I'm not one of your soldiers."

Just then, sufficiently certain that the Queen was indeed out of earshot for a few minutes, the soldiers began to speak to one another.

"I'm glad she's giving us a minute to breathe," one of them said. Kessara watched as he gave the man next to him a playful punch in the ribs. "My heart has been racing this whole time."

Good. I'm glad that she intimidates you.

"I confess to the same," Captain Drohma said, chuckling under his breath. "I haven't seen Kessara in a few years, but if she looks anything like Jinna..." He trailed off, glancing over at the study door as the others began to laugh.

"Wonder if Wes Cervos still plans to marry her."

"The Queen?"

More laughter.

"Kessara. Maybe the princess is a little less uptight."

She felt Alder's hand on her shoulder. "You don't need to listen to this," he hissed into her ear. She shrugged him off as the men continued. She felt sick to her stomach, but she couldn't bear to look away.

"Who cares," Captain Drohma said, lowering his voice a few notches. Kessara watched as he held a finger to his lips and glanced at the door. "I doubt the Envoy would care if she

43

wears a white dress on their wedding night, boys. That swine would still be getting quite the deal."

"It's not like he'd know what to do with a girl like that. Now me, on the other hand, I would–"

"Move," Alder said, placing a firm hand on her shoulder. "Now."

She pulled away from the peephole. "Don't touch me—"

He grabbed her by both shoulders and stared into her eyes, his face mere inches away. His green eyes were piercing. "If I hear another word," he whispered, his voice on the edge of wavering. "I am going to go down there and kick his teeth in. And that would be stupid. So please, let's just go."

Without further protest, she allowed him to lead her by the elbow toward the shadows at the back of the room. "I can defend my own honor, Alder," she snapped, shrugging away from his grip. "I don't even know you. This is really none of your business."

He released her and she sat against the wall, feeling the comforting softness of the tapestry against her back. She resisted the sudden urge to be sick. *All the time, this is what they were thinking of me. Perhaps even when I was a young girl.*

She was surprised at how violated she felt by their mere words. She had always thought that she was tougher than that, but this felt different, somehow.

"You don't know what these men are capable of, Kessara," Alder said, sitting next to her, his voice gentle. Part of her wanted to tell him to give her space, but she couldn't bring herself to say it. Another part of her was comforted to know he was close. Though he was indeed a stranger to her, Wes trusted him, and that went a long way in her book.

She swiped a tear from her eye. *I don't know what you're*

capable of, either. But I have little doubt you meant every word of your threat.

Neither of them said anything for a moment as the faint sound of jeers and laughter filtered up to the balcony. Finally, Alder spoke.

"I was with Captain Drohma on the day that I saw Wes for the first time," he said, running a hand through his red hair. He paused, beginning to speak before stopping again, as though the words were too difficult to say out loud. "All of the soldiers I was with were talking about this barmaid in the village we were in. Talking like this. Drohma included.

"Did they…" Kessara trailed off, unable to finish her question.

"No, fortunately, they were just talking," Alder assured her. "Wes still defended her, though. Told Drohma that she was a kind person."

He chuckled for a moment. "Men like that don't care about how kind a woman is. They don't even care that she's a mother, or a daughter."

"Apparently they don't care if she's a competent ruler, either," Kessara said, pressing her eyes together as new tears formed. Her mother was not naive, but still, she was glad that she'd been in the other room, safe with her father. Her parents had a tendency to bicker, but she was certain that her father's response to such comments about his wife would be no less violent than Alder's threat.

"No, they don't. Wes might be a bit naive," Alder said. "But still, even though he was by himself, he stood up for a barmaid in front of a group of warriors. At the time, I had no idea that I'd soon be fighting beside him, but I respected him for that."

Kessara nodded, feeling numb. She was glad to know that

Wes was safe, at least for the moment. What Alder said didn't surprise her. Wes was a good man, through and through. And he always had been. *I'd be lucky to be his wife.* She pitied whichever poor women the soldiers below had left behind in Aridmoor.

"I wish that more women had someone to defend them," Alder said under his breath, looking down at his boots. Kessara looked over at him, but he wouldn't meet her eyes. "And yet, I lived with these men. They were like my brothers. Despite everything they said and did, at the time, I would have died for them. What kind of person does that make me?"

She said nothing. After a moment, Alder continued to speak, as though unable to stop the torrent of guilt from pouring out of his heart.

"I don't know why I'm telling you this," he said, chuckling uneasily. "You're right. We're strangers."

"No," Kessara said, placing a hand on his arm for a second before removing it. "I shouldn't have said that. If you're Wes' friend, then you're my friend too. On top of that, you're a believer in the High One. I–I want to hear what you have to say."

Alder looked at his feet again, clearing his throat before he continued.

"I don't know what they did when the sun went down and they snuck off into whatever city or village we were posted in. I don't know where they went after the ale ran out and the card games ended for the night."

"But you suspect that they did more than talk about how good a girl looked in a tight dress," Kessara ventured. Now that he was telling her the rest of his confession, she wasn't so sure that she wanted to know.

46

"Yes."

"So why did you stay so long?"

She tried to keep the disgust from showing in her voice, though she couldn't decide if she was angry with him, or only with the soldiers that he'd served with.

Despite everything he said, she couldn't shake the feeling of comfort and safety that she had just being near him. She felt like nothing could touch her, so long as he stayed nearby.

What kind of person does that make me? She asked herself. *I say that I can take care of myself, yet here I am, wanting to be protected by a man that I just met.*

"You could have left," she added. "You could have said something, though I suppose it's not obvious who would even see their behavior as a problem if even your captain condoned it. Still. There's always some way to do what's right."

For a few long moments, he said nothing. He closed his eyes, and she watched as he clenched his hands into fists, knuckles going white. "My Princess," he started. She was waiting for a clever quip, or perhaps the sort of frightening calm he'd shown when threatening the soldiers, but instead, all she heard was the pain behind his words. *My title sounds strange when he says it, somehow.*

"Even if we're friends, you know nothing about me. For whatever mad reason, I feel like I can trust you, so I'm going to. In case you couldn't tell, I'm not really the sort of guy to mope around sharing his feelings," he said.

She nodded, so he continued.

"That's Wes' job," he added with a smirk. She resisted the urge to argue.

"I have made terrible choices in my life," he continued, placing his palms against the stone floor of the balcony.

47

Kessara could still hear the soldiers, but their words and laughter had faded into the background, no longer important. "Choices that you have never had to make. I'm not saying your life is easy, so don't get defensive."

"I'll try."

"You've never lacked for anything. You grew up in a palace. Your family is powerful. You've always worn the nicest clothes and had your hair braided by servant girls. And you've certainly never gone hungry a day in your life."

"Ah, so you're condemning my judgment of you by making one of your own," she quipped, trying to keep the tone light even as the hurt in her voice betrayed her.

"Am I wrong, my Princess?" he gave her a hint of a smile.

"No."

"Ever since I was a child, my father was always drunk, in jail, or both. Usually, he ended up there after giving my mother a few good hits to the face. He even tried it with one of my sisters once, though that was the last time before he died in jail. Anyway, as you can probably imagine, it was not an easy childhood."

"I'm sorry, Alder."

He continued as though he hadn't heard her. "My sisters and I had a governess, sort of—a woman who helped my mother around the house, watched us while she went to work in the city, that sort of thing. Anyway, even with her help, we barely survived."

"I'm sorry," she said again, cringing as soon as the words came out but unsure what else she could say instead. Even though they were alone, she found herself glancing around the room, listening for pauses in the soldiers' chatter below. She didn't want anyone else to hear Alder's words.

She wondered if he was simply unable to stop talking now that he'd gotten started, not that she minded. It would be easier to have him as an ally if she could truly call him a friend, and that connection was much easier to build with someone willing to open up to her. The whole conversation felt fragile, like it would end at any moment, never allowing her to see this side of her new friend again.

"I enlisted in the Aridmoor army at age fourteen. I saw an opportunity to provide for my family, and I took it. I'm not sorry for that part. I'm not. I was given a set of terrible choices in my life, and I took the best one that I could. Better to be a soldier than a bandit."

"Your family is fortunate to have you."

"Thank you," he said under his breath, not meeting her eyes. "But that was not the only choice I made. The King's Protectorate paid a much better wage than the general forces, and even after several years paying my dues, I still wasn't making anywhere near enough to pull my mother out of the business she was in."

He looked at her, his eyes filled with pain and shame, and her stomach sank as realization dawned. His mother had been given even worse choices than he was. *A woman he hadn't been able to protect.* Her heart ached for both of them. She could only hope that his sisters had not been forced into such a profession.

"Selection for the Protectorate had little to do with skill or training. I learned very quickly that even in King Radagar Ursa's day, the soldiers that were chosen were those who were the easiest to manipulate and control. And it's gotten even worse under Kylan's reign."

"I guess I can't imagine you as a man who is easy to control,"

Kessara said, trying to smile.

"Why, because I'm stubborn and do as I please?" he joked.

"No. Because I know that you believe in the High One, and that you were willing to risk everything to do the right thing."

"I guess so. I just hope I didn't do the right thing too late."

"What do you mean?"

"I betrayed King Ursa, Kessara. He hates Wes, and he hates Celesyria, but I assure you that he now hates me above anyone else," he said, his voice hard. "And all I can do is hope that he doesn't choose to punish my entire family for what I've done."

* * *

Alder rested his head against the back wall, feeling drained. It was rare that he spoke so openly with anyone, and he had not had a conversation like this since the day that he freed Celesyria. He could still hear the insipid chattering of the soldiers below, but he did his best to ignore them, focusing instead on Kessara's voice.

"They'll be okay," she said, tucking a few stray hairs behind her ear and laying back against the tapestries beside him. "You'll protect them. I have no doubt."

He coughed, looking at his feet. He couldn't bear to look at her for too long. When he did, all he could think about was how badly he wanted to protect her. She was not prepared for the world that was coming. *Wes has an inkling of it. I just hope he'll be able to protect her when she becomes his wife. He must.*

"Alder?"

"Yes?"

"Do you ever doubt that you did the right thing in the first place?"

"No, but maybe I should," he said, smiling and glancing up at the shadowed corner of the ceiling. "It is rarely a wise decision to chase after a god that you've met only in your dreams."

"I wish I had your faith," Kessara said, her voice barely loud enough to hear as she pulled her body in closer to the wall and tucked her arms around her knees. "I've doubted that I did the right thing. I've never stopped doubting. I woke up today, and I saw the sun rising over the North Sea, and all I could think about was that nothing could be greater than nature itself. It seems foolish, almost, to believe that there's something higher. Someone we can't even see."

She paused for a moment, glancing at him, as though waiting for a scolding, but he said nothing.

"I know that the dragons are dying, and I believe that Celesyria found fragments of what she thinks is the Codex Veritatis, and that it said what she claims it does. But just because I no longer believe that the Dracodei are really gods doesn't make it easy to have faith in another all-powerful creator."

"It's hard for me to relate, I guess," Alder said after an awkward pause. "For me, the High One is so real, it's like I'm talking to you when I pray to Him. I guess I've had moments where I think I'm just deluding myself, but…"

Kessara smiled at him, a sad smile that didn't touch her blue eyes. "A part of me thinks that the idea of a true God of Kaveryth makes sense, and the historicity behind that belief has gone a long way in convincing me. But is that really faith? Is it enough?"

Alder shrugged. "I'm a freak who has dreams. What do I

know?"

Kessara chuckled, giving him a weak punch in the arm. He felt his stomach flip at her touch. *I like making her smile.* The thought came to him unbidden, and immediately he wished that he was thinking something else, something that wouldn't be preparing him for so much pain. *Maybe this is how Kessara feels about the High One. Maybe her mind is telling her one thing, but her heart refuses to listen.*

"I wish there was someone we could ask about these things," she said, her cheeks red as she pulled away from him and leaned back against the wall. "I feel like I'm walking blind, just feeling my way through."

"That sounds like faith to me," Alder pointed out.

"I guess so. I just wish that I didn't fall asleep at night thinking about what it would be like not to wake up," she paused when she saw the expression on his face. "I'm not depressed. I'm not... no. Nothing like that. I've always thought about it, I guess. Thought about death as this endless sleep, this total emptiness that I wouldn't even know I'm in. Ever since I was a child, it terrified me, and all of my parents's talk of the Eternal Lands felt hollow. I guess I struggled to believe in the Dracodei, too."

She gave a visible shiver.

"Well, that's a cheerful thought," he joked, unsure what possible answer or even comfort he could give.

Before Kessara could reply, they heard the sound of the throne room's door swinging open and the thump of boots on stone. As they shuffled back toward the railing of the balcony, they heard the Queen emerging from the study at the back of the room.

"My apologies," she gave Drohma a nod as she strode toward

the door. There were four soldiers waiting there, dressed in the blue uniforms of Galeharbor's army.

"My Queen," one of them said, bowing deeply. "Forgive me."

Alder could see the murderous expression on Drohma's face, but the Captain said nothing.

"What is going on?" she asked, gesturing to the man to get up off of the floor.

"Bandits, my Queen," he said, rising to his full height. "Bandits have breached the gates of Windshear."

* * *

"Come out, boy," King Manta said. Wes emerged from the dark closet, trying to be silent as he pressed the door closed behind him. He could hear the sound of men's feet and new voices outside, but before he could ask what was going on, Queen Manta strode back out into the throne room.

He expected the King to follow, but he did not. Instead, the man walked over to a small liquor cart near his desk and grabbed two glass tumblers. He moved toward Wes and held it out. "No, thank you," Wes said, certain that his confusion was visible on his face. The King pressed the glass into his hands, placing his finger to his lips as he walked back toward the door, his footfalls surprisingly quiet against the aging, creaky hardwood.

He watched as King Manta pressed the open end of the tumbler against the door and placed his ear against it to listen. "Not very dignified, I realize, but it works," he whispered, casting a wistful glance back at his desk where he had just stubbed out a half-smoked cigar.

Wes followed suit, trying to give the King enough space as he found his own spot to press his glass. He closed his eyes and listened, feeling himself wilting beneath the man's gaze and confused by what was going on outside.

When the Queen had entered the study several minutes earlier, she'd told her husband that King Ursa wished to bring their men into his new Red Army. Wes had stood there stupidly for a few minutes, wishing to be anywhere else, until the King asked him if he could perhaps step into the closet so that they could speak alone. The Queen had given him an apologetic smile as he stumbled into the tiny, dark room and shoved the King's heavy fur cloaks and silken dinner capes out of the way.

He hadn't been able to hear much through the closet door, nor was he trying to eavesdrop, but he couldn't help but to catch the gist of Captain Drohma's proposal. He had to admit that it sounded very logical, and all he could do was hope that the King and Queen would be able to see through the facade and recognize that the plan was nothing more than a chance for King Ursa to gain more power for himself and for Aridmoor.

Now, it seemed, there were new developments. He pressed his ear harder against the glass, straining to hear as the Queen began to speak. He heard the snatches of an apology, though he was not sure to whom.

A moment later, there was a new voice, and it sounded like it was coming from a little farther away. He could scarcely make out the words, but one look at King Manta's face made it clear that he'd heard precisely what he'd feared.

There were invaders on the streets of Windshear.

He watched as King Manta clenched his free fist, again

expecting the man to bolt from the room. Instead, he kept listening, sweat beginning to bead against his brow.

The voices moved closer, and Wes began to make out the words more clearly. He could hear a familiar laugh that set his teeth on edge.

"It seems rather foolish of them to attack your city just in time for the best soldiers in the Four Kingdoms to arrive," Drohma said.

The Queen said something, but Wes couldn't quite make it out.

"Whatever political differences may exist between our Kingdoms, my Queen, I am hardly going to permit innocent people to be killed by these animals."

The King's face was red with anger, but still he continued to listen.

"Thank you, Captain," came Queen Manta's voice. "There is no time to waste. Soldiers, fall in with the Protectorate men, and do as they ask."

"That's it," the King hissed, slamming the glass down onto a side table so hard that Wes was amazed it remained intact.

"Please, out of my way," he said, pushing past Wes and heading into the throne room.

Wes pulled the door nearly closed behind him, leaving just enough of a space for one eye to peer through. He could hear better, too.

"My Captain."

Wes watched as the King walked up to the red-clad soldier, extending a tanned hand for him to shake. Drohma gave an awkward half bow before offering his own hand. "While we appreciate the concern, I assure you, my men are perfectly—"

"My King," Drohma said flatly, "Glad to see you back so

soon."

"What excellent timing, isn't it?" King Manta said. Wes could see him tightening his fists though he kept an easy smile on his face.

"Indeed."

"Gentlemen," the Queen said, stepping between the two men. "Bandits are out on our streets doing gods know what."

She gripped the King's arm and leaned toward his ear. "This isn't a sword-measuring contest, darling," she hissed under her breath, loud enough that even Wes could hear it from behind the study door.

Wes watched as the rest of the red soldiers smirked, no doubt amused to see the King being dressed down by his own wife.

"M—M—My King," one of the Galeharbor men stammered, clutching the sword hanging from his belt as though the weapon could somehow be used to ward off his secondhand embarrassment. King Manta tipped his head in his direction.

"There's something else," the man continued, his words tumbling together. "I saw elves. At least three, but there could be more."

Gasps filled the room, and Wes barely managed to suppress his own before it gave him away.

"Are you sure, boy?"

The King took two long strides toward the nervous soldier, who could barely hold his gaze. "Three elves. Right here, in the capital of Galeharbor. You realize that is a wild claim, correct?"

"Yes, my King."

"But that is what you saw?" Queen Manta prompted, placing her hand gently on the young man's arm.

56

"That's what I saw. I am sure of it."

For a second, no one spoke. Even Drohma was quiet. Wes shrunk back slightly as the Captain's eyes brushed over the room, including the shadowy end where the study lay, but he did not seem to notice anything amiss. He tried to reach out to Celesyria in his mind, wanting to ensure she was still safe, but he got no response. *Good. It means she's still too far away.* He had no idea where Alder and Kessara had gone.

"Alright," King Manta said finally. The Queen straightened up beside him. "If you still wish to help us, Captain, we will not refuse Aridmoor's aid. It's time to fight."

Chapter 5

Celesyria's eyes shot open as she heard a yell. The sound pierced the air, loud enough that for a second she feared her hiding place had been discovered. She tucked her wings into her body and made her way out from beneath the trees where she'd been resting. No one seemed to be nearby, but she could not calm the racing of her heart. She'd tried to sleep for the past hour or so, but it had been impossible. All she could think about were King Ursa's men, marching across Galeharbor as though this kingdom of sky and sea already belonged to them.

O High One, keep those wicked men away from my friends, she prayed as she attempted to stretch out her cramped legs, the manacles she'd been given in prison still attached to her ankles. There might have been a chance to have them removed in Auranth—the men of the city were known for their weapon-crafting and skill with metals—but it would have been risky to bring her to the forge where their equipment was located.

Since she could still function with them on, she assured Wes and Alder that she was fine with bearing the burden a little while longer. She wasn't sure she'd told them the truth. Though she could handle the discomfort, the constant reminder of how she still was not free weighed heavily on her heart.

There was another cry, louder this time, followed by another. Celesyria pressed herself as flat against the ground as she could go, the spikes of her back the only part of her that would show above the waving grasses as she made for the top of the little valley. The noises continued as she slinked toward the ridge. They were coming together now, coalescing into a visceral chant that seemed to shake the ground.

She raised her head, peering over the endless sea of green, and then she saw them. A black line, as far as she could make out from here, slithering across the grass like some great black snake. *A battle cry,* she realized, fear gripping her chest. She could make out a few words, but they were speaking in a language she did not recognize.

They're headed straight for Windshear. She laid back down flat against the ground as the wind gusted overhead. *Straight for my friends.*

She only barely managed to stop herself from letting out a bellow of frustration and anger. *If only the dragons were as numerous as we once were.* Tears pricked her eyes as she imagined a sky full of Guardians, rushing in to give aid to the people of Galeharbor. *No one would dare march straight through the Four Kingdoms like this in the first place. How much the world has changed...*

Painful thoughts crept in at the edge of her consciousness. *What if we've made things worse than they were before? What if we were wrong about the High One, and ceasing the sacrifices to the Dracodei only hastens the death of the few dragons who remain?*

She pressed her eyes closed for a moment, desperate to get ahold of herself. She sniffed at the air, tasting a hint of smoke and hoping that it came only from the invaders' most recent campsite. She smiled darkly. *The barbarians of this world may use fire as a weapon, and yet I cannot.* Like so many other things, it didn't make any sense to her, but there was no time to dwell on it.

She couldn't let these doubts paralyze her. She and Wes had told the truth. How could she expect that the truth would not bring painful consequences with it?

Even if the dragons still filled the skies, the Dracodei were not real. A prayer to them would not move them to command the Guardians to fight.

She thought of her mother and father, somewhere in the caverns of Whitespire. Were they worried about her? Were they still angry at the lies she'd told and the things that she had done?

She didn't know. But she had faith that one day, they would accept the truth of the High One. And when that day came, they would continue to fight as Guardians. Not because the usurpers had told them to, but because their physical power had given them the responsibility of protecting the innocent.

Celesyria rose to her full height, unfurling her great orange wings and looking toward the walls of Windshear. She was born with power, and it was her duty to wield it for good, even if it meant risking her own freedom.

She pushed off of the ground and leaped into the sky, heading toward her friends as fast as her wings could take her.

* * *

No more sounds came from the throne room. Through the crack at the edge of the door, Wes could see that everyone had gone, headed toward the violence that waited outside the safety of the palace walls. Wes moved to King Manta's leather chair, collapsing into it and grabbing a small bowl of nuts that he'd noticed on the desk. His mind was racing as he tried to put together everything he'd just heard, but he'd not had a chance to eat breakfast, and the hunger was distracting. He scarfed down a handful of the snack and returned the bowl to the desk, embarrassed to think that not so long ago he would have downed the entire thing.

Just then, he heard footsteps, and stood up from the chair just in time to see Kessara's head poking through the door. "All clear."

Alder stood waiting in the empty throne room, giving him a clap on the shoulder. Wes looked around at the empty room. Whatever was happening on the streets of Windshear seemed very far away as he looked at the huge blocks of sunlight that lit the stone floor, pouring in through the windows that lined the walls. Alder snapped his fingers, and they listened to the echo as the tiny sound reverberated through the huge space.

"Wow," Kessara said finally. "I've never actually seen this room completely empty before. It's beautiful. Peaceful."

Wes listened for some telltale sound of violence or pain, but nothing seemed to penetrate the thick walls. He thought of his childhood, before his parents were killed, back when the world felt safe. There must have been problems in Silverfell then, too, but he was too young to notice them. To him, the palace in Stronghollow was not only a home but a haven, a safe place to come back to every time that his duties as Envoy called him away across the world.

Until one day, without warning, it wasn't safe any more. His parents and his brother Roven were murdered, and the throne room was empty, just like this one. He used to sneak into the abandoned space and crawl up onto his father's throne, curling up and closing his eyes, letting the scent of ancient wood bring back memories of a time when his world had been alive.

"One empty throne room is enough," he said, his voice uncomfortably loud as it echoed against the walls. "Even the sound of gossiping nobles is better than the silence of hopelessness and decay."

"I'm not sure about that," Alder put in, grinning. "You've never had to listen to Queen Ursa's younger sisters—may the good Queen rest in peace—trying to explain why it should be legal to import elven cosmetics."

Kessara and Wes stared at him.

"Let's save the mopey poetry stuff for later," he suggested, shrugging his shoulders. "There are more important concerns. We all heard what the soldier said. No one has seen an elf in Kaveryth in years."

"There have been spies," Wes pointed out. Kessara nodded in agreement, but Alder waved his words away.

"Sure. But to be out in the open like this? It's unprecedented. I don't like it."

Kessara let out a long breath. "Do you think they're trying

to take the city?"

Until that moment, Wes hadn't considered the possibility. But it had happened before, when he was twelve. It had happened to his own city. And though the elves had ultimately failed to take control of Stronghollow, they had all but destroyed the House of Cervos. *I can't let the same thing happen here.* He looked over at the Princess. The woman his brother had loved. His friend.

"I don't know," Alder said, pressing his fingertips against his forehead. "But I do know that your people are in danger. And we have to do something."

* * *

"*We* don't have to do anything," Kessara said, taking a step until she stood between the two men. Alder raised an eyebrow. "*I* have to do something. You two have to stay here, out of sight. Both of you are wanted criminals."

"My Princess—" Wes started.

Alder began to laugh, the jolly sound of it echoing through the throne room. "I know you're a strong woman or whatever, but you can't possibly think that's how this is going to go."

The absolute nerve of him. Kessara balled her hands into fists until her fingernails left indents on the skin of her palms. *Every time I think I might be starting to like him, he reminds me that he's an arrogant brute.*

"He's right, Kessara," Wes said, not meeting her eyes. "There's nothing you can do. You can't put yourself in the line of fire just for the sake of it. We should stay here, try and find a lookout where we can—"

"Oh, come on," Alder said, giving an exaggerated sigh. "The

Princess can find a lookout. You and I are going to fight."

"I can take care of myself," she snapped. Wes said nothing, though she could see the blush that had bloomed on his cheeks. He was fiddling with the sword at his waist. She rolled her eyes.

"Oh, can you?" Alder said, his eyes still laughing though he had wiped the smirk off of his face. "You couldn't even lift my sword."

I really could slap him.

"I've trained with a bow since I was six," she said, refusing to let any more of her rage come through in her voice. *I don't even owe him an explanation*, she reminded herself.

Alder raised his hands in mock surrender. "Did you not hear what your own soldier said? There are elves out there. They aren't going to be taken down by the plinking of your arrows. Be rational."

"Oh, so women are stupid," she snapped, any semblance of dignity gone from her tone.

"No," Alder said calmly, rolling his eyes at her. "*You* are *being* stupid. There's a difference."

"Is that so?"

"Your mother handled Captain Drohma. Her gifts as a woman proved helpful in that situation. Your ability to shoot hay bale targets is not going to help fight off these bandits. You're just going to be in the way."

"How dare—"

"Will you both shut up!" Wes yelled, his voice thundering against the stone. "We don't have time for this. Kessara, you and I have things to discuss."

Alder said nothing, folding his arms across his chest and tapping the toe of his boot against the ground as though the whole conversation was boring him.

"Whatever you have to say, it can wait," Kessara said, forcing herself to sound calm. Wes was trying to protect her, and, unlike Alder, he wasn't actively trying to treat her as though she was inferior to himself.

"Wait until an elven knife ends up in your chest?" Alder demanded.

Wes raised a hand and continued to speak. "Your father still wants us to marry."

"I know. He's told me the same, many times."

"What's there to discuss?" Alder said, moving toward the throne room door. "This isn't a difficult choice. Kessara is the only chance that Silverfell has, and the survival of Silverfell is the only chance that Galeharbor has. Even a dummy like me can see that."

"Nothing is that simple," Wes said, catching Kessara's eye for a moment before looking away.

"On top of all of that, Kessara is the most beautiful woman I've ever seen, and believe me, I've seen a *lot* of women," Alder said as he pulled open the door.

"Be a man, Wes. Marry her. Do it today."

He moved to leave. "Wait," Wes said. They both looked at him, Alder nearly bouncing up and down on his feet in his eagerness to join the fray. Wes stared at the floor for a few long seconds.

"Celesyria just asked me not to be mad. She's here."

They rushed over to the window just in time to see a huge dragon flying past, her orange scales shimmering in the sun.

Chapter 6

A few minutes later, Celesyria flew over the city's outer wall, careful to stay high enough that she could avoid arrow fire while still getting an idea of what she faced.

At first, all she could do was stare, stunned by the beauty of Galeharbor's bustling capital. The buildings were intricate and beautiful, nearly all of them built with pale-white stones that seemed to gleam from within when the sun hit them. Even though the sea was miles away, nautical details were dotted throughout, everything from statues of sea-sirens to shell patterns carved above doorways.

The streets would have been beautiful, too, were it not for the nightmare that was unfolding on them.

"There are dozens of them, Wes," she said within her mind, hoping that he was still safe, hiding out somewhere in Windshear's palace. If he did come out, at least she'd be able

to give him a heads up about what to expect. *"All dressed in black."*

"How very original," Wes replied.

She circled lower and lower, watching. The narrow side streets were a press of merchants and peasants, all desperate to find some protection from the invaders, but there were just too many of them. Even from the sky, Celesyria could hear the screams of fear and pain as they picked people off from the edges of each crowd.

The main thoroughfares were filled with dozens of horses and a handful of deer, all wearing oiled black saddles and bridles that matched the uniforms of their handlers. She saw a large group of soldiers in Galeharbor colors standing off to the side, swords raised, expressions of confusion crossing their faces. She wondered why they weren't doing anything. Worse, she couldn't see how she'd be able to land so that she could fight back. Even the broader streets were narrow, and she was not invincible—if enough of the black soldiers could corner her, she'd be killed. For not the first time, she wished that she was wearing the dwarf-made armor of the Guardians.

No. She swallowed the sick taste in her throat. *I can't just rush in. I need a plan.*

Celesyria circled again, coming in lower to get a better look, but before she could, she heard a scream that rose above the pandemonium.

At the end of an alleyway, she saw a young boy, no more than twelve years old, struggling to make his way through the mob of people to reach safety. To Celesyria's surprise, his skin was the deep brown common to the people of Vilzan, an isolated corner of the mountain range that separated Silverfell from Galeharbor.

At the other end of the crowd, people were shoving past each other into a large building. There were two Aridmoor soldiers at either side of the door, shouting at the crowd to stop shoving and to let the women and children through first.

"They're working together?" she asked Wes, hoping he understood. She couldn't focus long enough to explain more clearly what she meant.

"Yes. King Ursa sent his Protectorate here for a meeting, and then the bandits showed up."

"Are you safe?"

"For now, yes. You?"

"I'll explain later," she said, watching with some satisfaction as one of the Aridmoor soldiers threw a black-clad dwarf off of a staircase, sending him flying toward the street far below. She looked away before he landed, relieved that she could not hear the crunch of bone hitting cobblestone.

She heard the scream again.

As she flew lower, she felt the flick of an arrow against her back upper leg and twisted out of the way before the unseen archer could get another shot in. Her mind flashed to the injury she'd sustained to her wing back when she and Wes had been captured. It had taken weeks to heal. She heard the boy's scream again as she felt another arrow, this time clinking uselessly against one of her manacles before falling to the ground.

As she doubled back and dove downward once again, she could no longer see the child that had captured her attention. The air was filled with other screams, other cries of pain as peasant men attempted to fight back with shovels and sticks only to be cut down by the bandits. Celesyria tried to focus on the invaders' faces, but each of them wore black masks

68

that obscured all but their eyes. She could see, however, that not only the dwarves carried axes rather than swords, but many of the men, as well. She couldn't see any elves for the moment, and she wondered if it had been an elven archer that had shot her. *Please, don't let it be one of their poison-tipped arrows,* she prayed.

In the chaos, none of the soldiers in either Galeharbor blue or Aridmoor red seemed to be paying her much attention, but she could see the occasional civilian pointing up at her, shouting. *It has been so long since they have seen a dragon. There was once a time when my presence would have been ordinary, a comforting reminder of safety rather than an omen of a world headed for war and death.*

And then she saw the child again, right beneath her, screaming at the several soldiers who surrounded him. She beat her wings in place for a moment, trying to figure out what was going on before she was forced to take another tight circle overhead. The boy's hands had been wrenched behind his back, and even at her distance she could see the red welts where the rope was cutting into his skin.

It all made sense. Slavers.

Wishing that she could speak to the boy in her mind and assure him that she was coming back, she circled back toward the wider street. The horses were still there, but now she could see that many of them now carried prisoners on their backs, mostly women and children. They were tied to the saddles, but it seemed to her that they had already given up getting away, their bodies limp and their faces dejected as the bandits moved the animals into an orderly line.

I could burn them. Celesyria looked at the dozen or so horses near the edge of the street that were not carrying victims. *I wouldn't have to get so close. It would work.* For not the first time, she wondered about the ancient oaths taken by the dragons when they were summoned to Kaveryth. For most of her life, she'd taken it for granted that using fire against humans was forbidden on pain of eternal punishment in the Wrathlands, but knowing what she knew now of the High One, she couldn't be sure.

Another question. Another reason we need to find the Codex Veritatis.

Whatever the oath may be, it did not bind her in how she exercised her power with horses. She'd used a similar strategy back in Silverfell, when she had set the forest on fire to allow Wes to escape the soldiers that hunted him. Still, she hated the thought of killing such beautiful animals, and worse, she couldn't do very much as many of them already carried prisoners. But it was the best option that she could think of.

"Hang in there," she said to the little boy, knowing he would not hear her. *"Maybe I can save even more of you."*

Even if she could make it back to him, what could she do? If it would be difficult to land in the main street, it would be impossible to land in one of the tight side roads. But she had to do something. He was so young, and so afraid. She hadn't known Wes when he was young, but she pictured him exactly like that, alone and terrified in a world that had suddenly gone mad.

Steeling herself for the arrow-fire that would almost certainly follow, she flew in as low as she dared, trying to keep her wings as close to her body as she could while staying aloft. Several of the horses shied and bucked as she got close. She watched as one of the women bloodied her nose against her mount's neck as he reared, unable to maneuver out of the way with her hands and feet secured so tightly.

And then she saw it. The reason that the Aridmoor and Galeharbor soldiers were standing around. The reason that the trafficked slaves were not even trying to free themselves.

* * *

Alder made for the door of the throne room once again. "Dragon or no dragon," he said, turning to face Kessara and Wes. "I'm a soldier, and I'm not going to hide myself away inside the palace while a city of the Four Kingdoms is overrun."

"Wait, Alder," Kessara said, taking a few steps toward him. "Don't be stupid. Captain Drohma is going to capture you and drag you back to High Keep. If he doesn't, he's going to kill you on the spot. Do you honestly think that after everything you've done, King Ursa is going to let you share the battlefield with Aridmoor's men?"

"She's right," Wes said, tearing his eyes away from the window. The fighting had begun in earnest, and it was drawing nearer to the palace. Even through the thick walls and windows, they could now hear the faint sounds of battle below. Alder stretched his arms above his head, itching to feel the weight of his sword in his hand. "The Princess is right. It's too big of a risk, and we need you to survive. We can't lose you."

"Killing yourself to prove your manhood isn't bravery," Kessara chirped. "It's nothing but foolish pride."

Alder said nothing, curling his hands into fists at his side. He loved Wes, he really did. Even Kessara was… he couldn't finish the thought. Despite her bratty attitude, he cared about her, too. *They're both spoiled nobles. Wes has been through the Wrathlands itself, but neither of them understand war. They don't know the cost of holding back.*

"Even without training as a Guardian, Celesyria is stronger than twenty men," Wes continued, placing a hand on his shoulder. "She will strike fear into even the elves."

Alder shook himself free of Wes's grip and strode toward the window, his footfalls echoing across the open space. "Look," he said, pointing toward the ground. Kessara peered over the edge of the next window over for a moment before sinking to the ground, her hand over her mouth. "Yes. Murder. That's what bandits do."

Wes came and stood next to him, facing the carnage that had now reached the outer wall of the palace. "But that's not what I'm trying to show you," Alder continued. "Look at the city."

"Okay, and?" Wes said, eyes roving over the expanse of glimmering white buildings that stretched into the distance. He put a hand to his forehead, shielding his eyes from the reflected sunlight.

"The streets, Wes. They're narrow. All of them are, even the main roads."

Kessara looked up, realization dawning.

"Celesyria is going to have a hard time fighting here. There's hardly anywhere she can even land, let alone move around and fight."

Kessara cursed, putting her head in her hands.

Wes went silent, and Alder was sure he was talking to the dragon. A flash of jealousy passed through him. He hoped that eventually he'd be able to do the same, but in the meantime, it annoyed him that he could only communicate with her using Wes as an intermediary.

"She told me she's alright, but she couldn't focus enough to say more," Wes said, his voice quiet as he moved to sit next to Kessara. "She told me before that talking to humans in her mind requires a different concentration than talking to another dragon." Kessara just nodded, bowing her head against her knees again, an awkward pause blooming around them. Alder remained on his feet, taking a few paces toward the door.

"Like I said," he stared at his friends. "I'm a soldier. I know how to fight, and more than that, I know how to strategize. I'm going. You and Wes can talk about getting married."

"So why haven't you left already?" Kessara snapped.

Because I want you fools to understand. He forced himself to hold back his tongue.

"Alder," Wes tried again, getting to his feet. "Say you help. Say that the armies of Galeharbor and Aridmoor manage to push the invaders out of Windshear. What then? What happens when they strike again, in some other city?"

"My father will accept King Ursa's offer," Kessara said softly. "It's only a matter of time. The situation in Kaveryth is too dire for him to continue to wait on my account."

Alder threw his hands up. "I thought we were here because we all believe in the High One."

"I do," Wes protested. Kessara crossed her hands over her chest, giving the faintest hint of a nod.

"So why do you insist on giving in to despair? I know that things look bad. They *are* bad. But our fate does not rest on the wiles of King Ursa or the scheming of the Septemvirate. It doesn't even rest on our own families," he paused, looking over at Kessara. "Our faith is in the High One. He created the whole world, and I have to believe that if that's true, He's still here, holding it all together. Even now."

"It's hard to believe," Kessara said, all of the fire gone from her voice. She rose to her feet and headed across the room, picking up an abandoned fruit from their breakfast, examining it, and setting it back down. The sounds of battle continued below, and Alder considered how strange it was that such hatred had come to Galeharbor on such a beautiful, sunny day.

"Have you had any of the dreams lately?" Wes asked.

"Yes."

"So it's easy for you to say that He's in control."

"Maybe so," Alder said. "But those dreams may not come to me forever, and dreams or no dreams, you need to stop cowering in fear. The High One has a plan for what is to come, and He will give us the strength to meet it."

"Did He plan for Zanek's death?" Wes said, his voice wavering as he stood up and moved closer, his dark eyes meeting Alder's own. "Did He plan for him to die at my hand?"

Zanek. The late Queen Ursa's illegitimate son. He hadn't known him well, but he knew that he'd grown up in the palace at High Keep with Kylan, raised as one of Radagar Ursa's own sons. Unsurprisingly, he'd grown up as a loyal soldier of his Kingdom. Wes had killed him in self-defense before being thrown into Stronghollow Penitentiary.

"I'm sure He didn't want it to happen," Alder said, trying to keep the irritation from his voice. "But He allowed it, just like He allows all sorts of evils. We live in an imperfect world, Wes. These things happen, but they all work out for our good."

The bitter echo of Wes' laughter filled the room. "You dream of the High One. You close your eyes and receive messages from the Eternal Lands. I dream of Zanek's face the moment he realized that his life was over."

"Wes," Alder said, raising a hand and taking a few steps closer to his friend. He watched as he blinked away a few tears. "You have to understand—"

"It's you who does not understand," Wes snapped. "I killed someone, and I can't shake it. I can't shake the dreams, and I can't shake the guilt. Maybe killing is easy for you, maybe you think it's stupid to be so saddened by the loss of criminals, but it isn't easy for me."

"You think it's easy for *me*?" Alder spat. "Why, because I'm a soldier? Because I had training in war before I had to watch men die at my hand?"

"By the way you talk about it, yeah, you make it sound like it's easy for you. You can joke around, brag about how brave you are, and fall asleep easily knowing the God of all Kaveryth will come and visit you, all while I suffer. So forgive me if I'm sick of hearing about the High One's grand plan," Wes said, his fists balled up at his sides. "He's already taken my parents. My brother. Odrigh and Lev. But that wasn't enough. No, I had to take a life myself. Maybe His plan is to break me."

Alder tried to focus only on the air rushing in and out of his lungs. *He's not angry at you,* he assured himself as he watched Wes walk toward the window again, wiping tears away with the back of his hand. It was easy to forget how much younger Wes was—seventeen years to his twenty-three—and how much of a difference it made. *He's been through things no one should have to face, and he hasn't had enough time to come to terms with the way things are.*

Alder thought of his own dark nights, back when he'd been

a fifteen year old soldier, forced to wound and to kill even earlier than Wes had. *You don't understand, Wes. It's never been easy for me.* He closed his eyes, leaning against the wall of the throne room. *I've killed dozens of people. I did it to protect the innocent, and the men I killed deserved death. But that doesn't mean their specters do not haunt me as I lay awake at night.*

He heard the sound of a heavy door slamming shut, and his eyes shot open. Wes stood frozen, staring back at him. He swore under his breath, cursing himself for getting roped into a pointless fight instead of paying attention to his surroundings.

Kessara was gone.

* * *

Kessara raced through the palace courtyard, trying not to trip on her skirts as she headed for the top of the keep. She glanced behind her, expecting to see Wes or Alder giving chase, but saw no one. She rolled her eyes. *At least Alder's penchant for arguing was useful for once. But they'll notice my absence soon enough. I have to hurry.* She could only hope that they wouldn't dare follow her all the way to the King and Queen.

She heard cries of pain from outside of the palace's outer walls, but so far, it did not seem they had been breached. She thought of the carnage she could see from the throne room's windows and fought back nausea as she continued to run, rounding a corner and rushing up a flight of narrow stairs. She knew she would see more when she reached even higher ground. She had to find a way to disconnect the blood and the broken bodies from the reality of human lives. War was coming. This was only the beginning.

Finally, she reached her destination and rested behind a short wall, her chest heaving with the effort. She forced herself to take a few moments to breathe and to think before rushing forward. She didn't have much of a plan, and she didn't want to cause more harm than good. She peered over the wall and watched where her father, her mother, and Captain Drohma stood. The Captain was being helped into heavy armor by two soldiers. She watched as a third one handed him a sword that looked nearly as long as she was tall.

She was higher now, and the sounds of battle below were dampened by the rush of wind that surrounded the keep. She didn't want to look down. "Did you know that a fugitive dragon was hiding within your borders?" she heard Drohma ask as he slipped on his thick leather gloves. She dared a glance around, but did not see Celesyria. "I hate to imply anything, of course, but I am certain that King Kylan will wish to know."

"Of course not," King Manta said, knitting his brows and frowning. "Had any of my scouts found her, I would have been informed immediately."

"It would have been dealt with," Queen Manta added. Kessara looked at her feet. Her parents were not lying—Wes and Alder had not mentioned that they had arrived via dragonflight—but she still felt a pang of guilt that she and her friends had not been able to share the full truth with them.

"Captain," one of the soldiers interrupted, pointing over the edge of the tower wall. "There she is."

Kessara shuffled toward the eastern edge of the tower and peered downward, feeling a rush of vertigo as she realized just how far away she was from the ground. She swallowed bile as she gripped the stone wall, thankful that the catwalk she'd found was fairly safe. She watched as Celesyria passed beneath them in a tight circle, the tips of her wings nearly touching the walls of the keep as she flew.

She saw clusters of black-clad bodies, swirling through the streets like a tide of ink. She forgot her terror at being so high, unable to look away from the destruction below. She watched as soldiers and bandits fought, the ring of clashing swords reaching her ears even over the sound of the wind. She watched the glint of the midday sun on metal helmets. The soldiers of Aridmoor and Galeharbor were intermingled, each man trying to kill as many of the black-clad invaders as they could. Even with her lack of knowledge when it came to military strategy, she knew that this did not bode well. *They're overrun.* She looked away as one of the bandits, a dwarf, swung an ax into the helmet of a Galeharbor soldier. *If they weren't, they'd be fighting in organized companies of their own men.*

She dared a glance over at her parents and the Captain. Her mother stood with her hand over her mouth, eyes wide, while her father and Drohma watched with arms crossed over their chests. "Elves," Captain Drohma said, gesturing toward a street that lay near the outer wall of the palace. They were close to the throne room. Too close. *Please, stay hidden.* Kessara hoped that Alder hadn't dragged Wes into danger as he'd planned.

Then she saw them. Not a single elf, but five of them, all converging on a group of three Protectorate soldiers with their backs pressed up against a wall. One of the men was already badly injured. She could see several huge gashes at his shoulder, blood dripping down his arm. He carried no sword. "No!" she heard Drohma cry out. She glanced over at him as he pressed his eyes shut, putting his head in his hands.

Even you have a heart.

She looked away from the imminent massacre of his men, unable to bear the sight of their faces as they met their end.

"Wait," Kessara's mother cried out, leaning over the railing until the King placed a restraining hand on her shoulders. "Look!"

Everyone on the tower rushed to the railing and stared.

Celesyria had landed, placing herself between the elves and the soldiers. For a moment, the elves just stood there. Kessara watched in fascination as they spoke to one another. They wore their hair long, and from a distance she could not tell if they were male or female, only that they were beautiful. Even from where she stood, she could see their sharp cheekbones and silvery skin, every movement of their bodies as graceful as a dance.

Celesyria roared, taking a step forward as the Aridmoor soldiers behind her rushed along the wall toward safety. Kessara wished she could speak to her, could find out what was happening, but it didn't matter. She could see that the elves were laughing amongst themselves, and a moment later, they turned and fled, heading back into the narrow streets of Windshear and out of sight. Celesyria wouldn't be able to follow them.

"Well, speak of the demon herself," Captain Drohma said as Celesyria leapt back into the sky. "At least the traitor did something useful." The vulnerability she thought she'd seen in his eyes was gone. Kessara got to her feet and called out to her mother as she breached the short wall, not wanting one of Drohma's lackeys to mistake her for a threat. "Kessara," her father hissed as she strode toward them, the dirty hem of her dress dragging across the gleaming stone. "Have you lost your mind? Go back to the palace. Now."

"You're not safe here," her mother said, grabbing her by the arm and pulling her in closer, away from the edge of the keep. "Listen to your father."

As if to punctuate the point, a volley of yells and screams sounded below.

"One of my men will be glad to escort you back to safety," Captain Drohma said. Kessara swore she saw the hint of a smirk on his lips.

"How dare you speak about Celesyria that way," she snapped, shaking free of her mother's grip and striding over to Drohma. "Have you no honor at all? She saved the lives of your men, at great risk to herself in such a confined space. You should be thankful."

"Kessara," her mother pleaded.

"Show some respect for the King's legate," her father added, his voice wavering slightly with what she knew to be a simmering rage. She ignored them both, meeting Drohma's eyes as she stepped in front of him. *I know the game. I know that King Ursa and his men hold all of the cards. But that doesn't mean I'm going to abandon what's right.*

"My Princess," Drohma began, extending a hand as though he was about to brush her cheek before thinking better of it. "Please, calm down."

"You know that I stand with Wes Cervos, and that I therefore stand with the dragon Celesyria as well. My father speaks of respect," she paused for a moment, swallowing a flash of shame as she imagined his furious eyes boring into her back. "But you have no respect for me, for the people of

Galeharbor, or for the truth. If you did, you would consider the claims made about the High One rather than blindly following King Ursa's orders."

"Kessara, that is enough," her father snapped. She could hear his footsteps behind her, but she did not turn.

"My King, I have not taken offense," Captain Drohma said, the half-smirk returning to his face once more. "The dragon has committed crimes of blasphemy and treason, but for the moment, we have a common enemy. If she wishes to shed blood for the sake of the Four Kingdoms before she is caught and returned to prison, I will not hinder her."

Kessara set her jaw, saying nothing as she allowed her father to usher her back toward the flight of stairs.

I knew that reasoning with him would be a waste of time.

Still, she'd felt that she had to try. A small part of her still believed that people could be reasoned with, that people would accept the truth if only they had the opportunity to hear it. She felt a pang of annoyance as she thought of Alder. Surely, he'd make some insulting comment about how women were naive and how this was the kind of problem that is ultimately solved by violence.

For the time being, she feared he was right.

"If you'll excuse me, my King," Captain Drohma said, kneeling on one knee. *Of course he acknowledged only my father.* "Our people have need of my aid."

"Very well," her father said, waving a hand until the Captain rose and headed for the stairs, sword in hand, followed by his men.

For several moments, Kessara stood at the edge of the tower, watching as Drohma reached the ground and headed into the fray. Within moments, he reached his first opponents. She

81

looked away, hearing the screams as he cut them down. *I will learn to face this. But not yet.*

"Kessara," her father said, his voice dangerously calm. Her mother said nothing as she turned to face them, the sounds of pain still ringing in her ears. "You had better get your friends somewhere safe. Now. Or I'm going to turn them in myself."

"Errol—" her mother started, placing a hand on his arm.

"No, Jinna, she needs to hear it," he snapped, his eyes never straying from Kessara's face. "You're still a child. You think of everything in terms of high ideals and fantasies of a happy world. But this is reality. Your people are in danger. And if you think I'm going to allow them to sacrifice their lives for the sake of some new God they have never known, you are sorely mistaken."

Kessara swallowed. *They have never known the High One because He has been hidden from them,* she wished she could scream at him. *Do they not deserve the truth?*

"Father, I know that this is a difficult situation—"

"This is an invasion."

"Yes."

"All of Kaveryth has been affected by what you and your friends have chosen to do. I will not repeat myself again. Wesley and the redhead had better stay out of sight until I can make up my mind about the best path forward. We will speak later. Now go."

"Yes, father," Kessara muttered under her breath as she headed for the stairs.

Chapter 7

Wes swore under his breath, pacing back and forth near the door of the throne room. "I'm going to find her," Alder said without hesitation, fingering the sword at his belt as though assuring himself it was still where he'd left it. "She doesn't even have the bow that she claimed to be skilled at using."

"If Drohma sees you, he will kill you."

"What do you care?"

Wes glared at the taller man. "I owe you my life."

"How's that?"

"You got Celesyria out of prison. Aside from that, we're a team. We serve the High One in a world where almost no one else knows Him. I'm not about to stand here and let you get killed."

Wes expected Alder to object with some line about how Wes didn't have the strength to forbid or permit him to do anything. Instead, he went quiet, raising a hand as he listened to a noise coming from the throne room's door.

Wes heard it, too. There was a tapping sound, gentle but insistent, interrupted by the occasional shout from the battle outside that had likely moved inside the palace walls. "Get your sword," Alder hissed under his breath, drawing his own in one fluid motion. Wes followed suit, cringing as the metal clanked against the buckle of his belt. Was it Kessara, wounded and needing their help? Was it a trap? Possibilities flooded his mind as he and Alder stalked closer.

"Get the door for me," Alder whispered, his voice so quiet that Wes barely heard him. He obeyed, taking hold of the heavy metal ring and pulling the great slab of wood inward. "By the Dracodei," Alder swore as he rushed out into the hall.

Immediately, he understood why.

Laying there, on the floor of the hall, was an elf, bleeding out of a massive wound in his stomach.

Wes stood, numb, as Alder rushed over to the elf's side, his hands shaking as he opened the front of his buttoned green shirt. "Help me," The elf said, coughing as his eyes roved from side to side as though unable to focus. "By the High One, have mercy." He placed a silvery hand on Alder's own, and Wes could see the desperation in his dark eyes. Alder shook his head and stood, looking up and down the hall. Wes heard the sound of stamping feet on stone, and the visceral roar of some indecipherable war cry echoing against the walls.

"Wes, keep watch," Alder said, bending and grabbing the man's feet.

Wes continued to stare down the hall, realizing that his sword was in his hand but feeling completely incapable of using it. He watched as Alder dragged the wounded elf into the throne room. He seemed rather heavy, despite his lithe frame, and Alder let out a string of curses as he dragged him over the slight rise of the threshold.

"Close the door!"

Wes obeyed, shoving his sword back into its sheath and hauling the door shut behind them. He was too shocked to object to Alder bossing him around. He lowered the wooden bar that served as a lock. *Not that it will be enough to stop them.*

He knelt next to Alder, who held the elf's face between his hands. *He's handsome,* Wes noted absently to himself, trying not to notice the blood that had begun dripping onto the stone floor.

"Who are you?" Alder asked.

Wes could hear a gurgling sound coming from deep within the man's throat.

He swallowed, fighting back the urge to be sick. Every part of his body was screaming for him to run, that it was a trap, that elves were dangerous and never to be trusted. But for some reason, he could not bring himself to run. He couldn't turn away from a broken warrior who had used the name of the High One.

And, it seemed, Alder couldn't bring himself to turn away either.

"You need to tell us if this is a trap," Alder said, forcing the elf to look into his eyes. "Speak the truth, or I will finish you myself."

"Wait," the elf choked, going into yet another coughing fit. Wes couldn't help but notice the blood again. It was all over the floor now, weaving between the stones like a miniature river of death splitting off in all directions. "I'm alone, I swear it."

"Do you swear by the High One?" Wes asked, trying to focus on anything but the reek of death.

"Yes."

"How did you get in here?" Alder asked again, rooting around in a leather pouch at his waist for something.

"I don't know," the elf choked out, giving a brief chuckle that transformed into another fit of coughing. Alder produced a liquor bottle, but the elf held up a hand. "I was led here."

"What do you mean? How—" Wes started.

"We heard of you," he said, pointing a trembling finger toward Wes. "Even in Nox, we heard of what you and the dragon have done."

Wes and Alder said nothing as the elf coughed again, clutching at his chest. Even though he was trying not to look, Wes could tell that it was too late to help. Not even the palace healers would be able to do anything for him now.

"I hadn't heard about the High One or the Codex in a hundred years," he continued, each word followed by a labored breath. "Until you defied the Septemvirate."

Alder caught Wes's gaze. For the first time, Wes could see a hint of fear in his green eyes.

"I didn't accept it right away. But when I was sent here, commanded to kill… I felt a burning in my heart. All of the old stories are true."

"What do you want us to do?" Alder said, his voice shaking as he glanced toward the door of the throne room. The sound of footsteps had faded. Wes hoped that they had moved somewhere else, at least long enough to buy them some time.

The elf said nothing.

"What do we do?" Alder asked again, taking the man's face in his hands and bending so close that their eyes were inches

86

apart. He shook him, his voice bordering on hysteria.

The elf was no longer coughing, no longer looking around wildly. His eyes looked glassy. Wes watched his chest rising and falling.

"Stop shaking him," Wes said, closing his eyes. "Wait."

"Celesyria," he called to the dragon in his mind. "I know you're busy, but this is an emergency."

For several seconds, she didn't respond. All that they could hear were the faint sounds of footsteps. Even the shouts of battle had softened.

"I can't get to you. I can't land," Celesyria said finally.

"There's an elf here, and he's dying. He says he knows the High One. He asked for mercy. I don't know what he needs. I don't know what—"

"Let me think."

Wes glanced at Alder, who had sat next to the man and grasped his hand in his own. There were tears in his eyes, and he did not attempt to hide them.

"Wes," Celesyria continued. "I've read about how a believer should die, but I can't remember what should be done. I'm sorry."

Wes swore. "She doesn't know what to do," he told Alder, his voice faint. The familiar tide of guilt threatened to overtake him as he watched the man struggling for air.

"I'm sorry" Celesyria repeated. "There's something else I have to deal with. Pray. I wish I could help."

Wes assured her that it was alright. For a moment, he said nothing, trying to force air in and out of his lungs.

"Please," the elf said, barely loud enough to be heard. Wes looked down at him, watching as his life began to fade away behind his eyes. Despite everything that had happened, then and now, he felt a spark of hope rising in his chest.

"All of my dreams," Alder said, shaking his head. "All of the revelations given to me…"

He trailed off, looking away from Wes, his eyes red with unshed tears.

"That doesn't matter now," Wes said, standing up and looking around the room. "Maybe you were right. The High One didn't bring this man here for no reason."

An idea began to bloom in his mind, a flash of memory that fell into place as he strode across the throne room. He hastened his pace until he reached the breakfast table, the remnants of the meal left behind. *There.* He grabbed hold of a crumbling biscuit, leaving behind a portion that was sticky with jam.

"I'm not sure he can eat, Wes," Alder said, giving him a strange look. The elf's breathing had worsened in the minute or two he was gone. There was not much time left.

"Just trust me," he said, breaking up the biscuit into crumbs on the palm of his hand. The elf moaned, trying to lift his head, and Alder rushed behind him and helped him into a half-sitting position. Wes could see blood and filth seeping into Alder's peasant attire, and at that moment, he was certain that the soldier would have had the same compassion while dressed in Aridmoor's finest regalia.

Wes shook his head. When faced with a world that hated you, it was far too easy to get angry at those whom you loved. *Forgive me, Alder. Brother.*

Alder helped the man to open his slackened jaw, his fingers gentle.

"O High One," Wes began, clearing his throat before going on. "I do not know the words, I do not know the way. I now obey You as much as I know how to obey, and I love You as much as I know how to love. I ask You in Your mercy to bring this servant to the Eternal Lands, forevermore."

He nodded to Alder, pressing a few of the biscuit crumbs into the man's mouth with his fingers. With Alder's assistance, the elf was able to work his jaw up and down, finally swallowing. He closed his eyes. For several moments, they heard only his breathing as Alder supported his body.

Soon, his chest rose and then fell for the final time. He was gone, and Wes could only hope that his journey would end in the presence of the High One.

* * *

Calesca bombs.

Celesyria circled again, trying to get a better look at the circular shapes that had been hung from the saddle of each horse. She'd read about them before, in a book in Whitespire's library called *An Encyclopedia of Vicious Weaponry and Mechanicals.*

The precise method by which Calesca bombs were ignited was not known, but the devastating results that they caused had been well-studied. They were also rather infamously made only in Galeharbor.

Celesyria shook her head. She wasn't going to risk setting off a chain reaction, and neither were the soldiers. The only way to rescue these prisoners without blowing up half of Windshear would be to pick off the bandits in other parts of the city one by one.

She heard the rush of air as an arrow flew toward her. She tensed up as she flapped her wings, bracing herself for the splinter of pain, but it never came. They'd missed. *"Time to go,"* she thought to herself, noticing that four of the human soldiers had taken bows off of their backs. One arrow rarely did her much harm, but a swarm of them certainly could.

A few moments later, she'd returned to where she saw the little boy.

She thought that she was too late, but then she saw a flash of dark skin against the gleaming white stone of the city.

There he was, standing on a ledge several stories above street level.

Alone.

He was cowering against the wall, his arms still bound tight behind him. Below, climbing a tall wooden ladder, was one of the black-clad soldiers.

The boy was still standing in place, probably trying to avoid slipping. It would be a difficult place to walk without the use of his arms for balance. *How'd he get away? Why haven't they already dragged him onto one of the horses?* The soldier was climbing still, slow in his heavy leather armor. *Where are the rest of them? Did the soldiers fight them off?*

There was no time to dwell on her questions. Celesyria closed her eyes for a moment, wishing that, just once, the High One would speak to her directly and tell her what to do. But she knew that there was only one choice. She flapped her wings, rushing forward, the air whipping particles of dust into her eyes as she got closer to the building.

She shot out a front claw and swiped the ladder to the side. Her stomach clenched. It was done. She circled, flying upward, trying to ignore the sound of bones crunching as the bandit's body hit the ground a second later.

When she headed back down, the boy was gone from the ledge. She caught a brief glance of him through a window, safe within the strong stone walls. She was relieved to see that he was well, but the realization of what she had just done threatened to overwhelm her.

She forced the painful thoughts away as she flew toward the city gate, hoping that she could pick off a few more of the bandits standing guard. Perhaps she could give a few of the captives a chance to flee.

As her wings pounded the air, she was once again reminded of just how uncomfortable her manacles felt. Even after all this time, she couldn't get used to their weight. It was strange. She was so large. Flying with Wes and Alder on her back was fairly comfortable. But for whatever reason, the iron symbol of her captivity seemed almost too heavy to carry.

Forgive me, she prayed, glancing out across the city toward the glimmering North Sea. She wasn't sure that she needed forgiveness for killing to save the life of another, but she knew that she needed something, some healing or hope that would remind her she was free.

Just then, she felt a jolt of pain rush through her tail and up her spine. She banked to the right as hard as she could without falling out of the sky, trying to see where the arrow had come from. *There.* She saw a flash of red hair in the corner of a doorway. She flew closer, and the woman noticed her, her bright green eyes flashing with hate as she felt around to her back for another arrow. She was beautiful, but there was a hardness to her face that made Celesyria shiver. A second later, the elf dashed into the depths of the building.

Celesyria circled again, blinking the sunlight from her eyes. *It would have been such a beautiful day.* As she looked down at the ground, it was clear that the fight was coming to a close. The ground was littered with the dead, and to her relief, most of the bodies seemed to be wearing black from head to toe.

She pitied the fallen Protectorate soldiers that she saw, thinking about how much evil in the world was caused by those who genuinely thought that they were doing the right thing. These men had chosen to become her enemies, but they weren't, not really, not in the same way that the black-clad invaders were. They were lost. They were in desperate need of the truth, and she was determined that she would continue to fight until that truth was known throughout all of Kaveryth.

She tried not to think about the people on the horses. There was no way to rescue them without causing even more carnage.

I will not forget about you. I promise.

* * *

"Wes, you need to hide," Celesyria said within his mind. He and Alder had not moved in several minutes, both lost in their own thoughts as the fallen elf lay dead beside them. *"The soldiers have kept control of the city, but I saw several of the bandits heading into the palace."*

"What about the soldiers of Aridmoor and Galeharbor? Were there a lot of casualties?"

"A fair few. King Ursa's men are sweeping the city to find any of the elves that may have survived. I saw them drag one out of a tavern a few minutes ago and tie him up. They're probably trying to get information."

She didn't have to say more. Wes knew that the black-clad invaders were coming for their own wounded. It would be better to kill them than to allow them to be captured and probed for information. The fact that this elf was already dead brought little comfort.

Wes told Celesyria to find somewhere to hide before telling Alder what she'd said.

"We have to hide him," Wes finished, gesturing to the body on the floor. He still looked handsome, somehow, with no color to drain from his already silver-toned skin.

"Wes," Alder said, shaking his head as he got to his feet and cupped a hand to his ear to listen. The footsteps were coming closer. They were out of time. "His soul is gone, off to wherever the High One wills for it to go. We have to leave the body. There's no time."

"We can't do that," Wes protested, lifting up the elf's arms and placing them over his chest. "The body and the soul belong together. We can't just leave him laying here like a piece of meat."

Wes remembered the funeral that had been held for his parents and brother when he was twelve. It had hurt to see them placed in caskets and lowered into the ground, but there had been something comforting about it, too. He'd had a chance to look at their faces one last time. A final moment to memorize them, to steel himself for the loneliness that would be with him until he met them again in the Eternal Lands. He knew that they couldn't do the same for the dead elf, but they could at least protect his body from being desecrated by his former allies.

Alder ran his hand through his hair, looking up at the high ceiling of the throne room for a moment before turning back to Wes. He rolled his eyes. "You're right. Grab a leg."

The two of them dragged the elf across the floor, and unsurprisingly, he was just as heavy as he'd been the first time, even with two of them carrying the weight.

"Why did you give him a biscuit before he died?" Alder asked as they reached the study door, his words punctuated by heaving breaths as he set the elf's legs down gently.

"Those kids I found," Wes started, opening the door. They could hear that the men outside were close. *Maybe they'll be intercepted by the soldiers before they can make it through the door.* "Holga and Gohr. In Boneshire. They memorized a prophecy, from the Codex Veritatis. It's been passed down in their family for generations."

"What was it?"

Wes said nothing for a few moments as they dragged the man behind King Manta's large desk and closed the door behind them. The sun was beginning to move lower in the sky, giving the back half of the room a shadowy look beneath the small windows. Alder pulled one of the tapestries from the wall and Wes helped him to lay it over the elf's body. The bandits could find it if they looked hard enough, but it was the best that they could do.

"After they told me," Wes started as the two men surveyed their work, listening to the sounds in the hall outside. "I wrote it down, memorized it myself, and destroyed the text. I couldn't risk someone finding it if…"

Alder nodded.

"So, this is what it says."

Wes began to recite, closing his eyes and feeling rather foolish.

"Stripped of all help, stricken with thirst, he will come. His tongue will be as sharp as his antlers, his eyes cast down with grief. He will leave his token to the earth, he will set the hopeless little ones

*free. He will bestow a crown, he will reverse the oath. He will bring
the bread of hope to all Kaveryth, even to a Kingdom long thought
dead. The usurpers will be cast out, the mighty will be brought to
lowliness, and the High One will rule forever."*

"Ah. The bread of hope," Alder said. Wes opened his eyes,
surprised that his friend had not found some way to make
fun of his stammering delivery of the message.

"I hope it was the right thing to do," Wes said, giving Alder
a brief smile. "It seems pretty stupid to think that a half-eaten
biscuit would suffice, but I didn't have any better ideas."

"It's not stupid," Alder said, looking over at the tapestry-
covered body. "The prophecy is obviously about you. Like
Celesyria says, the Envoy has some sort of special role in the
High One's plan. You did your best to fulfill it. And the High
One knows your heart. And his."

Wes said nothing, his cheeks burning as he fought back the
urge to dismiss Alder's compliment. He reached up and felt
the burn mark that had covered his moonscar. It was a new
scar, a new reminder that who he was went deeper than the
fate written on his skin. Alder and Celesyria had not been
given such an obvious calling, and yet, the High One was
using them. Even though sometimes it was hard to see, he
had to believe it. He had to carry on.

The sound of raised voices snapped him out of his reverie.
Wes gestured to the closet where he had hidden earlier and
the two men rushed inside, pulling the doors closed behind
them.

Chapter 8

Kessara awoke to the sound of banging at the door of her chambers. Before her mind could react, it seemed, she was already out of bed, her bare feet freezing cold against the stone floor.

"It's us," she heard her mother say before the pounding on the door continued.

"I'm coming," she called, trying to keep the fear out of her voice. After she had left the top of the keep earlier that afternoon, she'd hoped to look for Wes and Alder. Before she could even step foot in the palace, however, she'd been ushered aside by Galeharbor soldiers who assured her that she would be safe in her chambers with guards at the door until the crisis passed. Unable to convince the men that she could handle herself, she'd been led up to her rooms where she had promptly fallen asleep.

After locating a robe laying on a chair near her bed, she walked over to the window, drawing the curtain back slightly and looking out at the city below. The perfect sunny day had given way to a gorgeous night. The moon was nearly full, and its glow bathed everything in a gentle blue light. *How long have I been sleeping?*

"Kessara, we have to talk," her father chided from the other side of the door.

"Sorry," she said, stretching her arms over her head as she sauntered across the room and drew back the pin of the lock. "I was tired. I had only meant to rest."

"Good," her father said as they entered, his voice still as stern as it had been earlier. "You should be here, resting, away from all of this death and chaos."

"So… it's over, then?" she asked, not quite meeting his eyes.

For a moment, her father said nothing. Her mother patted his arm for a moment before walking over to sit on Kessara's bed.

"We've kept control of Windshear. With the help of King Ursa's men, our soldiers are sweeping the city in search of surviving bandits. So yes. It's over."

"I see."

"There were several hundred casualties, including civilians," King Manta continued, his voice brusque. "The physical damage to city property and personal property will require us to levy a large new tax that our people will struggle to afford. Worst of all, dozens of people were captured and taken away. Probably headed into Boneshire."

"Slaves," Kessara's mother added, staring out the window. "Women and children. Gone. I still wish we—"

"We couldn't, Jinna," King Manta said, slamming his fist

against the door frame. He breathed in deeply, walking over to his wife and resting a hand across her shoulder. Kessara stood stupidly by the door, her heart aching, remembering that two days before everything had seemed almost normal.

"I know you wish that we could have done more to save them. I wish the same. Our men were ready to die to save those poor people. And I know that some of the Aridmoor soldiers were as well. But they couldn't take the risk. A single Calesca bomb would be devastating, let alone dozens of them."

Our weapons. Made in Galeharbor. She couldn't bring herself to say it out loud. She knew that her people manufactured the best weapons in the Four Kingdoms. She didn't want to think how their enemies could have gotten hold of their technology.

She felt numb. All she wanted to do was crawl back into her bed, wake up to the sun pouring through her window, and go back to the way her life was before the dragon and the Envoy messed up her plans.

"Kessara," her father said, gesturing for her to come closer. She obliged, trying to hold back the tears that threatened to spill over. If she wanted to protect her friends and all of Kaveryth, she couldn't let her father see that weakness. She had to be strong. She had to hold fast. "I need you to understand something here."

"I'm listening," she said, looking out toward the window and rolling her eyes as soon as her father glanced away. *I understand perfectly. The dragons are dying, and the Four Kingdoms are losing control. And you refuse to believe in the one being who could save us.*

"This is not going to be a one time event. This is what happens before a full-scale war breaks out. Unless we do something to stem the tide, the powers of Nox are going to keep pushing. They are not going to stop."

Kessara glanced over at her mother. She was still staring out the window, tears pooling in her pale blue eyes. "Have you heard anything about your friends?" she asked.

"No. I left them in the throne room, but I wasn't able to go back," Kessara said. *Thanks to our soldiers treating me like a prisoner,* she wanted to add.

"No one was there when our men did their last sweep," King Manta said.

"Oh."

She could not think of anything else to say. For a couple of moments she just stared out the window, hoping that they had not decided to do anything stupid. Without wanting to, she thought of Alder, the image of his handsome face filling her mind where Wes' should have been. *It doesn't mean anything. The only reason I'm not worried about Wes is because he's smart enough not to rush out into a crowd of soldiers who want to capture him.*

"Kessara," the King said, clearing his throat. She looked up, noticing that her mother was also staring at her, her brows knit in concern.

"Yes, father?"

"I'm told that the Septemvirate has been given word of the raid. Elder Gunnan and Elder Qofi are on their way here to speak to me."

Kessara felt a knot forming in her stomach. She was not enamored with the Elders after what had happened to Wes and Celesyria. *At least they aren't sending Elder Bram.* He'd always been rather prickly to deal with, and he had treated Wes rudely for years, even when he was a young child.

Her father paused for a moment, giving his wife a warning

glance out of the corner of his eye before continuing to speak.

"They're going to ask for Galeharbor to provide soldiers to King Ursa's allied army. And I'm going to say yes."

"Errol—" Queen Manta started.

"Father, you can't!" Kessara said, nearly shouting, her voice large in the small space of her bedchamber.

"There is no other choice," he said. There was a hardness to his eyes. "None of the Four Kingdoms are strong enough on their own to hold fast against the powers of Nox. We need to unify."

"Around Kylan Ursa?" Kessara's mother said, incredulous, getting up from the bed and walking over to where her husband stood. "Under his father, perhaps, but Kylan? That boy is ravenous for power. You could see it in his eyes ever since he was a child! And after what happened to his mother—"

"Who else do we have?" the King snapped. "The Envoy is the only one left of the House of Cervos. The House of Noctua is already gone, and Boneshire can barely keep themselves from starving to death."

"What about you? What about us?"

Kessara listened to her parents argue, feeling numb. Her father was right, according to the factors that he was considering, but he was blind to the reality that went beyond what he could see. *How can I make him understand that You are the one who has set the stars in their places?*

"Jinna," the King continued. "Without Aridmoor's men, it would be futile. You cannot honestly think that King Ursa would be willing to bow to me of his own accord."

"Of course not," her mother snapped. "Why do you assume that I am stupid."

"I don't. But you're not thinking rationally."

"No? I'm thinking emotionally, like a woman, right?"

"Jinna—"

"I will marry Wes!" Kessara shouted, cutting them both off. "I will do it now. Mother is right, father. Kylan is dangerous."

The room went quiet for a moment, and they could hear the uncomfortable coughs of the soldiers in the hall who were keeping watch. *Nothing to see here. It's not as if you didn't know listening to my parents argue was part of the job description.*

"My daughter," her father said, rubbing at his temples. "That possibility is the only reason that I have not said yes to Drohma before now. What did you think it was that I was talking to Wes alone about?"

Kessara could hear the blood pulsing in her ears. She had known for a long while that this was what she had to do, but somehow it had never felt quite real until now, even when she'd accepted Wes' proposal in front of half of Stronghollow before temporarily rescinding it to appease the Septemvirate.

"Being noble-born is not a guarantee of an easy life," her father continued. "It can be a heavy burden. Kessara, you have made me very proud in your twenty-two years.. You have studied harder than any other youth in Windshear. You have advocated for those lowly people who may have had no one else who was willing to listen. But this is the true test."

"I know," she said, pretending not to stare as her father wiped a few tears from his eyes. Her mother only nodded, placing her delicate hand on Kessara's shoulder. "I will always be proud of you. We both will."

Kessara felt a tightness spreading across her chest. She looked to the door, and then to the window, wishing that she could run away, flee to the labyrinthine gardens that lay just outside of the city and find some little grove where she could be alone to think. She tried to keep her face stoic, but tears sprang to her eyes. *I need to be strong. But perhaps there is a way to use my tears.*

"Kessara," her mother started, sharing a quick glance with her husband. "I know that you miss Roven very much. We do, too. He was a good man, and his brother cannot replace him. But this is the right thing to do."

"Roven was wholly dedicated to the people of Silverfell," her father added. "He would want you to do whatever was necessary to protect them along with the people of Galeharbor."

Kessara did not need to pretend to sob as she thought of Roven.

They had met when they were only infants, and she couldn't remember a time in her life when she hadn't loved him. Until the very moment that he died, he had been a good man. Perhaps the best man that she ever knew. The unfairness of his death was so overwhelming that whenever she thought about it too long she ceased being able to breathe. This moment was no exception.

"Father," she choked out, rushing over to embrace him, leaning against his shoulder until her tears soaked his jacket. "I do miss Roven. But there is another reason for my sorrow."

After a few more moments of allowing herself to cry, she drew back, wiping snot from beneath her nose and facing her parents. "When the elves murdered the man I loved, they robbed not only Wes and myself, but the whole of the Four Kingdoms. They stole their future. They changed so many lives with the destruction of one family."

Her mother was crying, too. The King rested an arm over

her shoulders, pulling her close as Kessara spoke.

"If the Envoy is willing to marry me, I will marry him at dawn. I love Wes only as a brother, but my love of justice will sustain me in my vow."

"Good. I will need to notify the temple—" her father started.

"Father, please listen," Kessara said, rubbing at her stinging eyes. "I don't believe Wes is ready. We need more time."

"I have given you time," the King said, his blue eyes flashing.

"Not enough."

"For what? What can you say to him that has not been said? He knows how important this is."

"Yes. But he also knows that there is more to the plan."

Her father opened his mouth to speak, but she did not give him the chance. "If we can find the Codex Veritatis, we can prove that everything Celesyria said is true."

"Kessara," her mother pleaded. "I can believe that the High One is lord of all Kaveryth, but this is—"

"Think about it," Kessara said, trying to keep her voice calm and her face somber. "Even if Wes agrees to marry me and I become Queen of Silverfell, the Septemvirate will continue to insist that the people of the Four Kingdoms continue to worship these false gods."

"The religious beliefs of my people are not my concern here," the King snapped.

"Perhaps not. But the treasure that the Dracodei demands certainly is."

"In case you hadn't noticed, Wes has ceased making sacrifices already."

"She has a point, Errol," her mother cut in, looking up at the King. "If Wes marries Kessara, the Septemvirate will certainly intervene and force him to continue bringing the sacrifices for the Feasts of Offering."

"Exactly," Kessara said, feeling breathless. "We will be in a better position with me as Queen, to be sure, but we will still lack true liberty as long as the Septemvirate wields so much power."

"And their power rests upon the foundation of the Dracodei and the worship that the Four Kingdoms offer to them," her father finished, rubbing at his chin with his fingertips, his eyes looking off into space. "If you and your friends are right, and the Dracodei are imposters, we will be able to rule without the interference of Elder Dorold and his men."

"Exactly, father," Kessara said, allowing herself to give him a small smile. *Please, High One,* she prayed within her heart. *Help him to listen, to set aside his plans and to take a chance, even if his concern for the moment is only with power rather than the truth.*

"Kessara, you know that I have regard for you. But I have no time left to give," her father said finally.

"I understand. I know that my friends and I will have to move quickly. You just need to stall Captain Drohma."

"And the Septemvirate," her mother pointed out.

"Yes," Kessara said, a flash of annoyance prickling against her skin. "I know it will be difficult, but you are the most skilled diplomat in the Four Kingdoms. If we succeed, it could give our Kingdom and her people a fighting chance. Please, father."

King Manta walked over to the window and gazed out at the city as the room fell silent.

Chapter 9

The hooded figure leaned out of the doorway, trying to listen for signs of trouble, but it was of little use. The rain pounded against the street, filling his ears with an unending shushing sound that drowned out any hint of footsteps. Every few minutes, white-hot bolts of lightning seared the sky, followed by a crash of thunder.

He could not see the moon, but he knew it was late enough that the city was asleep. Mothers had long since tucked their little ones into bed. Fathers had left their rocking chairs empty before their hearths, giving the embers of their fires a final turn before heading off to their beds. The hooded man chuckled to himself as he gave a final glance up and down the narrow street. He ducked into the building and pulled the cheap wooden door shut behind him, eyeing the rusty bolt with suspicion as he attempted to shake water from his cloak.

It would have to be good enough.

The wicked men are still awake. It is never too late an hour to steal or to murder. No. They believe that the night belongs to them.

He made his way deeper into the dark building, holding up the torch he carried so as to avoid bumping into the cobweb-coated walls. The whole place smelled like rodent droppings, and every time the thunder sounded, he could hear a new rush of skittering feet that seemed to come from all directions. "Vile creatures. I should burn the nests," he muttered under his breath, his words breaking off as abruptly as he'd begun them.

The loneliness of his voice was even worse than the silence.

He passed several doors, some of them left ajar, gaping black mouths that bid him to enter the darkness. Most of them were shut tight with ancient, rusty bolts that would require a great bludgeoning in order to come loose.

He fiddled with the three objects in his pocket—one large and unreasonably cumbersome, and two small and smooth against his fingertips—until he found the door he'd been looking for.

It had not been opened in a while, but it did not look so abandoned as the others. The dust was thinner on the metal knob, and the wood beneath had been varnished within living memory. *I wish I had listened to you sooner,* the hooded man thought to himself, drawing out his hand from his pocket, a dainty key resting on his palm like an injured bird. *You too, father... I could have done so much more.*

He turned the key in the lock and entered the room, closing the door just as another burst of thunder sent the rats into a chittering fit. They were close to this room, but he scarcely noticed them now.

The thunder and pouring rain outside felt very far away. Deep within these walls, it was easy for the hooded man to remember. He thought of himself as a child, tripping over his clumsy limbs as he held his mother's hand as they followed his father into this very same room. It had been a ritual for so much of his life, but eventually, his parents had grown old, and the responsibility had been left to him alone. Ever since they'd gone to the Eternal Lands, he'd only made it here a handful of times.

The hooded man walked toward the far end of the room, the lamplight casting strange shadows in every direction as he moved. There were dozens of old objects covering much of the floor and leaning against the wood-paneled walls, forgotten things suited for the burn pile that someone had once thought important enough to keep. He nearly stumbled over a small wooden shield and sword that he could only assume were childrens' toys.

There, the man thought, listening for some unseen menace that he would have had no way of hearing over the rain outside. *Just as I left you.*

The wooden trunk had a lock. Reaching into his pocket, he drew out the correct key, a large one, with jagged-looking teeth at the end. He lifted the lid with some trepidation, as he always did. He chuckled to himself. As a child, he'd always imagined that someone might have snuck into this lost room and left some horrible immortal snake inside the wooden chest, curled up against the ancient velvet lining, waiting for his family to find.

Of course, there was no snake. The box was completely empty.

Once more he reached into his pocket and drew out the

heavy package, glancing beneath the flap of the fresh leather case he'd purchased and assuring himself that the ancient book within was as he'd left it. He set it in the bottom of the trunk, his movements gentle, as though he was setting down a babe in her cradle. He closed the lid and turned the key in the lock. The click was impossibly loud.

For a moment, he stood there, listening. Even the rats had gone silent. The thunder had slowed. He could hear the whoosh of his breathing. *Oh, father. I hope it's not too late. I hope that my actions, however flawed they were, did not make things worse for the people of Kaveryth.*

He paused, almost expecting an answer. None was given, but he was almost sure what his mother, at least, would have said.

The High One will forgive you. Even when you did not yet believe, you protected the Codex Veritatis in the best way that you knew how. It will be alright, you'll see.

He wiped a tear away from his cheek as he locked the door behind him and headed back toward the street.

Forgiven or not, he'd made his choices, and he would have to face them like the bracing cold of the storm.

Chapter 10

The battle was won.

Celesyria circled over Windshear as the moon rose, looking for bandits who remained within the city walls. She saw only bodies, and she wondered about the logistics of removing them and getting the city back to normal. She shuddered at the thought of people waking up and heading to the market for bread and eggs as though nothing had happened, as though their neighbors hadn't been carried off and sold into the most terrible servitude imaginable. How could these people ever feel safe again, when armed invaders could storm their city in the middle of a perfect summer day?

For now, at least, it seemed they were safe. Soldiers in red and blue patrolled every street, and if she missed any of the black-clad bandits she was confident they'd be taken care of. One of them waved a hand at her from below, and though he seemed friendly, she decided that it was time for her to return to her camp among the grove of trees.

She remembered the last time she'd been captured, the feeling of the ropes cutting into her flesh, of the manacles being snapped around her ankles. She had been promised that she was being restrained only for the comfort of the people, but it was a trap. She doubted that these men below, however numerous, would be able to imprison her again without such false pretenses, but still, she wasn't about to offer them the opportunity to try.

"Hello, Celesyria," a woman's voice said in her mind as she reached the edge of one of the market districts. She was so surprised that she nearly flew into the steep roof of the apothecary building.

"Kessara?"

The woman laughed. *"I would have loved to have been born a princess. What a life I could have led."*

"Who are—" Before she could say more, she caught a glimpse of red, stark against the white stone of a crumbling wall. It was not blood.

"Oh come now, dragon," the red-haired elf woman said. She was sitting on the ground with her back to the wall, doubling over as a fit of coughs wracked her body. Celesyria took a sharp turn, circling back to get a better look. *"Don't sound so surprised. There are a few of us elves that have the gifts required to speak to your kind."*

Celesyria knew this to be true. She'd read about it some-where, the title or even subject of the book escaping her memory. Still, it was strange to experience it. She didn't like the idea that the sworn enemies of Kaveryth were able to intrude into her mind.

"*What do you want?*"

"*Your help,*" the elf said as Celesyria passed by her again. She was clutching at her chest. This time, she noticed the bow discarded at the woman's side. It was the same elf who had shot her hours before.

"*With what?*"

"*I want to know the High One,*" the woman said, her voice gentle. "*I'm dying. I want to know Him before I meet my eternity.*"

Celesyria did not answer. She took another loop, wider this time, narrowly avoiding another collision with a nearby housetop before reaching the elevation she wanted. She had to think. *She's probably lying.* She felt anxious, expecting the elf's voice to invade her mind again at any moment. *It's a trap. She already tried to kill me today. Even if it wasn't, I've never read anything in the Codex fragments I've seen about elves being saved from the Wrathlands. I'm not sure that it's even possible.*

She thought of the elf that Wes and Alder had met. She had spoken to Wes about him briefly after the men had retired to King Manta's study closet for the night, and as far as she could tell, his change of heart had been genuine. She hadn't had the heart to tell Wes she suspected that elves, like dragons, had no souls that would permit them to enter the Eternal Lands.

Still, the advice she'd given him had been correct.

Pray.

There was nothing else that they could do.

She flew back toward the red-haired woman. The elf rested near an empty square, and Celesyria was able to land with enough room that she would be able to flee if she had to. She saw two soldiers passing by the edge of the street that demarcated the market district from a rough-looking street lined with taverns. The men only nodded to her before continuing on their way.

"If you so much as move, I will kill you," she said to the woman, leaning her head in close enough that the elf would be able to feel hot breath on her face.

The elf laughed, setting off another fit of coughing. She raised a gloved hand to her mouth as her chest heaved. It came away slick with blood.

"You're welcome to," the woman said aloud, giving Celesyria a gruesome smile. "A sword to the gut is a painful way to go."

"We don't have much time. We need to pray," the dragon said, continuing to speak in her mind as she looked over her wing. They were still alone.

"Oh, Celesyria," the elf said, speaking in her head again as she closed her eyes. Through the blood and the pain, Celesyria could still see that she was beautiful in an almost frightening way, in a way that didn't feel exactly real. *"So loyal to the High One, even though He hates you."*

Celesyria's chest tightened, but the elf did not give her a chance to respond.

"Unlike you and the Envoy, I have some dignity. Even now," she let out a mirthless chuckle, her eyes still shut. *"If the High One is real, he allowed Wesley Cervos' entire family to be slaughtered."*

"You don't—"

"Please, Celesyria," the woman said in the dragon's mind, her voice so loud that the dragon was certain it had been affected by some kind of sorcery. *"Let me finish."*

Celesyria said nothing. She knew that she should fly away, return to camp, and rest, but curiosity kept her rooted in place.

"The High One has treated you even worse," she continued. *"You know it yourself. You have no soul. When you die, there is no*

hope. There is only the Farplace. Only emptiness."

"We're not even sure where the Farplace is. We don't even know if it's a real place beyond the shallows or if it's something else. No one can claim to know what it's like to be sent there."

"Perhaps not. Perhaps it's not so terrible," the elf continued, coughing even as she spoke in Celesyria's head. *"But why is it that you are not welcomed into the Eternal Lands? You've risked everything for the High One, and yet He offers you no thanks. No mercy. No love."*

Celesyria's heart ached at the words. It was as though the elf was echoing back her own thoughts, the dark ponderings that she did not dare utter to anyone else, not even to Wes. She had to leave. The elf had clearly chosen the Wrathlands already.

"Your kind knows nothing of love."

The elf woman opened her eyes, laughing again. It was an ugly sound. *"You lecture me about love after you abandon your parents and put everyone you've ever cared about at risk?"*

"I had to do the right thing."

"How very noble of you. Then again, it's pretty clear where you got it from."

Celesyria felt sick.

"What are you talking about?"

"Your father, Celesyria. He is—or was, I suppose, I'm not sure if they've killed him yet—a noble fellow. Just like his daughter."

"Tell me," Celesyria screeched aloud at the elf, the force of her roar causing the woman's hair to flutter away from her face. At that moment, she could not bring herself to care who heard her. "Tell me what happened to him. Where is he?"

The elf smiled up at Celesyria, blood coating her teeth. A moment later, the light faded behind her green eyes as she went to meet her eternal punishment.

* * *

Alder's eyes shot open as he felt someone grab him. It was too dark to see anything. His hand flew to the knife at his belt before he could think.

"Alder," Wes hissed, shrinking away from him in the pitch-black closet. Alder's heart rate began to slow as he moved to a sitting position and took several breaths.

"I almost stabbed you," he snapped, attempting in vain to blink away the darkness. "You can't surprise me like that. I've been in battle—"

"Yes, I know," Wes said, making a shushing sound. "I'm sorry. Something's wrong."

"What? What happened? What time is it?"

"Late. I just woke up to Celesyria—"

"Is she okay?"

"Yes," Wes said, sucking in a breath. Alder could imagine him rolling his eyes. "It's her father. An elf woman told her that something's happened to him, and she said that she's going back to Whitespire."

"Now?"

"I told her to calm down, but she said that she can't wait. The soldiers have left her alone, but now that the battle is over, she suspects that Drohma's men will be after her."

"She's right," Alder said. He knew the man too well to think that he would let the dragon go, even after she aided his soldiers. She'd embarrassed King Ursa with her escape, and that was enough. On top of that, he was certain that the Septemvirate were eager to see her captured again for good.

"Maybe she should."

"What if she's captured? How will we find the Codex on our own?" Wes asked. "Besides, if she leaves, I will have no way to speak with her."

Alder cursed. "Is she sure that the elf is even telling the truth?"

"Of course not," Wes said. "I told her that she probably wasn't, but she doesn't want to take the chance with her father's life at stake."

"Okay," Alder said, trying to stretch out his legs in the cramped space. "So we go to her and try to convince her to see sense."

"She told me that the city is empty of bandits, but there are Galeharbor and Aridmoor soldiers swarming all over."

"Well, that complicates things," Alder said after a pause. "Tell her we're coming. We'll find a way out of Windshear."

Alder waited as Wes spoke to Celesyria in his mind. The closet reeked of sweat and cigar smoke. "Why are we still in here?" he asked, coughing as he got to his feet. He opened the door, the comparatively fresh air of King Manta's study filling his grateful lungs. Wes followed.

"She agreed to wait until dawn, but no later," Wes said, blinking quickly in an attempt to dispel the darkness of the closet from his eyes.

Alder looked up at the windows near the ceiling of the study. "Judging by where the moon is, that only gives us a few hours. We need to find Kessara."

Wes didn't answer.

He was standing behind King Manta's desk, using the toe of his boot to lift the edge of the tapestry they'd left spread over the elf's body.

"That closet must really stink if it's nicer to be out here with a corpse," Alder joked, moving toward the door to the throne room.

Wes shot him a look. "I wish we could give him a proper burial."

"We can't."

"What will they do with the body? Will his family ever know what happened to him?"

Alder turned to face his friend. "They'll burn him, Wes. Along with the others. His family will know whatever the surviving elves choose to tell them."

"Don't," Alder said as gently as he could as Wes stared down at the fallen elf, the edges of his eyes going red. "You need to be tough, Wes. There is no place left in this vicious world for men who cry."

I'm sorry, he wanted to say as he watched his friend straighten up, keeping the tears that welled in his eyes from spilling. *Sometimes I wish that I hadn't had to be the strength of my family. I shed no tears for my father, so that my mother and my sisters could. Men carry the pain on our shoulders, and no one gets to see how we're breaking. That's life.*

* * *

After grabbing a lamp from the King's desk, Wes and Alder made their way into the throne room, stopping for a few minutes at the abandoned breakfast table to eat whatever food they could find. Wes' stomach ached. He couldn't exactly remember when he'd eaten last, but it had been far too long. How strange it was to think that for his entire life up until a few months ago, his body had carried plenty of extra food

116

stores. Now, he had no idea where his next meal was coming from. He took what he could get.

"It's kind of strange to eat this bread," Alder said, his mouth stuffed full of one of the stale biscuits. Wes chewed and swallowed his own before answering, thinking that it was not half bad for having been left out all night.

"It makes me feel even more stupid about giving it to the elf in the first place," Wes said, shoving another biscuit in his mouth as quickly as he could. *I hope it helped him.* He felt a pang of worry at his own ignorance, unable to stop the final moments of the dying man from replaying over and over in his mind. *If You are the one who created the world, High One, I suppose it would not be difficult for You to transform bread into hope. Still, it is hard to believe what I cannot comprehend.*

"Alright," Alder said, grabbing a mug of cold tea and downing it in one swallow. "We need to move."

As they made their way out of the throne room and into one of the endless stone passageways, Wes was again struck by the emptiness of the place. It was night, of course. He didn't expect to see people roaming the halls, but there was something more than that. There was a hollowness here that reminded him of his home in Stronghollow, after the elf invaders had murdered his mother, father, and brother. *Maybe it's their very presence that leaves a mark on a place, like a dark smoke that won't quite clear.*

Wes followed Alder. Though the former soldier was heavy and easily a foot taller than Wes himself, he moved in near total silence. Wes, on the other hand, sounded like a dog on three legs as he tried to keep up.

He hoped that Alder knew where he was going. *At least the guards seem to be concentrated elsewhere.* Wes kept as quiet as he could as they pulled around another bend in the stone wall and ascended a twisting flight of stairs. When they pulled open the door that lay at the top, they were met with a darkness so heavy that their lamplight was scarcely able to penetrate it.

"Where are we?" Wes asked, his whisper sounding far too loud in the empty expanse that lay before them.

"The upper north wing. Kessara will be here."

"How do you know?"

Before Alder could respond, Wes continued. "And don't you dare say that it's because you were a soldier."

Alder made a noise under his breath that Wes suspected was laughter.

"Because I was in the Protectorate. The palaces of each of the four greater noble Houses are basically laid out in the same way. I've studied the builders' schematic for the one in—" Alder stopped, and Wes could see the shadow of his head bobbing back and forth in the lamplight. "I'll explain later. Be quiet. We're close."

Moments later, they arrived at a door. Alder knocked on it, paused, and then knocked again. There was no answer.

"Kessara," Wes called out, trying not to shout as the two men began pounding on the door with more force. "Kessara! It's us!"

They paused. All Wes could hear was the sound of his breathing, still somewhat winded after rushing up the stairs. Please, please let her be alright.

He reached for the handle and began to rattle it, but it was locked into place. Alder tried to do the same, to no avail.

"Where is she? Did something happen to her?" he asked as Alder handed him the lantern.

The tall man glanced back toward where they'd come from

before shoving his shoulder into the door as hard as he could. It made a fantastic noise.

"Are you insane—" Wes started as Alder pulled back and slammed his body forward a second time.

This time, the door flew open with the sound of splintering wood. Pieces of decorative shell shattered against the stone floor, sending bits of sharp, shimmering dust in all directions.

Alder snatched the lantern out of Wes' hand and moved into the dark room, with Wes following close behind. Wes expected to hear the sound of rushing footsteps at any moment, but so far, no one was coming upstairs.

They reached the bed and Alder held the lantern aloft. The sheets were in place and a blue quilt was folded over neatly near a mountain of pillows. No one had slept here.

"Where is she?" Wes whispered. "What do we do?"

Before he could say more, they heard the sound of boots clattering on stone.

Wes rushed over to the wall opposite the door and felt around until his fingers found fabric. Alder came up beside him with the lantern and did the same.

"Smart," his friend said, yanking on the heavy curtains as hard as he could. "I didn't even think of that. Yet."

Wes was glad that Alder could not see his smile in the darkness as he did the same, leaning backward with all of his weight until the pins holding the curtain rod tore free from the wall above.

The two men stumbled out of the way just in time for the metal pole to come clattering to the ground, so loud against the floor that Wes was tempted to cover his ears.

He heard someone shouting from below. More footsteps, though Wes couldn't tell how many men were coming. They still sounded like they were rather far away, perhaps near the front entrance of the palace.

"Let's move," Alder said, grabbing three of the long curtain panels and tying their ends together by the glow of the moonlight that was now coming through the window. Wes bent down to help, but his friend was already done. It wasn't a neat-looking rope, but it only had to hold for a few seconds. Wes moved to the edge of the Princess' balcony and peered over the edge. There was a courtyard below, dotted with various fountains and statues and surrounded on all sides by tall green hedges. *The labyrinth.* It had been one of Kessara's favorite places ever since she was a child.

A second later, Alder was beside him, throwing the makeshift rope over the side. "See," he said, taking the free end and tying it to a statue of an anchor that sat to one side of the balcony doors. "The High One has a plan."

Wes said nothing, looking down at the solid stone courtyard beneath them. *Only if He plans to keep me from falling off of this rope.* He rubbed his sweaty hands against the legs of his pants, trying in vain to keep them dry for more than a few seconds. He felt like he was going to be sick. It hadn't looked so far down before.

Alder stuck his head in through the balcony door, listening. "Sounds like they're at the bottom of the stairs. Move."

Wes stood by the railing, unsure of what to do.

"Wes," Alder said again, gesturing to the rope. "Go."

"You go first. I need to see how to do it."

Alder rolled his eyes. "How to climb? It's pretty simple. Just go."

"Really, you go," He said, swallowing back nausea. "I'll—"

"I can hold your weight if the statue doesn't hold."

"I can't, I—"

Alder grabbed him by the shoulders. Wes forced himself to hold his gaze. No crying, he reminded himself, using all of his willpower to stop the tears from coming. He's right. Men do not have the luxury of tears.

"The rope could hold an Aridmoorian bear. I know how to tie solid knots. It's that anchor I'm worried about. And if it breaks, I can keep you from falling," Alder said, his face revealing nothing. "Even if you could do the same for me, and you can't, it would be stupid. Your life is more valuable to Kaveryth than mine. Now be a man, and move."

Wes tried to ignore the shouts that were filtering through the balcony door as he clambered over to the other side of the railing, took hold of the rope, and pressed his eyes shut.

He hated that Alder was right. It brought back every old guilt that his soul carried. But there was no time to let himself feel it.

A few breathless minutes later, he was on the ground. He just barely managed to make it over to a potted plant before vomiting up his meager breakfast. As he wiped his mouth clean, he saw Alder standing there, arms crossed, with a grin on his face. "Men can puke. Just as long as they don't cry."

They heard men upstairs. It would be only a matter of seconds before they made it into Kessara's room and onto the balcony. "This way," Wes said, spotting a narrow path between two tall hedges, blocked by a wheelbarrow. He shoved past it, racing through, his heart pounding.

"Good call," Alder said from behind as they rounded one corner, and then another, until they reached a point where the path split. "Any brilliant ideas which path to take?"

Wes shrugged his shoulders. "Don't you have some fancy

Protectorate navigational training you could utilize?"

"Ha ha," Alder said, making his way into the right-hand path. "I think this will get us closer to the castle. Assuming Kessara is hiding out somewhere inside, and that's a big if."

The moonlight was bright enough for them to see by, but they could no longer tell which direction they were heading. Wes hoped it was the right one. Alder's guess was as good as his own. *Kessara would know the way, if she was here.*

"Do you think she's alright?"

"Look," Alder said, glancing over his shoulder as Wes tried to keep up with his long strides. "Drohma may not be a nice guy, but he's a good soldier. There's no way he would have let the royal family of Galeharbor come to harm."

Wes nodded as they continued to walk down the impossibly long passage. His legs were beginning to tire, and they still could not see the palace. He tried to reach out to Celesyria in his mind, but he could not seem to get her to hear him. *You had better just be sleeping or something.* He didn't want to alarm Alder with the news. He hoped that she wouldn't attempt to go to Umrym alone, but they were running out of time. Even with his view obstructed by the hedges, the sky was gradually becoming lighter. Dawn was coming, and he was losing hope that they would find Kessara.

They walked around a tight bend in the path, finding themselves mere feet from a door. For a moment they just breathed, looking up at the vast walls of the palace rising above them. Alder was the first to move, walking over to what looked like some kind of servant's entrance and grasping the door handle. It turned without resistance. "See," he said, opening the door. "Divine providence."

Wes moved to follow him, but before he could enter the

castle, Alder slammed the door shut. He had no time to react before he heard the heavy thunk of the bolt.

"I hate to do this, Wes," Alder called through the door. "But we're out of time."

* * *

Alder turned to head deeper into the castle, but Wes continued to pound on the door. The sound echoed through the empty room.

"Do you want every soldier in Windshear to find us?"

"What by the Dracodei is wrong with you?" Wes asked, his voice muffled by the wood that lay between them.

"You really need to work on your cussing. I learned a lot in the military, perhaps I could help you. And besides, we no longer believe in the Dracodei, so it seems rather silly to invoke them."

"Alder," Wes said slowly, pausing for a moment as though he needed to take a breath. "Let me in. Now."

Wes sounded so serious that Alder began to feel a little bad about his jokes.

"I'm going to find Kessara," Alder said, pressing his face close against the door so as to be heard through the thick wood. "It's nearly dawn."

"And why do you think you'll have any more luck finding her without me?"

"I have a plan."

"One you couldn't tell me about, of course. What if Kessara has been captured? What if she—"

"I swear on my life that I will keep your maybe-betrothed safe, if that's what you're worried about."

He felt an unexpected rush of emotion at the thought of protecting her, of hiding her delicate frame behind his bulky one, warding off their enemies. Wes had a good heart, but the thought of her having no one else but him to step in front of her when she inevitably faced danger made him feel uneasy. He rubbed at his forehead with his fingertips, glad that his friend could not see the confusion written across his face.

I need to be careful. She belongs to Wes, he chided himself, thinking back to what he'd said to Wes scarcely an hour before. *Whatever wild daydreams I may want to indulge in, she needs to marry the last remaining member of the House of Cervos. Not only do I barely know this woman, the very fate of the Four Kingdoms rests upon her choice of husband. I don't get to whine about the fact that it's never going to be me.*

"I'm not worried about your ability to protect the Princess," Wes was saying through the door. "I'm worried that you're too late."

"I have a plan, and you need to trust me," he said, struggling to keep any hint of his emotions from coming through. "We still need to find the Codex Veritatis. All of us hanging around in the same location is too dangerous, anyway. If they capture one of us—"

"You just got finished saying that my life was so much more important than yours. Do you actually believe that, or was it just a ploy to get me on the rope?"

"Both," he said quickly. "You are more valuable than the rest of us. You and Kessara both, which is why it makes logical sense for Celesyria and I to each protect one of you."

Wes said nothing.

"You need to get to the dragon. Fortunately, our little break-in has probably brought most of the soldiers standing guard close to the castle. Go back to the fork and take the left-hand path. My advanced navigation training indicates that it will get you out into the city proper, and you'll be fine from there."

"Fine," Wes said after another long pause. Alder listened for the sound of company. He could hear soldiers moving somewhere overhead, but he hoped he would be relatively safe in the servants' area of the castle.

"I knew you'd understand," Alder said. "We will see each other again in Auranth. Stay safe, and may the High One guide you."

Without waiting for a goodbye, he strode off into the castle, moving as fast and as silently as he could until he found what he was looking for.

Perfect. He forced his breath to slow as he observed the Protectorate soldier standing guard near the liquor storeroom. *Please don't fight me.*

Within a half second, he had his knife to the soldier's throat. He got his other hand around the man's body and dragged him inside behind some ale barrels. His captive was shaking so hard that he feared he would accidentally cut him.

"Don't move," he whispered, turning the man around so that he could face him. "I'm not going to hurt you. As long as you cooperate. You need to tell me where Princess Kessara Manta is. Now."

Chapter 11

Kessara awoke, but she did not open her eyes. For several moments, she lay in the dim room, pretending that she was comfortable in her bed upstairs. The straw mattress she was sleeping on was scarcely thick enough to stop the jutting stones of the dungeon floor from digging into her back. She wondered what time it was. Was she tired because she'd had such an uncomfortable sleep, or because she'd barely slept more than a few hours? Either way, the night had felt very long, and she was eager to leave the dank-smelling dungeon where she'd been sequestered.

She didn't even know where her mother and father had been taken. She was told it was too risky to keep them together, and that for the next couple of days, they would need to do their best to keep a low profile. The only freedom that she'd been able to negotiate was that her guards would stand watch at the staircase leading down to the dungeons rather than at the door.

She rose to a sitting position, picking pieces of straw out of her long blonde hair, wishing desperately for a warm bath. *Wonderful. I have no clue where my friends are, and no one is going to allow me to go and find them even if I knew the way.*

"You smell like the cadet barracks back home," a voice said from the shadowed corner of the cell.

She shot up from the bed, but before she could scream, she saw Alder's smirking face illuminated by the weak lantern light as he strode into the center of the room. Even in the poor light, she could see the laughter dancing in his green eyes.

"What kind of a gentleman watches a lady in her sleep?" she snapped at him, pulling her night dress more tightly around herself. She wished very much to pat down the halo of frizz that surrounded her hair, but she refrained. *I don't care how I look in front of him,* she told herself. *How dare he sneak up on me like this.*

"Darling," he said, stifling a yawn with his hand. "I'm not a gentleman. I'm a soldier."

A soldier who served in the King's personal army, who probably should have absorbed some basic etiquette, she wanted to retort, but she said nothing, folding her hands across her chest.

"Sorry for scaring you."

"I can tell by your grin that you're feeling terribly guilty."

"No, I really am," he said, his face growing serious. "I'm sure you were on edge last night, and you probably thought something terrible was about to happen. Hence why I opened with a joke."

"Actually, it was an insult," she said, stifling her own smile as

127

she sniffed at the underarm of her dress. *Lovely*. Heat rose to her face as she inhaled the unpleasant scent. "A true enough insult, it turns out."

"We'll find you a bathtub somewhere, Princess," he said, so serious that she was certain he was poking fun at her. "But in the meantime, you should know that Wes and Celesyria are heading to Whitespire as we speak."

"What? Why?"

"If it's any consolation, I had an even worse start to my morning than you did. Wes and I slept in a closet in your father's study, and I nearly stabbed him when he woke me up to tell me that Celesyria was about to fly the coop."

Kessara waited for him to continue with some explanation, but she doubted that he could produce one that would explain why her friends had felt the need to make decisions without so much as informing her of them. She would have liked to say goodbye.

"She met a dying elf woman after the battleground cleared out, and she taunted her. Told her that her father was in danger," Alder said, all of the humor gone from his deep voice. "Celesyria doesn't know if he's even alive."

"By the Dracodei," she whispered, playing with the ends of her tangled hair. "That's horrible."

"We don't know if the elf was telling the truth. Perhaps the creature was just trying to break her."

"Maybe. But Celesyria is not going to sit back and hope that that's all it was," Kessara said.

"No. In any case, Wes was able to convince her to wait until dawn before heading to Umrym."

"What time is it now?" she asked.

"Well after dawn," Alder said, glancing around the room as

though he might find a small window that he had missed.

Kessara put her head in her hands. "So they're gone. I didn't even get to say goodbye to Wes. He just left me here."

Alder took a few steps closer and extended a hand toward her. She didn't know whether to grasp it or not, and a moment later, he allowed it to fall to his side. "As much as I'd love for all of us to take a trip to Whitespire, there's only so much room on Celesyria's back. Two riders was difficult enough for her. Three would be dangerous."

"He could have told me he was leaving."

"Kessara," Alder said. Her eyes narrowed at his tone. It reminded her of someone talking to a small child. "We didn't know where you were. There was no time, and Celesyria wasn't going to wait. So we split up."

"And Wes preferred to go to Umrym than to stay near the woman he's supposed to marry to save his Kingdom," she said, feeling tears welling up in her eyes as fast as she could blink them back. Even if she couldn't bring herself to love him, it still hurt, somehow. It hurt to know that even though she was willing to offer her entire life and happiness for the sake of their people, he was unable to so much as talk to her about it.

"It's not like that, Kessara," Alder snapped. "What do you care, anyway? It's pretty obvious that you and Wes are hardly an inseparable pair. It's not ideal that you didn't get to talk to him, but it's not something that's worth your tears."

"It's nothing to do with us being a romantic couple," she spat. "My father has made it very clear that marrying Wes is not optional, not for me. And I understand why he feels so strongly about it. My people are being boxed in. My parents are being given no choice but to assent to King Ursa's tyranny if they want to protect Galeharbor—"

"I didn't mean—"

"You never stop talking, Alder," she said, not waiting for him to finish. "You need to listen. My feelings for Wes have nothing to do with my tears. My love for him has nothing to do with my feelings. You should know as well as anyone that duty does not always align with the longings of our hearts."

He said nothing. For a few seconds, they just looked at each other, his bright eyes gazing into her own. She looked away first, feeling as though she'd been burned. There was something about the way that he looked at her, like he was stripping away the lies that she'd had to tell herself from the moment they met.

I hate him.

He's a brute.

He's not good enough for me.

"Forgive me," he said, his voice so low that she could barely hear it. "You're right. And I'm truly sorry for mocking you. You're only fulfilling the duty that the High One has placed before you, and that is praiseworthy."

"So," she said finally, tucking a strand of hair behind her ear. "What do we do now?"

Alder straightened, all business. "*We* are not doing anything. *You* are going to do your best to stop your parents from selling their souls to Kylan Ursa and his Red Army. *I* have other things to attend to, in Aridmoor."

"My father will do what he has already set his mind to do," she said, shrinking away from one of the dungeon's walls as a large spider skittered past. "Perhaps he'll wait for me and Wes to marry, but perhaps not, especially now that he's taken off across Kaveryth. I've said my piece. My presence here can do no more good. Anyway, he told me that two of the Elders are arriving—"

"The point is, Kessara, I have an unexpected matter to attend to, and it's urgent," Alder cut her off. "I didn't plan to leave your side, but I promised Wes I'd keep you safe, and given these new circumstances, the safest place for you is here with your guards."

"So you don't actually think that I can change my father's mind. You just want me to stand around looking pretty while the world burns."

He looked at her for a moment, and she felt her stomach flip.

He doesn't think I'm beautiful.

She tried to convince herself that the intensity of his gaze meant nothing, that he was looking at her only because there was nothing else more interesting nearby. It was yet another lie.

"I want you to live long enough to become the future Queen of Silverfell."

"So you're saying that you're incapable of protecting me?"

Alder chuckled at this. "My darling, if you're going to appeal to my ego, don't insult my intelligence."

I hate when you call me darling.

"Fair enough," she said, returning his smile. "Surely you're clever enough to realize that you can't tell me what to do. I'm coming with you."

* * *

"How far are we?" Wes asked.

"It's still a while yet," she said, feeling the shifting of his weight on her back as she flew. It was much more comfortable

131

without a second rider, even if Wes had a tendency to yank out some of her small scales when she turned too sharply and he panicked. *"See the Wings of Noctua, there to the west?"*

"I do now," Wes said.

"If you look just to the left of it, there's a constellation known only to the dwarves. They call it the Mining Helm."

"I can see it! Those four stars curve over the top. It really does look like a helmet."

The simple happiness in Wes' voice almost filled her heart to bursting.

Celesyria had always loved the stars.

Ever since she was a hatchling, she'd been amazed by the majesty of the constellations. She would spend hours overground with her father, trying to learn them all by sight and by name. Her mother had not approved of her husband and daughter spending so much time outside of the caverns of Whitespire, and even her best friend, Gramnok Beastbane, had not understood, but she treasured the memories, not to mention the navigation skills that were the result of her instruction.

Despite everything, I hope that he's alright. The mere recollection of his name brought a stab of pain to her chest. Gramnok had betrayed her, but after the initial anger had worn away, she'd prayed to the High One for the strength to forgive him, and she had. She even missed him. Life had seemed so much simpler back then, when the two of them would laugh together in the shadows of the mining tunnels or pester the dining hall dwarves for a second serving of dessert.

She couldn't dwell on thoughts of her father.

Not now, not while she and Wes had to focus on reaching Umrym. The worries were too painful to bear. She couldn't allow them to pull her under.

"I still can't believe Alder locked me out of the palace," Wes was saying. She tried to focus on his words, wishing that the thoughts of the past and present fate of her loved ones would fade away. The High One was in control, so why was she still so scared?

"I'm lucky I even made it back to you. I could have easily been captured," Wes continued.

"Kessara will be alright," she said. *"I think Alder can handle protecting her, not to mention her guards."*

She listened to the sound of her wings pushing against the air, savoring the feeling of the night breeze lifting them higher. Mere months ago, she'd been trapped in the dungeon of Stronghollow, fearing that she'd never fly again. The manacles she still bore were a painful reminder of what she'd endured, but she knew that she'd been very fortunate to escape at all. Every time she flew, she made a point of thanking the High One. She'd taken her freedom for granted all of her life, but now she understood that it came at a price.

"I know," Wes said finally. *"It was probably the right call. But I don't like that we're all separated. We have no true allies but each other, and I guess four seemed a lot better than two."*

"I'm glad you're with me, so I don't have to be completely alone," she said. *"Without Gramnok, I have no idea how I'm even going to get into Whitespire without being seen. I'll probably be captured and hauled to our own dungeons before I can even find out what's happened to my father."*

She realized that she was crying, and she was glad that Wes could not see her face. He had enough reasons for tears.

"Whatever happens, Celesyria, it's going to be okay."

"Because the High One has a plan."

"No," Wes said, shifting forward as she banked across a current of warm air. *"I mean, yes, but that's not what I meant. However angry your mother is at you—"*

"For committing crimes of blasphemy and probably treason."

"Whatever it is she thinks you have done, she's going to be relieved that you're okay. You'll have a chance to explain, at least."

She looked over toward the western horizon. She could see the Severed Summits now, the great mountain range that surrounded her home. They were close.

"I will have to reach out to her in my mind," she said. *"When we're near enough. But I'm scared to face her. I'm scared that she's only going to shut me out."*

"I can go into Whitespire alone," Wes said after another long pause. *"You're too big to sneak around the caverns, but I'm not. I could look for the Codex, and try to find out what happened to your father."*

Celesyria was so stunned that she struggled to speak.

"That's insane. You cannot possibly think that is a good idea." As insane as it certainly was, she couldn't help but to be touched by her friend's offer.

"It isn't, but neither is your plan," Wes said, his words tumbling into her mind more quickly than she could absorb them.

"You'll be captured."

"I'm afraid I will be. I really am. But spending time with Alder... he takes risks. He makes the best choice that he can, but he doesn't wait for a perfect solution that will never come before he acts. He trusts the High One to carry him through."

Celesyria rolled her eyes. *"You don't need to compare yourself to him, Wes. You're two different people."*

"It's not about that. I know very well that I'm never going to be a handsome, muscle-bound warrior from the plains."

She wanted to remind him that he was handsome in a different way, but he continued before she could get a word in.

"I always play it safe, and every time I get into trouble, someone else has to take risks for me. Even to the point of sacrificing their lives. Perhaps it's time that I do the same, and have faith that the High One will protect me."

"You're very noble, and I'm thankful for the offer. But you know as well as I do that we can't risk any harm coming to you," she said. *"You're too important to all of the Four Kingdoms, and to Kaveryth itself."*

It was true. Many had lost their lives in order to protect the Envoy's own, but how many more would come to know the High One thanks to his courage in speaking the truth?

"Celesyria," Wes said, shifting in the leather saddle once more. *"They can't kill me. Elder Dorold will try and find some way to force me to offer the sacrifices, and he'll enjoy locking me up in the darkest dungeon he can find, but there's nothing worse that the Septemvirate can do, not to me. But they could kill you. Don't you understand?"*

"I know," she started again. *"But that doesn't—"*

"Even if I'm imprisoned, you and Alder and Kessara can continue to spread the truth about the Dracodei. You can find more allies who will stand beside you. Eventually, you can find a way to set me free."

She paused for a moment, trying to think of what to say to convince him that this was madness. She knew that in the end, however Wes and her other friends would protest, she was expendable. Wes was not. She had so often felt guilty for being jealous of him and of his special role in service of the High One, but now, she began to understand why being the chosen one was such a difficult weight to bear.

As much as she was tempted to think that his offer to go to Whitespire alone was nothing more than an act of masculine ego, she knew that the truth was much more complicated.

Wes wanted to choose.

He wanted his destiny to be in his own hands, to walk through the storm and come out on the other side by his own power. But that was not the life of someone who served the God of all Kaveryth. Wes knew it himself, however much he wanted to push back against it. To serve the High One was to give up your own ideas about how life should be, and embrace the path that was laid before you.

She only wished that she could be at peace with that reality herself. Whenever things got quiet, thoughts of the bandit she'd killed back in Windshear filled her thoughts. She'd made a choice, and now she would have to bear the burden of the consequences. Wes had to do the same.

"My friend," she began, casting a glance over her shoulder at him. He was riding much better than he had been just a few days ago when they left Windshear, but as always, his face was pale and his fingers were clutched too tight to the leather holding straps. *"I appreciate everything you are willing to do for me and for my family."*

"I'm not asking your permission, Celesyria," Wes said.

"Now that sounds like something Alder would say," she quipped, unable to resist a reptilian smile at the stars spread out before her. *"I never said that you needed my consent to go to Whitespire. You may seem very young to me and my 137 years, but that doesn't mean I don't view you as an equal."*

"So what do you want me to say? I can't allow you to take all of the risks, Celesyria. You will pay a higher price for capture than I

will," he said.

"The people, dwarves, and dragons of Kaveryth will lose everything if the Dracodei continue to usurp the worship of the High One. We need you to find out what He wants of you, and to fulfill the Envoy's calling. We need you to marry Kessara, and save the House of Cervos. And I need you to be okay, because you mean the world to me, and I wouldn't be able to bear it if I not only lost my father and Gramnok, but you as well."

To Celesyria's surprise, her eyes were blurry with tears. It was true. In just a few short months, Wes had become more than a dear friend. Despite their difference in species, she could not think of him as anything less than a brother.

Wes said nothing for a moment. She listened only to the beat of her wings as they flew, dawn and the mountains of Umrym drawing nearer.

"If I don't go, what is your plan?" he asked finally.

"I don't have a great one, but it's a start. I need to speak with my mother, preferably face to face. I need to find out where my father is and what we are up against."

"Okay," Wes said. "You're right. We'll be careful, and we'll find a way."

Celesyria let out a deep breath, sending a plume of smoke swirling off into the night sky.

* * *

"Can you remind me again why we couldn't have just borrowed some horses?" Alder asked as the deer he was riding jostled him nearly out of the saddle for the umpteenth time. He had never ridden one of the huge horned beasts before, and it was much more difficult than he'd expected.

137

"I believe that the word you're looking for is 'stolen,'" Kessara chided him, shifting her body weight as her own deer moved beneath her, stepping over an old hollow log that lay across the path. "Most of Windshear's horses are being used by Galeharbor's army at the moment. Two of the remaining animals going missing would certainly have been noticed. In any case, as I told you, these two beautiful boys were gifts to my mother from a Lesser House noble in Silverfell. Actually, I think he was trying to bribe her into a questionable alliance with some of his merchant friends, but in any case, she won't mind us using them."

"Oh," Alder said, clamping his thighs against the saddle as hard as he could as his own deer followed Kessara's. "So your parents know that you decided to follow me to High Keep?"

Kessara said nothing, falling behind him for a moment as they passed through a narrow stand of trees. They had been traveling for two days already, and had only just reached the eastern border of Aridmoor. Soon, they would leave the safety of the forest and reach the wide open spaces of the Plains Kingdom.

Home.

They would have to stop and make camp soon. Alder looked up at the sky above the canopy of trees, already longing for the feeling of insignificance he always felt when he rode across the plains. Now, with the aid of his faith in the High One, he was sure the experience would be even more awe-inducing.

"I couldn't tell them," Kessara said finally, though he had already known by her silence that their little journey was not something they had approved. "I left them a note, so they wouldn't worry."

"They will worry anyway," Alder pointed out.

"It would have been nice if I'd been able to tell them why we were going in the first place."

Alder sighed as his deer wandered off of the path and toward an apparently delicious-looking plant. "They wouldn't have understood, Kessara," he said, yanking the creature's reins until he cooperated. "I didn't exactly want to tell them about the soldier that I threatened at the point of my knife."

"You knew him, didn't you?"

"Yes. He was part of my command a couple of years ago. We also grew up in the same corner of High Keep."

He felt a pang of guilt about scaring poor Calen half to death.

Alder had only intended to use his threat to gather information about Kessara's whereabouts. Instead, he discovered that the younger soldier had been given a message from his mother to deliver if he happened to run into Alder. Calen insisted that she'd only said a few words, and had asked him to spread the message to other soldiers who might still have some regard for her son despite his defection from the Protectorate.

The message was simple.

Raela is dying. Tell no one. Hurry.

"Deermaster Lev delivered these deer to us, before he died," Kessara said after several seconds of silence. "Sometimes our world feels so small."

Alder set aside his worries about reaching Raela in time, glad for even a small distraction from his racing thoughts.

"Nothing is a coincidence," he said. "Even a humble Deermaster has a role in the High One's plan. Had he not been willing to offer his life to protect Wes, you and I would have continued to live our lives in service of the false gods."

Deermaster Lev had been killed assisting Wes during the

spring Feast of Offering, leaving his family without a husband and father. Alder's heart broke for them. He knew how they felt, but at least their family's patriarch had died an honorable man, doing what he thought was right.

"That's true. But his death had a deep impact on Wes," she said. "I'm not sure he's ever going to get over it."

"He will, in time. He has to."

"You're a soldier. You've seen death," Kessara said. He could tell which way her questions were going, and he steeled himself. "Does none of it bother you, like Wes assumed? Do you fall asleep and think about the men that you killed?"

They haunt me every day. They rise up to follow me at dawn. I can never shake the ghosts.

"No," he said instead, looking forward as he urged his deer to walk faster. "The men I killed deserved to die."

"They were still human."

"They acted like monsters. They forfeited their right to live."

"But don't you feel guilty?" Kessara asked, riding up until she was right beside him again, her deer obeying her subtle commands without a fuss.

Alder chuckled, the sound hushed against the thick trees. "Men don't have the luxury of acting based upon our feelings. Our world would fall apart if we did."

"You sound like my father," Kessara said, glaring at him.

"Good. So long as I never sound anything like my own father, I'm happy."

"Women aren't stupid, you know," she snapped. "We use logic, too."

"Kessara," he chuckled again, and he watched as she gazed straight ahead, her tanned skin gleaming in the dusk-light. *By*

140

the Dracodei, why is she so gorgeous when she's mad at me?

"I'm well aware that you speak four languages, including ancient elvish, and that you do advanced mathematical puzzles for amusement. Don't be silly."

"Who told you that?" she turned to him in the saddle, her cheeks pink.

"About the math?" he stifled another laugh. "Celesyria, actually. Though I assume Wes told her. What else do you do for fun? Do you pop over to the Academy at Vaevar for thrilling lessons in advanced chemistry?"

"I would punch you if I could reach," she grumbled, but she was smiling.

"I would pretend that it hurt," he countered.

"I would—" she started to say, leaning toward him slightly as their deer fell in more closely beside each other. Before she could say more, she stopped herself, pointing ahead toward a small clearing.

"Th—th—this looks like a great place to make camp," she stammered.

He flashed her his brightest smile.

I would kiss you and make you mine.

They rode forward in silence, gazing up at the open sky overhead. The sun had already dipped below the horizon, and the crickets had begun to sing their nightly song. After a couple of minutes, they had reached the far side of the meadow, and they started to unpack their camp supplies beneath the dark shadows of the trees.

As he began to set up his own bedroll, he watched as Kessara struggled to lift the specialty deer saddle down from her mount. He wanted to help her, but held himself back. *It's not that I think women are too stupid to think logically, or too weak to carry something heavy,* he wanted to say. He wished he could make her understand.

He hated the way that so many men acted. So much of the evil in the world was done at the hands of his own sex. And yet, it seemed that for women like Queen Manta and Princess Kessara, the goal of a better world could only be achieved if women became more like men. He found the whole idea completely backward.

You shouldn't have to think about everything from the standpoint of cold logic, he wanted to say. *You should be able to find a place in the world where the tenderness of your heart is valued. You shouldn't have to carry heavy burdens. Not because you are weak, but because it is beneath you.*

"Alder?" Kessara asked, pulling him out of his thoughts. He moved to help her with the saddle after all, but before he could, she managed to heft it onto the ground. She had torn a fingernail in the process, and he watched as she stuck it in her mouth to suck the blood away without so much as a flinch.

"Yes?"

"Where do you plan to take your family? That's why we're going back to High Keep, right?"

He felt the familiar twinge of worry fluttering in his gut.

"Yes. And I have no idea. If things keep getting worse, there will not be any safe havens left in the Four Kingdoms. But in the meantime, the mother and sisters of a traitor would be wise not to live under King Ursa's nose."

Chapter 12

As dawn drew near, they made camp in the foothills of the Severed Summits. Until they reached Whitespire, they would have to travel only at night. They could not risk Celesyria being seen.

"Are you going to hunt?" Wes asked her, happy to be able to speak out loud for a while. It was easier for him than speaking within his head. He settled in next to the small fire he'd built, rubbing his hands together near the cheery orange flames. Despite the daytime heat of the summer, the nights were cold in the mountains. The high peaks ensured that much of the land remained beneath a constant veil of shadow, even at the height of the midday sun, and beneath the moonlight, the entire range grew frigid.

"I have to," Celesyria said, stretching out her wings as she attempted to draw warmth from the flames. Despite her ability to breathe fire herself, she was still as cold-blooded as any other reptile. "At least it will be nice and warm while we sleep today."

"Nice for you," Wes said with a snort. "I'm going to have to try and find a spot that's hidden in the shadows unless I want to bake myself alive. These rocks take in so much heat."

"At least you can regulate your own body temperature."

"Perks of being human," he said with a grin, reaching for his pack and drawing out some of the dried meat that he had brought.

His smile faltered as he took a bite of the bland food, remembering the journey back toward Silverfell after the spring Feast of Offering. His Witness, Odrigh, had insisted on sharing his disgusting salted fish with him. Aside from his affinity for local Galeharbor cuisine, Wes had liked the sailor very much.

His death at the hand of bandits had shattered Wes' heart, and he was still trying to find a way to live with his guilt.

"Are you alright?" Celesyria asked, glancing down at him with one enormous eye.

"Sure," Wes said, smiling up at her. "I'm fine. Just need to finish eating, I'm famished."

They relaxed into a companionable silence as Wes choked down the rest of his meat and a large portion of his stored water. Celesyria would keep an eye out for a nearby stream where he could refill his waterskins when she left for her hunt.

Just as he was taking a final bite of dry bread, he noticed an orange glimmer on a mountain to the south. "Do you see that?" he pointed, squinting, trying to see clearly through the darkness. Celesyria got up from her spot near the fire and clambered onto a large rock to get a better look.

"Oh, I see it," she said, her voice cold. "And there are at least four more, most of them right between us and Whitespire. They look like fires."

Wes felt his heart begin to beat faster. Something was wrong.

He knew Umrym as a deserted, empty place, a place where you could cry out and listen to the echo of your voice until it faded away. It was well-inhabited by dwarves and dragons, but both species preferred to spend almost all of their time in their underground cities. Anyone on the surface drew immediate suspicion from those who lived their lives below.

"Perhaps they've had similar troubles with the elves," he suggested, raising a hand to his brow and looking to the west, where the shores of Nox were hidden by the huge mountains. "They might have put up some guard posts, to keep an eye out."

"Maybe," Celesyria said. "It could be that, or it could be something worse."

Wes let out a slow breath. The bandits that had invaded Windshear had been able to kill hundreds of people and to capture dozens more. If they were gathering in large numbers in Umrym, would even the dragons be able to extricate them from the mountains? There were so many places that they could hide. It would be like herding cats.

"So what do we do now?" he asked as Celesyria continued to count several new fires she'd spotted in several directions. The sky was growing lighter, and soon, they would not be able to know where their potential enemies lay.

"You need to hunt," Wes said, finally, realizing that she had no more of an answer than he did. "We can't afford to let the

145

day get any lighter.'

"Alright. I will stay as close as I can. As soon as I tell you that I am soon to return, get ready to leave. I think it will be safest if we cut north, toward Helmm, and double back toward Whitespire."

"I'll start packing up as soon as I'm done eating," Wes promised, trying to shake the fatigue from his arms and legs. It had been a very long day, and he'd been looking forward to sitting down somewhere other than a dragon's saddle, but there was nothing that could be done about it now.

He watched as she took off into the sky, making her way out of his line of sight within a matter of seconds.

Helmm. Wes focused on the question of geography for a moment, trying to imagine a map of Kaveryth. He knew about the city, though he'd never had any reason to travel there. Celesyria had visited their Great Library, and though the place had not been so grand as the name suggested, it had contained a long-forgotten portion of the Codex Veritatis.

Helmm lay directly across the West Strait from Nox. The thought of being so close to the land of the elves sent a shiver down Wes' back. He had never heard of anyone who visited the elven homeland and lived to tell about it. Only rumors and speculation had survived, clouding the place in a fog of mystery and suspicion.

Even Celesyria had not been able to find out very much about what Nox was actually like. Most of the books in Kaveryth shied away from the subject. Whatever the truth was, it was not a place Wes ever wanted to end up. The thought that bandits might be bringing human slaves there made him feel sick.

Before he could fade away into his own guilt, he noticed a

flash of movement behind the rock that Celesyria had been standing on not long before. Before he could register what he was seeing, the intruder had fled the camp, knocking over one of his packs and sending his provisions scattering across the stone.

"Hey!" he shouted, struggling to his feet and giving chase.

"*A spy. You need to land and hide, Celesyria,*" he said to the dragon. The effort of mindspeaking combined with the sudden sprint made his lungs heave, but he kept going, rushing into the field of jagged stones that surrounded their camp.

"*I'm coming to you,*" Celesyria said.

"*Don't, I'm fine. Please.*"

There was a flash of black hair. *I'm gaining on him.*

Wes tripped up a hill, curses pouring from his lips as he fell. He blinked back tears as he regained his footing, watching as tiny pieces of sharp stone fell out of his newly-raw left kneecap. His pants were torn and covered with droplets of his blood.

For a moment, he thought he'd lost the intruder. He looked around, trying to catch his breath, until he saw the flash of black again, on the other side of the stony field. He ran as fast as he could, but within a few seconds, he realized that his quarry was no longer moving.

It's a woman. As he drew closer, he saw that her ankle was stuck between two rocks, and she was struggling to pull herself loose.

"If you're going to kill me," she said, her voice gentle. "Do it now."

* * *

Kessara stared out over the moonlit water as a gentle breeze tugged at her hair. Lake Darro was massive, and she couldn't shake the irrational fear that some horrible creature was lurking in its depths, waiting to swallow her whole. She shivered as she bent low, filling their waterskins with the clear water. It splashed against her fingers, so cold that she wondered how it did not freeze. *Hardly a place for a night swim, monsters aside.* She wiped her hands against the bottom of her dress, her fingertips feeling stiff and clumsy.

Her back tensed as she heard the cry of an ironwolf, somewhere across the lake. Two more of the wolves joined in his mournful song, their voices ringing in her ears after they went silent. She knew that they were too far away to hurt her, but she still found it difficult to relax when she heard their howls. She glanced over at Alder.

"Of course you're sleeping right through it," she said out loud, her voice small in the wide open space of the Aridmoor plains. *You're strong enough that the wolves fear you.* She didn't dare carry on with any more of her imaginary conversation out loud, as she could never really be sure that he was actually asleep. She'd basically had to force him to take a rest in the first place and let her keep watch.

She reached into one of the pockets of her pack, drawing forth an old perfume bottle she'd taken from her chest of drawers. She poured a few droplets of the substance into each of the waterskins, shaking them up until the liquids were well mixed. *O High One, forgive me if this herbwoman's potion offends you,* she prayed silently. She had always been taught that the Dracodei hated the sorcerers that roamed Kaveryth, but she didn't know if the High One felt the same way about them. She wasn't even sure that the woman was a sorcerer at all.

It seemed more likely that she was a typical country healer, using ancient natural remedies to cure physical ailments.

After she finished with the water, she returned to the warmth of the fire, gathering up their tin dinner bowls and wiping them clean. Alder had caught a rabbit, and she had prepared it for the both of them, to his—and her—surprise. He hadn't even asked her to do it, but when she saw him rounding the nearest hill, carrying the fresh meat, she'd wanted to turn it into a feast.

Despite growing up with a team of cooks and servants preparing her meals, she enjoyed cooking for herself from time to time, and had practiced at it ever since she was a little girl. She'd been able to replicate a recipe for rabbit stew, and even though it was missing several ingredients, it had turned out much better than she'd expected. To her surprise, she'd felt great satisfaction in watching Alder devour his portion, his enjoyment written all over his face. He'd even offered to do the dishes, but without even thinking about it, she found herself insisting that she would take care of it.

Perhaps he's not as much of a pig as I assumed.

She put away the rest of their dinner utensils and sat down near the flickering fire. He told her that he'd been raised by his mother and sisters, not by his father. As she watched him sleep, his eyes pressed closed, his teasing mouth quiet, she could imagine him as a child. She could imagine how helpless he must have felt, watching as his father knocked his mother around, unable to do anything to stop him.

Is it any wonder you grew up wanting to be strong enough to fight back?

She drew closer to Alder's sleeping form, as though pulled in by magic. He was so handsome in the firelight that she found it fascinating that he'd chosen the brutal life of a soldier. He said that he'd joined the Aridmoor army, and later King Ursa's Protectorate, for the money, but she found that hard to believe.

With his charm and good looks, she had no doubt that he could have found his way into an actor's troupe, or some other profession that didn't entail risking his life. He would have made much more money that way, accepting tips from rich city women as he made them laugh.

No. She watched him breathe, his chest rising and falling calmly, as though the world of his dreams held none of the cares of his waking life. *You chose to be a soldier because you had to find a way to fight back against men like your father, whatever the cost.*

She knelt beside him, butterflies fluttering in her stomach. She could tell herself over and over again that she did not want him, but that didn't mean she could believe her own lies. She thought of Wes, halfway across the world by now, trying to help Celesyria's father and search for the Codex Veritatis at the same time. *Is it fair for me to marry him, even when I know I will never love him in the way that I'm beginning to love...*

She let the thought fade away. She couldn't bear to acknowledge the rest, not even to herself. She moved to get up, but before she did, she leaned forward to pull Alder's wool blanket back up over his chest.

A second later she was pinned to the ground, a knife held over her chest.

Alder swore, dropping his weapon into the grass. "What in the Wrathlands is wrong with you, Kessara!" he shouted, clambering to his feet. "Speaks four languages, can't figure out not to wake up a man sleeping in the wilderlands on high alert. Typical noble." He shook his head as he gathered up the blanket and shook out the pieces of grass.

She yanked it out of his hands and stormed off to the far edge of the camp without another word, laying down against the damp grass and pulling the comforting wool around herself. She could hear him trying to apologize, but she ignored it.

I'm letting romantic feelings cloud my judgment, she chided herself as she closed her eyes. *I need to remember that my first impressions are always correct, in the end.*

* * *

"It's an elf," Wes told Celesyria, keeping a generous distance between himself and the wounded being. *"A woman. And she's hurt."*

"Be careful. Elves are far stronger than men, even when wounded."

Wes took a couple of cautious steps closer to the sharp rocks where the elf woman's ankle was caught. They were dotted with blood. Despite the grimace of pain on her face, she was so beautiful that for several seconds all he could do was stare at her. Her face was silvery in color like most of her kind, and her hair was as black as raven feathers. But most lovely of all were her eyes. Even standing several feet back, they seemed to pierce right through him, as cold and wild as the North Sea in wintertime.

"Please," she choked out between gritted teeth as he took a few tentative steps closer. "Make it quick. I'm in a lot of pain."

"Unlike your kind, I don't believe in executing defenseless people without a fair trial," he said, stepping onto one of the rocks that trapped her. He knelt down, trying to see how bad the damage to her ankle was, but it was hidden in shadow.

"But your kind certainly does," she said, offering a weak smile. "The race of men kill the innocent more often than either of us would like, but that doesn't mean every human is guilty of the crime."

"I suppose," he said, laying on his chest on the rock and reaching for the woman's calf. Her black trousers were slick with blood.

"You seem to be a decent person," she continued, crying out as he pulled at her leg. "Do you assume that I can't be innocent, just because elf blood runs in my veins?"

Wes didn't answer for a moment, instead pressing his own legs into the crack and shoving at the stone on the opposite side. It began to move, inch by inch, as his thigh muscles screamed for him to stop. A second later, she was able to pull herself free, and he collapsed onto the stone, breathing hard.

"I suppose if you didn't think I was innocent, you'd be running away by now," she continued, pulling her soft leather boot off of her injured leg. Wes observed the damage, trying not to be sick as he looked at a piece of bone that had stuck straight through her skin.

"I don't know that you're innocent, considering that you were spying on my camp," he said, removing his cloak and tearing off a thick strip from the bottom. "But I've met a good elf before. Not so long ago."

To Wes' relief the woman did not ask for more detail. Instead, she accepted the piece of cloth and began winding it around her leg without so much as cringing at the pain. "I didn't really need you to wreck your clothes, but thank you, anyway," she said, smiling over at him.

"What do you—"

She pulled back a bit of the material. Wes could still see the red patch of blood, but the bone was no longer visible. He could not see so much as a cut on her shimmering skin.

"We heal much faster than you do."

"Apparently."

Wes stood awkwardly for a moment, trying not to stare at her beautiful face. He wondered if it was possible that she was putting him under some sort of spell.

"My name is Aelrie," she said, taking a few steps toward him and extending a hand. The skin of her palm was soft, and she wore dainty silver rings on several of her slender fingers. "Who are you?"

Wes didn't answer. There was something in her eyes that made him think she knew exactly who he was. Why else would she have been following him, had she not known that he was the Envoy?

"Why were you following me?" he snapped, drawing his own hand back. "Why are you in Kaveryth at all? Don't you have some slaves to whip in Nox?"

Her easy smile fell away, and immediately Wes felt a pang of guilt. He couldn't decide if he'd really been too harsh, or if she was playing some kind of trick with his emotions.

"I just want to talk for a little while," she said, looking off at the mountain peaks hundreds of feet above. Dawn had broken, and the land was bathed in a soft pink glow. "I want to tell you more, but I can't. I promise you that I do not wish you any harm."

Wes considered this. *"She won't tell me why she was watching me,"* he told Celesyria. *"But she says she just wants to talk."*

"Let her," the dragon replied. *"If she wanted to hurt you, she*

153

would have done it by now. I found a deer, and I'll be heading back to camp."

"Okay," Wes said.

"Try to get information, but don't trust her. Don't trust a word she says."

The elf woman was giving him a funny look. "Are you okay?"

"Er, yes," Wes said, smiling stupidly. "We can talk. Are you sure that your ankle is alright?"

She gestured for him to sit on the rock that had crushed her ankle moments before.

"What's a human boy doing in Umrym?" she asked instead of answering him.

He sat on the rock opposite, trying to read her expression. *She knows who I am. Why won't she admit it?*

"I'm from Stronghollow, the capital city of Silverfell."

"That's not an answer," she said, her voice stern, but she was smiling.

"I want to tell you more, but I can't," he said, returning her grin.

Before they could speak any more, Celesyria's voice sounded in his head.

"Wes, you need to run. You need to get out of sight, right away."

"What?" he asked, trying not to allow his feeling of alarm to show on his face. He wasn't about to tell Aelrie that he was traveling with a dragon. *"Where are you?"*

"I landed while I was hunting. I picked up the scent of men, or perhaps dwarves. I can't make out how many, exactly, but it seems to be more than two. I'm not sure if they were waiting for me to come down in order to trap me, but they still seem to be at a distance. I can't hear them yet."

Wes felt the muscles at the back of his neck go tight. *"Can you hide?"*

"I'm trying. I chased a duskmink down a passage, and now I can't turn around. I'm hoping there will be more space to move as I reach the end."

"Tell me if you need help," he said, glancing up at Aelrie, who had a look of confusion on her face.

"Just stay out of their way, Wes. Please."

Chapter 13

A few hours later, Alder shook Kessara awake.

He had lingered there for a couple of minutes, watching her. Her tanned skin looked so pretty, bathed in the moonlight, and her face bore a beatific expression. He wondered what kind of dream she was having, not wanting to wake her up and remind her that she was camping in the Aridmoor wilderlands, her normal old life fading away into memory as the winds of the world shifted.

"I have to leave now," he whispered as she opened her eyes, shivering as she sat upright and pulled the blanket more tightly around her shoulders.

"I'll be ready in a minute," she said, her voice heavy with sleep.

"Absolutely not," he said, shaking his head as the Princess got to her feet and stretched her arms out above her head.

"You're staying here. You can guard the deer. I'm going to head in on foot."

It would be a long walk, but he hoped to be able to make it back by lunch time. The moon was still high, and provided that he steered clear of ironwolves, he assumed that he would be able to make good time in the hours before dawn. He'd have to move more slowly as he drew nearer to the populated area surrounding High Keep.

"I'm coming with you," Kessara said, gathering up their camp supplies and shoving them into leather sacks.

"I let you come in the first place because I promised Wes I'd keep you safe. I'm not going to be able to do that while I'm sneaking into the city."

"I can take care of myself."

"I know you can. I'm sure you can manage our camp just fine. Do you want me to start a fresh fire before I leave?"

"You really are a…" Kessara said something under her breath that he could not quite make out.

"Scoundrel? Fiend?" he asked, smirking as he pulled on his tattered peasant's cloak, hiding his bulk beneath the loose, threadbare fabric. The clear sky promised good weather, but he wanted to draw as little attention to himself as possible.

"Alder. I'm not just going to sit around here making tea until you return. That's not who I am," Kessara said. There was a flash of something in her eyes that he couldn't quite read.

"I'm walking in the belly of the bear. I'm going to be in danger, and if you're near me, you're going to be in danger, too."

"I figured that part out, thanks."

"King Ursa has a soft spot for you," he reminded her.

"What does that have to do with anything?"

"It's one of the few advantages we have, and we can't afford to lose it. Something tells me that Aridmoor's king is not going to look at you the same way if he catches you traveling with a traitor who abandoned his personal army."

"He's not going to find us."

"We don't know that, Kessara," he said, the teasing smile gone from his face as he tightened his fists in frustration. *It's like it's all a game to her. She's never really had to fear for her life until a few days ago. Even when she broke Wes out of prison, she knew that there would be no physical consequences. She doesn't know what it's like to bleed at the end of a knife.*

"Still—"

"You've never heard what he says about you," he added, trying not to let his anger show so much in his voice. He had to make her understand. "He's just as bad as his men. High Keep will be full of them, not to mention the drunks and the thieves that roam the streets."

"I'm a woman, Alder," Kessara said, shaking her head. She had tidied the camp, and now stood opposite him, her arms crossed over her chest. "The lustful thoughts of men are not a surprise to me."

"Of course not," he started, trying to find a way to speak tactfully, but there was none. "But the consequences of their vile thoughts is not something you have had to face. You live in a palace, separated from the streets of Galeharbor. Even when you do leave, you have guards. And even if you didn't have guards, you dress as a greater House noble. No one would dare touch you. If you come with me to High Keep, you'll be a peasant in their eyes, but your beauty will remain."

"No one is going to find us," she said, taking her own tattered traveling cloak and pulling it on over her simple brown dress. She did not try to dismiss his compliment. "And even if they did, you're not going to let anyone harm me."

I'd rather die. He was surprised at the fierce determination that he felt. He had no doubt that he meant it.

"High Keep is becoming more dangerous by the day, just like every other city in the Four Kingdoms," he said. "The world is not as it was. I would do anything to keep you safe, but I'm not invincible."

Kessara looked out at the lake for several seconds. The water was so calm that it resembled a huge mirror, reflecting the pinprick lights of a thousand stars. He had to get moving if he wanted to cover significant ground before dawn.

"I appreciate that you don't want women being treated like pieces of meat," she said finally, meeting his eyes with her own. "I only wish you didn't treat us like decorations to be placed in the rooms where men rule the world."

"Do you honestly think that is how I see you?" he asked, taking a step closer until their faces were inches apart. Her eyes searched his own, but he could not read them, could not understand what she felt.

"It seems that way," she said, her voice faltering as she broke away from his gaze. "Instead of expecting men to be good, you expect me to hide away in the shadows."

At any other moment, he would have laughed at this. Mocked her naivety, smirked at her ignorant idealism, but this time, he couldn't bring so much as a teasing smile to his face.

Instead, he reached out and took her hands in his, trying to still the shiver that ran up his back at the touch of her skin against his own.

"Kessara," he said, giving her tiny hands a gentle squeeze. "I wish that men did not steal. I wish that they did not kill. And I certainly wish that they did not harass and rape."

She squirmed a little in his grasp, and he released one of her hands. "It is a tragedy that women must be the ones to be careful, to avoid traveling at night, to seek safety in numbers. I agree with you. Men should be the ones who change their behavior."

He cupped her chin in his free hand, looking into her eyes, hoping that she could read the unspoken words in his own.

I know that what I feel is crazy, but it's true. I would fall apart if anything happened to you. I couldn't bear it. I need you here, where you're safe. Where I can come back to you.

"That is not the world we live in. We live in a world where people must lock their doors. We live in a world where we must carry weapons to protect ourselves from violence. And we live in a world where we cannot place women's safety in the hands of those who would seek to harm them. We cannot expect honor from criminals. It is a fool's daydream."

Kessara opened her mouth to speak before closing it again, searching his eyes with her own.

"I do not see you as a decoration, darling," he said, letting his hand fall away from her face. "I see you as a woman, who should be free to go through life and leave the worst of the burdens to men like me and Wes."

He offered her a sad smile as he stepped back, hoping that the magic was broken while wishing more than anything that it wasn't. He took a breath and spoke once more.

"When the time comes that you must defend yourself and take your safety into your own hands, I know that you are strong enough to manage on your own. All I ask is that you don't seek those moments out. You're better than that. You're smarter than that."

Without another word, he turned toward the direction of High Keep and strode off into the darkness.

* * *

Wes looked over his shoulder, scanning the stones for any sign of movement. He could not hear anything but the sound of his own breathing. Celesyria had gone silent in his mind, allowing his new worries to fill the space.

"Aelrie, we need to go. People are coming," he said, getting to his feet and offering the elf a hand. She accepted, getting to her feet with some difficulty and leaning against him. Despite the cold appearance of her silvery skin, she felt warm as she draped her arm across his shoulders.

"How do you know?" she asked as they walked toward the nearest mountain foothill, trying to keep to the shadows of the craggy stones jutting up from the ground. "I cannot sense them. Usually I can hear far better than any human."

But I assume you cannot smell better than a dragon.

Wes kept that detail to himself as he guided the woman over a treacherous bit of terrain. It wasn't safe to tell her the truth, of course, but for whatever reason, he wished that he could. She had such a gentleness about her, an aura of trustworthiness that made him want to bare his heart at her feet. It was dangerous.

"Are you safe?" Celesyria asked after several minutes of walking, interrupting his swirling thoughts.

"Safe enough. Please stay hidden. With any luck, the intruders will pass you by and I'll be able to find you then."

"What of the elf? Is she gone?" Celesyria asked, but he did not answer. There would be time to discuss their conversation later.

"We need to hide. It looks like there might be a small cave over there," he said aloud to Aelrie, gesturing toward a thick shadow that lay between two dragon-sized rocks, pressed up against the mountain.

"Right," she said, taking some of her weight off of his shoulder as they reached their destination. They darted inside the shallow cave's mouth, and Wes tried to blink away the sudden darkness from his eyes as they sat on the cold stone floor.

"Close them," Aelrie suggested, reaching out an unseen hand and touching his arm. "Your sight will adjust faster."

He obeyed, closing his eyes and saying nothing. He could hear the intruders himself now, the sound of boots hitting stone. It sounded like there were a fair few of them, but he doubted that they would find them here. He only hoped that Celesyria had gotten herself well out of the way.

He glanced over at the elf, now able to see the faint outline of her body in the dark. *What if this is some kind of trap? Perhaps these are her friends, and she's going to call them right to me.*

"Thank you for helping me," she said, a smile in her voice. "It was very kind. I've never experienced kindness at the hands of a human before. Then again, I suppose my folk have never given you any reason not to hate us."

Wes wasn't sure exactly what to say to that. He cleared his throat before he spoke.

"Seems like you didn't need my help much in the first place," he pointed out. "I'm sure you would have been fine, had you waited for a few minutes."

162

She laughed, a tinkling sound that seemed to light up the damp, cold cave.

"I'm kind of a simple girl that way," she said. "When a handsome man offers to help me, I figure it's best to take it."

Wes blushed, glad that she could not see his face clearly in the dark—unless, perhaps, elves had some sort of night vision powers that he was unaware of. She wouldn't have found him very handsome a few months ago. He'd been quite fat up since he was a child, and it was only a stint in Stronghollow Penitentiary that had finally helped him to shake his stubborn extra weight.

Even without the fat, I'm still too young, and my face looks every bit as childish as I feel. He was glad that elves, to his knowledge, could not read minds.

"I need to go," the woman said suddenly. He heard her shuffling to her feet.

"What? It's not safe. You can't go out there!"

Wes could hear the sound of jeers and laughter from outside as the company drew closer. He imagined that they must be traversing the rocky field by now.

"I told you that I couldn't explain everything, and I really can't," she said, reaching out a hand again and resting it upon his shoulder. "But I'm really glad to have met you."

Wes stood up, taking a few cautious steps toward the entrance of the cave and peering out. Even though it was barely dawn, the light was bright enough to nearly blind him. She took hold of his hand and pulled him back into the safety of the shadows. It was strange to touch her. Though he could not see it, he could imagine how strange it would look to see her silvery hand clasping his own.

163

"I have to leave now," she said, letting go of his hand. "Perhaps one day we will meet again."

Wes sighed, sitting back down in the corner of the cave. "Can I ask you one thing before you go?"

He imagined that she nodded, though of course he could not see it. "Yes. Anything."

"I believe you, about what you said. Some elves are innocent. But are you?"

She didn't respond for what felt like a very long time.

He heard her moving to leave the cave, to walk right into the open air where he could hear the stamping of men's feet.

"No," she said.

Her voice was sad.

* * *

He thinks that he's won.

Kessara strode through the waving grasses, feeling the midnight dew seeping into the bottom of her dress. *Is it a lie to hold back the truth?*

She felt a pang of guilt, but she ignored it. She couldn't think of another way. Wasn't the safety of the Four Kingdoms more important than being honest with Alder?

She was sure that it was, but still, she found herself unable to think of the High One and what He might think of her.

She thought instead of the two deer, which she'd decided to call Boris and Barry, hoping that they would be safe where she'd left them. They had the lake for water, and fortunately, Aridmoor was the perfect place for any creature who enjoyed eating grass. It was only the ironwolves that they would have to avoid.

Clouds had begun to gather across the sky, obscuring the moon. She could smell rain, but for the moment, she remained dry. She could see the tallest spires of King Ursa's castle in the distance, across the flat lands, and that was all she needed to find her way there. She was sure she'd given Alder enough of a fair start so as not to catch up to him on the plains, but still, she hoped that he wouldn't venture beyond the poor part of town where he'd told her his family lived. With any luck, he would never even know what she'd done.

Not until he sees the results, anyway, she corrected herself.

The walk was boring, but occasionally she experienced a moment of blind terror as one of the ironwolves howled across the plains. She had her bow with her, and a couple of short knives, but she knew that she stood little chance against the massive creatures. Especially if they attacked as a pack.

She passed the time thinking about her family, and thinking about Wes. She could picture her father, sitting in his study, offering a cigar with Captain Drohma and telling him that Galeharbor would provide the men that the Red Army needed. Her mother would be outside, pacing around the throne room or perhaps the palace gardens, furious at her husband. She felt bad for both of them. Though she hoped that her father would hold out a little longer, she understood that she was asking a lot of him, and a lot of her people.

She hoped that Wes and Celesyria were safe. She doubted that they would come to any harm on their travels—It would take ten ironwolves to do any harm to the dragon, and most of the men who sought her remained in the eastern half of Kaveryth—but she feared for what would happen once they reached Umrym.

Alder had explained to her what the dying elf had told

Celesyria about her father's fate, and unlike the men, she didn't think it was likely that the words were a mere attempt to wound the dragon. If they were true, if elves were in Umrym, exerting control over even the Guardians, it meant that her friend was in grave peril.

And so was Wes.

She thought of his face, of his dark eyes, the curls that always fell out from beneath his helmet when he wore the ceremonial armor common to the greater House nobles. Even after all that had happened, it was hard for her to shake her memories of a Wes that no longer existed. For so much of her life, he'd been Roven's kid brother. He had been shy when he was a child, but over time, as he grew more accustomed to his burdens as Envoy, he'd started to come into his own.

Until his parents died.

Until Roven died.

Her life, and Wes' life, had been torn apart at the seams. Even after five long years, the brokenness she felt had not completely healed. She doubted that it ever would.

Marrying him would take every bit of strength that she had left, but she knew that if the High One blessed their espousal, everything would be alright. Perhaps it was the sorrow that they had suffered together that would enable them to create something beautiful.

She thought of children, running through the halls in Stronghollow's palace, chasing each other through the strange indoor forests. She thought of what it would be like to hear the laughter of little ones again, in a city that had suffered from low birth rates for decades.

Their children would bring hope.

They would bring the promise of life to a people who

166

desperately needed it.

The House of Cervos would rise again.

But try as she might, she couldn't help but picture her children with fierce red hair and pale, freckled skin.

My Lord, my all, she prayed as she saw the walls of High Keep rising before her. The rain was beginning to fall in earnest, and she drew her cloak more tightly over her hair. *Give me the strength to let go of the dreams of my heart, so that I may seek what You have planned for me.*

She shook her head, as though she might be able to knock the worries loose. She couldn't dwell on the mess that was her romantic life any more.

She had only a couple of hours before it would be time to try and talk sense into King Kylan Ursa. He wouldn't listen to anyone else, but she might have a chance. She had to try.

* * *

"Wes, there's a problem," Celesyria said in her mind, trying to focus on speaking to Wes at a distance while simultaneously listening for the approach of their enemies. The men—elves, dwarfs, whatever they were—were close now.

"What's going on?" Wes replied.

"I'm trying to get to an open space. I can hear them. I might need to fly. If they make it to me where I am now, I won't be able to fight them off."

"I'm close to you. I can hear them from where I am," Wes said. *"Wait for me. I'm coming as fast as I can."*

She did her best to direct him to where she was, hoping that he'd be able to stay hidden himself. Despite his brave offer to go into Whitespire alone, she didn't want to leave him without her in the mountains unless she truly had no other choice. The Severed Summits were a dangerous place for a single human to travel, and even if he made it out of Whitespire, it would still be a long walk to Auranth.

She looked around, trying to see if anyone was coming behind her. So far, the little passage remained empty, but she had no way of knowing what the men's route was. Overhead, the morning sun had dawned, painting the sky a beautiful, cloudless blue. There would be no way to avoid detection with the men so close, but at least if she could fly away it would take another dragon to even attempt to bring her down. She'd be far above their heads before they could so much as draw their bows.

For several minutes she waited, trying to calm her loud breathing every time she heard a snippet of rough conversation floating on the wind. *As usual, here I am alone, waiting on someone else in order to act.* An unwanted, familiar rage rose in her chest. *Despite all of my physical power, I find myself helpless once again.*

She imagined her foes rounding the corner, dressed in the same black clothing as the bandits back in Windshear, rushing down the stone passageway. She could kill them all with a single blaze of fire from her throat.

Why would You give me such power if I am forbidden to use it? She asked the High One. *Or is it just another lie that I've been forced to believe, because You have refused to give me another answer?*

"I think I'm close. I reached the pile of round stones that you mentioned," Wes said. The High One, of course, said nothing. It would be much simpler if He would just talk to her. Or perhaps, like Alder, he could reach out to her in a dream. It

seemed that He was interested in neither.

"Okay, you need to find the tall—"

Before she could finish her thought, she heard the sound of laughter echoing through the passage from the direction she'd come. *Not yet. No.* She tried to shuffle farther down the path. Up ahead, she could see a bend. With any luck, it would lead to a more open space where they could fly away. *We need more time. He's so close.*

As she pressed herself forward, she felt the delicate membranes of her wings scraping against the rough rock walls. She gritted her sharp teeth together and pressed on, unsure of what else she could do.

As she inched her way forward, she thought about how her life had looked mere months ago, back when she'd spent most of her time curled up in the libraries that were spread throughout Umrym. It was one thing to be stuffed into a ball when examining an illuminated list of ancient Claim designs, but this was simply infuriating.

She was a dragon, a member of the most powerful race of creatures in all the world, the daughter of Guardians, and yet her size and strength had caused her nothing but trouble.

I should have never left Whitespire and gone to Wes about the truth of the Dracodei. Perhaps I could have reached him with mindspeak while he brought the treasures to the great spire. I would have had my research close at hand, and Wes could have still sought Kessara as an ally.

Instead, she'd had to be at the center of things, and it had cost everyone dearly. Now, she'd put her family at risk. Her father might even be dead. And it was all her fault.

She heard more talking, more pacing feet, more shouts. She pushed forward, cringing as she felt what she hoped was a small tear on her left wing as she brushed against a particularly jagged piece of rock. She was close now.

"I think this is a shortcut," a voice behind her said. He was close.

"You blithering fool, we've been this way!" said another.

"No, the passage we found had weeds growing up the cracks."

"What cracks?"

"Exactly."

"The point is over his head, what else is new," a third voice added.

More laughter.

"Wes," she said as she reached the bend. She stuck her face through. On the other side lay a huge open expanse, a smooth lake surrounded by gentle rock rises. She'd made it, just in time. *"You need to hide."*

"I'm right here, I had to go around, I could see a group of elves and—"

"Do not let them find you," she interrupted him. *"Do not go to Whitespire. Stay where it's safe."*

She could hear him saying more, but she couldn't make out the words. She was too afraid to think clearly, and besides, there was nothing to say. It was too late. If she was lucky, these men would take her to Whitespire alive, and perhaps she could find out some information from her prison cell.

She pressed her wings as tight against her sides as she could, trying desperately to get her body through the too-narrow space. The manacles on her ankles kept catching on the rock, sending jolts of pain up through her legs. The men were teasing and joking behind her, making fun of one of their companions who was apparently called Helgaec. If they hadn't seen her already, it would be seconds before they'd be upon her. Without the use of her claws, she'd be defenseless.

Even if she wanted to risk eternity in the Wrathlands, she couldn't use her fire. She couldn't turn around. Her head and neck were free, breathing in the fresh morning air, but she couldn't move.

She lifted her head, looking up at the sky as they came.

It was perfect.

She could not see a single cloud.

Not even a stray bird marred the open, endless blue sea that rested between the mountaintops. She closed her eyes, wanting to capture that memory, to hold it until the end came. She would not think of the ground. She would not think of the pain.

Chapter 14

The streets of High Keep were quieter than Alder remembered.

Even before dawn on a gloomy day such as this, there were usually people off to begin the day's more urgent business. Men would head out to the fields to work as soon as there was enough light. A few industrious housewives would hurry to set out the milk bottles.

Today, there was no one. He saw a few soldiers at the gate of the city when he arrived, but they paid him no attention. *They probably should have.* He made his way deeper into the maze of neat stone streets, feeling rather unimpressed with the quality of the men who guarded his home city. Then again, his height and bulk were not so out of the ordinary among other Aridmoorians as it was in Galeharbor or Silverfell, and he gave them no other reason to be suspicious of him.

The neighborhood where he'd grown up was not a nice one. He braced himself as he turned the corner that led toward his street, expecting the usual company of drunks and other various riffraff, but even they were nowhere to be seen. Alder shivered. It had begun to rain a little, though not enough to explain the lonely feeling that enveloped the place.

Everything about the architecture of High Keep reflected stability, strength, and order. The streets were set in a tidy grid, they were almost always kept swept and clean, and statues of their various war heroes marked many a corner. It was a bizarre contrast to see it so empty, like mother's neat kitchen left empty with breakfast on the table.

At least no one will remember me when the King's men come knocking. He strode toward his door, listening to the lonely sound of his boots hitting the ground. In this part of the city, the homes tended to resemble those found in the smaller rural village, usually made of cob rather than wood or stone.

As a child, he would play out front with his sisters Violet and Marya, who promptly ignored him as soon as their older, more interesting friends arrived. Back then, there were children everywhere. Though the neighborhood had never been particularly safe, it was at least alive, and he'd never had much trouble so long as he stayed away from those his mother called the 'hollow-eyes'.

"Now, girls, you keep your brother away from those hollow-eyes, hear?" she would say, looking up from her baking and resting her rolling pin on her hip. "Most of them are drunks trying to take the pain away–"

"Or they're tinkering with the black craft," Marya would finish, promising that they would stay far away.

A smile rose to Alder's face. He and Marya always fought,

but they were alike, too. They were both stubborn when they knew what they wanted. It always bothered her that Alder was not only older, but also a boy. Still, he was thankful that he'd been the oldest, able to protect her and their youngest sister, especially in those early years. To this day, Violet and Marya had never found out what their mother had done to put food on their table, and he planned to keep it that way.

He missed her. He missed them all.

Even though he lived in the nearby barracks while he was in the Protectorate, he wasn't permitted very much free time where he could go out and visit. Things got even busier than usual when Wes abandoned the Feasts of Offering. *And now, I'm a fugitive.* Alder knocked at the door, shielding his face with his cloak. *Makes it a little difficult to pop in for tea.*

His mother's house was one of the shabbier ones in the neighborhood. As he waited for someone to answer, he examined the soggy-looking boards around the door frame and the sagging cob along the roof. They would need to be repaired soon or they would risk a cave-in. He had little money left to give, but he hoped he could convince his mother to take it. Isla Cadogen was a proud woman now, ever since his father had died. It was as though her old timid personality had died with the ceasing of his insults and blows.

She and his sisters had always worked to support the family as best they could. Though his mother had been forced into a dishonorable profession before he'd joined the Protectorate, those days had passed, and she now labored in a laundry. Violet did mending for a seamstress a few streets over, and Marya had managed to become the only female blacksmith's apprentice in High Keep. *Kessara would love them.* His mind wandered to thoughts of her, curled up against his chest after

174

her ordeal, trusting him even when she was vulnerable in sleep. He hoped that she was safe out on the plains.

When no one came to the door in a few moments, he knocked again, worrying that he would rattle the door straight out of its frame.

He looked over his shoulder, expecting some soldier to question why he was slinking around in the pre-dawn hours, but no one came. The rain was getting stronger, though, and he could feel his cloak and pants growing damp and sticking to his skin.

He knocked again, leaning his face to the edge of the door and calling, "It's me."

Finally, there was Marya in a shabby yellow nightdress, her hair sticking out every which way.

"What in Nox is wrong with you? Scaring us half to death like that!" she snapped, gazing at him up and down for several seconds before diving into his arms for a hug and promptly bursting into tears.

* * *

"I've been captured," Celesyria said a few minutes later, her voice subdued. *"I got stuck. They have me bound."*

"I can come. I can find you."

"Wes, you need to run. You need to get to Auranth somehow—"

Without warning, her words were cut off, leaving nothing but a ringing in his ears. *They've taken her into a cavern.* Wes hoped that she would be brought to Whitespire and not one of the other cities in Umrym, where he had at least a vague idea of where to go. Still, it was clear now that he would have no way to contact her without going beneath the surface himself.

For what felt like a very long time, Wes sat alone beneath the perfect blue sky, thinking.

Waiting. For what, he didn't know.

Resting against a large stone, he pulled his knees up against his chest as he listened to nothingness, his heart aching for the sound of leaves rustling in the wind.

He remembered the last time that he sat just like this, five years before, in the depths of the Citadel in Stronghollow. That time, he hadn't even been able to hear what was going on outside. He had been tucked away like a set of fine teacups that no one could risk breaking, all while his family was torn apart.

Usually when he pondered those moments, he thought of Dorold coming to tell him that his world had been destroyed, but this time, alone in the darkness, he thought of the waiting.

The hours of uncertainty, the hope mixed with bitterness and hatred, the longing to rip the moonscar from his face.

He reached up and touched the scar. At least he was free of the symbol at last, though he wasn't sure having it burned away by hot coals hurt any less than removing it by his own hand would have.

"Celesyria says that the High One has a special plan for the Envoy," he said to the sky, not caring how loud his voice sounded amid the scattered rocks. "So what is it? Because so far, it seems like my role is the same as it always has been. I get to sit around and watch those I love get hurt, is that it?"

He buried his face in his hands. He wanted to cry. He longed for the release, the taste of salty tears rolling across his lips, the lingering headache that always followed. For once in his life, the sobs did not come.

176

He breathed in and out, letting the fresh mountain air fill his lungs. He could imagine the blood pulsing through his veins. He felt the stone against his boots, solid and secure.

And that was all.

He waited for some acknowledgement from the High One, some balm from the heavens to sooth his soul, but nothing came. He was still here, he was still alive. But he had never imagined he was so completely and totally alone.

Maybe Dorold and the Septemivirate were right all along. Maybe the Dracodei are the true Gods of Kaveryth, and the Codex is nothing but a collection of old bedtime stories.

He glanced around the stone field as he got to his feet, making sure that he was alone as he began walking in the direction he hoped would lead to the site of Celesyria's capture. After several minutes of difficult hiking, he found the passage.

This has to be the one. He rushed forward, halfheartedly glancing behind him as he went. He felt reckless, like he wanted to storm the caverns and drag Celesyria out by her feet, but he knew that it would do her no good if he was captured out of fearlessness.

As he ducked into the passage—narrow for a dragon, not so narrow for an average-sized human boy—he could smell the remnants of pipe-smoke. *Dwarves.* He listened to the singing of the air as it rushed overhead, like the sound of a child blowing across the top of an empty bottle. The walls were steep, and rose several feet higher than he could reach. If he ran into trouble here, there'd be no possibility of climbing out.

Maybe this is all my fault. He continued to journey deeper along the path, the lingering smoky smell assuring him that he must indeed be close. *Maybe it was ceasing the sacrifices that brought all of these elves into Kaveryth and emboldened the traitors among dwarves and men.*

As he rounded a tight bend, he saw a huge blood mark against the stone.

He rushed over, taking an old cloth from his pack and swiping at it. He ducked out of the shadow of the wall and leaned into a ray of sunlight, squinting at the blood. *Celesyria.* He watched as the barely-visible flecks of gold dried against the fabric. As a member of a greater noble House, he'd been expected to complete a much more rigorous education program than most of his peers. It would seem that learning about the scientific makeup of dragon's blood–and the simple trick used in identifying it–had finally been put to some use.

There were a few other marks, some of them near enough to the ground that he wondered if they were dwarven or human, but there was no time to waste checking them. He didn't know exactly how far from Whitespire he was, and without being able to fly on Celesyria's back, he was sure it would take him a good while to reach it.

As he continued forward, he realized what Celesyria had been trying to do.

Just beyond the narrow part of the passage where she'd been captured, there was a lake that stretched hundreds of feet across. It reflected the clear sky above, rippling gently as the breeze blew across it. On all sides, he could see a lip made up of jagged but traversable rocks. He felt like punching something.

She could have made it. She was so close to making it.

On the horizon, near the mountains that jutted up at the far side of the lake, he could see the great spire. It looked to be about a half-day's walk away. He could get to her. He put a hand to his forehead and looked at the sky, trying to figure out the exact position of the searing-bright sun. *We must be on the north side of the city.*

He and Celesyria had talked about her home to some degree, but now that he was here without her, he struggled to remember very many useful details.

Even as the Envoy, he had never been invited into the actual caverns before. He only knew the layout of the tower, where no one else—save for a few dwarf-women servants—was allowed to go under any circumstances.

As he refilled his water sacks, taking care to add some of the strange medicine the herbwoman had given them back in Galeharbor, something else caught his eye, a little closer, to the west. In the elevated valley between two mountains, he thought that he could see several dots of orange firelight.

He squinted against the competing sunlight, wishing that he had time to head over and investigate further. Still, as he looked more closely, he grew more certain of what he saw. Amid the firelights, he could see several small buildings. He noticed a few that looked half complete, with open sections of their stone walls revealing hearth-fires burning within.

"By the Dracodei," he swore under his breath.

It seemed that there was a new settlement in Umrym. And unlike all of their other cities, it was overground. Which meant it was filled with humans, or—more likely—elves.

* * *

Celesyria clamped her jaw shut as she felt the chains wrapping around her body, pinching skin and tearing off scales. She

179

MAJESTY

wouldn't give them the satisfaction of hearing her cry out. They had urged her forward into the clearing, and she could see now that there were two dragons and several dwarves with her. One of the dragons was a large male that she did not recognize, with green scales and a quiet demeanor. *He must be from Rowek.* One of the dwarves clipped a chain to her existing ankle manacle with quick precision, all business.

The other dragon, she knew. Her name was Jaconial, and she'd hated Celesyria long before she'd run off to tell Wes about the Codex. The two of them had hatched within a couple of years of each other, and Jaconial had always been nasty and jealous of Celesyria during their early training. Celesyria had later been recruited to the Guardians, and she had not. It was not surprising that Jaconial was taking a particular pleasure in her role as traitor-catcher.

"Tighter," Jaconial snapped at two of the elves, who were trying to pin Celesyria's wings in against her sides so that she could not lash out at them. "The chains should be tight enough that she's on the edge of bleeding."

"I'm not going to try and run, Jaconial," she said out loud. *Not for the time being, anyway,* she amended.

"You know her?" the green dragon asked, giving Jaconial a sharp look.

"Not well," Jaconial said, not meeting Celesyria's eyes. "We trained together as hatchlings, that's all. I've always suspected that something wasn't quite right with her. Seems my instincts were correct."

"Sure seems that way," the dragon agreed, giving Celesyria a brief glance that she could not decipher. Both of them were wearing the armor common to Guardians, she noticed. It was rare for anyone trained for the role to be rejected as a

180

Guardian upon reaching adulthood, but even stranger for someone who did not make the cut to later be recruited. *Even more dragons must be dying.* It was hard to imagine things being worse than they were when she left, but she supposed it shouldn't be surprising. All of Kaveryth seemed to be coming apart at the seams.

"Can't say I took her for a blasphemer, though. Her parents have always served the Dracodei well. At least, until recently," Jaconial said, chuckling.

Celesyria tensed up against her restraints.

"Jaconial," she said, forcing herself to keep her voice calm. A few of the dwarves looked up briefly before returning to the task at hand. "I know that you don't like me. Will you please at least tell me what has happened to my father."

Silence fell. The green dragon raised a scaly eyebrow at Jaconial.

"Stop talking," she said instead, gesturing to the dwarves. "It's time to go. I'd like to get to the city before supper. I'm starving. I'm sure there will be a special meal prepared for us in celebration."

Celesyria bit back a growl as the dwarves began to tug on her bonds, dragging her forward toward the eastern edge of the vast lake. She stumbled a little, feeling off-balance with her wings pinned so tightly to her body, but she wouldn't fight back. Not now.

She knew that being captured was a risk that she'd taken flying into Umrym. Sometimes, there was a time for running away, for hiding, for waiting for the right moment to act.

And sometimes, there was a time to be bold, to walk straight up to your enemies with your head held high, come what may.

She had chosen the latter, and any further decision with

how to proceed was out of her hands. It was up to the High One now. All that she could do was follow the path that was laid out before her, one clumsy step at a time.

* * *

For the next few hours, under the burning heat of the afternoon sun, Wes traversed the eastern edge of the lake, seeing no one. It was so quiet that he almost wished for an ironwolf's call to split the silence.

Before long, he'd passed through one of the mountain valleys, making his way onto the lower plateau of Whitespire just as the sun began to set. He found a hidden spot close to one of the cave entrances, and dined on some of the food he'd brought, looking up every few moments, certain that someone was about to discover him. As darkness poured over the massive valley, he grew more and more anxious.

I have to go in there soon, he thought to himself, gulping the cool lake water from his watersack. *I have to walk right into the home of the dragons.*

He remembered his conversations with King Manta and with Alder. Both of them had reminded him that people, especially men, must do what their duty states, even when they don't feel like it. He certainly didn't feel like marching into the caverns of Whitespire, but that wasn't exactly his biggest problem.

He didn't feel like the High One was with him.

Sitting there, alone in the darkness, he wondered. Was everything he had been through in the past few months nothing but a coincidence? Or was the God of Kaveryth there, but choosing to be silent?

He couldn't decide which possibility was worse.

Do I have a duty to the High One even when I'm carrying such doubt?

He thought of Celesyria, bound in chains somewhere far beneath the heavy layers of dirt and stone. She had sacrificed so much to tell him what the Codex Veritatis said. She had trusted him to help her, even when he at first tried to push her away.

Kessara had walked right into prison in order to set him free, willing to bear whatever consequences may have come.

Alder had given up his entire life, even putting his own family at risk, in order to follow what he believed to be the truth.

He wished that he could hear the call of the High One as loudly as the warrior could, but perhaps it wasn't necessary.

As much as his heart was telling him that it was all a mistake, that he'd been duped, that the world was as cold and hateful as he'd spent the last five years believing it was… there was something else, too. A nagging hope that would not die.

His friends had sacrificed everything to protect him and to bring the word of the High One to the people of Kaveryth. Whatever he felt, whatever he feared in the moment, that was something that he couldn't ignore. Their blood, their sweat, and their tears had watered the dry earth of his heart.

He had to believe that it was enough to keep his faith alive, growing up through the cracks.

Eventually, the rain would come. Or maybe it wouldn't. But until he knew for sure, he would keep moving forward.

Chapter 15

Rain pattered against the roof of the little cob house as Alder sat with his mother and his sisters. His mother had revived that evening's fire, putting on a pot of tea and busying herself with making everyone comfortable. Even in such dangerous circumstances, Alder was comforted to know that his mother's hospitality and warmth could always be counted upon. His home was a safe port in the waves, and the thought of asking his family to leave it behind, perhaps forever, made him feel awful. But there was no other way.

He wanted to tell his mother that he'd received her message, but for the moment, he kept silent. It was more important that he get them out of the city as quickly as he could.

"I don't know how to say this," he said after a few minutes of hugs and greeting, laying back in his favorite chair and accepting a cup of the warm tea. "I wish that things did not have to be this way, but the most important thing to me is this family. I cannot allow you to be harmed. You are no longer safe in High Keep. You need to leave. As soon as you possibly can."

"Alder…" his mother trailed off, her eyes staring into the fireplace, thinking. She seemed far away, and Alder felt a pang of guilt prodding him in his gut. Her mother had lived in this city her entire life, and in this house since she'd gotten married as a teenager. He couldn't imagine how she felt having her missing son turn up in the middle of the night to tell her that she had to leave it all behind.

"So, you betrayed our King and the Protectorate, and now we need to uproot our lives," his sister Marya said, taking a sip of tea before she could say anything worse. He should have known that many of the details of his defection from King Ursa's army would have reached his family's ears, and he doubted that his fellow soldiers' version of events would have painted him in a positive light.

"Oh, don't be like that," Violet said, playing with the end of her long red plait. She looked like she could almost be Alder's twin, but in reality she was his youngest sister at only fifteen.

"You don't get it, do you," Marya snapped, setting her mug down hard on the table in the middle of the small living room. "Some of us like our home. Some of us want to raise families here."

"Marya," Violet started, reaching a hand over from her own chair and laying it on her sister's arm. "Alder is alive. He's safe. Aren't you happy he's here, despite all of that? He's our brother."

"Of course I'm happy he's alright," Marya said, her voice wavering as she swiped at her eyes with the back of her hand.

"I've missed him. But I didn't think that he would be coming back to tell us that we had to leave everything behind."

"I know, darling," their mother said from her place nearest to the fire. Her voice was so quiet that Alder had nearly missed it.

"I'm sorry," he said, not sure what else he could add.

He knew that he was asking his middle sister to sacrifice the most of all of them. Marya was nearing eighteen, and before he'd left High Keep, he knew that she'd been courting the son of the blacksmith she worked for. Leaving would mean leaving her work and her future behind. Alder couldn't blame her for being angry with him. His choices had impacts that went far beyond himself. But that didn't mean that they weren't the right ones to make. He only hoped that his family would be able to understand that before it was too late.

Outside the living room window, he heard the yelp of a dog. Marya stood up from her chair and peered through the curtains, listening.

"You're certain that no one saw you?" she asked in a whisper. "There are guards, you know. Even in this neighborhood."

"Yes. I was careful," he said, trying not to let his annoyance show. Even after years in the Protectorate, his sister still assumed he would make the errors of a new cadet.

"So," Violet said after several moments passed with no other sound from outside. "Where would we go?"

"I haven't decided that I'm leaving," Marya said, shooting her little sister a glare from across the room. "I'm not convinced that any of this High One nonsense is even true in the first place."

"How much have you heard?" Alder asked.

His mother and sister recounted almost everything that had

186

happened at the disastrous meeting of Wes, Princess Kessara, and the Septemvirate, including details that he himself had not heard. Some of the information he assumed was nothing but gossip repeated many times over and later taken as fact, but still, in a way it was good to know that the very idea of the High One was getting out, even if most did not know any real details. The very idea that the Codex Veritatis could actually be true had been enough to scandalize half of the population.

Even on a vast continent such as Kaveryth, it was incredible how quickly information could spread. *We just need to find a way to use that to our advantage.*

He tried not to think of how Wes and Kessara Cervos would be able to use their roles as King and Queen of Silverfell to do just that. Even though he was confident that they would use their royal resources to defend the cause of the High One, he couldn't shake the sting of jealousy that lanced through him.

"Things have gotten so terrible here," his mother said, her brow furrowing with concern. "The crime, the bandits, all of it. It's like the very Wrathlands have been unleashed here in Aridmoor, and I hear it's just as bad everywhere else. If the High One wants us to follow Him, why is He letting so much evil befall us? It seemed for a while that things were looking up, when King Ursa became Steward of Silverfell, but it didn't take long for things to fall apart and become worse than they were before."

"She's right," Marya said. "And the summer Feast of Offering is approaching within a matter of weeks. How much worse will things get if the Dracodei are denied their treasures?"

Their mother gestured to a little shelf near the door, where Alder could see an expensive-looking velvet pouch, no doubt filled with coins—his family's contribution to the offering.

"The Septemvirate plans to bring the treasures to the great spire even without the Envoy," his mother said, reaching down to feel the little sack as though to assure herself that it hadn't been emptied in the night. "They won't be able to enter the tower, let alone the sacred cave, but their hope is that the Dracodei will accept our treasures anyway. They've even chosen a Witness from Redvale, in Boneshire. The other greater House nobles wanted someone from a more respectable Kingdom to be chosen, but the Septemvirate insisted on confirming the Witnesses in turn, as usual."

Alder forced himself to wait until she was done speaking before allowing any of his anger to show. "How dare those pompous old fools think that they are still entitled to your treasures," he snapped, grabbing the bag from the shelf and pouring it out into the little table. There were enough coins there to feed his mother and sisters for a month. It was not money that they could afford to freely spare. "This is an outrage."

What he didn't tell them was that he'd just sent Wes and Celesyria straight toward Whitespire, a stone's throw away from whichever agents of the Septemvirate were assigned to bring the treasures. He swallowed a sick feeling that was rising in his throat. *Brilliant plan, Alder.*

"Have you ever considered that maybe you and your friends are wrong?" Marya asked, her green eyes flashing with anger.

"You've never even cared about worshiping the Dracodei," he countered, leaning forward in his seat. Violet had shrunk backward, pulling her knees up to her chest as though she could curl into a ball and hide, just as she'd done when their father was alive. His mother pretended not to hear their bickering as she poked at the fire. "Have you ever even gone to a temple of your own accord?"

"I've always done my duty! I don't have to be perfect to be entitled to an opinion," Marya said, her voice rising several decibels.

"Maybe not, but it sure makes you sound like a hypocrite."

"I'm a hypocrite? Since when do you care about being all moral—"

"Since it became clear that I had to follow the truth."

"The truth that led you to abandon us?"

"I didn't abandon you! I was coming home as fast as—"

"Whatever. You can't just storm in here and—"

"Shut up! Both of you!" Violet shouted at them. The little house fell silent at once, and Alder watched as his youngest sister peered out the window to be sure that they hadn't alerted any of the neighbors of trouble.

Alder's mother stared into the crackling fire for a few seconds before settling back in her chair and placing her head in her hands. Her hair looked a lot more gray than the last time he had seen her.

"I'm sorry that I have to come home and make such demands," Alder started after a few breaths, reaching out to take Marya's hand. She drew back, crossing her arms against her chest, but she allowed him to continue to speak. "I know that you all have been suffering since I left, and I am genuinely sorry for that. We were barely getting by with the help of my Protectorate salary, and now you have the entire weight of our household on your shoulders."

He looked between his mother and his two sisters.

"You shouldn't have to provide for yourselves," he continued. "My father should have been here, but since he decided that the bottle was more important than his flesh and blood, the responsibility fell to me. And whatever good I sought to do out in the world, I failed to take care of my household. I really am sorry."

Alder wanted to say more, to continue to defend himself, but decided against it. The family sat there for a little while, listening to the crackling of the fire and a couple of dogs barking somewhere outside.

"It must have taken a lot for you to walk away," Marya ventured after several long, tense minutes. "You've done a lot for us, big brother. I'm sorry for seeing the worst in you."

"If following the High One is so important to you, I am willing to try and do the same," Violet added. She looked so much younger than her fifteen years as she sat there in the firelight, fiddling with her hair between her well-bitten fingernails. She was so trusting, so willing to take a step in the dark, so long as someone that she loved led her by the hand. Alder could only hope that her goodness would not lead her into peril.

"I can't say what I believe any more," his mother said softly, speaking for the first time in a long while. Finally, she met his eyes. "The world is shifting so fast beneath me that I've begun to question everything I've ever assumed to be true."

"I know exactly how you feel," Alder said, giving her freckled hand a squeeze. "You spend your whole life thinking that everything will carry on as it always has, until one day, it doesn't."

"And I've lived in the old, stable world a lot longer than you have, my son," she said, smiling until it reached the corners of her eyes. Green, like his own. "It's going to take me a while to find my footing again."

Violet stood up from her chair, padding across the rug until she stood facing the rest of her family. "Whatever security and comfort there is to be found, we need to find it together. I don't care where we must live, so long as my family is with me and we are safe."

Alder couldn't bring himself to meet her eyes. *I wish I could stay with you, little sister. I wish I didn't have to leave you alone again.*

"I don't have much of a plan," he admitted. "But I know that we don't have much time. I came here from Windshear, over in Galeharbor, and I captured one of my brother soldiers at knifepoint before I left. He'll tell Captain Drohma and the others I was there, and it won't be hard for him to guess that I might come here next."

"You captured a Protectorate soldier at *knifepoint?*" His mother asked, her jaw falling open.

"I'll explain later," he said, hoping that he would not have to. He had not mentioned Kessara's more recent role to them, not yet. "He's fine. I let him go."

"If we're going to go, we should leave before dawn," Violet said, peering out of the curtains again. The sky was still dark from where Alder stood, but he knew that it wouldn't be for long. Every hour he spent in this house he was putting his family at greater risk.

"Dawn? Today?" Marya asked, her eyes nearly bugging out of her skull.

"It would be best," Alder said.

Without another word, she rushed to the door and lifted her cloak from its pin, putting it on over her night dress and slipping her feet into a pair of bear-leather work boots. Alder went to speak, but she held up a hand. "I'm bringing Kristoff, or I won't come. He will understand. He will leave everything behind if I ask him to."

He knew that nothing he would say would change her mind. He could only hope that she would not come to any trouble on the way.

As she swept out of the door and into the cold rain, the room fell silent again, each member of the family lost in their own thoughts.

"I know one place we can go," his mother said, her voice so quiet that it was nearly drowned out by the spitting and sparking of the fire.

Violet looked up at her mother, clasping her hands together across her chest.

"Raela's farm, out in Claghan village. She'll help us."

Alders eyes met hers, but he could not read her expression.

"I got your message, mother. You chose loyal men to deliver it," he said.

And I repaid one of them by scaring him half to death. He still felt guilty. Any loyalty the soldier had to him before would be long gone now, but what choice did he have?

"That's why you came?" Violet said, her brow furrowed with confusion.

"No," he said quickly. "Only partially. I knew that I needed to come here as soon as I could. You've been in danger ever since I left the Protectorate. Her message only spurred me to move faster. But what of Raela? Is she…"

He let the words trail off. He couldn't make his mouth form the words. Raela had practically raised him for most of his childhood, staying with their family and watching him and his sisters in the daytime while his mother worked. When they'd gotten older, she moved out of the little cob house, but

192

stayed nearby on a small farm in the nearby village of Claghan. Now she was dying.

"No. There was an accident. She is still alive, but I don't think she has much time."

He felt some relief, followed by the urge to run out into the rain at that very second and go to her. He looked up at the ceiling, saying a quick prayer of thanks to the High One that he would have a chance to say goodbye.

"She will be glad that her last days were spent helping us," Violent offered, taking a couple of steps in the direction of the bedroom that she and Marya shared.

"Okay," Alder said, downing the dregs of his tea. "It's settled then. I'm leaving now. Grab your things, and wait until dawn breaks to follow me. It's not safe to travel by night. I will see you in a few hours."

He moved to the door and stuffed his feet back into his boots, bracing himself for the chill of the wind and the rain. "Thank you," he added, giving his mother and Violet a pinched smile. "Thank you for trusting me."

Without another word, he slipped through the door and into the night, glancing behind him as he disappeared into the shadows of a nearby street.

* * *

Kessara did not see another soul as she moved through the streets of High Keep, trying in vain to shield herself from the torrent of rain that had begun to fall. *At least no one else seems to be out here tonight.* She shivered as she took a brief respite beneath the canopy of a shoemaker's shop. She did not doubt what Alder had told her—any big city was bound to be full of dangerous individuals, best met in a busy crowd with the aid of daylight, if one had to run into them at all.

The castle was easy to find. Like Windshear's palace, it rose above all of the other buildings, a stone sentinel that could be seen far across the plains. Though the entire city was walled in heavy stone as well, it had been easy to slip into a small merchant's entrance that lay to the west. There had been a single guard present, who looked scarcely old enough to need to shave, and he'd readily accepted her excuse that she was visiting a friend. *It wasn't even a lie. Kylan Ursa was my friend, once. A long time ago, before power corrupted his heart.*

As she left the market district—and the relief from the driving rain that many of the shop awnings offered—and drew deeper into the side streets of High Keep, she began to notice how dark the buildings were. Here, she was lucky to find even a single candle set in a window for light. Fortunately, the castle was well lit by torches and signal fires, and she was able to press on in the right direction.

As she ducked into a narrow alleyway, she had to rest her fingertips on the right-hand wall until she reached the end of it, scarcely able to see her own feet in the oppressive shadows, even with the aid of her lamp's light.

The next street was brighter, with a few crumbling stone window sills sporting oil lamps. The houses here looked much nicer, with their stoops swept clean and their stone facades in good repair. She let out a slow breath of relief as she hurried on, confident that no one could hear her booted footsteps over the pounding of the rain.

How she was going to explain to the castle staff why the Princess of Galeharbor was dressed as a peasant and soaked from head to toe was anyone's guess, but she figured that she would deal with that problem when she met it.

"Hey! Yes, you!" a voice shouted over the rain.

For a second, she stopped short, looking around and over her shoulder, trying to figure out where the words had come from, but then, she hurried on.

"Wait! Don't be like that," she heard as she trotted forward, not sure whether or not to break into a full run and draw more attention to herself. "It's a slow night, isn't it?"

A slow night? She thought to herself, puzzled.

For a second, she heard nothing but the patter of rain on stone, and she slowed back to a fast walk, holding her lantern as far ahead of her as she could. The little circle of yellow light was of little use. The neat stone houses disappeared in a few moments as she rushed past, replaced by grubby cob homes with rotting wooden door frames.

"How much, love?" came another voice, this time from ahead of her. She stopped short, nearly dropping her lamp to the ground. "Don't worry, we'll pay top dollar. Call it a group deal."

Kessara swore, panic rising in her chest as she broke into a run. The men continued to leer at her, and she could not tell from which direction their voices came.

"I know just the spot, out of the storm."

Their voices seemed to come from everywhere at once. There had to have been at least three of them, maybe four. "Leave me alone!" she screamed into the darkness, running as fast as she could.

The walls were tight around her.

She could no longer see the palace in the distance. She spun, trying desperately to catch sight of a signal fire or even a candle lit in the window of a house, but there was nothing.

She'd gotten turned around somehow, and she no longer knew which way to run.

They all laughed. "Look, we can do this the easy way or the hard way, but the customer is always right," one of them said. He was close. She could practically taste the reek of his breath.

"I am the Princess of Galeharbor!" she shouted into the rain, holding her lantern up and moving it every which way. She tried to illuminate one of their faces in the darkness, but they slithered back into the shadows before the light could hit them. "If you don't run now, you will face the power of the crown. King Ursa will have your heads!"

More laughter. Never before had Kessara realized the power of the royal clothing she usually wore, the trappings of her family's wealth and power. Without them, she was nothing in their eyes, only an object to be used.

Just as Alder said.

"Sure, Princess," one of the men said. This one had a gruffer voice than the other two she'd heard before, and she decided that there were indeed three of them. Three men. Three men to fight off with nothing but a useless bow and a hidden knife. "Say we believe you, and we don't, what changes? Do you see any of Ursa's soldiers nearby?"

She held the lamp steady, refusing to glance around and to confirm what she already knew. She had seen hardly anybody on the streets before now, and if there was anyone on patrol, they'd be guarding the better areas of the city.

A hand shot out of the darkness, grabbing her arm and knocking her lantern to the ground. For a second she watched as the pool of spilled oil burned against the stone, but then it was gone, extinguished by the rain. "Help!" she screamed again, using her free hand to reach beneath the hem of her tunic. She felt the comforting weight of her blade in her hand, yanking it free of its sheath just as one of the other men lunged for her.

She heard a yelp of pain as she swiped with the knife. She felt it connect with something solid, but in the dark, she couldn't see which part of his body she'd hit.

"Careful, men," the gruff voice said. "This one's a *warrior princess*."

She spread her feet out to steady herself as she whirled around, slashing her knife as fast as she could, blinking away the rain. She heard more of the men laughing as she hit nothing but air and water.

Just leave. She wouldn't beg, not out loud, but inside she was screaming. She tried to stab in the direction of the voices. They sounded close enough to touch, but she could not see them. All she knew was that she must be in the middle of them, or they would have lost sight of her, too. *Just go back to the gambling den or the inn or the gutter. Just walk away. Please. Please, High One, make them leave. Call them away. You have the power to do it.*

Someone grabbed her from behind, pressing a meaty hand into the front of her neck, making her gasp. She lifted the hand with the knife over her shoulder, stabbing backward. This time, she felt the knife hit home. The man roared with pain, and though she could not see him, she hoped that he was stumbling backward, stemming the flow of blood from a wound to the face or neck.

For a second, the men went quiet. *Have I killed him?*

Her chest was heaving, but she struggled to register what had just happened. It felt like she was watching someone else act through a piece of cheap, bubbled glass.

No one was laughing now. One of the men called her a filthy name. The other grasped for the arm that held her knife, but she managed to wound him, though by his cry it was clear that she had done little real damage.

"Your friend needs a healer!" she shouted, swallowing after she choked the words out. She felt like she was going to vomit at any second. The adrenaline was still pumping through her veins, but the resulting strength seemed to be waning. She couldn't fight them back much longer. She could feel her hand trembling, and she grasped the knife tighter, desperate to keep hold of the slick, wet handle.

"Help!" she tried to scream again, but the sound caught in her throat. The rain was too loud. This part of the city was too isolated.

She tried to stand firmly in place as one of the men lunged again, but he was too strong. He took hold of her hair in his fist, yanking her head back so hard that she felt that her neck would snap in two. Before she could react, one of the other men took hold of her wrist, twisting it until she felt the knife slipping from her fingers.

She squirmed, kicking out with her feet, trying to bite the man who gripped her wrist, but then the laughter began anew. "I'd say it was worth it," the man behind her said with a chuckle. "Brodon didn't need that eye anyway, ugly mutt he is."

She felt more hits, and a punch that landed squarely against the back of her skull. It didn't hurt very much. She could no longer differentiate between the blows.

She wanted to keep going, to keep lashing out with her legs, to keep screaming until someone woke up and came to her aid, but she couldn't. She felt slow, like her brain was not connecting properly with her limbs. The fire had gone out of her.

Alder was wrong. One of the men picked her up, releasing his grip on her hair. *I couldn't take care of myself. Not when it counted.*

She closed her eyes, feeling the rain against her face. She tried to pray to the High One, but she couldn't focus. Everything had taken on a dreamlike haze. She was no longer sure of anything.

A darkness that wasn't quite sleep overtook her as the man carried her along, off to a kind of pain and violation that she couldn't manage to think of by name.

Chapter 16

Elder Dorold looked out of the window at the driving rain. Though he was sure that dawn had to be near, no sign of the sun could be seen beyond the heavy cover of clouds.

"Thank you for meeting with me at this unholy hour," he said to King Ursa before taking a deep drink from his coffee mug.

"You could have chosen better weather."

"Indeed."

For a moment, the two men sat in companionable silence, both sipping at their hot, bitter coffee. The King's servants had produced a full breakfast, and after his long journey from Stronghollow, the Elder was grateful for his host's hospitality.

King Ursa's study looked different than it had when his father, Radagar Ursa, was King of Aridmoor, but Dorold could not pinpoint exactly what had changed. The desk was the same as it had always been, a massive wooden structure covered in old red paint, the outline of a bear carved into its surface. The walls were unfussy, with a few wooden animal-shaped carvings hanging at intervals. The floor was covered in warm rugs, making the whole room feel cozy.

It was the opposite of the way that Dorold decorated his own office—when people visited him, he wanted them to know that he was in charge and that they should keep their wits about them—but Radagar Ursa had a different style. Many years ago, he'd told Dorold that he wanted the place to feel welcoming, because anyone who was close enough to the King to spend time in his personal study deserved to see him as a mere mortal as well as the leader of a nation.

The babbling of an old fool, Dorold had thought at the time, smiling and nodding all the while.

"So," King Ursa said, setting his empty mug before him on the desk and sitting back in his chair. "To business. What does the House of Manta think of my Red Army?"

There was a teasing grin tugging at the corner of the young King's mouth. Kylan was so unlike his father in temperament that, were it not for their physical similarities, Dorold would have doubted the legitimacy of the family bloodline. Kylan's very presence in the office was enough to bring a chill to the air.

"They don't like it, especially Jinna," he said, giving a quick smile of his own. "But Errol is no fool, and they see the necessity. I assume you received word of the raid that took place shortly before I arrived?"

"Yes," the King said, pressing his large hands against the red-painted wood. Dorold could see the maelstrom of anger forming behind his green eyes. What Dorold couldn't figure out was if he was merely concerned about the abuse of innocent people, or if the invasion served as a fearsome political omen. "Slavers and the rest. Not to mention the fact that my men allowed the traitor dragon to aid them rather than recapturing her immediately."

"I'm sure that Captain Drohma did not think she'd be able to get away, my Lord," Dorold said quickly. He wasn't sure where the young Captain was at the moment, but he was sure to receive a harsh reprimand whenever he came within view of the King. "By the way King and Queen Manta described it to me, they were completely outnumbered. Were it not for the timely arrival of your Protectorate, Windshear would have been taken."

King Ursa smiled, pleased. *Good. His ego, as always, remains intact. Shame that he cannot see it for the weakness that it is.*

"I suppose," the King said, waving a hand. "We will catch her and the Envoy in the end. Kaveryth may be vast, but they cannot run from us forever."

"Exactly, my Lord."

"Anyway, in light of the bloodshed, I assume that my friends have agreed to provide the soldiers that I sent Drohma to request?"

"Yes, my Lord," Elder Dorold said, pulling his gray robe more tightly around his shoulders. Though a fire burned in a small stove set in one corner, the room was still rather frigid to his old bones. He supposed a hot-blooded young man such as Kylan did not notice such things, but those days had long since passed him by. He feared that soon traveling itself would

202

be off the table, and he would have to send one of the younger members of the Septemvirate on such missions. "They agreed to the eleven thousand that you asked for. The first three thousand will be sent here as soon as they can reasonably be spared from the Galeharbor army. Another thousand will be pulled from the navy, if you wish it, or they can direct those ships toward the West Strait immediately," he paused.

King Ursa nodded, waving a hand and beckoning him to continue. "I'll speak with my military advisers and come up with a strategy, now that we know we'll have the men."

"Right," Dorold said, clearing his throat. "As for the remaining seven thousand, Galeharbor's forces cannot bear to spare any more men, so they will have to be conscripted. This may take weeks."

"We have the time. But will they be able to find competent men?"

"Galeharbor is a Kingdom of treasure-hunters and fisher-men," Dorold said with a tight smile. "If there was ever a group of men more suitable for the naval force, I can't envision who they would be."

"A fair point, Elder," the King said, chuckling softly. He paused for a moment, ringing a bell that rested against the wall and pushing the picked-over breakfast tray toward a young female servant who entered the room within seconds. "Thank you, Corinne," he said to the girl, who bowed her head before scurrying back out into the hall with their leftovers.

"I suppose the bigger question is if there are enough men who aren't already part of Galeharbor's armed forces."

"The seas have been quiet," Dorold said. "And only recently has Galeharbor begun to feel the pressure that the bandits have been placing on most of Kaveryth. There are plenty who will jump at the chance to serve. I doubt we will even need to offer a high salary."

"Excellent," the King said, his eyes searching Dorold's.

I know that look, he wanted to say. *I'm not going to cease the sacrifices, even if they must be dumped at the base of the great spire. The dwarves and Guardians will demand their pound of flesh, and we must not allow the people to become accustomed to spending the treasure that they have always earmarked for the Dracodei.*

"There is one other thing," Dorold said.

"Oh?"

"The King and Queen will only agree to this alliance if Princess Kessara is offered full immunity from any charge being brought against her, including treason or heresy," he said, drawing a rolled piece of fresh parchment out from inside his cloak and laying it on the desk. "They had a contract drawn up before I even arrived in Windshear."

"Done," the King said, leaning forward in his chair and grasping a quill pen from a cup that sat on the other side of the vast surface. He signed the line at the bottom of the contract without reading so much as a paragraph. *Not surprising.* Dorold watched the King form an intricate signature in dark-red ink. *He's always fancied the Princess.*

Dorold took the document and rolled it back up again, leaving it laying on the desk. "I trust you can have a messenger return it to Windshear?"

"Of course."

"So that's settled," Dorold said. "There is one more thing. There's a young boy in Boneshire—in a little town called Rill, I think—who seemed to have fallen severely ill from the water before recovering rather miraculously. The healers cannot figure out another explanation."

"He actually survived?" the King asked, knitting his eyebrows together.

"Yes, my Lord. It would seem that this child is very strong. As of late, I've heard of dozens of deaths, many of them of adult, healthy men. He's hanging on, and the rest of the Elders and I figured that it may be worth bringing him to Vaevar to see if he can be studied scientifically. It may help us to find a cure."

"You need my approval?"

"It seems silly that we would," Elder Dorold said. "But the Academy faculty have demanded royal permission in order to begin their studies."

"Whatever for?"

"Human experimentation, my Lord. It is unlikely that the child would go willingly. He is an orphan, and he would be leaving behind a sister."

"I suppose it's for the greater good," King Ursa said, reaching out a hand for the second contract that Dorold withdrew from the interior pocket of his cloak.

"Of course, my Lord. But it is the law that a member of the ruling greater House must give special assent for any such scientific inquiries."

King Ursa only nodded as he signed the document, barely taking the time to read what it said. The Elder thought he seemed somewhat on edge, and figured that it would be best not to overstay his welcome.

"Very good, my King," Dorold said, glancing over the signature.

"Alright, Elder," King Ursa said, rising to his feet and ringing the servant's bell once more. "Are you prepared to take your turn in securing more soldiers?"

"Absolutely. My stag is being cared for in your stables. I will be on my way just as soon as my Lord gives his leave."

* * *

By the time Wes reached the edge of Whitespire, the late afternoon sun was nearing the horizon. In the distance, to the south, he could see great dark clouds amassing amid the peaks of the Severed Summits. The air tasted metallic against his tongue, and all around him, he noticed that the birds had gone more quiet than usual. The air was heavy with heat, and after walking for miles in the hot sun, he could feel sweat pooling up against his back. His feet ached within his boots, and he was sure that when he took them off—if he ever again got a chance to rest—his toes and heels would be covered in blister sores.

At least I'll be out of the storm. He clambered down a small hill, trying to avoid twisting his ankle between any rocks. Stretched out before him was the great city of Whitespire, but he could see little of it on the surface. The great tower was there, holding court over the silent city, the point of its spire seeming to touch the approaching clouds. Though he had seen the tower dozens of times, it was disorienting to look at it from this direction, from the north. The mountain that pressed into its backside looked smaller from here, which set the humongous structure apart from its surroundings even more.

As he reached flat ground on the bottom of the valley, he found it easy to believe that the spire had not been created by the skilled hands of dwarves or men. He had always felt that the spire was otherworldly, had always believed it when he was told growing up that it had been crafted by the Dracodei themselves. *Only the High One could have created this.*

The doubts were not gone, but he had to admit to himself that every time he really looked at things, he saw new evidence of what he hoped was true. He choked back unexpected emotion as he strode deeper into the city.

Maybe Celesyria is right. Maybe part of my true role as Envoy in the eyes of the High One has always had something to do with the great spire. Maybe once it was something like a temple to Him. Maybe the Dracodei simply took it for themselves.

But there was no point in speculating. He would not get any reliable answers unless he and his friends managed to find the Codex Veritatis, and if they wanted to do that, he had to rescue Celesyria. He had no idea how he was going to manage it, but finding her presented enough of a challenge to focus on at the moment.

Most of the city was hidden beneath the surface, and Wes had never seen any of it. Up here, there was nothing but the entrances to a dizzying number of interconnected caverns, little plain buildings stuck halfway out of the ground. As always, the surface of Whitespire reminded him of a field blooming with great stone caskets.

He did not see anyone else nearby, which was not unusual—for many years now, the skies had been empty of the dragons that usually patrolled them, and dwarves avoided going overground unless they had a very good reason to be there—but he couldn't shake the feeling that he was being watched. He probably was. The elves that had set up camp throughout Umrym probably had a presence here, too, somewhere that he could not see.

It was time to go into the caves.

He walked between several of the entrance buildings, not sure exactly what he was looking for, but hoping that he'd know the right place to go when he saw it. Most of them, he ruled out immediately. Their doors were made of solid stone, and considering that they were large enough for a dragon to enter, he would not be able to lift them open. The ring-shaped handles, meant to be gripped by dragons' claws, looked themselves to be heavier than his sword.

Somewhere in the distance, he heard the crack of thunder split the sky. Overhead, the sky still looked clear, but the thick storm clouds had drawn closer since he last checked on them. He knew that Whitespire had trouble with flooding on the surface from time to time, necessitating that all of the doors be closed. He stopped for a moment, rubbing at his temples, trying to think of where he might be able to get in before it became too late.

Some part of him thought that perhaps he should pray to the High One for guidance, but he dismissed the idea as soon as it arose. He was so tired of stumbling through the problems that he'd been swept up in, and somehow, it felt even worse when he asked the High One for answers and received only silence and indifference in return.

He glanced over to the southeast, where the storm had already begun in earnest, lightning flashing across the sky and making up for the dimness left by the setting sun. Over those hills was the path that led through Boneshire, back toward Aridmoor, and then onto Silverfell. To Stronghollow. *Home.*

Would he ever be able to return there again? Would he ever be able to go back to the palace where he'd grown up, to step back into the only sort of life that he'd ever known?

The last time he'd come to Whitespire, he had left two men behind, their bodies abandoned amid the stone, the dirt, and the silence.

Odrigh and Lev never got to see their homes or their families again.

Even though I refused to act as Envoy and deliver the treasures of the Four Kingdoms to the false gods, I still ended up back here. A chill raced down his spine as he peered at the door of yet another cavern entrance.

He thought of Kessara and Alder, wondering if they were alright and if they had managed to keep King and Queen Manta from joining King Ursa's Red Army.

He closed his eyes for a moment as rain began to fall upon the city, Kessara's pretty face filling his mind. He thought of her dancing blue eyes, her smile, the bubbly laugh that had always come so easily to her when they were children. He could see why his older brother Roven had fallen in love with her. In fact, he couldn't remember a time when the two of them had not been in love. They had always been so connected, like two halves of a single soul. Everyone had always known that they would live their lives together.

If I'm supposed to make her my wife, I'm going to need some kind of sign. I'm going to need to know with certainty that it's the right thing to do.

He hoped that the High One was listening.

As the rain began to fall faster, leaving the ground slick and treacherous to navigate, Wes rushed forward, searching each entrance for a door that he could open. He wanted to scream. He was so close, and yet he may as well have been back in Galeharbor for all the good it did him.

He glanced back at the great tower as he raced toward the

southern end of the city, into the depth of the storm, where there were still entrances that he had not checked. Whether he lived or died, whether Celesyria rotted in a prison far beneath the surface, the tower would carry on.

It would watch.

It would wait.

Chapter 17

As Celesyria was dragged through the tunnels of Whitespire, she remembered the last time that she'd felt just as helpless, back in Silverfell, when she and Wes had been thrown into prison. The soldiers had treated her roughly then, and she'd managed to tear her wing membrane as she tried to reach her friend.

Though Jaconial and her companions were somewhat less violent toward her, she couldn't help but feel that this particular capture was even more of an insult.

She watched the various halls and cave offshoots passing by as they went, her wings cramped and aching beneath her bonds. She recognized almost everything that she saw. This was her home, the only one that she'd ever had, whatever its flaws. And now, it had become her prison. She had lost not only her freedom, but the dignity of who she was.

Not so long ago, she'd been the respected member of a legacy family of Guardians. Now, she was nothing but a traitor, a blasphemer—and worse, her father was being treated as though he was the same as his daughter.

She had given up on trying to get Jaconial or the green dragon to tell her anything about his whereabouts. It was clear that they were not willing to cooperate. Instead, she passed the dreary march in silence, turning to the High One in prayer when it became clear that no one here in the world below wanted to listen.

Soon, they reached the heart of the Guardian quarters, and Celesyria wondered if her mother was close by, safe and sound in their sleeping cavern. She did not dare reach out to her in her mind. Not yet. She did not want her mother to be in trouble if she was willing to help her daughter, and if she was not... Well, she would have to figure that out if the time came.

The fellow leading their little parade—a fat male who was very short, even for a dwarf—gestured toward a narrow hallway that was almost hidden behind a cluster of bright blue orb-lights. "In here, men," he said, as the dwarves holding onto her chains began urging her forward.

She followed without resistance, curious as to where they were going. She had never noticed the corridor before, and she wondered if the orb-lights had once covered the entrance entirely. She could not remember exactly how this far-flung corner of the Guardian's quarters had looked the last time that she saw it.

As they entered the tunnel, the orb-light faded behind them and it became very, very dark. Two of the dwarves near the front took hold of wooden torches from the walls, reaching into their pockets in search of tinder boxes.

"You're kidding, right?" the green male dragon asked, his chuckle making the tight walls seem to shake.

"Oh—well—right," one of the dwarves said, lifting his torch in front of the dragon's face. The other one did the same, and for a moment the tunnel was filled with a bright yellow glow as the green dragon let forth a small stream of flame from his jaws.

Torches lit, they continued into the darkness. Celesyria noticed that the angle of the floor was growing steeper, leading them down into the belly of the mountains. She wanted to ask where they were going, but what good would it do? She couldn't so much as turn around in the tight space even if she were to try and flee.

Finally, after several minutes, the dwarves walking ahead stopped at a huge, wooden door. It looked very different from the old-fashioned style usually seen closer to the surface. This one was sleek and clean, as though it had been freshly varnished and set on its hinges that very day.

It's probably a dungeon. She tried to swallow the panic in her throat as the fat dwarf reached into his pocket and produced a keyring tinkling with dozens of shining, new keys. *A dungeon usually accessed only by dwarves, if the key is any indication.* Dragons preferred to use great metal turning-wheel style locks most of the time, as they could be maneuvered without the need for opposable thumbs.

Usually, criminal trials were held in the Hall of Assembly, in the southeast end of Whitespire. The Guardian meetings were held there, too, as well as general meetings of the governing councils. Dragons were huge creatures, and it did not take very many of them to fill a space. It was necessary for them to make as much use of a single large space as possible, be it a dining hall or a courtroom.

Finally, after several moments selecting the correct key, the dwarf managed to turn it in the silver padlock and began dragging the door open with the aid of his companion. "Watch your head this time, Jaconial," the green dragon rumbled from somewhere behind her as she was pushed toward the doorway.

"Very funny."

"It would be, just not for you."

Celesyria was surprised to hear a hint of happiness in Jaconial's voice. She wasn't usually the type who took kindly to a ribbing, so most never attempted to include her in their jokes.

"Okay," one of the leading dwarves said, "Keep your tail straight as you pass through. The walls here aren't the most stable, and if you bring them down, we'll all be buried."

Celesyria did as she was told, stepping through the tight doorway, trying not to panic as she felt the edges of the wooden frame pressing against her sides. She wanted to breathe deeply to calm herself, but she feared that if she did, she would get completely stuck.

A second later, she was through, stretching her legs out as they made their way down a dimly-lit passage wide enough that the dwarves could walk directly at her side and monitor the placement of her chains.

"They really do need to move it somewhere better," the green dragon was saying to Jaconial as Celesyria glanced at them from over her shoulder. Jaconial had slipped through quickly, but her friend looked for a second as though he'd gotten completely stuck. *Move what?*

"And you really do need to stop eating like such a pig,"

Jaconial retorted.

"Don't insult me. A dragon can eat far more than a tiny little pig!"

"It's an expression, Nazzan."

Before she could hear whatever it was he said next, the dwarves in front rounded a bend in the path and Celesyria followed. Suddenly, the walls were gone, the ceiling was gone, and most of the floor was gone. Celesyria stopped short, almost knocking one of the dwarves beside her to the ground.

They were in a massive natural cavern, probably some sort of mining pit, with rough unfinished walls and wooden catwalks stretched across the chasm. The space felt so vast that Celesyria experienced a sudden rush of vertigo, though she was still standing several feet back from the edge. It was a strange sensation for someone who was accustomed to flying.

In the center of the room, sitting on a huge platform that looked big enough to fit fifty dragons with ease, was a black obelisk.

"Let's get moving," Nazzan said from behind, and Celesyria obliged, taking careful steps toward the wooden bridge that the dwarves had stepped onto. Like the door, it was crafted with gleaming new wood. Even the nails that held it together shone. Still, even though she knew it would hold their weight, Celesyria forced herself to look straight at the obelisk rather than glancing at the pit beneath, taking the most careful steps that she could manage.

This room is obviously new. But that obelisk...

As they reached the edge of the massive center platform, she was able to get a closer look at it. It was as pure black as the darkest sky, and yet, the surface seemed to shimmer and move, like a mixture of night and smoke. She felt a dread in

215

her heart the longer that she looked at it, but she couldn't turn away. It reminded her of the spire, far above them, where Wes brought the sacrifices to the Dracodei. It looked ancient, like it had watched the very birth of the world. But while that tower was beautiful, this one was ugly, though not necessarily for reasons that she could name.

She thought of Wes, somewhere up there on the surface, alone in a land not meant for men. She began to reach out to him in her mind.

She was already nearly certain that it wouldn't work with miles of rock and earth resting between them, but what she didn't expect was the sudden crash of pain that screamed within her head as soon as she tried.

* * *

The rain began to abate somewhat as Alder hurried through the streets of High Keep, looking over his shoulder as often as he could to ensure that no one was following. Only after a few minutes of walking where he did not see another soul did he allow himself to relax a little.

It's my mother and sisters I'm worried about. He pulled the hood of his cloak from his head, pausing for a moment to ring out the water out of it before replacing it against his red hair. *Please, High One, do not let anyone see them. Do not let anyone follow them.*

It would be suspicious for three women to be traveling alone in the predawn hours in the city, let alone venturing beyond its walls, but there was no other way. If they waited for daylight, there would be soldiers everywhere, and they ran a greater risk of being asked what they were doing and where they were going. In any case, if Raela truly was nearing death, he didn't want to waste any time in getting to her.

She was a lovely woman, almost a second mother to him and his sisters. Even though she'd been very busy taking care of the house and doing small home-work projects when she could get them, Raela always treated each child as though he or she was her special favorite. He could remember standing beside her in the kitchen of the little cob house, helping her wipe the plates and pans after she washed them.

As he got a little older, she began to teach him his letters, and his sisters were soon old enough to be taught the same. Most of the poor in High Keep were illiterate, including his mother, but Raela could read and write perfectly and as a result, so could he, Marya, and Violet.

He remembered asking her about it once, when he was nine or ten years old. He knew that Raela was from Boneshire, and that if anything, peasants in that Kingdom were even less educated than those of Aridmoor. She'd never given him an answer, probably distracting him with a taste of cake batter or an offer to bring him with her to the importer's market.

He thought of it now as he made his way through the streets, wishing that there was more time to answer so many of the questions that he'd never bothered to ask. All his mother had told him was that Raela had been in trouble with her father, and that she'd needed a new home just as their family needed some help.

What could have happened to her that brought her to the gates of death? His mother had not said anything about the nature of the accident, and he'd been too focused on getting everyone to safety that he hadn't asked.

She probably burned herself at her kiln, he speculated, taking shelter beneath an alcove as a fresh torrent of rain burst from the sky. He wanted to wait for the weather to calm again, but after a few minutes it was clear that the respite from the worst of the rain had only been temporary. *I told her that a woman of her age deserved a gentler profession. So did mother, not that she'd listen to either of us.*

After Alder and his sisters had grown up, their mother had not needed Raela to live with them anymore, so she had returned to the small farmhouse that she'd purchased years earlier, outside of the city limits. Still, she'd needed money, and a job as a limeburner had opened up soon after she left. They'd all been trying to find her something safer ever since.

Stubborn woman. Alder smiled as he rounded a bend in a narrow street. It was darker here than it had been closer to his house, and he held his lamp aloft as he walked, trying to see where the entrance to the street he was looking for was.

I have to be close, surely. He stopped to read a couple of the signs, the words barely legible between the peeling paint and the reflection of his lamplight in the slick of the rain. *Okay. Miller Street, which means Bear Street is just past the clockmaker's shop—*

A woman's scream sounded over the rain, jolting him from his thoughts. He heard it again, a little quieter this time, and before he could even think about it he felt the familiar weight of his sword in his hand. He pressed himself close against the nearest wall, walking slowly toward where he thought the sound may be coming from. He blinked against the darkness, trying to get his bearings again. *The soldiers will help her.* He hesitated, feeling the comfortable weight of his blade against his palm.

She screamed again. A few seconds later, he heard the

218

muffled sound of laughter. Men's voices. More than one.

He held the grip of his sword more tightly. Another scream. *No one is coming. I can't let this happen.* He rushed along the wall and ducking into an alleyway, trying to quiet his breathing. He was almost sure he was behind the little courtyard where the city tinker usually peddled his goods, and if he was, there was an alley just to the east that should take him in the right direction.

He could no longer hear screams, and he could only hope that she had not been dragged too far from where he'd first heard her. He strained his ears against the pattering rain as he ran down the alley, kicking an old bucket out of his way and causing a huge ringing sound as it crashed against a stone wall.

Then he heard the men's laughter again, impossibly close. He slowed his steps, keeping both his sword and lantern pointed ahead as he checked over his shoulder periodically. The alley remained deserted.

He could hear the sound of vile curses, the sort that scandalized even his well-worn soldier's ears. It made him sick to think that they were directed at a woman who they planned to harm, if they hadn't done so already.

As he rounded another bend, he saw it. A door left ajar, with a sliver of yellow lamplight peeking through it. On his side of it, there was a small window, the glass panes long since broken. He crept over to it, peering over the sill, careful not to let his lantern or his sword sound against the wall.

In the far corner, he could see two men crouched low, their backs to him. There was a third man sitting nearby, cradling his face as blood trickled from between his hands. Between them, he could see a flash of blonde hair. The woman was laying on the floor, unmoving. He didn't have time to watch for a sign of breath rising in her chest. He pulled back, making for the door.

He shoved it inward with a shoulder, leaping into the room with a yell, sword raised. The men nearly fell onto their rear ends as they spun around, the leering smiles falling from their faces as they realized what was happening. In an instant, they were drawing their own weapons, but Alder barely took note of them.

The blonde hair belonged to Kessara. He stood there stupidly for precious seconds, watching as her chest rose and fell. She was alive, but her hairline was crusted with blood, and her face was pale. As the men strode toward him, their boorish grins returning as they realized he did not come with other soldiers at his back, he thought of what he had told her.

He thought of the soldiers that he knew, the soldiers that had joked about assaulting women, just like this. He thought of those men who he suspected would actually go through with it.

He thought of all of the times that he could have done something to stop them, but chose not to.

A roar broke from his chest as he dropped his lantern to the ground, sword flashing as he lunged at the men. They stumbled backward, their eyes going wide as they gripped their weapons and narrowly avoided the tip of his sword. Two of them gripped knives in their shaking hands, including the one with the bleeding face. The other, the least grubby-looking of the three, held a club at face-height, unwavering.

Before Alder could react, the man dashed forward and swung the club low, narrowly missing his kneecap. Alder howled with pain as he felt the heavy wood connect with his femur, but he recovered quickly, lunging to one side and striking down the already injured man in a single stroke. He collapsed to the ground, blood pooling across the stone floor.

The other man with the knife took off for the door, dashing around Alder and out into the night. He wanted to chase him, to put him down like the animal he was, not caring who saw it. For all of the times he had caused death, for all of the battles that he had fought, he had never felt such rage. It blinded him, hampering his reaction time as the man with the club rushed to the corner, toward Kessara.

He forced himself to take two breaths before rushing forward. One wrong move, and she would be killed.

The man tripped over Alder's discarded lantern, his club nearly falling to the floor. Alder pounced like a cat, raising his sword up near the ceiling before swinging it down on the man's neck. He listened to the telltale thump, and then the room went silent.

He looked at Kessara for a second, making sure that she was still breathing before turning to the opposite corner and emptying his stomach against the floor.

The other man was still out there, unharmed. He would do it again. Men like that did not stop until someone made them stop, and if crime rates in his home city were any indication, that was something that his fellow soldiers were finding harder and harder to do.

He pressed his eyes shut, trying to breathe, trying to get his heart to stop racing. He wanted to think of the High One, but he couldn't face Him. Not now. Not with his hands stained with blood.

He strode across the room and lifted Kessara into his arms, pulling her face close to his chest, knowing that no matter what else happened, no matter who she married, he would make it his life's mission to make sure that no one ever dared to hurt her again.

* * *

Celesyria tried to speak again, this time to Jaconial. The pain was even worse. It felt like there was a pulsing orb behind her eyes, expanding and shrinking until it exploded into a million shards of light, driving out all other thoughts. She swore out loud, and the sound echoed off of the rough rock walls. The other dragons and all of the dwarves turned to look at her.

"I wouldn't try speaking with your mind again, unless you want to spare the inhabitants of Umrym the inconvenience of your trial and execution," Jaconial said aloud, the edge of her lip curling over her front teeth like a feral dog. Seeing Celesyria's alarmed expression, she continued. "Don't worry, Celesyria. It will be a fair trial. But blasphemy is a serious crime."

Celesyria bit back the insults she wanted to hurl at her old rival. It would do no good now.

I knew that I was putting myself at risk by coming back, but... execution? She thought to herself, turning the word over and over in her mind. It tasted strange on her tongue, like a foreign word in a language that she did not speak.

She pictured herself being dragged back up overground, to the Obitus Field, where dragons dealt with their worst criminals. It had been many, many years since someone had been executed. As far as Celesyria knew, it had not happened in her lifetime. She knew from her research that most of those who were killed at the hand of the councils had committed terrible torture against humans in war, or killed a spouse, or something equally heinous. She knew that in their books of law, crimes of blasphemy carried similar weight, but she'd never heard of them being enforced within living memory.

Then again, I've never heard anyone else publicly deny that the Dracodei are the true gods of Kaveryth, she thought to herself, snapping her head up as she heard footsteps coming from across the other side of the cavern.

She tried not to think of the terrifying methods of death that had been in use at the time of the Boneshire war, let alone those which were in use even earlier. As she heard the sound of echoing voices, she closed her eyes, forcing deep breaths into her lungs.

Somehow, they are able to stop me from speaking to other creatures. But I know that they cannot stop me from speaking to the High One.

She did so, there in the very bowels of the world, speaking to Him from the depths of her heart.

Death is not the end, she said to Him, trying to comfort herself. *Even the Farplace is not so frightening, compared to the thought of dying and fading into nothing. But You don't have to send me to the Farplace. You could create a soul for me, with no more than a word. You're the true God, the Creator of all. Everything rests beneath the power of your hand.*

"Pay attention," the green dragon, Nazzan, whispered to her, his voice gentle. "It's time."

She opened her eyes, the brief peace she felt while praying to the High One fading away like morning dew touched by the sun. Her heart began to pound in her ears as she saw the others crossing from the opposing catwalks and striding toward the center of the platform.

There were three dragons, three dwarves, and three elves. As all nine of the creatures moved to kneel before the obelisk, Celesyria's breath caught in her chest as she noticed the faces of the elves.

Their flesh was so rotten that it had begun falling off of their bones.

Chapter 18

Kessara saw Alder's face again, through the fog and the pounding of her headache. He was just as handsome as he ever was, but there was a tightness to his jaw, and his eyes were looking off elsewhere, somewhere ahead. They were moving. She could feel his body, his legs carrying them forward, his arms pressing into her sides and back. She smiled as she closed her heavy eyelids. His chest felt warm. It was a nice dream. She liked that he was there.

Some time later, she awoke suddenly, her chest clenching as she tried to even out her breathing. There had been a dream, a horrible nightmare, but already it was fading away, off to wherever forgotten dreams went. The more that she tried to grasp at the details, the less she could remember.

She could feel grass beneath her now. Alder's warmth was gone, replaced by a damp chill that was soaking into her clothing and little prickles where weeds poked up at her. She was very tired, but after a couple of moments trying to get back to sleep, she could not. There was something, something important, right on the outside of her thoughts—

She sat up, eyes wide, trying to see where she was. Wavering grass, everywhere, as far as she could look. Cold. Everything soaked by some recent rain.

Within a second, Alder was beside her, holding out a trembling hand as though unsure whether she would shatter if he dared touch her.

"Princess," he started, his voice filled with an emotion she was too confused and exhausted to place. "Lay down. You need to rest."

She did not lay down. Instead, she started to cry. The tears came pouring out of her before she knew why they were coming, but she could not stop them. In a moment she was sobbing, her throat raw, her lungs burning, unable to stop.

"Shh, shh," Alder was saying, coming to sit nearby, cradling her body against his own. "It's okay. I'm here."

She blinked a few times, trying to get the torrent of tears to slow long enough to get a good look at him. He was no dream. The grass and the cloudy night sky above them were real, too. Her mind felt slow, like she was picking up information but not able to find the right place where it fit.

Details began to pour back into her mind. The darkness. The streets of High Keep, the cobblestones against her feet. The jeers of unseen men. She pressed her eyes shut, trying to sort it all out.

The men had attacked her. She had attacked them back.

A clear memory stuck out in her mind, bright as lamplight. She could feel the sensation of stabbing one of them, of her knife meeting the soft resistance of flesh.

The tears slowed as she remembered them taking her, bringing her to a room in some decrepit house or perhaps an old shop, laying her against the floor in a shadowed corner.

She reached out a hand to grasp his, and he accepted it, enclosing her small hand inside his large one.

"Shh," he said again, stroking the back of her hand with his thumb. "You're not badly hurt. You're going to be okay, promise."

His touch steadied her as the last of the swirling memories fell into place. She could think of the general order of events... at least, until she reached the end. The corner. The hardness of the floor pressing against her spine.

She wanted to cry more, now that she knew why she was crying, but her eyes had gone dry. Perhaps she was out of tears.

"You were right," she choked out, looking up at him.

"No," Alder said, blinking faster than was natural. He swore then, pressing his eyes tight. "No. You should have been safe. You were in my home city. There should have been soldiers patrolling the streets. Those worthless pieces of filth should have—"

"I couldn't control any of that," she said, glad to find that her voice was still in good working order. "But I could have listened to you. I could have waited—"

"This isn't your fault, Kessara," Alder snapped, squeezing her hand a little too hard before softening his grip again. "I'm sure you had your reasons for going into the city. You should have been safe, whether you listened to me or not."

"But that is not the world we live in," she said softly, giving him a sad smile.

Alder said nothing. She felt the warmth of his hand around hers, gentle now, but if he wanted to, he could do more than squeeze her a little too tight.

A good man is not one who is too weak for violence. A good man is one who has the power to destroy, but chooses to protect instead.

"They didn't… do anything to me. I don't think," she said after a while. It wasn't a question, not exactly, but she found herself wanting an answer.

Alder cleared his throat. "No. You were fully dressed when I saw you, as were the men. I don't think they got a chance."

"Thank the High One," she whispered.

She was tired. The rising and falling of Alder's chest was comforting, as was his warmth. She allowed herself to try and relax, breathing in and out, trying not to think any more about what had happened. The more she tried to avoid the memories, the more that they intruded on her mind, unresolved, relenting.

"What happened to the men?" she asked after a while, her voice heavy with tiredness. Her body was crying out for sleep, but she couldn't, not yet. The final questions had to be answered before she could bring herself to rest.

"I killed two of them," Alder said. She felt his body tense against hers. "One got away. I wanted to go after him as badly as I've ever wanted to do anything, but I didn't."

"I was going to try and talk to Kylan," she said, feeling foolish. Alder said nothing, so she continued. "You know it yourself, he's always had feelings for me, at least on some level. It was clear even when Wes was first arrested that he was not going to allow me to face any legal consequences for defending him. I thought I could get him to listen to reason. It wasn't like I could allow you to escort me."

228

She listened to Alder's breathing for several seconds, feeling the warmth of his body against hers. She took a few slow breaths herself, trying to soak in the peaceful feeling that seemed to radiate from him.

"I understand," Alder said finally. "I don't think it was wise, but I understand."

He seemed about to say more, so she waited until he spoke again.

"As long as we're getting all of our secrets out in the open, I should tell you something."

"What?"

"Wes didn't agree to go to Umrym without saying goodbye," he said, looking away from her and tilting his face toward the clouds. "I locked him out of the castle, and I can only hope that he went to Celesyria in time, because she really was about to leave. I thought it better for us to split up, and Wes wasn't about to listen to me of his own free will."

She closed her eyes, deep in thought. On a logical level, she was angry. He shouldn't have manipulated Wes, and he certainly should not have lied about it.

What if Wes is still in Windshear somewhere, unable to get to Auranth to meet us? But she couldn't bring herself to lash out at Alder. Not now. There would be time for that tomorrow, whenever this endless, gloomy night ended. For the time being, she really did need to sleep.

She said nothing else, listening to the soft sounds of Alder breathing and the occasional chirping of a night bird until her eyes grew too heavy to keep open. She lay there, her hand still entwined with his, and despite everything, she felt the glimmer of a butterfly in her stomach as she relaxed into a dreamless slumber.

It seemed she had been asleep for only a few minutes when Alder's body shifted beside her, and she felt the weight of his hand stroking her hair.

"I'm sorry. We're running out of time," he said as she yawned, trying to stretch out her tired back. She thought she could see the barest hint of dawn light on the eastern horizon, far beyond the ocean of green. "We have to go."

She blinked sleep from her eyes, unable to remember if she had dreamed. All she knew was that she didn't want to leave. She wanted to stay right here, with Alder's arms wrapped around her.

Safe.

* * *

Wes was not surprised to find that the first cavern he entered was deserted. The entrance—a dwarf-sized wooden door with a normal handle—had been placed in a far-off corner of the city. Wes had found it just before giving up entirely on getting into the underground part of Whitespire.

Outside, the rain had started in earnest, and the crashes of thunder had begun to come with greater regularity. Here underground, though, it was silent. If he didn't know that Celesyria was in here somewhere, taken captive like a common criminal, he could almost find the caverns peaceful.

Celesyria had told him about her home city before, and he knew that in a lot of the older areas, the rooms were lit by nothing but hundreds of individual candles. This room was one such place, all ancient rough stone and gleaming yellow pricks of light against the darkness. The candles gave off more heat than he expected, sending beads of sweat rolling down from his forehead. Still, it was beautiful.

He looked around the large room, trying to get his bearings. Already, he forgot exactly where the door leading back to the surface was. It was lost within a sea of lights, but he could see another opening far across the floor, and he walked toward it. It wasn't a door, only a small cave passage leading farther down. His cloak, which had mere seconds ago been almost too hot to tolerate, was not thick enough to counteract the sudden damp chill that pressed into his bones as he walked through it.

There were a few torches here along the walls, already lit, burning neatly in their holders, but the heat they provided could not overcome the damp chill that filled the air.

Wes saw no one as he made his way down the tunnel, but he knew he might not be alone for long—someone had to have lit the torches and kept watch of the candles, but whoever that individual was, they were off somewhere else for the time being.

As the grade of the floor grew steeper, Wes felt a wave of apprehension rushing over him. It was cold, and the darkness seemed to grow more complete as he went. He feared that eventually he'd reach a place in the path where he would need to carry a torch just to see enough to keep his footing.

Celesyria needs me. He pressed on, trying to push aside the other, unhelpful thoughts of the doubting variety that plagued his mind.

Not so long ago, he and Celesyria had both been imprisoned, and the worst part about it was how he had grown complacent during his time in captivity. He'd almost been able to convince himself that a life within the status quo wouldn't hurt as much as a life lived free, whatever it cost him. *Celesyria won't feel the same way,* he reassured himself. *Her faith is too strong. She's not going to waver, whatever they say to her.*

The thought brought him comfort, but there was a fear, as well. Celesyria would keep fighting until the bitter end, but Wes couldn't help but fear that the cost would end up being her life.

Finally, after what felt like hours alone with the patter of his footsteps and the swirling maelstrom of his thoughts, he reached the end of the path.

There were three passageways ahead, each leading in a different direction. All of them had torches waiting nearby, but he could not see any more light coming from within the tunnels. He saw a small sign beside one of them, to the far left, in dwarvish. He stood there, trying to puzzle it out, the memories of his schooling muddled and mixed in with all of the other information he'd had to make sense of in more recent days.

"Sparkle pit?" he tried out loud, feeling quite silly. "Glitter hole? Shiny chasm?"

It was obviously something to do with a mine, at any rate. Not what he was looking for. He turned to the other two tunnel entrances as they stared back at him, their gaping black mouths seeming to mock him in the dark. They did not bear any sort of label as to where they led. Wes took a few steps into one, breathing deeply, and then did the same with the other.

Well, that's a start. He repeated the process, just to be sure. Up or down. *The stink of long-buried gasses or the fresh smell of the air circulating nearer to the surface.*

In the adventure story books he'd read growing up, the prisons were always held in some filthy dungeon, with moss and mushrooms growing against the wet walls. Perhaps that was the case for dragons as well. However, he also had exactly one lead on someone that might be willing to help him, and that person was Celesyria's mother, who was more likely to be in the Guardian's quarters. Wes remembered Celesyria's description of her home, and from what he could tell, it had to have been nearer to the surface.

And filled with dozens of dragons, he reminded himself as he took the torch from the wall and headed into the fresher-smelling tunnel.

* * *

Alder gripped Kessara's hand as they walked, not wanting to let go, even for a moment. He told himself that he was supporting her weight, helping her to stay standing after her ordeal, but that was a lie.

With every step they took, her hand clasped warm and secure in his own, he was more certain of the terrible truth.

He was falling for her, and there was nothing he could do about it.

She had to marry Wes. The two of them had to protect their people. He couldn't stand in the way of that, no matter what his heart screamed at him from within.

He glanced over at her as they pressed forward, noticing that her regal posture had not changed in the least. As always, she walked with her chin held aloft, her back as straight as a sturdy tree, her eyes facing the world head-on.

How could I have ever been harsh with her? Was it all just an act, a way to push her away so that this wouldn't happen in the first place?

Some good it did. In fact, her reaction to him had only made him more interested in her. She had seen the worst parts of him, the anger and the stubbornness that would have driven most people away... but she was still here. She was still holding his hand, walking beside him, racing the dawn.

They were close now, but the plains had a way of making even short journeys seem to stretch out. He found it difficult to be bothered. Here, he could enjoy the warmth of her skin, admire the delicate features of her face.

It will be the last time, he told himself as her eye caught his, a smile pouring over her face like sunlight. *I cannot indulge this any further. It's not fair to Wes, and it's not fair to her.*

Some self-pitying part of himself wanted to say that it wasn't fair to him, either, but he pushed the thought down deep. He could never remember a time when his life had been fair, and he doubted that it was going to begin to become so now. There was so much evil in the world, so much darkness. It was hard to imagine that what little light was left would be able to overcome it.

And part of it was his responsibility.

He remembered the rage that had coursed through him when he'd found Kessara, like a fire that spread through his bone marrow, urging him on. Urging him not only to kill, but to torture, to tear to pieces, to utterly destroy.

He was a soldier. It was not the first time he'd killed someone, not by a long shot, but it was the first time he had wanted to do it so badly. The men were wicked beyond comprehension, that much was not in doubt. They had ganged up on a woman and sought to violate her in the most demeaning and humiliating way possible, but they were not animals as he had thought to himself at the time.

They had souls, despite everything, and I should have remembered that when I put them down. He wanted to seek forgiveness from the High One, but at the moment, he felt unable to pray. Guilt coursed through him, mingled with his blood.

On one level, he knew that the actual actions he had taken had been justifiable. But the thoughts that lay beneath the surface as he acted... He couldn't convince himself that it was alright. It wasn't. His thoughts alone convicted him.

"Are we going to be there soon?" Kessara asked, her voice faint, mingling with the early birdsong that had now begun in earnest.

He cleared his throat. There would be time later to reflect on the deceits of his heart, his guilt, all of it. For now, Kessara needed him.

"Yes, Princess," he answered, not wanting to say her name. "Raela's farmhouse is just beyond that rise." He pointed toward a few stray trees at the top of a hill, jutting out into the sky against the flatness of the grasslands.

"Will this woman help us? Who is she?"

"She is like a second mother to me," he said, rubbing his thumb softly against hers, savoring the final moments of being able to touch her skin. "And yes, she will. You'll meet my mother and my sisters as well. I asked them to follow a few hours behind us. They won't be too long now, considering our delay."

Kessara nodded, and Alder thought he saw tears forming in her eyes, but no tears came. Perhaps he'd only imagined it.

He guided the Princess up the base of the hill, feeling exposed in the open space, looking down at the plains of Aridmoor that surrounded them. Soon, all of the women that he cared about would be together in Raela's exposed farmhouse, with the entire world against them. It was all his responsibility.

No matter what he had to do, he would keep them safe. He would protect them all.

Chapter 19

"What's wrong with their faces?" Celesyria whispered in Nazzan's direction, hoping he would pity her enough to answer. Jaconial turned to her instead, her voice a low hiss. "It's the obelisk," she said, rolling her eyes as though it pained her to give her old rival even a moment of her time. "It prevents anyone from being able to mindspeak, both in this room and in the perimeter around it, to prevent spies. We can't fly here, either, though I'm not sure how they managed that effect. But it also removes the elves' glamors. Satisfied?"

"What's glamor?"

Jaconial did not say more. Most of the others in the room were still bowing before the great black obelisk, but two of the dwarves had already gotten to their feet, perhaps signaling to her captor that the meeting would soon proceed.

"They use some kind of sorcery to maintain their beauty,"

Nazzan leaned his head toward her and whispered, his rumbling voice quiet enough that Jaconial could not hear. "Elves live for hundreds of years, but their bodies eventually decay. When they come here, honesty is demanded from them, even in their appearance, just as dragons must speak out loud for all to hear."

Celesyria watched as the rest of the company got to their feet. "What about the dwarves? What effect does the obelisk have on them?"

Nazzan said nothing, instead straightening his neck so that his head was no longer in easy whispering distance. The elves, dwarves, and dragons walked over to their places, each member of the strange gathering moving as though they had joined a well-choreographed dance. *Whatever this place is, they know what they're doing.*

"Jaconial, Nazzan," a huge black dragon thundered, his voice sending fresh ripples across the surface of the obelisk. "We must ask you to return to your duties. Thank you for your service in apprehending this criminal. Dwarves, you may go as well."

She felt her chains being loosened and then removed, allowing her wings to unfurl into a more comfortable resting position. As always, her ankle manacles remained, but at least they were no longer attached to heavy chains.

None of her captors said a word, only bowing as they left through the same door that they entered by. Despite Jaconial's general unpleasantness, Celesyria had found her familiar presence almost comforting, and Nazzan did not seem like the needlessly cruel sort. Even the dwarves who had aided in her capture intimidated her less than those who had just joined the meeting. She wished that they'd been permitted to stay.

She wanted to run, but she knew that it would be pointless. If she made for the narrow tunnel, reinforcements would be called in to block her at the other side. Even here, she was heavily outnumbered. Instead, she took a few tentative steps forward, her claws clacking against the smooth floor of the platform. She did not know what to expect from this unknown assembly, but she didn't want them to know that they intimidated her. She would keep her head held high.

"Well, Celesyria," the black dragon said, shaking his head back and forth before going quiet again.

"She already knows everything, Dajin," one of the elves said after a moment. "I suppose it matters little what she hears." With their long hairstyles and gruesome faces, Celesyria relied on the tone and depth of his voice to inform her that he was a male. His features were frightening to look at, but she forced herself to meet the twin pitted holes in his skull as he looked toward her. *How does he see without eyes?*

"Knowledge is important to you, isn't it?"

"Y—yes," she said, the single word sticking in her throat.

"The Great Library at Helmm is gone," he continued. Celesyria thought he frowned, but she could not be certain. "There was a terrible accident. I'm sorry to bear this news. I'm told that you enjoyed going there to study."

She clenched her jaw. *All of those books. All of the history, all of the traditions that dragons and dwarves struggled to remember... Gone.*

"Fire devours books, it couldn't be stopped. A pity," said one of the other dragons, a female with orange scales similar to Celesyria's own. A flash of recognition coursed through her. She knew this dragon. She was a low-ranking member of one of the Whitespire administration councils.

So what is she doing here?

"It was for the best," a male voice chimed in. It was one of the dwarves, but Celesyria didn't recognize him. "It's difficult to build a future with the bones of the past surrounding us. The Kingdom of Boneshire knows that all too well. I wish that our own archives would go up in smoke—"

"That's a lie," Celesyria snapped, unable to contain her anger. She stopped short as she noticed everyone staring at her, their gazes unwavering. She realized that she recognized a dwarf that stood at the furthest end of the platform. He had worked with Gramnok on a recent project in the sapphire mine that lay just south of the city, though she didn't know his name. "Progress requires a foundation to build on."

Before she could say more, one of the elves began to laugh, a rickety, hollow sound. She could not tell if they were male or female.

"Be quiet," the orange female dragon said, her voice echoing against the walls. "The fate of Umrym is not your concern."

Celesyria bit back a retort. She thought of Wes, Alder, and Kessara, out in the world, with the knowledge of the High One burning in their hearts. Whatever else she did or could not do, she had already impacted the fate of Umrym, and there was nothing those at this meeting could do to take that back.

"The settlements are going well," the first elf who had spoken said. His voice was still beautiful, despite the ugliness of his body.

The fires. A chill rippled down Celesyria's tail. Their fears had been correct. Elves were amassing their forces within Kaveryth itself, right under the noses of those who were supposed to protect the people. *What is going on? Why aren't the Guardians pushing the settlers back?*

"And the Guardians and my fellow civil servants are turning a blind eye, just as we hoped," the orange dragon chimed in as though answering her unspoken question, her voice filled with an unsettling mirth.

"I really didn't think it would be so easy," the dwarf that Celesyria recognized said.

"We told you, Girnac," the dragon continued. Most of the others stayed silent, watching her. It was not apparent by the layout of their meeting who was in charge, but the orange dragon spoke with a confidence that drew all eyes toward her. "Even with the mountain of treasure they'd amassed from the offerings, they were still so willing to accept elven jewels in return for keeping quiet."

"What do you mean?" Celesyria said, unable to keep quiet a moment longer. *Did the Guardians already know that the Dracodei are false Gods? Do my parents know?*

The orange dragon ignored her, but the black one, Dajin, took a few steps toward her. He was the largest in the room by far. Even in the cavernous space, his bulk was intimidating. "Surely you're not so naive as to think that the Guardians and the dwarves don't get a cut of the treasure," he said. It wasn't a question, so she said nothing, waiting for him to go on, but the look of surprise on her face had clearly betrayed her.

"Come now. Think of all the work that is done to facilitate the Feast of Offering. You yourself helped to fill the treasure caverns. That treasure is often used as a personal bank account for various administrators, dwarf and human alike. And for Guardians, as well."

She opened her mouth to speak, but he continued before

she could get a word in. The others present in the meeting kept their eyes on him, caught on his every word. Maybe the orange dragon was not in charge after all.

"Oh, it's not so bad," he said, revealing a sharp-toothed smile. "Many of those in charge use the money to improve the community, believing it to be a blessing for serving the Dracodei faithfully. Others use it for their own wicked desires. It's never been a big problem."

He paused, giving her a pitying look. "Until recent decades, there's just been so much money, Celesyria. Enough to bathe in. How could we deny those who keep it flowing an occasional trip to the mistress, or to the gambling cavern?"

"My parents," she said, swallowing. "Do they know of this?"

The elf laughed again, his humorless chuckle rattling against the walls.

"Of course they know about the Guardians' access to the money," the orange dragon chimed in. "They were some of the good ones. Not to worry. They used the treasury to care for their fellow dragons and the dwarves, especially now, with the deaths and the need for imported food."

A brief flicker of relief mixed with horror filled Celesyria's chest

"But, my dear," the orange dragon said, tilting her head. "The good can still be stupid."

"What do you mean they 'were' some of the good ones?" she choked out, forcing herself to keep her tone calm.

Dajin cleared his throat and glanced over at her.

"Your mother has continued to be loyal to her race and to the dwarves in our community," he said, giving her another humorless grin. "But your father...He refused to see sense. He's been exiled."

"To the Farplace?" she asked, pressing her claws into the floor, the urge to tear the black dragon apart rushing through every muscle in her body.

"Oh, no. Death would have been too cruel a punishment for his misdeeds, at least for now. We sent him to Nox. Perhaps there he will learn how the world really works."

* * *

Raela's house was tucked away behind a sweep of a hill. Had Kessara not had Alder to lead the way, she would have missed it. The rain had finally stopped, and the clouds that had covered this part of Aridmoor since their arrival had finally floated away on the wind.

Her head ached and she longed for a few more hours of sleep, but as they approached the tidy red door, she felt some energy returning to her body.

Dawn would be there soon, and the light always made her feel more alive. It reminded her that there was still hope, that just waking up every day was a gift. It had never felt more true than it did that morning. She had been so close to the end.

"You ready?" Alder asked, interrupting her morbid thoughts as he raised a hand to knock. She nodded, anticipation building in her belly as he rapped at the wood.

Even after everything they had been through together as of late, she did not know Alder very well. It was one thing to be told something about a person. But it was quite another to experience their past for yourself, to slip into a life that they had lived long before meeting you.

It was different with Roven. There was never a time when I

243

didn't know everything there was to know about him. The same is true for Wes. It's like we're already part of the same family.

The thought made her cringe involuntarily as she listened for the sound of movement inside the small cob-walled house.

She tried to stop thinking about the impossibilities of her love life as Alder knocked again, looking over his shoulder at the visible edge of the road leading out of High Keep. They had not run into anyone on their trek, but still, she was glad that he was so careful. She could respect that about him. Though he was clearly more than capable of putting up a physical defense, he was smart enough to know it was better to avoid violent confrontation when you could.

Alder smacked himself on the forehead with the palm of his hand and moved toward the side of the house. "She's ill. I doubt she can leap up and come to the door. Wait here a moment."

She did as she was told, leaning her body against the wall, unable to stop the corner of the windowsill from jabbing into her back. *It's probably better if I don't fall asleep on my feet, anyway.* She fiddled with a small wind chime that hung from the top of the round, red-trimmed window.

Alder did not return for several minutes, and she could hear no signs of life from inside. Icy fear gripped her. What if they were too late? What if they were visiting the body of a dead woman? Or worse, what if one of King Ursa's lackeys had gotten to her?

She stood up straight, her hand moving instinctively toward the hidden leather strap which held her knife. Of course, it was no longer there, and her hand met nothing but the fabric of her dress. It was back in High Keep, either in the alleyway or in that miserable building where the men had taken her.

She couldn't remember the details.

I don't want to remember. She straightened the hem of her shirt with her hands. Every time that she thought about what had transpired, unfamiliar emotions bubbled to the surface. She would have to deal with it, but not here. Not this night. For the time being, her mission was the same as Alder's. They had to make sure that his family was safe.

Is that even possible? Will the wicked forces of the world ever allow us to support the cause of the High One without putting ourselves in grave peril?

Before she could ponder the issue further, the red door swung open, and Alder stood on the other side, gesturing that she come in. With a glance over her own shoulder at the deserted walking path and the road that lay beyond, she stepped over the threshold. Like the door, it was red, and for a moment, it reminded her of a line of blood spilled across the dark wooden floor.

The blood of soldiers who defend this land. The blood of their sacrifice that keeps you safe.

* * *

Alder was not prepared for the sight that greeted him as he entered the back bedroom of the house. With Kessara at his heels, he walked toward the bed, the fall of his boots disrupting the silence. "My love," Raela said, opening her swollen eyes into slits as he came up beside her and took her hand into his own. "Sorry I couldn't let you in. Oh, what I'd give to be able to make you a cup of tea and sit by the fire..."

There was no fire at all, not now. The house was freezing cold, and Alder doubted that the worn quilts Raela rested under were enough to drive the chill from her sick body.

"G—good idea," Kessara said, a little too brightly, as she turned on her heel and headed back to the main room. "I'll get a fire on, at least."

"What happened to you?" Alder said, examining the woman's face. The sockets of her eyes were blue and purple with bruises, and one of her cheekbones was sunk inward. He had assumed that she'd been injured at the kiln where she'd worked as a limeburner. This was much worse. He tried to bite back the rage that was rising in him as he looked her over. Her arms were covered in bruises, scrapes, and cuts. He doubted that the rest of her body, hidden beneath the blankets, was in any better shape.

"It doesn't matter now," Raela said, giving him the hint of a smile.

"Of course it matters! Whoever did this to—"

"There's no time," she said, gripping his hand with surprising strength. "I was afraid that you wouldn't make it here at all. I was holding on, waiting for you."

She said nothing else for a moment. Alder looked at her face, trying to focus on the pretty brown of her eyes rather than the damage that surrounded them. He wanted to do something, to rush her to a healer, to save her, but he knew that was a childish wish. Had there been a chance it would help, he was certain that his mother, Marya, or Violet would have done so already. Perhaps they had already tried and failed.

"Ask your woman to come in," she choked out. "The weight of my eternity is too heavy for one person to carry."

He let go of Raela's hand and took the two steps toward the doorway of the room, beckoning for Kessara. She had managed to light a small fire, enough to warm the air in the small house until the sun rose high enough to come in through the windows. "Mother and the girls are coming. Should we... wait for them?" he asked, unsure exactly what she was asking him and Kessara to do.

"Please tell them I love them...after," she replied, looking up at the ceiling as she breathed in and out, a wet sound emanating from her chest. *After you die.* Alder tried to keep his expression stoic as tears threatened to spill over. "They won't understand what I need."

Kessara was glancing over at him, as though unsure whether she should run or hold his other hand. She decided on the latter, pressing her fingertips in between his as Raela began to speak.

"I am dying, of course," she said, smiling as she allowed her eyes to fall shut. "I need your help, but first, I need you to promise that you will take care of something for me."

"Anything," Alder said as Raela opened her eyes, reaching for the table laying at the other side of her bed. Kessara let go of his hand and rushed over, grasping the folded paper that Raela was trying to get hold of with weak, clumsy fingers.

"Yes," Raela said, relaxing back against the pillow and closing her eyes again. "Take this letter. Please read it when I am gone."

"Of course I will," Alder said, taking the crumpled rectangle from Kessara and sliding it into the pocket of his trousers. He had a thousand questions, but he did not want to make the woman speak any more than necessary. Drawing each breath seemed to take an extraordinary amount of energy, and he was certain that talking was worse.

She went on. "Do not let it fall into the hands of our enemies.

The information I have given you can change the world. I need you and your wife to promise me that you will go to Boneshire and make use of it."

Wife? Kessara glanced up at him, her cheeks pink. She said nothing. Alder swallowed fresh tears that were threatening to pour over.

Raela had always been intelligent. She taught him and his sisters how to read and how to do arithmetic. She was better at academic subjects than anyone he'd ever met, a fact that she had never wanted Alder or his family to share for reasons that she had never explained. To see her like this now, unsure of what she was saying, pained him more than he could have imagined.

"We will. I promise," Alder said.

"Thank you, my love," Raela said, not opening her eyes. "It's the end. I know that this will probably not make sense to you, but I need you to help me to go home to the Eternal Lands. There's a loaf of bread in the kitchen. Please bring it."

Kessara and Alder glanced at one another. Normally, when a believer in the Dracodei died, their family had to bring an offering of coins or jewels to one of the local temples as payment for the trip that their soul would take to get to their place of rest.

As Kessara rushed out of the room to fetch it, Alder thought back to the palace in Windshear, where he and Wes had met the dying elf. He hadn't even told Kessara about how Wes had given him bread to help him make his way home in death, and now it was happening a second time. *How extraordinary.*

"Thank you," Raela said, her voice raspy and faint. *Time is short.* "I don't know exactly what to do, but I hope it's enough."

"Anything you ask," Alder said.

"Take a piece of the bread. Ask the High One for the gift of the bread of hope. Pray with me for forgiveness," she said, punctuating each word with a rattling inhalation of breath. "Trust in the mercy of the true God."

Kessara tore a piece of bread off of the loaf, sending crumbs scattering across the worn floorboards as she passed it to him.

I can't do this. He set his jaw, afraid to say the words aloud and make things even worse for Raela. *Wes did it, but he's the Envoy. It's not the same. What if she is sent to the Wrathlands? What if—*

"Alder," Kessara prompted, clearing her throat. She looked over at him, and to his surprise, there was a soft smile on her lips. "You need to try."

He took the bread, closing his eyes for a moment, trying to remember the prayer that Wes had used. It didn't come to him, but then again, it wasn't as though Wes had known what to say, either. Kessara was right. If the High One was who He said He was, they had to trust that He would be merciful, even if he got the details wrong.

"It's okay," Kessara said, casting a glance over at Raela. Her breathing was growing more labored, the breaths coming several seconds apart. "He kept her alive long enough to bring you here, didn't He? That must mean something. He hasn't abandoned us."

He nodded, taking a few small crumbs from the bread and kneeling beside Raela.

"High One," he started, shifting his weight against the floor. "Please forgive this woman for whatever evils she has done in her life. Please cleanse her and prepare her for the second life. Please allow her to come home to You."

For a few seconds, no one spoke. In the living room,

Kessara's fire crackled, and Alder could see light beginning to trickle in through the windows. His mother and sisters would arrive soon. "Amen," he added. Kessara said the same, and Raela murmured her assent.

He used a thumb to draw her jaw open, placing the crumbs on her tongue. The woman swallowed, and for a few seconds, they rested there in the silence, waiting. Alder prayed silently, begging the High One to accept his attempt at leading his old nurse home to the Eternal Lands. The very fact that she knew of Him was a miracle in itself, certainly she had never confessed to any forbidden faith before. He had to hope that what they had done had been enough.

Raela's breath slowed, and by the time Alder returned to a standing position, she was gone, drifting off to sleep, the hint of a smile resting on her lips.

Chapter 20

As Wes walked deeper into the tunnel, he grew more hopeful that he had chosen the right path. The ground began to gradually slope upward, getting steeper as he went higher. He figured that the passageway must belong to dwarf servants, as he doubted even the smallest dragon would be able to fit through it.

As he carried on, he tried to focus his mind on the High One, waiting for some guidance, some solution to the impossible problem that would lay ahead of him even if he did find the Guardian's quarters.

Will Celesyria's mother listen? Perhaps You can open her heart. He wondered whether he had the depth of faith or even the mental energy left to come up with a decent prayer, but he had to try. Whatever he was feeling, the High One already knew about it, anyway.

Surely a God capable of visiting Alder in his dreams and speaking to him has the power to hear even the weakest prayers of men. So, if You're listening, please help. Please help me to figure this out. Celesyria has given everything to help You be known throughout Kaveryth again.

As he trudged on, his lungs burning from the long uphill trek, he remembered something that Celesyria had told him, not long after they had met for the first time.

Dragons did not have souls. They were not like men, dwarves, or elves. They had been created to live in the Farplace—for what purpose, Wes did not know—until they had been summoned to Kaveryth in order to protect it from the elven forces of Nox.

How can she maintain such hope when her end is already decided?

Of course, there was no answer but the shuffling of his feet and the occasional skittering of some insect that lived here in the deep. Some part of him wanted to pray again, thinking that perhaps it would help him not to feel so alone, but the thought exhausted him. He tried instead to reach out to Celesyria in his mind, figuring that perhaps it would be more likely to work closer to the surface, but it was no use.

It would be dangerous to try and reach out to her mother without warning her ahead of time, especially considering that she had no idea that he could mindspeak at all. He had to stay hidden, at least for now.

What if she's not in her quarters at all? What if I'm caught as soon as I leave the tunnel? His thoughts tumbled together into a haze of worry and doubt. Moments later, a beat-up old door came into view at the edge of his lamplight.

He stopped there for several minutes, trying to get his

labored breathing to slow. Now that the moment of walking into the fire had come, all he wanted to do was to run back the way he came. He could find his way back to the surface. He could find food and make for Auranth, just as Celesyria had told him to do.

Then we could come back. A mixture of relief and guilt flooded his chest at the very thought of leaving the strange, subterranean world of the dragons. *If Alder was here, we could save her. We'd still be outnumbered, but I'd have a decent fighter beside me. And I've already been in here, so I could navigate at least part of the way. We couldn't risk bringing Kessara in here, but her knowledge of ancient languages would help us to research ahead of time. It could work.*

He let the thoughts hang in the air, waiting.

Here, alone in the dark, he found himself expecting an answer like he'd received so many times before. His connection with the High One was never like what Alder had. He didn't dream, see visions, or hear His voice.

But now, in the absence of His gentle light, he realized that the High One had been beside him all the way through. He'd come to rely on the little nudges, the hints that he was doing the right thing or about to make a horrible mistake. It had always been subtle, subtle enough that he'd miss it if he wasn't listening.

No matter how hard he tried to quiet his thoughts, they were all that he could hear. His own fears, hammering between his eardrums, unwilling to give him a moment's peace.

Maybe no one was listening this time.

After his lungs had stopped hurting and his heartbeats had returned to normal speed, it was time to move.

As he moved to the door and pulled at the handle, he realized that despite the emptiness he felt, he still had a choice. He could have chosen to run, but instead, he was stepping forward in faith. That had to count for something.

The door swung toward him without resistance, bathing the passage behind him in a soft blue-green light. He hung his torch on a wall peg that was hidden behind the path of the door.

As soon as he crossed the threshold, the sounds of an earthquake assaulted his ears. The rumbling sound came from every direction at once, disorienting him as he stepped forward. *Snoring.* A smile rose to his lips as he thought of how loud Celesyria usually was when she slept.

He was in some kind of main hallway, empty of furnishings other than the huge green and blue spheres of light that hung from the ceiling on black cords, far over his head. After a couple of minutes, he grew more used to the sound of the snoring, and found himself able to listen more closely to where each specific rumble was coming from.

All along the sides of the hall, he could see doorways leading off toward other rooms. *Celesyria's mother is probably through one of them.* He quickened his pace and walked over to the nearest door. It was not like the others he'd found before—this one was a simple swinging barricade made of a light material he did not recognize. With just a light touch of his hand, it swung inward, and he peered through the crack at the sleeping form that lay farther within. He spotted purple-toned scales.

Celesyria's mother is orange, like she is, he remembered, tiptoeing back and moving to the next doorway. This time, the sleeping dragon inside was pure white. As he moved along the side of the hall, he continued to glance over his shoulder, hoping that no dwarf would come bursting from the tunnel. The place felt deserted, and so far, none of the sleeping creatures noticed his intrusion.

Okay. He reached the final doorway and crossed to the row on the other side of the room. *I can do this. If she's here, I'll find her, and then I can—*

Before he could so much as finish his thought, he felt a hand clapping over his mouth from behind.

"Quiet," a voice hissed from below his ear. He squirmed, trying to get free, but the dwarf's grip was too strong.

No, not now, please, he pleaded to the High One as his captor dragged him toward a dragon-sized passage on the far side of the room from where he had first entered. *She's here. I know she is.*

He stopped struggling for several seconds, trying to keep his footing as the dwarf pulled him into the mouth of the other passageway. Once they had walked a little farther along, the dwarf spun him around so that they could see each other. Wes' heart was pounding so hard that he could hear it in his ears. It was over. They would imprison him, at best. Sneaking into the Guardians' chambers as they slept might even be a capital offense, though he doubted the Septemvirate would permit his execution.

"Have you lost your mind?" the dwarf snapped under his breath, his face revealing that he was as surprised as Wes felt. "Screaming would be a bad idea," he added. "If I let go, will you stay quiet?"

Wes's heart continued to hammer away, but he nodded, and the dwarf let his meaty hand fall away from his mouth. His captor looked to be of typical dwarf height, his body thick with muscle. He had a brown beard, and his matching brown eyes did not look angry.

"Ok," Wes said, his voice sounding strange in his own ears after so much silence. He glanced back toward the way they had come, but saw no one. The snoring was just as loud as before. "Who are you?"

"I'm Gramnok Beastbane, of course," the dwarf said, knitting his heavy eyebrows together as he crossed his arms against his chest, pulling at the strap of the heavy-looking leather bag that he wore. "And if you don't want to spend the rest of your life imprisoned at a convenient distance from the great spire, you'd better follow me."

* * *

Her father had been sent to Nox.

Celesyria tried to breathe, tried to stop the panic from overtaking her, but she could not. "No," she said, her voice rising until it was nearly loud enough to shake the walls. "Not Nox. You wouldn't. Such a thing has never been done. Our courts handle criminals here, you have no right—"

"Shut up!" the male elf screeched at her, his voice losing any semblance of its usual gentle elven timbre. He walked toward her, coming to a stop near her feet.

"No need to wake the rest of Whitespire," one of the dwarves put in from across the platform.

"Everyone," Dajin said, with the sort of tone one might use to corral unruly hatchlings. "Please be quiet."

Celesyria obliged, though she had to clamp down her jaw to stop herself from burning the nightmarish elf alive where he stood. It would be so easy. Even without fire, it would not be difficult to kill him. He was so close to her sharp claws, glancing up at her with a cruel smile twisting his already horrific visage. A stench seemed to emanate from his body, like rotting flesh mingled with fish.

"You're so clever, Celesyria," the elf said. Dajin did not interrupt him. "You figured out so much, all on your own. It's a pity that your loyalty to your so-called 'High One' was more important to you than your own family. Perhaps your father could have been spared."

Celesyria sucked in air. *What if he's right?* She thought to herself, trying to look anywhere but at the demented creature at her feet. No one else on the platform said anything or moved from their places. *Would it have been better for me to wait, to be patient, rather than marching up to Wes and setting the world on fire?*

Guilt pooled in her gut. From the very start, she'd been reckless. Now, even when Wes had cautioned her to be patient, she had continued in the same pattern. She could have tried to form a plan back in Windshear, but instead she'd raced into danger with scarcely a thought, so certain that the High One had to be on her side.

We need an army if we want to change the world, not a handful of dissidents. She, Wes, and Alder would already be outnumbered here in this room, without even considering the other elves, the Septemvirate, and whoever else may be conspiring against them. Their entire strategy had been naive right from the start.

"Where is my mother?" she asked finally, refusing to take the bait, at least, not out loud. Whether she'd been foolish or not, it was too late now. She could only keep going.

"Your mother is fine," the elf answered. "But I'm the one talking here. And unless you want one of the guards outside to pour oil on your wing and strike the flint, you need to be quiet."

A shiver ran through her body at the thought. She doubted the threat was idle. "In case you've forgotten," Dajin cut in. "I'm the one in charge here, Falloren. Get back to your place."

With a brisk nod to the black dragon, the elf strode off toward the far end of the platform, giving a quick bow to the obelisk as he passed it. Celesyria glanced up at the structure briefly before looking away. She couldn't bear to let her sight fall on it for more than a few seconds, but she was not sure why.

"Your curiosity is rather unique among our kind," Dajin continued, striding into the center of the space and looking at her directly. He was so large that it was hard to believe that they were part of the same species. "Perhaps if you'd been born an elf like the others here—" he gestured to Falloren and the other two elves, who had remained quiet—"it would have been seen as admirable."

He paused. Celesyria swallowed, not sure if she was expected to say anything, but Dajin continued.

"It's a pity that is not the case," he said, shaking his head briefly before going on. "Still, I see no harm in fulfilling that curiosity in the time that you have left."

Celesyria met his eyes, refusing to allow her gaze to falter. She was terrified, but she couldn't resist the longing for answers. All her life, she'd been told lies. The very foundation upon which her entire worldview had been set had turned out to be false. How many other truths had she been denied?

"A little history lesson, shall we?" Dajin said, looking at the others assembled in the room. No one objected, though Celesyria caught one of the dwarves rolling his eyes. "In the

258

beginning of Kaveryth, the first four kings were men, just as they are now. Silverfell was given to the King of Earth, Aridmoor to the King of Air…" He trailed off for a moment, cocking his head at Celesyria, who gave a nod indicating that she could figure out the rest.

Though their ancient names had been lost to history, the names of the Elf-Queens that they had married had continued to the present day. The mixed-race progeny of those ancient kings now made up the Houses of Cervos, Manta, and Ursa. *And the House of Noctua, until recently,* she amended herself.

"Right. Anyway, it did not take long for challenges to arise. Alliances were broken, food production was mismanaged, much of what could go wrong did. Man was suffering—"

"And the Elf-Queens found the perfect chance to take over the Four Kingdoms for themselves, going so far as to demand to be treated almost as gods by the people before turning their backs on them," Celesyria finished, shooting a quick glance at Falloren and the other elves. She was well aware of the accepted history of Kaveryth, that the Dracodei had created the continent and entrusted the Four Kingdoms to man from the beginning. Now, of course, she knew that at least part of that accepted belief was false, particularly in regard to who created the world itself. But would Dajin answer the questions that had always burned in the back of her mind, or would he add fresh lies atop the old ones?

"Do not speak of what you don't understand," one of the other elves snapped. Celesyria realized that it was a female by her voice, though she could not see her face from where she stood.

"It really is such a pity," Dajin said again, ignoring the outburst. "All of the inhabitants of Kaveryth are fed so many lies. I find it…unsavory. But I understand that it is necessary to preserve peace."

"So you're saying that the Elf-Queens did not come in those turbulent days?" Celesyria asked, trying to keep her tone as calm as Dajin's, though she was certain he could see the annoyance written across her face.

Dajin gave a grim smile. "No, they did come then. That part of your studies was accurate. But the Elf-Queens were not evil."

"Of course they were evil," Celesyria said with a snort. "They saw something broken, something they could control, and they came and took it for themselves. They could have lived in harmony with man, but instead, they chose to turn against them for the sake of power."

"How do you think that the Four Kingdoms began falling apart?" Falloren asked without expecting an answer, taking a few steps toward the center of the platform where the obelisk lay before Dajin could order him back. "It was the corruption and stupidity of men that lay waste to all Kaveryth. The Elf-Queens took pity on them, and agreed that an alliance by marriage was the best way to bring peace and stability back. The men were all too happy to take the elves as wives, their beauty alone sufficed to please them."

Celesyria took a couple of breaths, wanting to measure her words carefully. Much of what the elf said was nonsense.

While it was true that the Four Kingdoms had been in turmoil in those days, it was not solely the fault of men. She had no reason to doubt that all of the creatures of Kaveryth had played their role.

The dwarves had been given the land of Umrym before the dragons came, and they quickly plundered their mines to the very limit in search of wealth. They weakened the mountains so much that it later allowed for the destruction seen during the Battle of the Severed Summits, when dragon and dwarf grappled for control of Umrym.

The dragons had been greedy, seeking the same wealth and control of territory that the dwarves had. Though they had eventually forged an alliance that would go on to last for centuries, much harm was done in just a few years of war.

"Everyone was corrupt and stupid," she said finally, meeting the elf's face, unable to look directly at the remains of his eyes. "Not only men. Then as now, there were those of every race that put greed and power over doing what was right."

"The elf-women who married the first kings were superior in their intellect, and they knew that there was a way to create a world where people were equal and material wealth was bountiful," Falloren said, pausing to spit at the ground. Celesyria said nothing.

The rest of the assembly was listening, too, each of them with the exception of Dajin poised as though ready to tackle the elf to the ground If he dared to tell her too much. Celesyria dared a glance in his direction. He looked calm, probably secure in the knowledge that even Falloren would obey his word if he gave an order.

"There was so much good that they wanted to do for the people, but the men kept getting in the way, especially the kings, but even the Septemvirate. They couldn't allow their grip on the Four Kingdoms to be weakened, not even for the sake of their own people," Falloren continued. Despite the erosion of his features, Celesyria could see a look of genuine distress on his face.

Could some of this be true? Perhaps it's not so black and white.

261

I've been lied to about the nature of the world so many times that it's hard to know what to think.

"They could have made the Four Kingdoms better. They could have made Umrym better," he paused, giving a quick glance toward the nearest dwarf and the nearest dragon. "But they didn't get the chance. Corruption and greed were entwined in every institution. When the first kings died, things grew even worse. The race of men grew too numerous to feed."

Too numerous to feed. As though they're farm animals that must be culled when the grain prices go up.

"They wanted to fix things. Even as Kaveryth fell apart, they continued to serve as queens of the Four Kingdoms. They bore heirs with different men as the years passed, taking on the duty of women with courage. The sons and daughters of the noble Houses grew as numerous as the stars."

But they never married these men. They did not pass on the rule of the Four Kingdoms to their children. They only wanted to grow the power and size of their Houses with the help of man-blood because pureblooded elves breed too slowly.

It was strange to think about the fact that Wes and Kessara had elf-blood in their veins. She had always known it to be true, but now, looking at an elf face to face, especially without the shield of his glamor, the thought made her sick.

"I thought that men were already growing too numerous to feed," Celesyria said, unable to resist getting at least a small point across to all who were present. "Or was it just the peasants that didn't deserve to live?"

"You must see it from the point of view of those who sought the greater good of all of the people," Falloren said, waving a hand as though those lives were of no real consequence.

"Resources are finite. Every choice has a cost, sometimes a painful cost. And sometimes the innocent among us must be the ones to pay it."

He paused for a moment, and she noticed the look of distress set against his twisted features once again. No one spoke, and she caught a glance passing between one of the dwarves and the white dragon that stood nearest to her. *What else have they been willing to do to keep the population down?*

A shiver rippled through her back and down her tail.

"But men are blind," the elf continued, sneering up at her. "They live only decades, not centuries. They make choices for the short term, never realizing the implications of their decisions. The dwarves have developed a broader sight, living side by side with dragons. But men have not. Even when the Elf-Queens lived side by side with them, tried to teach them how to see beyond their own noses... they would not listen."

Celesyria swallowed, glancing around the room again, feeling disoriented. She'd forgotten the time of day, but hunger pangs filled her stomach. Not that it mattered now.

"They allowed the men to persist in their foolish religion, sending their Envoy to carry bread to the great spire every season, hoping that in time they would abandon their superstitions of their own accord. Of course, many would not. Even some of the elves participated in such nonsense."

Celesyria suppressed a smile. Even Falloren had acknowledged the High One. Despite everything, she and Wes had been right. However the worship of the Dracodei fit in, the true God of Kaveryth existed, and He had been worshiped from the very beginning.

He had just been forgotten.

"So, the Elf-Queens began to exile those who wished to

destroy the future of the Four Kingdoms. Not only men, but other elves, as well. The blindness had spread far enough," Falloren continued. "But the Elf-Queens had become too weak. They were driven out eventually, exiled to what became Nox."

He paused for a moment, another joyless smile spreading across his hollow face. "Such a shame. Even with the power of the dragons on their side, it was not enough to maintain elven control of Kaveryth."

Chapter 21

They sat there for a long while, keeping vigil. Kessara found a clean white sheet in a basket nearby, and laid it gently over Raela's body. She and Alder sat side by side against the wall, unsure what to do with themselves, their silence shrouding the room like mist. After what felt like a very long while, Alder cleared his throat.

She looked over at him, but let her gaze fall just as fast as she noticed the gleam of tears in his green eyes. In the periphery of her vision she could see him swiping the evidence of his sadness from his face. *It's okay to cry once in a while,* she wanted to tell him. *Even for a man as strong as you.*

She waited for him to speak, watching as the pink light of dawn filtered in through Raela's simple white curtains. Kessara thought that the little house was beautiful, from the flower-filled glass bottles that lay on the windowsill to the worn but well-swept floorboards. She wondered if perhaps one of Alder's sisters had come by to tidy up once Raela became too sickly to take care of her home herself. By what she knew of them, it seemed likely.

"Kessara," Alder said, looking down at his hands resting in his lap as he twisted them together and pulled them apart.

"Yes?" she prompted after a full minute had passed.

Finally, he met her eyes. The tears had dried, but there was a pain behind them that seemed to pour out from somewhere deep within his soul. "You need to convince Wes to marry you. You need to make him understand that he doesn't have any other choice. It's the only way that we'll be able to protect the Four Kingdoms."

She didn't say anything for a long time, forcing herself to breathe in and out. She'd told herself the same thing every day. For that matter, she was certain Alder had said the same words before.

But this time, it was different.

There was a finality to his command, and she could tell by the set of his jaw that there would be no changing his mind. Until that very moment, she'd thought that she'd already made up her own.

She thought that she was strong enough to marry a good man like Wes, even if she couldn't love him as a wife normally would.

She thought that all of her years spent learning how to be a princess would come together in the end, helping her to do what was right.

She thought that the deeper joy of serving her people would win out over the personal happiness of true love and little red-headed children.

But here, now, sitting next to this warrior of the plains, she knew that she'd been lying to herself.

Despite all of the reasons that she shouldn't, she was falling in love with Alder Cadogen. Even though she had not known him long, she'd never felt so strongly about anyone since Roven had been stolen from her.

I thought that my ability to love at all had died with him, she wanted to say. *But then I met you. And you taught my heart how to beat for another person again. I'm not even sure you did it on purpose. It's just who you are.*

She didn't say those words. She couldn't. They hinted at a promise that she would have to break, a vow that he wouldn't accept in the first place.

"I know," she said instead, forcing her eyes to meet his. The air in the room felt heavy and light at the same time, like some unseen force was rippling between them, drawing them together.

She thought of paper, lamp oil, flint striking steel. Fire devouring oxygen.

He was too close, and not being able to hold him almost hurt.

"He will marry me," she said, letting her eyes drift away, the intensity of his gaze burning through to her bones. "He'll do the right thing. *I'll* do the right thing."

Alder just nodded, twisting his hands together once again, his knuckles white.

"But just for a moment," she started, swallowing the tears that threatened to fall. "Just for a moment, can we pretend that the world is not so cruel?"

Her body wanted nothing more than to kiss him. Her heart ached to be near him, to consume him, to burn together into ash.

He took her hand in his, allowing her head to rest on his shoulder. She savored the warmth of his skin and the mingling of the air they both breathed.

"I don't have to pretend, my Princess," Alder said after several minutes had passed in heart-pounding silence. "I do love you. The love of a friend is not an inferior love."

"'To love is to will the good of the other'," Kessara choked out, the tears finally breaking free as she pressed her eyes closed and gripped his hand like she would never let go. "My parents taught me that. I know they're right."

But my God, my Lord... O High One, please give me strength. This kind of love hurts so much.

Minutes passed as the sun rose higher outside the bedroom's window. Kessara listened to the chirping of early birds, inhaling the scent of fresh grass as a breeze made the curtains flutter. She didn't let go of Alder's hand until they heard a knock at the door.

He let go first, and as soon as he did, she felt like she'd been hollowed out from within.

He won't hold me again. She laid back against the wall as he went to go and answer the door, the distance between them feeling suddenly vast. *Even friendship will be a risk for us, knowing we feel as we do. He will be careful now.*

She couldn't bring herself to think of the word he used to describe how he felt about her.

"Did you make it alright? Did you arouse any suspicion?" Alder asked from the main room, and Kessara got to her feet, casting a glance at Raela's body on the bed.

"No one saw us," one of the women said. "Only the guard at the gate. He was a brother of one of Marya's friends, so he

268

didn't ask us anything."

Kessara stepped into the room. The young woman who had been speaking, Violet, looked up at her, a flicker of surprise crossing her features before she dropped to her knees, followed by her mother and sister.

"M—my Princess," Alder's mother stammered, bending her face toward the floor as she knelt before her. "Forgive us. We did not expect you, of course."

"Please, stand," Kessara said, forcing a friendly smile despite her sorrow. Even here in Aridmoor, some of the common people knew her face. It had been easy to briefly forget her status as a member of the royal family when she'd spent the last couple of days sneaking around like a criminal.

The women got to their feet, patting their hair back with their hands and straightening the hems of their dresses.

"As you wish, Princess Kessara," the girl she assumed must be Violet said, shooting her sister an almost giddy glance.

"Raela is gone," Alder said with a bit of an edge to his voice, as though he wanted to get them back on track before they flew off into some other conversation about life in Windshear's palace.

The mood in the little cob house fell somber as Alder's mother headed for Raela's bedroom, her daughters following close behind. Kessara and Alder looked at each other as they waited for the women to say their goodbyes. She wanted to talk to him, to say anything at all, however insignificant, but she could not make herself speak.

When Alder's family returned to the living room, their faces were red and puffy with tears. They guided Kessara and Alder into two of the chairs that sat near the struggling fire, and Violet moved to the kitchen and asked if they wanted tea.

Kessara didn't think that she wanted to eat or drink any-thing, but she accepted when her stomach gave a loud protest.

"You need to eat," Alder muttered, leaving her alone in the living area and following his family into the tiny kitchen. "I'll find you something. I'm hungry myself."

Fighting off assailants and staying up all night takes a lot of energy. She sat alone, listening to the sound of clinking glass dishes and companionable words passing between family members. *Killing must be even more exhausting.*

When Alder held her hand, she'd managed to forget what had almost happened to her. In that moment of mingled grief and joy, she'd been able to push the whole night away, deep down where it didn't bother her. Now that she was alone, the feeling of terror came flooding back with surprising force.

A sob caught in her throat, and she pressed her eyes shut, forcing the tears to stay where they were. *You're okay,* she told herself, glancing up at the door that led to the kitchen and to Alder. *No one can get to you here.*

Her skin prickled beneath the sleeves of her dress as she thought of what they'd said to her. They had not feared retribution. They had known that law and order was falling apart, and they wished to exploit the current state of High Keep to fulfill their own sick desires.

She tried to focus on that element of the crime rather than on what had almost been done to her. It was easier to think about how she might help her people rather than about how she hadn't been able to save herself.

We need to make things better, for the sake of the common people who will face the gravest consequences for the bad decisions of those who rule over them. She tried to get her breathing back under control and into a steady rhythm, with limited success.

The kitchen door flew open as Alder kicked it with his foot, carrying a tray of tea in his arms. She jumped in her seat at the sound, and his eyes met hers. "Are you alright?"

"Yes. Fine," she said, getting to her feet and waiting as Alder set the tea and bread down on a round table with a floral-print cloth covering it.

Before the rest of the women had fully made it to their seats, Kessara had begun to cut the bread into messy slices. She took three for herself, and poured several spoonfuls of sugar into a mug of the dark tea before returning to her seat. She only just managed to wait for the others to get their own food before swallowing the first slice of bread in about three bites. She was even hungrier than she thought.

"To Raela," Alder's mother said, lifting her tea mug high. They all repeated the gesture. Silence fell for a couple of minutes as everyone ate, with Alder getting up at intervals to peer out of the window. So far, they remained completely alone.

"So," the older-looking sister, Marya, said. "She's gone. We need to send word to the temple, to get her body blessed and buried properly."

Alder let out a long breath. "There's no time, Marya. You are in danger, and the longer we stay here, the greater that danger will become."

"We can't just leave her body!"

"We have to. Someone else will take care of it," he put his head in his hands, plunging his fingertips into his thick red hair. "Does anyone else visit her as frequently as I assume you do, Violet?"

Violet shook her head. "No. I've been bringing her water every morning, but most afternoons when I have time to come back I do run into Mrs. Lobelia."

"So she'd notice if you didn't come?"

Violet nodded.

"It's settled," Alder said, glancing over at his mom. Kessara suppressed a smile. Even such a stubborn, bossy man sought the approval of his mother. "We have to leave this morning."

"Where exactly do we go?" Marya asked, crossing her arms across her chest and glaring at her brother. "I told Kristoff to meet us here, we need to wait for him."

Her husband, perhaps? Kessara noticed that she was not wearing the customary silver ring on her left hand that denoted marriage in Galeharbor. Perhaps Aridmoor had a different custom.

"Marya, we don't have time. We're in even more danger if he knows I'm here."

"He doesn't," their mother cut in. "She didn't give him any details. She just asked him to trust her, and he agreed. He will be here. He had to go to his father and leave him a note, saying goodbye."

Kessara noticed that Marya had tears in her eyes. *There must be so much that they have to leave behind. All because of us. All because of the choices that we've made.*

"Fine," Alder said with a brisk nod, casting another glance out the window. It was already late.

"If there's anything of Raela's that we can use, we should take it," he added.

His family got up from their chairs, tossing the remaining pieces of bread into a cloth bag to eat later. As they busied themselves in the kitchen, gathering supplies, Alder moved closer to Kessara.

"I don't have a plan," he said finally, giving her a half smile.

"But I don't want to scare my family any worse. Do you know of anywhere in Galeharbor that we could take them? Somewhere quiet, where King Ursa would never think to send his spies?"

For a second, she hoped that he would touch her hand again while his mother and sister were out of the room. Perhaps even kiss her. But he didn't.

Kessara didn't have to think long for the answer to come to her lips, but she was not eager to say it.

"They can go to Graveheim," she whispered finally, glancing up at the door to the kitchen. "To the city of the dead."

Chapter 22

The tunnels of Whitespire were so numerous that Wes found it difficult to keep his bearings. Every time that he was certain they were going north, or heading east, Gramnok would dash around a corner and he'd be disoriented again. The tunnels that the dwarf used were much narrower, not big enough to fit dragons, and it seemed they could be used to access the entire city. Fortunately, they were tall enough to fit Wes, though he was relieved that his recent weight loss had given him a bit more space between his body and the suffocating stone walls.

Though Gramnok led him on quickly, he was willing to talk. Already Wes had come to learn a great deal during their short hike, much of it too painful to dwell on until he had some time to think.

"They tortured you?" Wes asked, thinking back to how

betrayed Celesyria had felt back in Silverfell, when King Ursa had told her and the entire crowd that Gramnok had reported her as a liar and a blasphemer.

She will be so relieved to know that it wasn't so simple.

Wes tried once again to reach out to her mind with his own to no avail.

"They did," Gramnok said, slowing for a moment as he looked between two tunnels and selected the one on the left. "But I should have held fast. I told them what she knew of the High One, and I don't know if He will forgive me for that. If He's real, anyway."

Wes wasn't sure how to respond, and in any case, his own chest was heaving as he tried to keep pace with the surprisingly nimble dwarf. With his legs shorter than Wes' own, he had to run to stay ahead of him, but his voice never betrayed a hint of tiredness.

"At least I survived," Gramnok continued as he made his way down a steep incline. Wes followed, moving much slower as he tried not to trip. "But they haven't left me alone since. They're always watching, and I don't know if I can even trust my friends not to turn me in if I let the wrong word slip. So I've stayed quiet."

"Until now, presumably," Wes managed between heaving breaths as they finally reached the bottom of the long, sloping passage. The walls were even tighter here, and he could feel the damp stone brushing his shoulders every so often, sending a chill through his neck. He didn't want to dwell on the topic of torture. He could sense the dwarf's guilt, though he was sure that he would have caved to the pressure even earlier.

"Until now," Gramnok echoed with a nod of his head. He slowed to a stop as they reached another fork, looking back and forth for a second before leading them into the leftward passage. Wes knew that they were heading deeper into the ground, but he could not keep himself from a foolish hope that one such turn would bring them to the surface. He longed for fresh air and room to breathe it. He couldn't imagine living in such a place. "An old dragon friend of mine, Nazzan, was part of a detail that captured Celesyria somewhere overground. He wouldn't give me much more than that, but he hinted as to where he had taken her before he had been dismissed."

Wes was overcome with relief. *Thanks be to the High One. At least we know where she is.* He wondered how Gramnok had found him, but there were more important questions to consider.

"This room contained a magical object I had heard of before, though before now I questioned if it existed," he added, a flash of anger crossing his features.

"Do you have any idea how we're going to get her out?" Wes asked the dwarf, trying to push aside his curiosity about the other cryptic details for the time being.

Gramnok's steps faltered for a moment as he stopped to look at him. For a second he didn't say anything, his eyes flicking between Wes and the tunnel that lay ahead.

"What?" Wes asked, fresh worry settling in his stomach like a stone.

"There's another passage coming up in a few paces. It leads into an old silver mine. Nobody comes here any more, but it will bring us directly beneath the room where Celesyria is, assuming they haven't moved her."

"How close are we now?" Wes asked, swallowing back dread.

"Close enough," Gramnok said, his eyes finally meeting Wes'

own.

Wes tried to reach out to her in his mind for several minutes. Gramnok leaned against the damp wall, using the tip of his boot to roll a tiny stone back and forth across the ground. Without the sound of their footsteps, Wes could hear the gentle tinkling of water droplets somewhere deeper in the cave.

Gramnok looked up at him, and he shook his head in defeat. He could not hear Celesyria.

"Are you sure she's here?"

"Yes," Gramnok said, not bothering to finish his thought before getting up and continuing down the passage. Wes hurried to keep up. "And no. My friend was scared of telling me too much, and I don't blame him, but he did say that there were many others present, dragons, dwarves, and elves. There was going to be a meeting, perhaps even a trial. It seems unlikely that they'd haul her all the way down here only to take her to one of the prison areas immediately."

Wes didn't want to ask the next question. Gramnok answered it before he could.

"Look, Wes. If she's alive, my plan will give her at least a chance to escape. If she's dead, it won't matter anyway."

Wes wished he could close his ears, wished that he could stop the terrible word from getting into his head.

Death.

Every mention of it interrupted him, pulling him out of wherever he was in time and space, reminding him of everyone he'd lost. The faces of his family members would flash by, followed by those of his companions. Now, the face of Zanek—the man he'd killed—loomed largest of all.

"What's the plan?" Wes forced himself to ask, pushing aside

the faces, the memories, the loss. Celesyria wasn't dead. She couldn't be. And unless and until he had proof that she was, he was going to do everything in his power to set her free, just as she'd done for him when she taught him about the High One.

"It's not going to be a tidy operation," Gramnok said, glancing down at his leather bag as he slowed to a stop. There was a door cut into the sidewall of the passage, braced with crude wooden beams. The entrance looked only barely big enough for a dwarf to pass through. "As soon as I found out where Celesyria was held, I knew what I had to do. I had gone to the Guardians' quarters to warn Sharsi—Celesyria's mother—to head overground, but she wasn't there."

Is he about to put the entire population of Whitespire in danger in his attempt to save Celesyria? Wes eyed the stuffed bag the dwarf carried with renewed suspicion.

He did not get a chance to ask anything else.

"Stay here and keep watch," Gramnok ordered, heading into the small tunnel. "If I don't come back after, go back the way we came and look for Celesyria. She will most likely exit into the Guardian's quarters."

"After what?" Wes asked, ducking his head into the tunnel, holding his lamp ahead of him as Gramnok's own circle of light moved ahead at a rapid pace.

Gramnok paused for a moment, looking over his shoulder at Wes, his expression a mix of terror and wild excitement. From all that Celesyria had told Wes of her best friend, this was not the reaction to her capture that he'd been expecting.

"You'll know when it's done. Trust me. And no matter what happens, tell Celesyria that I need my little sister to understand that I had my reasons for what I have done.

278

Reasons that go even deeper than my love for her."

What reasons, aside from the obvious? How am I going to find my way back? How am I going to meet up with Celesyria?

Again there was no time to ask.

Gramnok gave Wes a pointed look. Without another word, he tore off at a run down the tunnel, heading deeper into the blackest shadows of the earth.

Perhaps there are some secrets best discussed in the light.

Wes continued on, shivering as his lamplight flickered against the walls.

* * *

Celesyria stared at the elf in front of her, her jaw hanging open.

No. It's not possible. He's lying, my race could never side with his. They wouldn't!

Falloren was saying something else, but she didn't hear it over the rushing of blood in her ears.

"What do you mean, 'with the power of the dragons on their side'?" she blurted out, anger cresting in her chest. She struggled to focus on his response over the pounding of her racing heart.

The elves are the sworn enemies of the dragons. Even though the Dracodei are usurpers, my parents and many others have been willing to risk their lives to protect the peoples of Kaveryth. For that matter, we are bound by our oath to do so. This is impossible.

"It's as I said," Falloren answered, giving Dajin a brief glance as though expecting a reprimand for telling her too much. "When the dragons were summoned from the Farplace—"

Before he could finish his sentence, a great booming

sound tore through the room. Celesyria closed her eyes and stumbled to the ground as another explosion sounded, this one strong enough to shake the floor beneath her. She felt pain searing through her ankle as most of her weight landed on it, twisting it sideways against the thick metal of the manacle.

She tried to lift her head, to get her bearings, but she couldn't see.

The room filled with clouds of black smoke, stinging at her eyes. She pressed her nose as low as it would go, managing to find a thin layer of breathable air that rested across the floor.

She tried to cry out, but she couldn't stop coughing, unable to keep the dust from getting into her lungs, but at least it didn't burn as bad as the smoke did. Just as the ringing in her ears began to go quiet, there was a third explosion, louder than the first two.

She heard the sound of splintering wood, the woosh of objects falling through the air, the sounds of destruction joining with cries of fear. She couldn't decide if she felt sorry for the others or not, and there was no time to dwell on it.

She had to get out.

She got to her feet, closing her eyes against the smoke, only opening them every few steps so that she could keep her bearings. She could scarcely see through the stinging tears.

The dust had settled somewhat, and between the narrowed slits of her eyelids she could see the black obelisk in the middle of the platform, abandoned. Despite the haze that surrounded it, and despite her own smoke-muddled eyes, she could see every glimmer on its surface, rippling like a thick black ooze of watery blood with streaks of silver.

Her ankle screamed as she tried to put weight on it, so she

held it aloft, wishing it had been one of her front feet. She shuffled forward, the ringing in her ears transforming into a dull hum.

She couldn't see anyone else on the platform. As the dust continued to settle, she could see that many of the wooden catwalks were still intact. She could hear shouts from the far side of the room as her hearing returned, coming from deeper within the tunnels. She found herself relieved. It sounded like most of them had gotten out.

Huge chunks of stone fell from the ceiling of the room, hammering down on the platform mere feet from where she stood and shattering into innumerable pieces. Every few seconds, she heard sounds of clattering and smashing coming from far below.

I have to get out. There's no time to sit here and worry about the pain, she told herself, forcing her ankle to accept the weight of her body. Either the platform would collapse and she would fall to her death, or it wouldn't and her captors would return with chains eventually. She had been given a single chance to escape, against all odds. She had to move fast.

After several moments of blinding pain, she reached the edge of the platform, where one of the large wooden catwalks was still intact. She wanted so badly to fly over the gap instead of putting her weight on the damaged wood, but if Jaconial was correct, she wouldn't be able to do so with the obelisk in such close proximity.

O High One, I need you to help this bridge to carry me, she prayed as she took a step forward. As soon as half of her body was on the catwalk, she began to hear the sound of splintering wood. Far behind her, somewhere in the tunnel on the opposite side of the cavern, she could hear the thundering sound of fallen rocks.

Whatever had caused the explosion, it had been strong enough to cause major structural damage. Whitespire was not built like a city one would find overground. It was all interconnected, hundreds of small tunnels that could impact the larger whole. If even a few of them collapsed, it could be enough to cause catastrophic damage.

She thought of her mother, who was most likely sleeping in the Guardians' quarters.

Please, please let the innocent dragons and dwarves of Whitespire get to the surface, she added to her prayer as she looked down at the catwalk. As much as she wanted to escape, she could not bear the thought that hundreds of citizens might die in order that she might be free.

She refused to look down as she rushed forward, putting all of her weight on the cracking wood, ignoring the agonizing pain as she ran on her injured ankle. Within a few strides she was across, just as the center of the catwalk began to buckle, pieces of wood sliding into the abyss below.

She didn't wait to see it fall, but she hoped that the platform and the disturbing black obelisk would go down with it.

She tried to reach out to Wes and to her mother as she stumbled through the passage, thankful that there had not been too many twists and turns on the way in. It was dark, but at least she knew that the passage moved upward in a relatively direct fashion.

Her injured ankle slowed her progress, but fortunately, the walls of this particular tunnel seemed relatively intact, at least for the moment. She finally had a few seconds to breathe.

Far behind her, however, she could still hear the crashes of falling stones. Nowhere in Whitespire would be safe for long if the chain reaction continued.

No one answered her as she reached the wooden door she'd remembered on the way in. It was laying flat against the floor, no doubt torn off of its hinges and trampled by a dragon on their way out.

She pushed her way through into the tunnel, forcing herself to breathe in and out as the walls seemed to close in around her body. It was so dark here that she could not see an inch in front of her eyes, and she feared using her fire to light the way, lest it burn up too much of the excess oxygen.

If there is a collapse anywhere near this tunnel now, I'll suffocate to death anyway.

For the first time in her life she felt truly claustrophobic. She put weight on her bad ankle, not wanting to slow herself down, trying to think of the constellations that dotted the night sky, far above. She would see them again. She just had to keep moving.

As she headed upward, the air began to smell better as it rushed into her nostrils. She had to be close now. Somewhere up ahead, she thought that she could see the telltale blue-green glow of orblight.

Her ankle hurt every time she slowed, but as long as she was moving the pain seemed to go numb. She shuddered to think about the long-term damage she could be causing, but there was no other choice. The sound of collapsing stone echoed up from behind her, somewhere far below.

When she reached the opening that led back into the Guardian's quarters, the light was enough to make her squint. When she was able to see again, she realized that she had nearly trampled Gramnok and Wes, who were standing just outside the entrance.

"Oh thank the High One you're alive," Wes said, rushing up to press a hand gently against her side and laying his head against her orange scales. "I wasn't sure you'd make it."

"Told you," Gramnok said from a few feet away, looking up at her as though scared to get close. He was covered from head to toe in gray dust, while Wes looked slightly cleaner. Neither of the men were severely injured, though Celesyria could see sections of dried blood peeking out along Gramnok's hairline.

Even though you betrayed me, I'm glad you're alive. How he came to be here standing beside Wes, she had no clue, but there wasn't exactly time to discuss it now.

"It's not over yet. We need to get overground," Wes said, heading for the large tunnel that led past the sleeping rooms.

As if to punctuate the point, a great crashing sound came from directly beneath their feet. All three looked at each other before breaking into a run, Celesyria staggering on her injured foot, her claws clattering on the hard stone floor.

"I need to go to my quarters," Gramnok announced as they reached the far end of the main sleeping hall.

"No. You'll be killed," Celesyria snapped before he could get the entirety of the last word out. "There isn't anything so important that—"

"I went to Helmm, little sister," Gramnok said. "Just as you used to do. Just as I should have done when you were still here. Anyway, when I was there, I found a portion of the Codex Veritatis that you have not seen. It explains so many things, and I risked my reputation to find it."

"You stole it?" Wes asked.

"For safekeeping," Gramnok said, his voice a low growl. "And it was a good thing I did, considering the fire. It talks about you, Wes. About the Envoy. About the true role he

284

serves, and about what the High One asks him to do."

Wes looked up at Celesyria. "We can't leave it behind. It could change everything. We could help Kaveryth, just as we've set out to do from the beginning."

All three of them knew what he was not saying out loud. If Whitespire continued to collapse, it was possible that any remaining copies of the Codex would be buried forever. All of the risks they'd taken to come here would be for nothing.

Celesyria said nothing, glancing behind her as the floor rumbled again. *How could I have missed a portion in Helmm?* She'd spent many hours poring over the documents in the Great Library, but it was a lot more difficult for her to study the human-sized books, scrolls, and loose papers than it was for Gramnok to do so.

In any case, it was too late to worry about it now. The library was gone, and her home city was falling to pieces. They had to get any information that they could.

"I'm coming with you," Celesyria said finally, watching as four dragons and a dozen or so dwarves ran past them, paying them no attention as they raced to the surface. She called out for her mother with her mind, but there was no answer.

Please let this mean that she's on the surface already, she begged the High One, looking up at the orb-lights hanging above.

"No, you're not," Gramnok said, planting his legs firmly against the stone. "I've betrayed you once already, and I'm not going to allow you to be hurt anymore. I'm sorry for everything. So much of this is my fault—"

"You're already hurt, Celesyria," Wes cut his words short, gesturing toward her ankle. She glanced down, noticing the ring of blood that lay behind the black metal of the manacle. The scales had been mangled even more as she moved. "I'll go with him. You need to get off of that leg."

"It'll be easier for me to get there. You need to get to the surface and fly away from here until we can come up with a plan," Gramnok said.

"How will I find you afterward?" Celesyria objected. "I still want an explanation for why you sold me out to the Septemvirate. And besides, you're injured yourself!"

"I will tell you everything, because I'll be fine," Gramnok said firmly. "It's just a scratch. One of my explosives went off too early and a rock hit me. Apparently, my skull is harder than stone."

"You did this?" she asked, incredulous, taking a couple of steps toward him as she heard another rumble from the depths below. His joke was not the least bit amusing. Upon closer inspection, Gramnok's wound looked even worse than she'd originally thought. It was shocking that he was still on his feet at all. "You blew up Whitespire and put hundreds of dwarves and dragons at risk?"

"Apparently," Wes cut in, raising a hand as though he wanted to hold her back from lunging for the dwarf. "But he had his reasons."

"What could possibly justify—"

"I will explain everything," Gramnok said quietly, his face pale. "I promise, Celesyria."

Without saying anything else, her two dearest friends in the world headed off toward Gramnok's quarters, the hammering of fallen rocks obscuring the sounds of their footsteps.

Celesyria could not find it within herself to pray as she headed for the surface.

Chapter 23

The sound of falling rocks grew quieter as Wes and Gramnok raced through the tunnels of Whitespire, but it was of little consolation. Much of the damage seemed to be concentrated farther below, where the mines were dug and the treasures of the Feast of Offering were stored, but eventually, Wes was sure that the whole city would be lost.

He had so many questions for Gramnok, so many things to discuss, but he could not voice them. Not now. His chest ached as they ran, and Wes saw Gramnok putting a hand to his head every few moments to contain the bleeding.

"We need to get you something to use as a bandage," Wes called as the dwarf raced ahead.

"Let's get to my rooms," Gramnok replied, not slowing his pace.

The caves were much darker here than in the Guardians'

quarters, lit with candles rather than orb lights. Many of the ceilings were reinforced with the same sort of old wood that he saw in the old miner's passage where he and Gramnok had parted earlier, and Wes feared that the area would soon collapse despite its relative nearness to the surface.

As they reached one of the narrower passages, a group of dwarves rushed by, nearly knocking Wes off of his feet. They turned back, slowing as they stared at him. A couple of them even pointed their fingers until Gramnok gave them some gesture that Wes did not recognize.

"Ignore the gossip," Gramnok said, coming to a stop near one of the small doors. "We have no time to worry about it now. Frankly, neither do they, but I suppose that's not stopping them."

Gramnok reached into his pocket, producing a key and inserting it into a small padlock. As the door swung open and Wes ducked his head to enter, another group of dwarves, mostly women, came racing up the passage.

"You should have been out of here as soon as the collapse started," Gramnok muttered at their backs, gesturing to Wes to close the door. Wes glanced around the small but comfortable room as Gramnok moved to open another padlock that secured a trunk at the foot of his short bed frame. It was sparsely furnished, with no decoration to speak of unless one counted the various mining tools set up neatly along one wall. It was the bedroom of a man who dedicated most of his life to his profession.

"Help me for a second," Gramnok said, his head deep in the trunk as he threw various pieces of clothing onto the floor. *All of this will be gone.* Another thundering sound in the distance made the ground shake slightly beneath their feet. *Thousands of lives, cut off from their home, from everything they've ever known. And after what Gramnok has done, he would have never been able to come back here anyway. He's a criminal now, just like us.*

Wes knelt beside the dwarf.

"It's here, underneath the false bottom. I can't get it loose," he said, grunting with a final effort before accepting Wes's aid.

The two men took hold of the trunk and lifted it, tipping it upside down and pounding on the bottom until the piece of wood broke free. A parcel of parchment bound with twine tumbled onto the floor, several of the pages becoming bent in the process.

"Forgive us, High One," Wes said, cringing at the damage as they set the trunk aside. Gramnok reached for a leather case that sat on the bed.

"You take it," he said, taking the pieces of parchment and thrusting them into Wes' hands. "Hide it, under your clothes."

"Why? It's going to be damaged."

Gramnok gestured to the sturdy leather case in his hands, opening the top flap to reveal several sheafs of old-looking paper covered in scribbled dwarvish and bound with twine. *A decoy,* Wes realized.

"If something happens on our way out of here, you are the one who must live. Your role as Envoy makes you more important than I am, especially knowing what I know now."

The desire to read the rather substantial Codex fragments in his hands was overwhelming, but he did as Gramnok asked, placing the bundle of parchment beneath his vest as carefully as he could. He breathed a sigh of relief after he'd adjusted his pants and tunic without ripping anything.

Gramnok held up the leather case again. "Now, I will guard this worthless case with my life."

Without so much as a final glance at his home, Gramnok made for the door. Wes scurried after him, forcing his hands to rest naturally at his side rather than against the hidden Codex.

As soon as they opened the door, it was time to test their plan.

Elder Dorold, head of the Septemvirate, stood in the hall.

* * *

The crash of thunder and the heavy pattering of rain met Celesyria as she reached the entrance of Whitespire. She leaped into the sky, putting weight on her shattered ankle for a final time before her strong wings beat the air, pulling her aloft.

Great sobs broke from her throat as she rose higher and higher, followed by a cry of rage and pain. She saw several dragons and dwarves she recognized rushing to the surface as she had, but none she knew personally. None that were her mother.

They had stared at her as she stumbled past, but none wasted any time yelling at her for her crimes of blasphemy and treason. It seemed that defending the honor of the Dracodei was not worth it to them, not if it meant risking their own flesh.

Somehow, despite the fact that the Dracodei were nothing but imposters, that fact bothered her. She had been willing to risk everything to tell them the truth about the false gods that ruled over them, but they couldn't even be bothered to shout at her in their defense when their own safety was in question.

She shook her head, trying to call out to her mother again now that she was on the surface, but there was no answer. The feeling of the rain was a relief against her sore body, but the thunder only obscured her ability to hear what was going on below.

Every time that lightning struck, she cringed, worried that she was about to be hit and jolted out of the sky. Flying in a thunderstorm was incredibly dangerous, but seeing as she could not walk on her ankle, she could see no other option but to pray and to be careful as she flew.

She circled overhead, trying to watch for her friends or for her mother, but she could see nothing but hundreds of dwarves, dragons, and a few elves milling about on the ground.

So far, none of the other dragons had taken to the skies, but they would as soon as the storm ceased. And if those from the strange council were among them, they would come after her. She doubted they'd attempt to capture her with their prison below destroyed. She imagined she would be executed on the spot. Unlike Wes, they were not compelled to take her alive.

She considered reaching out to Jaconial in her mind, wanting to know if she had lived. She did not like her, to be sure, but she did not deserve to die. Few residents of Whitespire did. They'd been raised in a culture built on lies, and she knew better than most how difficult it was to seek the truth for oneself.

So why did Gramnok do this? She took a final lap near the entrance, squinting through the rain in hope of spotting Wes towering over the sea of displaced dwarves. *Why destroy everything for the sake of punishing a few? How could he be so reckless?*

As soon as the thought came, she realized that she was asking herself the very same question. She was not innocent in this. She, too, had been reckless. She, too, had put others at risk in order to achieve her own objectives, however noble they may be.

And now, she feared she would never see her mother or her friends again.

* * *

Wes opened his mouth to speak, but no words came. *How could he find me here?*

Dorold took a couple of steps closer, his lined face twisting into a grimace. He was dressed as he always was, in the long gray robe typical of his office, which made his unexpected presence even more unnerving.

"Oh, Wesley," Dorold said, lifting a hand and pressing a fingertip against Wes' shoulder. "How I wish that things had been different. How many years I spent caring for you, all for you to grow up and betray us all."

Wes pressed his mouth into a tight line. There was no point in arguing. It had become clear after his imprisonment that Elder Dorold was beyond being reasoned with. Whether he had been secretly wicked from the start or merely corrupted by his lust for power, the man that Wes had grown up seeing almost as a second father was gone.

"Who are you?" Gramnok said, taking a step between the two men, clutching the leather case against his chest.

The walls vibrated as another crashing sound coursed through the city. "How typical of a dwarf," he said, sneering.

"Holed up in his halls of stone and unable to recognize a member of the Septemvirate."

"Despite your rudeness, I suggest that you get out of here. We're running out of time," Gramnok said, rising to his full height and staring up into the older man's face.

Dorold laughed, the hollow sound echoing along the passage. Two dwarf women and a group of several children rushed by them, and Wes said a silent prayer that they would make it to safety. Children of any race were a blessing, and the thought that a single one could be harmed thanks to their actions horrified him.

"You must know why I'm here, Gramnok Beastbane," he said, giving Gramnok a glance up and down before turning to Wes. "Perhaps your dwarven friend should have been more careful. I have eyes everywhere in Kaveryth, and I knew that he was friends with the dragon traitor. It was only a matter of time until he led me straight to the Codex."

"It's just a fragment. There are copies everywhere. You've put your life at risk coming here, for nothing," Gramnok snapped, his ears flushing pink.

"So give me that one, and I will let you live," Dorold said, his voice dropping to a near whisper.

Gramnok looked up at the much taller man's face. Wes could see their eyes meeting, neither wanting to be the first to look away. "The people of Kaveryth deserve to know who the true God is. Wes deserves to know what the true role of an Envoy is."

"It was this dwarf who betrayed Celesyria to us. Amusing that he now has the gall to lecture me." Dorold said, glancing over at Wes with a mocking frown.

"You ordered his torture. I do not hold it against him, and

293

neither will Celesyria when she finds out the truth," Wes said, taking a couple of steps toward his former mentor.

How dare you act as though you have the moral high ground here, you lying snake, he wanted to add. He had never wanted to hit someone so badly in all his life.

"Get out of our way, Dorold. I don't want to hurt you."

"Relax, Wes," Gramnok said, taking a couple of steps back through the doorway as another group of dwarves rushed down the hall. "Elder Dorold is an old man. It does not seem he is armed. Surely we can discuss this like gentlemen."

"Even after what was done to you at his command, you doubt his power?" Wes asked, following Gramnok back into the bedroom, not wanting to take his eyes off of Dorold even for a moment.

"He's right, Wesley," Dorold said, releasing a sigh. "I know that you do not understand the choices I have made, but I am far too old to thirst for violence."

"So get out of our way. Go to the surface. Get back to your scheming. You don't have much time."

"He's right," Gramnok added, facing them both with his back to the far wall of the room. "One of the deepest mines in Whitespire is dug right beneath this section of the city. When it collapses, this whole place is going down with it."

The sounds of falling rock were coming more steadily now, and Wes thought that the crashes indeed seemed to be moving closer. Other dwarves were still passing by in the hall, but they were beginning to thin out. He hoped that no other stragglers remained stubbornly behind.

"Give me the Codex, Gramnok," Dorold said after a moment, holding out a hand as though he was asking him to pass the table salt at dinner. "If we don't get to the surface soon, we're all going to be buried anyway."

"I'd rather die than let the Codex fall to you," Gramnok said, his voice calm.

Dorold moved to grab the leather case from the dwarf's hands. Wes rushed forward, taking his mentor's arm and yanking him backward, but Gramnok caught his eye and raised his thick eyebrows ever so slightly. *If only you could mindspeak.* Body language would have to do.

They had to convince Dorold that the case was what he was after without going too far, too soon.

Wes released the man's arm. "If the Codex is just a legend, why does it matter?"

Dorold laughed again, this time with genuine amusement. "Surely we're beyond that, aren't we? We had our reasons for what we taught to the people, including you. It's for their own good that things stay as they are."

"How could it be for—" Wes started just as a massive rumble sounded somewhere far below. The floor shook, and another crash followed as Dorold's mining supplies hit the floor. Wes noticed that the pickax was now only a few feet away from where he stood.

"There's no time for any more stupid questions," Dorold snapped, lunging forward again. "Give it to me, you bearded halfwit!"

"That's not going to happen, Elder," Gramnok said, stepping back again until his back pressed against the wall. With another cryptic glance at Wes, who was standing there stupidly, unsure what to do, he drew a dagger from one of the leather belts that crossed his trousers.

Dorold reached into his own cloak, pulling out a round bottle with a cork stuck in the top.

Time went still.

Wes stood, rooted in place, unable to make his feet move as Dorold heaved his arm back and threw the bottle toward the back wall.

Wes fell to the floor, pressing his eyes closed, expecting the sound of shattered rocks, the feeling of shrapnel embedding into his skin, but it did not come. He took in a few ragged breaths, his nose pressed against the stone, the sound of his heart thumping in his ears.

He saw a little trail of liquid slithering between two stones, rushing toward him.

He smelled lamp oil.

"I'm sorry. I really am," Dorold said.

"Wes, run!" Gramnok yelled. Wes clambered to his feet, nearly slipping on the oily floor.

"Dorold, don't—" Wes stretched out a hand, watching as Dorold's deft old fingers struck a flint. The room seemed to inhale all at once, the air consumed by the sudden inferno. Wes's eyes stung as smoke filled the space, black and choking. Everything in the room was being eaten by the fire, the greedy flames leaving only black soot and gray ash in their wake.

Wes couldn't bring himself to look at Gramnok. He never had a chance.

Instead, he turned and ran, remembering the precious words that were cradled against his chest. He wanted to cry, but there was no moisture in his eyes. He wanted to scream, to ask the High One why He would let something like that happen to an innocent person, but the bite of the smoke held his tongue.

He had taken a few steps into the hall before he heard the sound coming from the burned bedroom.

He turned, unable to keep going.

It was the most horrible scream he could imagine. Dorold stood in the doorway, fire burning up the bottom half of his cloak. Wes gaped for a moment, thinking that it looked like the man had been pulled only halfway into the Wrathlands. "I'm sorry," Dorold gasped, the hem of the cloak disintegrating as the fire made for his torso and face. "It's more complicated than you think—I never wanted—please—have mercy!"

Before he could say more, he stumbled over a loose stone, screaming as he fell to the floor. The fire was rushing up his sleeves now, leaving gruesome destruction behind as it moved beyond his hands.

Wes rushed forward toward the flames, taking several steps before stopping again, unsure what to do. He didn't know how he could help. He didn't know if he should.

Before he could decide, there was a crash.

The walls began to shake, and the floor moved so much that Wes almost fell himself.

As he regained his footing, he watched in slow motion as a huge chunk of the ceiling fell in front of him, landing directly on top of Elder Dorold Eli.

He did not make a sound.

Wes raced for the surface, clutching the fragments of the Codex Veritatis safe against his chest. There was no longer any reason to look back.

Chapter 24

"Please tell me you're alive."

Wes' voice sounded in Celesyria's head as she flew high above Whitespire. She was so relieved that she nearly faltered in the sky. She expected the tears to stop, but instead, they came harder than before. She wanted to thank the High One that Wes had lived, but she knew by the sound of his voice that he was coming to meet her alone.

Gramnok had been left behind.

She didn't know how to form the words to respond. Her emotions were as murky and impenetrable as the storm clouds surrounding her.

"I'm here," she managed, shifting her weight as a fresh torrent of rain pelted against her wings. *"I'm coming. Do you know where you are?"*

After a few brief instructions, she found him, standing

near the same entrance that she'd come out of. Most of the other dragons, dwarves, and elves had cleared out of the area, probably making for the hills that ringed the valley. Fresh collapses in the caverns below had left deep crevasses in the surface, sending heavy hunks of stone tumbling across the ground. Whitespire was no longer habitable, not even on the surface. She suspected that it never would be again.

Putting the fate of Gramnok and the displacement crisis that her race and the dwarves now faced out of her mind, she focused on finding a safe place to wait out the storm. Wes' weight felt comforting against her back, and she tried to fly as carefully as she could, though he had assured her that he was not injured.

He said little else until she landed on a stone outcropping against the interior side of the valley, making her way toward a small cave that she'd spotted in the brief flashes of illumination that the lightning strikes provided. The weight of her body against her ankle burned with every step, but she hoped that with Wes' aid that she would be able to heal in time.

As they made their way inside, she lowered her body so that Wes could get to his feet. As soon as he did so, he nearly collapsed against the stone wall, putting his head in his hands and erupting into tears. She lay down beside him, stretching out her ankle away from her body, saying nothing as the sobs wracked his frame.

You were strong when you used to cry all the time, she would tell him when he was ready. *You were strong when you took control of your tears. And you're strong now, even when you've been bent far enough to finally break again.*

She bowed her head, touching Wes' forehead gently with

her nose and crooning to him that it would be alright. After several moments had passed, she forced her tired body off of the ground and walked toward the cave entrance, trying to avoid putting weight on her ankle.

The storm continued, but it was calmer now. It was still night, and she had no way to tell how soon the dawn would come. She could not see the stars.

She returned to Wes' side and tried to get comfortable again, but her entire body ached. She glanced down at her manacles with a flash of annoyance. Even after all that they'd faced, she was not truly free. She wondered if she ever would be again.

Her ankle was in desperate need of attention—though without supplies, she doubted that much could be done—but she didn't want to rush her friend. Whatever he'd been through in the caverns had been terrible. She could see it by the pallor in his face and the haunted look in his eyes.

"I wonder if my mother made it out," she said in her mind once Wes' tears and sobs had slowed. *"Or if my father is still alive, wherever they've taken him. I have never been able to learn as much about Nox as I would have liked, but I suppose I'll have to figure out my way around now."*

"We'll find him," Wes said, lifting his head from his knees to face her. "And I think your mother is fine. There was a long warning period before the populated areas of the cavern really began to collapse, I would imagine that most of the citizens were able to get to the surface in time."

He chose to speak aloud. Even with all of his practice, she knew that mindspeak was much easier for dragons than it was for humans.

Wes paused for a moment. She desperately wanted to ask about Gramnok's fate, but she could tell by the desperate look

300

on his face that he would speak when he was ready. Instead, she glanced out of the cave entrance again just as a fresh bolt of lightning lit up the sky.

"Gramnok died defending the Codex Veritatis," he choked out. "Elder Dorold killed him."

Celesyria couldn't respond. She couldn't breathe. She couldn't make herself do anything at all. She had suspected the worst, but to hear the words made it real.

Gramnok Beastbane, her best friend in Umrym, her only friend for years, was dead. She'd never had a chance to speak to him after he'd betrayed her to the Septemvirate, never got to look into his eyes and tell him that she'd already forgiven him for what he'd done.

It was too late.

And worse, Wes' former mentor and the man he'd once loved like a father had been the one to murder him.

"O High One, please lead him to the Eternal Lands," she whispered out loud, closing her eyes against the tears that were beginning to fall again as Wes stroked her side. "Please forgive him for what he has done here today. Please have mercy on him."

"He told me that he had good reasons for causing so much destruction," Wes said, resting his palm gently on her shoulder. His touch was comforting, especially after the terror of being captured by Jaconial and the others. Despite the tragedies they now faced, she was thankful that they had each other once again. "But now I guess we'll never know why. He did tell me that he betrayed you only under torture, at the hands of elves."

Celesyria jolted at that, sending pain through her mangled ankle. "So it's true. The elves and the Septemvirate are working together somehow."

Wes got to his feet, stretching his arms toward the ceiling before beginning to pace in the dark cave. "I just wish I understood how everything fits together or where anyone's loyalties really lie. Dorold appeared out of nowhere, saying that he had spies throughout Whitespire and that he'd been waiting for Gramnok to lead him to the Codex. Obviously, the Septemvirate was involved with Gramnok's torture. But I'm still confused about the big picture. All I can tell is that everyone seems to be against us, and against the High One."

Celesyria told him everything that she could remember about the strange council meeting that she'd witnessed, and about the black obelisk. Finally, she explained to him that according to the council, the elves had, at least at one time, been allied with the dragons.

"We'll figure it out," Wes said when she'd finished. "Together. And I know where we can start getting answers."

Celesyria's scaly brow furrowed in confusion as she watched Wes begin to unbutton his vest, the hint of a smile spreading across his face as he drew out a bundle of wrinkled but mostly intact writings.

"You saved the Codex," she breathed, watching in awe as he laid the parchments on the ground, spreading out the rumpled pieces. Outside, the thunder had grown even louder, and rain had begun to seep into the front half of the cave, but she didn't notice. Nor did she care about the weight of the exhaustion spreading through her limbs.

Finally, they would find out more of what the High One wanted them to do.

* * *

"I know little of Graveheim," Alder admitted, stretching out in his chair as his mother and sisters returned to the room.

Marya nearly dropped the cloth-wrapped bundle of cheese she was carrying. "The city of the dead? I've heard more about that place than I ever wanted to know."

Alder wondered how exactly a peasant from High Keep had become so intimately aware of obscure Galeharborian geography, but then again, he supposed it wasn't entirely surprising. Marya had always been smart.

"That surprises me," Kessara put in, fiddling with a few strands of blonde hair. Her voice sounded smaller than it usually did, and Alder wondered if she was alright. He knew that she would not easily forget the trauma of the previous night. "Even the people of Galeharbor want to forget that such a frightening place lies within our borders."

"The reality of death is something faced by every man and creature," his mother, Isla, reminded them. "Wherever the soul may go—" she cast a glance at Alder, as though warning him not to start a debate about the Dracodei or the High One—"the body must be dealt with. And I for one am thankful that we have those who serve our people even after their awareness is gone."

Violet shivered in her seat. "I suppose. But I'm still afraid to see what it's really like there."

Alder cracked a smile at his youngest sister. "It'll be an adventure, Vi. Not very many people can say they've been to Graveheim."

"Will we be safe there?" Marya said, knitting her eyebrows across her forehead and glaring at Kessara. "Forgive me, Princess, but presumably you know that the people who live there form a very tight-knit community. It's not as though

303

we can just rent a cottage on the edge of town and continue life unnoticed."

"You're correct, Marya," Kessara said gently, clearing her throat and shifting a bit in her chair to avoid the beam of warm sunlight that was now coming in through the window. Alder felt the urge to get moving. Every minute they spent talking made him more nervous that they would be found out. "There is no chance that you will be able to slip in unnoticed. However, the Cenobites who live there are not only dedicated to the service of the Dracodei, but to the greater House nobles, as well."

"If they serve the Dracodei, why would they be willing to help you after you allied with a blasphemer?" Alder asked. He knew almost nothing of the recluses who lived in Graveheim, caring for the bodies of those who had died throughout the Four Kingdoms. In his mind, their existence had taken on the haze of myth. It was strange to imagine his family dwelling among them.

"If I were to approach them directly, they would not," Kessara said, reaching toward a piece of paper a quill pen that sat on a side table. "May I?"

Alder's mother nodded, and Kessara continued.

"The Abbess of their women's house, Priya, will help us. She's not only a fellow noble, but the daughter of my late uncle. She chose to serve with the Cenobites when she was eleven, so I didn't meet her until much later, when she took one of her rare visits home to Windshear. But she and I have always been close, despite the age difference and the difference in our vocations."

"Will the other Cenobites go along with her? What will happen to Marya's betrothed?" His mother asked.

"Though the order as a whole must serve the good of the Dracodei and of the noble Houses, the individual female and male members vow to obey the Abbot and the Abbess of their respective houses. Priya will accept you, Marya, and Violet as temporary visitors on retreat from the world—which is not unusual for their community—and you will be expected to assist them in their physical labors. I am confident the Abbot of the men's house will accept Kristoff to do the same."

She paused, no doubt expecting Marya or Violet to object in disgust. Alder smiled. Whatever other flaws that they may have, both of his sisters were hard workers, willing to do whatever was needed to care for their family. They'd had to be, growing up with their father in jail.

"I will not tell Priya any more than I need to. I cannot and would not command her to lie, and I don't wish to put the Cenobites in danger, but it does not matter. It's not going to be an issue. King Ursa is not about to send his army into Graveheim." Kessara lay a blank sheet of the paper on the table, beginning her letter to Priya as she spoke.

"You will not be compelled to worship the Dracodei while you are there, but you are free to participate in their temple services if you so choose," she added.

Alder set his jaw, hoping that his mother and sisters would trust him in regard to the High One and stay far away from the worship of the usurpers, but for the time being, it was not a fight worth having.

"This sounds like a reasonable plan," his mother said finally, giving Kessara a slight smile. "If Alder thinks it is wise, I am willing to do as you suggest. I expect my daughters will be willing as well."

Marya and Violet both nodded, though Violet looked a bit

sick.

Alder breathed a sigh of relief. It was not the sort of plan he ever would have guessed that they would come up with, which only underlined its brilliance. No one would ever think to look for them in the city of the dead.

The eyes of the four women fell on him, waiting.

"I trust Kessara with my life," he said, getting up from his chair. "If she thinks that the Cenobites will help, that is what you should do."

"What will you do?" Violet asked him, getting up again herself and beginning to pull blankets from a chest of drawers that stood near the fireplace. He glanced over at Kessara, who nodded. He felt a ripple of joy fill his chest. She trusted whatever his answer would be before he even said it.

"We're going to Auranth to find Wes Cervos," he said, continuing before anyone could ask any more questions about the errant Envoy. "And after that, we need to go to Boneshire."

"Boneshire? Why?" Marya asked, making a face like she had smelled something sour.

Because Raela told us to, and I suspect the letter that she gave me will explain why.

"There's no time to explain," Kessara cut in with a tight smile before he could say anything, finishing up the final words of her letter and folding it into an envelope that rested nearby. "There are two stags tied up by the large lake, on the north side of High Keep. I named them Boris and Barry."

She took out a fresh sheet of paper and began scratching out a map before handing it to Alder to check. He grinned at her hideously messy writing and the wobbly lines of her sketch, but the map was legible enough.

"Assuming that they're still there, you need to ride them to

Graveheim as fast as you can and ask for Priya. Give her this letter," she handed it to his mother. "She will take care of you."

"Raela's pony is strong. She will carry my weight easily enough. She's the only animal here that hasn't been sold yet," Violet said, getting to her feet.

"Wait," Alder said, kneeling down and grabbing his leather pack from where he'd left it near the fireplace. He drew out a vial and handed it to Violet. "Add a couple of drops of this to your water. There's an illness spreading through Kaveryth, and no one knows exactly which water sources are still safe to drink from."

For several minutes, silence filled the house as the women rushed around, gathering a few final odds and ends and adding them to their packs. Alder paced, looking out the window every few moments. Kristoff was taking too long. The sun was already high enough to indicate mid-morning. If they wanted to make it to the forest by nightfall, they had to hurry.

"I'm afraid, Alder," his mother said after a while, joining him at the window just as a man came into view on the path along the horizon. "I've spent so much of my life in High Keep. I seldom venture beyond the city walls, let alone cross the Kingdom's borders. How are we going to find our way? How will we know what to do? What if the Cenobites refuse to aid us?"

Alder pulled his mother in for a hug. He could not remember ever seeing her so vulnerable before, even after all that their family had survived.

"You're the strongest woman I know," he said finally, pulling back so that he could look her in the eyes. "My sisters, too. You're going to make it, and everything is going to be fine.

307

Besides, the High One will take care of you. You're not alone."

"That's what you believe, son," his mother said, shaking her head slowly. "I don't know what I believe any more. I feel like everything has been torn out from under me, and I'm still trying to get my feet back on the ground."

"Mother, it's—" Alder started to say, unable to avoid the twinge of frustration that bubbled up inside him.

"I know how you feel, Isla," Kessara cut in from where she sat nearby, twisting the ends of her hair through her fingers. "Alder is so certain of his faith. The High One even speaks to him when he sleeps, sometimes. I can't even imagine such a thing. I've just had to go along, doing the best that I can, even if I don't have all of the answers yet."

"Princess, I think that's perhaps the most courageous kind of faith," Alder's mother replied, smiling at Kessara. Alder felt the tension in his shoulders ease. *Kessara always knows exactly what to say. Especially when I am about to say the perfectly wrong thing.* "I would appreciate it if you both would pray for me, and for my girls. And Kristoff, of course. We're asking a lot of him."

Just then, there was a knock at the door, and the man himself appeared. Kristoff was a couple of inches taller than Marya, with the same green eyes and red hair that they all shared. He rushed over to hug his sister, and to Alder's surprise, he came to hug him next. The two men shared a somewhat awkward embrace, but Alder found himself grinning as he pulled back, unable to spurn Kristoff's friendly smile.

Proper introductions were made, but there was little time to talk. Alder was relieved when Kessara reminded everyone that they had a long way to travel before nightfall.

"I hope we'll have a chance to get to know each other soon,

seeing as we are going to be brothers," Kristoff said to Alder, giving him a handshake as he gathered up his pack and moved toward the door. "I have to go and ready my horse, and I figure I'll get Violet's mount saddled while I'm out there."

"Thank you," Alder said, placing a hand on his shoulder. "Any man willing to leave behind his entire life to take care of the woman he loves is good enough for my little sister."

When he had left, Alder turned to his family. "There is not going to be an easy way to say goodbye, so let's do it quickly," he said, blinking back a few stray tears. "I'm sorry that our reunion must be so short. And I'm sorry for the mess I've caused you."

Violet and his mother both took turns hugging him, burying their heads in his chest and holding back their own tears. "I love you both with everything in me. We will see each other again. Until then, try and make the best of your time with the Cenobites."

"Maybe it really will be an adventure," Violet added, picking up her large leather pack from the floor and pulling the straps across her shoulders. "I've never been to Galeharbor. I'm kind of excited."

Marya stood near the window, arms crossed, watching Kristoff head toward Raela's barn. Finally, she turned to face her older brother. Her mouth was set in a thin line, but as soon as he extended his arms toward her, she gave him a reluctant half-smile as she fell into his hug.

"I like Kristoff a lot," Alder said.

"He's a good man."

"I can see that. I really can. If you want my opinion, you should ask one of the Cenobite men to marry you both while you're in Graveheim," he said, surprised at himself. *Ordinarily,*

I'd be telling her to wait another decade, but these are not ordinary times.

"The thought had crossed my mind," Marya said as they parted, her brows knitted in a show of consternation that was betrayed by the beaming smile tugging at her mouth. "Not that I was asking for your permission."

"I didn't say you needed it," he said, smiling back.

A few months ago, he would have argued with her, told her that as the man of the house he did have a say in who his sisters married, but now it seemed a silly thing to argue about. By the look on her face he could see that she'd wanted his approval and advice, and it felt good to give it.

"So that's it, then," Marya said after a pause, gathering her own pack and helping her mother to put hers on. The three women traipsed into the back bedroom to pay their final respects to Raela before heading to the front door.

After another round of hugs, encumbered by heavy packs and restrained sobs, they were gone.

Kessara stood at the window for a while after they left, watching wide-eyed as though some monster might snatch them up before they could even get away from the farm.

"Come on," Alder said, opening the door and gesturing for her to follow.

Together, they sat on the little stoop, watching until the group reached the horizon and disappeared beyond it. They left behind nothing but waving grasses, stretching for miles beneath a perfect blue sky.

They would have to leave themselves in a few minutes, and he was still trying to decide what route would be safest. *Do we go toward the mountains and try to sneak through the woods of Silverfell, or do we risk the straight cut across the Aridmoor plains?*

He found himself unable to think of a satisfactory answer.

He reminded himself that the High One would guide them, just as he'd told his mother. If they were meant to make it safely to Auranth, they would find a way.

Kessara sighed softly, and he dared a glance over at her. Her blonde hair shone in the sunshine, and her hand rested against the old stone step, inches from his own.

I will keep you safe, Princess Kessara Manta. Even if it kills me.

She wouldn't meet his eyes, wouldn't dare move any closer, but it was clear what she wanted. The inches between them seemed to spark with energy, pulling him in. He gripped the stone with his fingertips.

He wanted more than anything to take her hand in his, to pull her close, to smell her hair, to kiss her. But he didn't dare touch her.

If he did, he wouldn't be able to let go.

Chapter 25

By the time that Wes and Celesyria had finished reading the fragments of the Codex, the storm had settled into a gentle pattering of rain. The sky was no longer pitch black, but dawn had not yet arrived. They had not seen or heard another soul since escaping Whitespire, and Wes was thankful. There was so much to take in, and he wanted time to read through the confusing parts of the text multiple times until he understood.

Celesyria got to her feet after a while, trying her best to avoid putting weight on her injured ankle, and stretched out her neck far enough that she reached the ceiling. *"I think I need spectacles,"* she said as she crouched back down, putting her face as close to the pieces of parchment as she could without tearing them with the scales on her chin.

Wes suppressed a chuckle at the mental image of a dragon in reading glasses before settling back down beside his friend.

It felt good to be together. It felt good to be alive.

"I'm sorry about Gramnok," he said as Celesyria stared down at the parchment. *"I know I didn't get much of a chance to meet him, but I know that he cared about you in the end. When it counted the most."*

Wes watched a tear beading up on the edge of Celesyria's huge right eye before she blinked it away.

"I'm sorry too," she said finally, releasing a slow breath that ruffled the papers. *"It still hasn't quite sunk in yet. I can't believe he's gone."*

"It takes a while," Wes said, taking one of the pieces of parchment in his hand and reading over the final paragraph for the fifth time. *"And then, just when you think you've figured out a way to stop grieving, there will be some smell or a color or a type of flower on the side of the road that reminds you of them, and it will all come flooding back. You live your life with an open wound."*

Such a moment had happened to Wes himself, a few days before, when they were nearing the border of Umrym. They'd dipped low over a meadow in Aridmoor, filled with purple and white foxgloves. His mother's favorite. He and Roven used to pluck them for her when they'd find them on the palace grounds, leaving them in vases all over the dining room. He smiled at the memory.

He continued, *"It doesn't get easier in the way that you'd expect. You don't get tougher. You're still bloody and raw, and your heart is open to things that never used to be able to hurt you. But there's a deeper ability to love that you gain, too. When the person you care about is no longer beside you, you experience their love as a whisper, usually while you're busy with something else."*

He smiled, meeting Celesyria's eyes. *"Grief teaches you to love as the High One loves. He embraces us like a storm, sometimes, tearing through everything else. But he also loves like the touch of a shadow, just a little reminder that this world is not all that there is."*

Celesyria closed her eyes for a moment as Wes touched a hand to the side of her scaly cheek. *"That's nice to think about,"* she said after a couple of moments, the hint of a smile flitting across her face.

"I wish I could say that I knew he was safe in the Eternal Lands despite what he did at the end of his life, but I do have faith that the High One knows his heart. And the best way to honor his legacy is to do what the Codex tells us."

Wes smiled at her, gathering up the most pertinent pieces of parchment and laying them in a neat row. She was right. Gramnok had lost his life for the sake of bringing the truth, even though he barely had the chance to experience it for himself. The least that they could do was to keep fighting. There would be time for melancholy later.

"Okay," Wes started, clearing his throat as he began to speak out loud. For some reason, he thought that such talk needed to be witnessed, even if it was just by the walls of a lonely cave. "From what I can gather—the fragments aren't complete, nor are they linear—the role of the Envoy has been important from the very beginning."

"I told you so," Celesyria said, her usually sweet voice sounding rather reedy from disuse.

He cleared his throat again. "It says that from the beginning, there was always one Envoy, he was always male, and his task was to…" He trailed off, pointing to an unfamiliar word in the text. He thought it looked like some form of Elvish, but neither he nor Celesyria knew exactly what it meant. "Perhaps

Kessara will know what the exact word says. If it's ancient Elvish, anyway. I think we can figure out the general idea from the context."

He continued, "Much of what we know of the Envoy now was true then, as well. From the beginning, they were to be educated in Silverfell by the Septemvirate from a young age. They each bore the moonscar. They were to bring the sacrifices to the great spire. They were forbidden from any sort of ruling power, even if they were born as nobles."

"And that's about where the similarities end," Celesyria finished, her eyes roving over the small, neat script. "The sacrifices the people gave were defined as trinkets in the text. It mentions pins, stones, and single coins. Nothing at all like the treasure demanded now."

Wes got to his feet again, bringing along one of the sheets of parchment. The rain had finally stopped, and the early morning sunlight seeping in through the cave entrance was bright enough to read by. "The real focus of the Feast of Offering was not as much about what the people gave to the High One," Wes said, his voice shaky with excitement. "The focus was on what the High One gives to *us*."

"The bread of hope," Celesyria chimed in, her voice a reverent whisper. "Just like you and Alder gave to that elf in Windshear."

"The High One used to give it to us all," Wes said, astonished at the implications of what they were reading. Finally, talking it through with Celesyria, it was all coming together in his mind. "It doesn't go into detail about the logistics, but the Envoy was to take the bread back with him, and it was to be offered to everyone, in every corner of Kaveryth. Even the dwarves. Even the elves."

Celeysria was quiet for a moment, her face pensive, but she did not speak. "I'm sure that the dragons have a role to play," he added quickly. "But this isn't the complete Codex. This text tells us that the dwarves were originally created to guard the great spire. It briefly mentions that the elves were originally created to counsel men, but it doesn't give any details about that, either."

"I know," Celesyria said, her voice a little too bright to be entirely convincing. "I'm glad we got some answers about your role in this, but we're still missing so much information. If the remaining full copies of the Codex are in Whitespire, we've missed our chance to get them."

Wes thought of the destruction they'd left behind, feeling rather insensitive for not having discussed it. Celesyria had lost her friend, her mother was missing, and she didn't even have a place to go home to even if she could be free. Still, the Codex was more important, at least for the time being.

"The prophecy that Holga and Gohr told me about makes a little more sense," he said. "Though not all of it is clear. The part about bringing the bread of hope 'to a Kingdom long thought dead' must refer to Boneshire, but I'm still not exactly sure how I'm going to do it. The Codex doesn't say how the High One gives the Envoy the bread."

"I was kind of hoping we'd learn more about this oath that you're supposed to reverse, the one mentioned in the prophecy," Celesyria ventured. "But fulfilling the rest of it, about marrying a woman and bestowing a crown, might be a good start as we try and figure out the bread of hope part."

"It's connected. I know, okay?" He snapped, feeling the familiar twinge of anxiety rising in his chest.

Celesyria drew back at his tone.

"Sorry," he added, setting the parchment back down and patting Celesyria's shoulder. "I guess some part of me was secretly hoping that the Codex would tell us that there was another way that doesn't involve marriage."

"It's okay. I understand," Celesyria said, giving her head a slight bow in his direction.

"Celesyria, a long while back, when we first met, I remember you mentioning a group you called the remnant," Wes said, remembering something. He was glad for an excuse to change the subject.

"Yes. They were given the thousand year prophecy. The High One told them that for a thousand years He would permit the people of Kaveryth to persist in their evils, but after that period, He would restore worship to Himself and bring peace to His people," she summarized for Wes' benefit. He was quite sure that she had the entirety of that particular Codex fragment memorized.

"Right," Wes said. "So why don't we try and find them as well, rather than strictly looking for the Codex? Perhaps they know more about how the Envoy is to go about bringing the bread of hope to the people."

"They probably have complete copies of the Codex Veritatis," Celesyria said, sending Wes a small smile. "The only problem is, I have no idea where to find them. The Codex portions I read in Helmm only mention that they were exiled by the Elf-queens to the east."

"Where the map ends," Wes added. "Very helpful directions."

"In any case, we just have to keep looking. Perhaps we will find some other fragments of the Codex in a place we don't expect, or we'll pick up a lead on how to reach this remnant—"

"—If they still exist," Wes finished.

"Right," Celesyria continued. "We need to find my mother, and by what I was told in the council meeting I was dragged to, my father is imprisoned in Nox."

"What? How?" he stammered, incredulous. *A prisoner from Kaveryth taken to Nox?* He had never heard of such a thing.

"That was my reaction, too," she said, frowning. "I'll tell you about it later. I was privy to some revelations that I doubt they would have shared had they realized I was going to escape alive."

Wes forced himself to take a deep breath. *How close did my best friend come to death?*

"Anyway," she continued, letting out a sigh that ruffled his hair. "Before we do anything, we need to get to Auranth again, as agreed. We need to talk to Alder. And Kessara."

"Can you make it? Once we're there, I'm sure we can find a trustworthy healer who will help with your leg. If not, Kessara is a quick study with such things, perhaps she can—"

"Wes," Celesyria cut in, brow furrowed. She spoke slowly, as though waiting for him to get angry with her again. "Are you going to marry her?"

"I have to. It's the right thing to do," he said, forcing a smile. "She's a wonderful woman. Beautiful, too. I could do a whole lot worse."

"The right thing to do is almost always difficult," she said, poking at his brown curls with the tip of her snout. "But that doesn't mean the hardest thing is always the right thing."

He didn't know how to answer that, and Celesyria offered no further clarification, instead turning to examine the Codex portions further. After a few moments, he began to take a few steps toward the front of the little cave.

He could hear the gentle noise of Celesyria humming a

tune from behind him as she pored over the documents. Even after everything that had happened, she still found hope in the words of her creator, still found a reason to be curious and to keep learning.

Wes reached the entrance, daring to venture a couple of steps onto the stone platform where they'd landed. He breathed deeply, enjoying the taste of fresh air after rain.

It was a glorious morning.

The sun was just beginning to peek over the tips of the Severed Summits, casting their rocky sides in shades of pink and orange and leaving the shadowy places a deep, cool blue.

I know that this world is not all that there is. But oh, High One, there's so much beauty in it. No matter how dark things become, no matter how difficult the path you place before us is to follow, what a comfort it is to know that dawn always comes.

Epilogue

My Dearest Alder,

If you are reading this letter, I am no longer well enough to speak. Most likely, I am dead. I know you, your mother, and your sisters will weep for me, but I hope that your sorrow does not hinder you. It is—I suppose, it was—frightening to think about death, but it is a comfort to pray about it. All my life, I worried about the judgment, wondering if I would reach the Eternal Lands or if I would be exiled to the Wrathlands.

A strange thing happened when I came to believe in the High One. I knew in my mind that He would judge me when I met death, but then my heart would remember that, above all else, He created me and all of us because He wanted to save us. He wanted to love us, more than we could ever love ourselves.

So now, I hope I have done what I planned to do: to fear Him in wisdom as my judge, but to cleave to Him in faith as my Savior.

Weep for me, Alder, my beloved one, but do not weep for long. I believe I am in the Eternal Lands now, where all is joy. I hope in that, as I write these words. I trust in that, because I trust in the One who has set me free.

I suppose that you will wonder how I came to believe in the first place, which is part of why I wished to write this final word to you. If your mother or sisters read this letter—and I give you permission to allow them to, after a time, when it seems right—it is my hope that my testimony will help them to follow the High One when they are ready.

You had a lot to do with this, my beloved. My dear Violet would come to visit me, and she never spoke of what you had done, how you had befriended a rogue dragon and defied King Ursa. I suppose she feared it would have upset me, would have brought shame to my thoughts of you. She is a good sister. But I overheard her speaking to your mother, and I knew the truth. And oh, how I hoped that your defense of Celesyria meant that you had come to know her God!

Not long after that, I had a dream. The High One told me that you were indeed following Him. And He told me that it was time for me to come home to Him, too. In this life, and in the next.

I must confess something to you, Alder. Well, I must confess many things, but let us start with only one. I am very, very tired.

I have known the High One since I was a teenager. Well, perhaps it would be better to say that I have known of Him. I did not always follow. I was not always faithful. But I always knew that the Dracodei were not the divine rulers of Kaveryth. I worshiped them along with everyone else because I was a coward. I turned aside from the true God, and in so doing, I obscured knowledge of Him from your family—our family—the people who are most important to me in all the world.

I hope that you will forgive me, and I praise the High One that my wickedness was not enough to keep you from Him forever.

I could say so much more on that topic, unburden this old sinner's heart, but there is not enough time. I have been writing this letter for a few days already, a little each morning when I am at my strongest. I hope that you can read the wobbly script. My body is falling apart, and I suspect my mind will soon follow.

Before that day comes, Alder, there is another tale I must tell. I must explain to you how I came to know the High One. Bear with me. This part of the story could have an impact on every man, woman, and child in Kaveryth, at least, if you obey my wishes.

I've started this part of the letter over and over again, crumpling pages and throwing them into the fire, my cheeks burning with shame as I try to get the words down. I love you all more than anything, and my pride hates the idea that I must confess something that might make you think less of me. But this suffering has taught me that no one can truly outrun the evils they've done, not forever. Not unto death.

So here it is, my beloved: when I was sixteen years old, I met a somewhat older young man. I fell for him. We were stupid and reckless. We did what those who are not married should not do. I can barely bear to etch such words in ink, but it is the truth.

I met Victor at the market in Rill, a little town in the south of Boneshire. It was innocent enough of a meeting, a handsome boy hidden deep within the shadow of his tent, working away at his craft. Catching my eye, beckoning me to come and see what he had made. I didn't see the harm, people were all about, so I went in.

He showed me his tapestries, all beautiful geometric shapes in every color imaginable, and typography that seemed to come alive. But then I saw something I was not meant to see. Something I probably should have left alone, that caused a cascade of decisions that I cannot say I regret, but perhaps should.

There was an image of an owl, hidden along the back of his tapestry. Then I saw another nearby, and then another, all cleverly woven in amid the messy back-threads.

I looked at him then, interrupting his flirtatious talk, and I told him everything.

I told him things that I should never have said, that I never would have dared to say if I hadn't been so enchanted by him.

I told him that I knew that owl, knew that it was the ancient, forbidden symbol of the House of Noctua.

I told him that I was one of the last two members of that noble House, along with my father, that we were masquerading as a wealthy merchant family. That our bloodline had not been destroyed, only damaged, and that my father had plans for me. That my father had brought us to Rill when I was a tiny babe, to hide us in plain sight.

Though he was the rightful heir to the throne, he said it was not the right time for restoration. He made me promise to marry and to bear as many children as I could, hoping that I would produce a generation strong enough to take back control of our homeland, and that if I failed, perhaps my grandchildren would be able to take up the crown once again.

My father made me promise never to tell even my future husband the truth about who I was, just as he had kept our bloodline secret from my mother before she died in childbirth. He knew that if the people found out that we lived, we would be targeted. By corrupt bandits, by slavers who wanted the path through Boneshire to remain clear, by the administrators who enjoyed their petty powers, perhaps even by the Septemvirate.

There were only two of us, and we were not safe. We had to wait, to find me a respectable man to marry, capable of raising heirs with decency and wealth even if we would have to hide their nobility from the world.

Instead, I told our darkest secrets to a stranger, because I knew that he secretly supported the old ways, the old monarchy, the relative freedom that Boneshire had once had, a very long time ago, under the House of Noctua.

I fell in love with him, even though he was basically a peasant, and then the irreversible deed was done.

I said nothing of Victor to my father until my belly grew too large to hide any more. He was furious, of course. He told me to see a young herbwoman called Malka, barely a teenager herself then, who he knew would keep things quiet. Of course, she assumed that she was dealing with a child that threatened our wealth and status, not a child who bore noble blood.

He told me that I must take a potion and get rid of our child (such words shake me to my core, even now). He feared that I had destroyed any chance of restoring the House of Noctua, and it was a fear that I understood.

Though there had been bastard nobles throughout the history of the Four Kingdoms, they were rarely permitted to rule, and it would make it nearly impossible to restore our particular monarchy from the ashes if our oldest heir was born out of wedlock to a peasant, especially if it was a son. But even if my child could be accepted, it did not matter.

I would never find a proper man who would marry me in the first place, not when I was already a mother.

I refused to kill my child. I told my father that the life inside me was precious, no matter what else happened. He was furious.

He was even more angry when I told him that I was going to marry Victor the tapestry maker, whether he approved or not. I confess that I did not treat him with the respect that he was due, but that does not excuse what came afterward.

My father told me that he was tired, and that in the morning, we could discuss the matter further. He'd been sick for years, with an illness that none of the physicians or herbwomen knew how to cure, and I feared that the revelation of my pregnancy might send his health over the edge.

So I went to bed.

That night, robbers went to Victor's tent as well as to the rooming

324

house where he slept. They slashed every tapestry to ribbons, and they killed him in his bed.

You will see tears on this letter now, and I make no attempt to hide them. Even after all these years, even after all of the stupid choices and mistakes that we made in those few short months together, I loved Victor with all of my heart. I still do. I hold onto hope that he asked the High One for forgiveness before he died, so that we may meet again in the Eternal Lands.

You see, Alder, Victor believed in the High One already. He knew of the owl, the symbol of Boneshire's restoration, but he knew even more powerful things about the truth of our broken kingdom and all Kaveryth. He and his sister, Lysha, were descendants of those who were sent to the east, the remnant of believers that were exiled hundreds of years ago.

I wish I could say more about those people, for they have a story of their own, but there isn't time. You will find them if you begin to look, and they will have answers to give you.

In any case, Victor taught me all he knew about the High One, which wasn't much, but it was enough for me to fall in love with his God. I knew that his sister, Lysha, and her husband Dallan believed as well, but she and Victor had not been getting along as of late (due, I suspect, to his sinful behavior, but I never found out for sure) and we never got the chance to meet.

The very day after Victor was murdered, before I could bring myself to confront him, my father died from his illness. I know it was he who ordered the execution, but I could do nothing about it. He was already dead, and so was the father of my child. What good would the truth do then? I understood that he wanted to do good, to preserve our noble blood, to help our people... but you cannot make good out of evil.

You cannot kill to bring life.

Even if I wanted to tarnish my father's name in death, I doubted that anyone would listen to me.

Instead, I hid.

I went to Malka just as my father had suggested, and instead of helping me to kill my child, I asked her for advice as to what to do. She helped me, and despite what she would have been willing to do to my little baby, I am thankful to her. She knew Victor's sister and had helped her with some fertility problems. She assured me that however Lysha felt about Victor's mistakes, or about how I encouraged him to persist in them, she loved her brother and she would love his child, legitimate or not.

This next part of the story, this next thing that I must confess, was difficult to write. I went to bed after trying to find the words for a while, only to wake up with no greater grace or clarity.

The simple truth will have to be enough.

I hid in Lysha's home for a couple of months, I had my daughter with the aid of Malka, and I gave her to Lysha and Dallan to raise as their own.

We all agreed to name her Holga.

She was the most beautiful thing I had ever seen. For a few blissful weeks, I got to hold her in my arms. I got to nurse her, to smell the back of her head, drinking in all of the love that flowed between us. I could never get enough of her, never play with her tiny toes enough, never kiss her perfect rosebud lips enough.

My grief over Victor's death was washed away in the tears of joy that I wept for my daughter, sitting by the fireplace alone at night, knowing that I was loved by a family that could have so easily hated me or at least resented me for what I cost them.

Letting go of her was the most painful thing I have ever experienced, before or since. Time heals many things, my beloved Alder, but it can never take away the pain of a mother who has lost her child—even if that child had to be lost for her own good.

I never told Lysha or Dallan that Holga had noble blood. They assumed only that I was a rich girl in trouble, afraid of the shame that would follow me, afraid that I would never find a husband. They never judged me for that. They showed me only love. I had expected them to cast me out hours after I had Holga, wanting those earliest moments with her for themselves, but they didn't. They waited, taking their time with her only when I needed to rest.

I could not have given my daughter better parents. They would raise her to know the truth about God, and I knew that I had done the right thing.

I heard, years later, that despite their infertility they'd been able to have a son of their own, a little brother for Holga. I know that the High One must have rewarded them for what they had done.

I'm sure you still wonder why I gave up my daughter, why I ran, even though my father was dead. It was not because I feared shame, or because I feared being alone. Sometimes, even I don't know the reason, and I second guess myself about the choices I have made. I had skill in business, I could have supported myself and Holga even if we ended up poor.

I was not ashamed, but I was afraid. Of so many things.

I was afraid of what my father feared, afraid that if I accepted her status as an illegitimate child that the House of Noctua would never be restored. I did not want her to carry the burdens that I spent my life carrying. You must understand how heavy a secret can become—so heavy that I spilled it in the corner of a tapestry maker's tent, to the first man I had ever met who truly wanted to hear me.

I wanted more for Holga. I wanted her to live life on her terms, to fall in love with whoever she wanted, to be raised by people who not only knew of the High One, but actually followed Him with *everything they had.*

I was not ready to do that yet.

I was not ready to be sorry for the sins I had committed, and I confess that until very recently, I still never felt entirely ready. I hope you will realize far sooner than I did that to stand before the High One with a peaceful heart is more important than anything else. Anything at all.

The rest of the story is much simpler. I am thankful, for all I want to do now is to sleep, but my pen is moving and the tears have slowed. I may as well finish.

Lysha knew a woman when she was a child who had married an awful man and moved to High Keep. You know that man well. Your father was always stealing and drinking, always in jail, even then. Your mother welcomed me into your home as a housekeeper and a governess—my education as the daughter of a rich merchant was very useful—and I left my old life behind. Left my daughter, in hopes of saving her the pain of knowing me.

You knew only that my father had been terrible to me and that I had left home as a teenager.

Now you know the entire truth, even the darkest parts of it.

I do not have time to explain why I am dying. It was not a tumble down a staircase nor an accident at the kiln. It was my own fault, but I have asked the High One for forgiveness, and I must content myself with His mercy.

I am tired.

Even my mind is tired.

Alder, you must find Holga. You must tell her who she is. She deserves a choice, and she is strong enough now to know the cost of making the right one.

Please tell her how much I love her, and please ask her to forgive me.

Yours,

Raela

Dear Reader

Thank you so much for reading *Majesty*, the second book in the Storm & Spire series.

If you enjoyed this book, I humbly ask you to consider leaving an honest review. It can be just a sentence or two if you like. Reviews are an author's lifeblood, especially independent authors, and *especially* those who write in smaller genres like Christian fantasy. =)

Thank you from the bottom of my heart for your support & encouragement.

If you want to stay up to date with my writing (including Storm & Spire book three!) or want to have input on future books, please consider signing up for my newsletter. One of the new characters in this book, Aelrie, was actually named by my newsletter subscribers, and they recently named a sea monster that will be featured in book three. :)

You can sign up at https://authorstefanielozinski.com/news letter

In Christ,
  Stefanie Lozinski

Behind the Scenes

Book two was a lot of fun to write, and I feel like I have learned a lot and grown as a writer since working on book one!

The stats...

This time around, I kept better records, so I can tell you that Majesty required **27 hours of plotting, 81 hours of drafting, and 18 hours of editing**. That doesn't include formatting, figuring out cover design, uploading to retailers, updating my website, and all of the other million little tasks that go into publishing. :)

It feels good to know that, by the grace of God, I can do hard things and persevere through a long-term project like writing a book.

I love seeing how deeper themes emerge as I write my books.

I have a special place in my heart for Kessara's story. As a woman, I've definitely experienced the pressures from the world that tell us we have to be everything a woman should be AND excel at historically male-oriented things on top of that.

Kessara has been artificially sheltered from just how impossible and unfair to women this is "in the real world", so it was really interesting to see through her eyes as she experienced the challenging vulnerability of being female.

I also really enjoyed watching Alder's story come together.

Alder has grown up without a father, which has impacted him deeply though perhaps not in the way I expected when I started writing. I tend to think that Isla did a great job as a mother, despite the horrible choices she felt she had to make, but that doesn't mean Alder wasn't negatively impacted by his dad not being in the picture.

Alder has a ton of courage and works hard. In a lot of ways, he's a very virtuous character. But on the other hand, he never got to truly *be a child*. He was always the man of the house, and that led to his fear of vulnerability - he never got the chance to lean on someone else in the same way that most children (including Wes) do.

In a way, Alder and Kessara actually have a lot in common.

Speaking of Alder...

Alder was not supposed to become a major character. He began his life as a briefly mentioned side character in book one. But after I began actually drafting the scenes he was in, I realized, hey, I really like this guy. He has potential to be a great, more traditional male character for Wes to play off of.

He definitely evolved as I plotted book two. Somehow, he and Kessara began to fall for each other, which is really messing up my plans. Not to mention the fate of Kaveryth!

The bread of hope

I love writing Christian fiction. I love having the freedom to explore issues of faith directly in my stories, even if it isn't always explicit. In most of book one, I would say the allegorical content was more subtle (though they were definitely there - including things readers have pointed out that I didn't even notice while writing!).

In book two, however, as we really delve into a world where

the status quo of the Dracodei has been upended, I loved getting to explore holy communion / the Eucharist in a more obvious way.

There are so many bible verses I could share on this issue, but this one from John 6:53-58 was on my mind a lot during the drafting of this story:

> *So Jesus said to them, "Truly, truly, I say to you, unless you eat the flesh of the Son of Man and drink his blood, you have no life in you. Whoever feeds on my flesh and drinks my blood has eternal life, and I will raise him up on the last day. For my flesh is true food, and my blood is true drink. Whoever feeds on my flesh and drinks my blood abides in me, and I in him. As the living Father sent me, and I live because of the Father, so whoever feeds on me, he also will live because of me.*

Wes and Alder really had no idea what they were doing when it came to giving the fallen elf (and later Raela) the bread of hope. There were more questions than answers. But they had to go on faith that the High One meant what He said and trust Him accordingly.

It was hard for me to write those scenes without giving a lot of clear cut answers, and that's how I feel in real life sometimes, too. I like certainty. I like to be able to reason everything out intellectually and tie it up with a bow! But that's not always what it's like when you're following Jesus. Sometimes you have to obey, even when your human sight can't see what God sees.

I can't wait to see more of what the High One does for the people of Kaveryth as Storm & Spire continues.

About the Author

Stefanie Lozinski lives in Ontario, Canada, with her husband, two young children, two cats, and a whole lot of books. When she isn't homeschooling her little ones, you'll find her on a long walk, drinking coffee, praying a Rosary, or working on her next novel.

You can connect with me on:

🌐 https://www.authorstefanielozinski.com

📘 https://www.facebook.com/authorstefanielozinski

🔗 https://www.instagram.com/lozinskistefanie

Subscribe to my newsletter:

✉ https://authorstefanielozinski.com/newsletter